The Only Way Is Up

The Only Way Is Up

CAROLE MATTHEWS

headline
review

First published in 2010 by HEADLINE REVIEW
An imprint of HEADLINE PUBLISHING GROUP

1

Cataloguing in Publication Data is available from the British Library

Hardback ISBN 978 0 7553 7377 2
Trade paperback ISBN 978 0 7553 7378 9

Typeset in Bembo by Palimpsest Book Production Limited,
Falkirk, Stirlingshire

Printed and bound in Great Britain by
Clays Ltd, St Ives plc

Headline's policy is to use papers that are natural, renewable and recyclable products and made from wood grown in sustainable forests. The logging and manufacturing processes are expected to conform to the environmental regulations of the country of origin.

HEADLINE PUBLISHING GROUP
An Hachette UK company
338 Euston Road
London NW1 3BH

www.headline.co.uk
www.hachette.co.uk

To Dawn Watling

18 April 1964 – 1 April 2010

A friend, a maker of mish-mash, a keeper of bees,
a watcher of birds and a plotter of excellent walks.
Someone who will always be remembered fondly.

My thanks go to the very lovely Tina Sorrell for advice about the process of becoming homeless. And to Mr Christopher Cherry for lending me his wonderful name. My real life Christopher Cherry, as far as I know, has no involvement with organic vegetables other than eating them, and I don't believe he has ever worn corduroy. He is, however, handsome and charming and writes and sings a mean ditty. Thanks to you and Caroline for being our friends.

Chapter 1

'This is the life,' I say, gazing out over the picture-perfect Tuscan countryside from the comfort of my sunlounger.

'I'll drink to that,' my friend Amanda agrees. 'More Chianti, Lily?'

She splashes some of the rich, ruby wine into my glass. The sun – unbroken since we've been here – is beating down again and that, combined with the wine, is making my eyelids pleasantly heavy. The fragrant scent of lavender that wafts from the hedge bordering the terrace is adding to the soporific effect of the sun. If I'd gone completely native in the last two weeks of our holiday, it would be a good time for a siesta.

I lower my sunglasses and gaze across the terrace and the garden beyond. My children – Hettie and Hugo – and Amanda's – Amelia and Arthur – are playing happily together in the azure pool just beyond the terrace. We've tried desperately to keep them from burning in the fierce sun, smothering them all in Factor 30 a dozen times a day but, despite our ministrations, they're all sporting a golden glow and kisses of freckles across their noses.

The children attend the same school – Stonelands, one of *the* very best private schools in Buckinghamshire – and get on famously, but you can never be entirely sure whether that will last over an extended holiday period. The girls are both eight, the boys ten years old – the age where they all like to squabble ceaselessly. But I have to say that they've all been angels. Amanda and I haven't had a cross word either and that's always difficult when you're bringing two families together. It was their idea – the Marquises – to join together for a holiday, and it's been a great success. I'd certainly like to do it again next year.

The villa is magnificent. Amanda chose it. The place is a restored Tuscan farmhouse just outside the film-set village of San Gimignano, and no expense has been spared on it. The old stone walls blend beautifully into the vine-smothered rolling hills that cocoon us. It has eight bedrooms so we've had more than enough space not to be on top of each other. The pool has been a great hit with Hugo and Hettie and the Marquis children.

We've fully enjoyed the life of ease here. Someone comes in every day to set out breakfast and lunch, and a couple of times she's left us homemade pizza bases and a host of fresh ingredients in the kitchen, so we've had great fun trying our hand with the outdoor oven. In the evenings we've taken our cars for the short drive into San Gimignano, sampling a different and usually excellent restaurant every night.

It's been just perfect.

'Look at those two, Lily.' Now Amanda lowers her sunglasses and gestures with her glass of wine towards our respective husbands, and laughs. 'All they ever do is work, work, work.'

Ah, yes. One small glitch in paradise.

Amanda's husband, Anthony Marquis, and my own dear husband, Laurence Lamont-Jones, are pacing relentlessly at the other side of the pool, Blackberrys clamped to ears. Anthony's voice is raised but, thankfully, he's far enough away that we can't quite hear who he's shouting at or what.

Amanda and I tut indulgently and exchange the familiar look of the hard-done-by spouse.

But secretly I know that we're both extremely proud of our husbands as handsome men at the top of their game. Laurence has classic good looks – it's one of the reasons why I fell for him hook, line and sinker the minute I clapped eyes on him. We were both at university. Laurence was malnourished and impoverished and, despite that or because of it, I knew he was The One. He still wears his dark hair swept back from his face – rather unfashionable these days, I think, but it suits him. Anthony has more rugged, rugby-player looks and is slightly more portly now – due, I'm sure, to an excess of corporate hospitality over the years. Laurence is still relatively slim, but there are slight signs of a businessman's paunch developing. Once upon a time, he used to run daily when he came home from work, usually in the dark and wearing one of those little high-viz vests. But now he has no time to maintain his fitness as he's back so late and is so exhausted. He's also been drinking much more lately – and not just on this holiday, where the wines are temptingly divine – and the pounds are slowly starting to creep on. Too much good living, I joke with him.

It's fair to say that our other halves have failed miserably when it comes to succumbing to the truly heavenly delights of the Podere Cielo. But then relaxation has never been Laurence's strong suit – that's why I was so keen for us to get away together. Both men brought their golf clubs but, in two weeks, haven't even managed to fit in one round. My husband was always such a charmer, always ready with a warm laugh, but there hasn't been much evidence of that recently. His work seems to be grinding the life out of him. And he's taken to chain-eating indigestion tablets. I must get him to go to the doctor when he has a moment. I'd hate to think he was getting an ulcer.

'They're cut from the same cloth.' Amanda shakes her head, exasperated. 'They work so hard.'

'It's very difficult out there,' I concur. 'So Laurence says.'

'Hell,' Amanda agrees, and takes another sip of her wine.

Watching my husband pace, I can't help but feel a shadow cross over me. This holiday has been, even by our standards, extortionately expensive, but I thought it would be money well spent as I hoped it would bring us closer together. We've been drifting apart – a terrible cliché, I know – but that's exactly how it happens. You drift. Slowly, but surely. Circling leisurely out of each other's reach. There's no deliberate intention to form separate lives within your marriage but, over time, that's what happens. Laurence might be at the top of his game, but there's no way he can rest on his laurels. I fully appreciate that. But the downside is that Laurence is never at home. He's a fund manager or some such thing in the City and his work takes him all over the world. One week he's in New York, the next in Hong Kong. Very rarely is he with us at our beautiful house in Buckinghamshire.

But then he tries to make up for it in other ways. His not insubstantial salary pays for all this. I take in the breathtaking sweep of the Tuscan hills again. The children board at Stonelands even though it's relatively close to home, we all have the most wonderful horses and stables at the house – we pay for someone to come in and exercise Laurence's – and I have more jewellery than I can ever wear. We really are very lucky.

My husband snaps his phone shut. I see his shoulders sag and my heart goes out to him. They never leave him alone for a moment. He strides over towards us. I had hoped that at this late stage in the holiday – we're going home in a few more days – he would be in relaxation mode, strolling or perhaps even reclining, but the pacing has never gone.

Perhaps we should think about a change of lifestyle for him when we get back from holiday. Cut back on the booze, persuade him to come to the health club that he pays royally for but never visits, have some hot stone massages. Amanda says that she knows a great holistic acupuncturist.

He comes over to the terrace where we're splayed out on the loungers.

'Everything okay?' I ask.

'Fine.' The word is crisp and says that all is *not* fine.

'Bloody office,' I mutter sympathetically. 'Can't they manage without you for two weeks?'

'I need to go back,' he says bluntly. 'There's something urgent I have to attend to.'

'Can't someone else do it?'

'If there was someone else, Lily, I wouldn't need to go back.' He doesn't try to hide his exasperation with me. 'I could get a flight later today and be back tomorrow.'

This is the last straw. 'No, Laurence.' I lower my voice as

4

I wouldn't want the Marquises to know that things aren't quite right between us. Their relationship is marvellous – Amanda tells me so constantly and I want to give the impression that ours is perfect too. 'I'm putting my foot down. This is our family holiday. The time should be sacrosanct.'

'I have to do this,' he says.

'No. I won't have it. Nothing can be that important. You've spent most of your time here on the damn telephone. We'll be home in a few days, anyway. Can't it wait until then?'

Laurence says nothing, but the sigh that escapes his lips is ragged.

'It's not all about money,' I remind him tightly. 'Your children, your wife are important too.' He's also been irritable with the children as he's so unused to spending any extended period of time with them and I want that to change. 'Sometimes you just have to say no.'

'It is *absolutely* all about money, Lily.' His lips are white, bloodless. 'I really need to do this.'

'No. And that's the last I'll hear of it.' I settle my sunglasses on my nose. What on earth will Amanda think if my husband just trots off at a moment's notice and leaves us stranded here? 'You'll stay here for the rest of the holiday and sort out whatever needs to be sorted out when you're back in work on Monday.'

My husband looks defeated, but I take no joy from it. He shouldn't even be thinking about abandoning us and jetting back on his own. This is our family holiday, for heaven's sake. Is it too much to ask that he enjoys it?

I stifle a sigh. 'Is that the end of it, Laurence?'

'Quite probably,' he says enigmatically. 'Quite probably.'

'Have a glass of this.' I proffer the Chianti as a peace-offering. Cutting back can start another day. 'It has healing properties.'

He gives me a doubtful look, but picks up a glass anyway.

Then Anthony rejoins us and the discussion is closed. Laurence is not flying back home for a day. How ridiculous. I won't allow it.

'Don't bother with the Chianti, my friend.' Anthony Marquis

5

slaps Laurence on the back heartily. 'Champagne is in order. Just clinched a deal for ten million.'

I have no idea what Anthony actually does, but he's in the same sort of line as Laurence – something or another in finance – and, although they move in different circles, they do have a few mutual acquaintances in the City.

'Champagne?' Amanda, who was starting to doze, opens her eyes. 'Wonderful.'

'Congratulations,' I offer.

'All in a day's work.' Anthony allows himself a delighted guffaw.

'You're supposed to be on holiday,' Amanda chides with an indulgent tut.

'Well, now that's sorted, I can kick back. Maybe we'll even get that game of golf in now, Laurence.'

He nudges my husband with his elbow and I note, with some embarrassment, that Laurence hasn't yet offered his congratulations to Anthony.

'Hmm. Perfect timing. It looks like lunch is served.' Anthony nods towards the covered dining loggia on the terrace where the housekeeper is setting out plate after plate of delicious-looking food. He rubs his stomach appreciatively. 'I've eaten so much bloody pasta I'm going to have to spend a month in the gym after this.'

We all laugh. Except Laurence, who's surprisingly quiet. All this fuss about not being able to fly back. I think that my husband needs to get his priorities right! Then, when I look at him closely, I note that there's a bleakness in his eyes that I've never seen before. I stand up and touch his arm.

He pulls away from me.

Amanda and Anthony take towels over to the children and chivvy them out of the water. Then they all wander off to the loggia. Laurence and I fall into step beside each other and start to follow them.

'This is the right thing to do, Laurence,' I say gently.

'You have no idea,' my husband says scathingly.

I soften. I have won this little skirmish and it wouldn't hurt to be gracious to him. 'Want to tell me about it then? What's so important that you feel you have to dash back?'

'When have you ever taken an interest in what I do, Lily?' He turns to me and his face is grim. 'There's little point in you starting now.'

I'm so taken aback that I can't come up with a suitable reply. And, as we go to the loggia for lunch, the sun suddenly disappears behind a cloud.

Chapter 2

We all sit down at the teak dining table beneath the white canopy, and a welcome breeze billows the fabric. I help Hugo and Hettie to pour themselves some freshly-squeezed orange juice – though at their age, they're perfectly capable of managing without my assistance. It's so beautiful here and school holidays are precious days for me as it's the only chance I get to spend quality time with my children – *and* my husband. I had hoped that Laurence might feel the same way too.

Clearly not.

'Have you had fun here?' I ask, smoothing my daughter's wayward hair from her eyes. Hettie's hair is the same shade of titian as mine, but there the similarity ends. Mine is styled in a sleek bob that I keep cropped short whereas Hettie's is an untameable tangle of curls provided by some genetic mystery that must go back generations. At least I know that our green eyes come from my mother.

'Oh, yes,' Hettie says. 'Alice is going to Barbados, but I think this is much nicer.'

'I like this as much as skiing,' Hugo informs me. My son favours his father and is dark-haired, with eyes the colour of the Tuscan sky. 'Can I try snowboarding this year?'

'Let's get one holiday out of the way first,' I chide, laughing. Laurence sighs and I know that he is annoyed that they don't stop to enjoy one thing before they're wanting the next. That's what children are like these days and, if he was around to talk to them more often, he'd know that. 'But, yes. If you want to do snowboarding, then I don't see why you can't try it.'

'Coolio,' Hugo says.

'Maybe we could all go skiing?' I suggest. This has been a resounding success. Other than the unseemly spat between Laurence and me, that is. I don't see why it wouldn't translate to the slopes. A snow-sprinkled chalet in the mountains for the Marquis/Lamont-Jones crowd sounds wonderful. Laurence has to learn to appreciate that we need these breaks together as a family.

Amanda shrugs her agreement. 'We know a lovely place in Klosters. The Robinsons go there every year. But we'd need to be booking up soon.'

'We should do it the minute we get back,' I agree.

Laurence shoots a dark look at me. Well, let him. And if he wants to spend the entire time with his phone clamped to his ear while we're on the slopes, then that's up to him too. One of the reasons that Amanda thought it would be a good idea to rent a villa together is that she too has spent enough holidays trying to entertain the children by herself while Anthony's mind was back at the office.

I use the orange juice pouring and food dishing up as a distraction technique, so that I don't have to sit down and face my husband, as I still feel stung by his comment. In some ways he's right though – we never find time to talk to each other any more. On holiday *or* at home. It's never the right time, is it? There's always something else to do. The minutiae of daily life doesn't stop just because you're going through a bad patch, does it? I did think that we'd find time to address our relationship difficulties while we were here in Tuscany, but then Laurence has been tense the whole time and I didn't want to spoil our marvellous time here by bringing up something unpleasant.

Laurence and Anthony sit at the far end of the table and it looks like they're already talking business. Again. I love my husband though, whatever little faults he may have. I'm sure I'm not perfect myself.

9

Amanda ties a sarong around her white bikini that shows off a figure that has been honed by hours in the gym. I know because I'm usually there alongside her.

My friend and I go to the same health club and spa – the only decent one in the area. It's expensive – what isn't? – but the facilities are truly marvellous. Laurence is a member too, of course, but never finds the time to go. I don't think he's graced the place once yet this year.

Amanda is always glossy and groomed. Her tan, at the moment, may be down to the Mediterranean sun, but it's maintained at this level all year round by judicious applications of St Tropez by a lovely young girl at the health spa. Even in her swimsuit, my friend is wearing a full complement of gold and diamond jewellery and designer kitten heels. On Amanda's recommendation, I go to the same hairdresser as her and have subtle slices of blonde put into my classic bob to keep me on the right side of being classed as a redhead. At thirty-eight, Amanda is two years younger than me, but she's already the leading light in the local Women's Institute and is a force to be reckoned with on the school committee. As well as going to the health club we also ride out together two or three times a week. Amanda is of the Hollywood, stick-thin breed whereas I consider myself elegantly curvy. We go to a little boutique together in Woburn Sands and she helps me to choose what suits me as, to be honest, I've never had much of a clue.

I don't know what I'd do without her. She introduced me to the 'in' crowd and I remember how lonely my days were before I met her. The house is a bit out on a limb and the only person I ever seemed to talk to was my cleaner – a darling woman from the village, but she was obsessed with her bunions and one quickly ran out of chit-chat once that topic had been exhausted. Of course, there was my hairdresser and massage therapist, but no one I could really talk to, not like I talk to Amanda. We share everything. Although, of course, I wouldn't dream of confiding in her that everything wasn't tickety-boo with Laurence. What would I do if our other friends found out?

The table is groaning with dishes of pasta – one with fresh

pesto sauce, another with a basil-scented ragu. There are salad leaves and a plate of ripe tomatoes with buffalo mozzarella and avocados and some pungent garlic bread. Anthony disappears into the kitchen and moments later returns bearing four flûtes and a bottle of fizz, he then splashes it out for us.

'To business,' he cries.

We all raise a toast. 'To business!'

My husband is late. 'To business,' he says alone.

'And thank you for a lovely holiday,' I say. 'Let's have a toast to us.'

We raise our glasses again. 'To us!' I try to catch Laurence's eye, but he looks away from me.

'This has been just wonderful,' I add. 'I hope we can do it again.'

'To next year,' Anthony proposes.

'To next year!'

'Do you think we could top it and find somewhere even more amazing?' Amanda wants to know.

'This is idyllic,' I say with a contented sigh. 'I can't see how we could better it.'

'Come on,' her husband says. 'Stop chatting, you girls! Let's tuck in. All this toasting is making me hungry.'

While Anthony digs into the pasta, Amanda helps herself to some salad – her low-fat, no-carb diet hasn't, it must be said, been abandoned for one moment since she arrived.

She passes me the dish. 'I hate to raise this,' she says, dropping her voice so that only I can hear her. 'Especially now. But all this talk of "next year" brought it to mind.'

I wait as she pauses. 'I gave you the invoice for your share of the villa, didn't I?' my friend goes on.

'Yes,' I murmur back. It was for an extraordinary amount of money. This sort of luxury doesn't come cheap, but this place is as high-end as high-end comes.

'Some time ago,' she adds.

The balance was due six weeks before we flew here. I distinctly remember putting the statement on Laurence's desk. I feel myself colour up.

11

'Hasn't Laurence paid it?'

'I'm afraid not.'

'I'm so sorry, Amanda. It must have completely slipped his mind.' Laurence is never normally like that. 'I know that he's been under a lot of pressure lately.'

She goes to speak.

I hold up a hand. 'That's no excuse. I should have remined him. The minute we get back, the *very* minute, I'll ask him to give me a cheque.'

Amanda pats my hand. 'Thank you, darling. I knew you'd understand. It's an awful lot of money to have outstanding.'

Thousands and thousands of pounds. The villa rental was over fifteen thousand pounds for the two weeks, and on top of that was the car hire, the food, the considerable quantities of booze. Anthony didn't want to slum it by flying budget airline. They are so used to business class, I'm sure they're physically allergic to economy, so that cost extra too. There'll be little change out of forty thousand pounds – for a two-week holiday. But that is for *two* families. Even for us, it was a stretch though. Laurence was very grudging when he agreed to it. But it was money well spent as it was beyond perfect.

I worry at my nail. Amanda has paid for all this in advance and we, it seems, haven't yet stumped up a penny. I had no idea. Obviously, I thought my husband was seeing to all that. I had all the new clothes to buy and the packing to do. He can hardly expect me to deal with the money side of things too. That's not how we work. I feel awkward that Amanda has even had to raise it. That's terrible of us. I hope this doesn't make her think any less of me as a friend. Also, this is the first time that Amanda has ever mentioned money to me before. Maybe I'm reading too much into this, but perhaps things are tighter in the Marquis household than she's admitting. I wouldn't be entirely surprised. Anthony did seem to be sweating on that deal. He must be so relieved that it's clinched.

I feel so sorry for them if things are difficult – goodness only knows that we're all over-extended and the current economic climate isn't helping much. So I believe. But that's just life, isn't it? We're all living on someone else's money. That's what everyone does. My dear parents, if they were still alive, would baulk at the way we spend; they could have lived for a year on what we get through in a week. I was brought up to watch the pennies – goodness only know where *that* went wrong. My monthly credit-card bill alone is like the national debt of a small developing country. Most families would struggle to pay it. For all their outward show, it seems that the Marquises aren't immune to the credit crunch. Surely this fabulous contract that Anthony has just landed will take the pressure off them. I do hope so, for their sakes.

'You know, Amanda, if there's ever anything we can do to help,' I say it almost as a whisper. I would hate for Anthony to think that I know they're having difficulties. 'You only have to ask.'

And I have no idea how those words will come back to haunt me.

Chapter 3

Laurence has a regular driver called Peter. He's a kindly, middle-aged fellow who ferries my husband to and from the airport when he has a business trip or sometimes brings him back home from London when there's a late-night dinner and the trains have stopped running, or my husband has had one over the eight. We give him a little extra cash in hand to drop us off and collect us when we go on holiday.

He usually turns up at the airport in our own Mercedes but, this time, he's in the company people-carrier. As soon as he sees us, Peter takes Laurence to one side.

'What's wrong with our car?' I ask.

Peter avoids my eyes.

'Nothing. I'll sort it,' Laurence says tightly. 'Get in.' And, dutifully – even though he's avoided answering me – we all pile into the people-carrier.

'I hope we go back to Tuscany soon, Mummy,' Hettie says. 'It was too wonderful.'

My daughter is destined to be on the stage. Everything in her life is a drama.

'I'd like to marry an Italian.'

'Yuk,' is Hugo's verdict. 'I never want to get married. Then I'd have to kiss a girl.' My son makes vomiting actions.

Let's hope his opinion stays the same for a long, long time. I don't want him getting some loose-moralled Stonelands girl pregnant at sixteen.

We set off – Peter driving, my husband letting his head drop

14

back on the seat next to me. But he's not sleeping, he's just staring at the roof. His fists are clenched, the knuckles white – probably tense from travelling with our offspring rather than doing his own thing.

The children are dozing as it's been a long journey back from the Podere Cielo and we all had an early start. As we turn onto the motorway, I lower my voice.

'This might not be the best time to discuss it,' I begin, but think, when is? Laurence is back at work tomorrow. He'll be on the train just after six in the morning and, if he decides to stay up at our apartment in London, I probably I won't catch sight of him until next weekend. 'We still owe the Marquises for our share of the villa rental and the car and the flights,' I go on. I don't mention all the food and wine.

Laurence lets out a breath that vibrates shakily in the car. 'I know.'

'You do?' I turn to look at him, but my husband's eyes are now closed. That's not what I expected. 'I thought it had slipped your mind.'

'Am I likely to forget a bill for nearly twenty thousand pounds?'

'Well, no.' But something is niggling me. 'So why haven't we paid it?'

'*We*? Why haven't *we* paid it?'

'You know what I mean.'

'Let me worry about that, will you?' Laurence turns his head and stares out of the window.

Shutting my mouth, I slink down in my seat, sorry that we're tetchy with each other the moment that we're back on British turf.

I love to go on holiday. We have been to some fabulous places in the past, like the Turks and Caicos Islands, the Maldives, Thailand, Goa – all with the family. Then Laurence and I try to sneak in a few grown-up weekends every year if we can negotiate a reciprocal childminding arrangement with some of our other friends. Our date weekends have taken us to Paris, Prague, Barcelona, Budapest, Rome and Reykjavik. But, even though we've travelled the world, I do love to come home too.

We have a beautiful place. Absolutely beautiful. Ten years ago, I found the plot of land in a lovely Buckinghamshire village called Morsworth, on the outskirts of the thrusting city of Milton Keynes. It's perfect commuting distance for Laurence. Easily accessible for London, yet when he's here, it really feels like an escape to the country for him. We're at the end of a winding lane, opposite a medieval church, and we can hear the bells ring when we're curled up in bed on a Sunday morning. Not that we often curl up in bed these days. Laurence is either out on the golf course at the crack of dawn or seeing to something in the office.

We had the barn built to our own specification. Gosh, what a price though. We poured all of our savings and more into it. But it was so worth it. The resulting house has all the charm of an old building and all the high-tech convenience of a modern one.

There are five spacious bedrooms, each with its own en-suite bathroom, an office for Laurence and a gorgeous, farmhouse-style kitchen for me. The children have their own playroom with a half-size snooker table. Outside we have a formal garden bordering the house with clipped box hedges and pink standard roses. Then there's an acre that I designed to have a more informal style with a sweep of lawn, meandering herbaceous borders and a sprinkling of acers to provide some shade.

Beyond the lawn, there's a stile that leads to a wood of silver birch trees that we planted shortly after we moved in and which is now flourishing nicely. A woodland walk wanders through it and, for our anniversary, we sometimes choose a sculpture to put in there too. When we got the first one we trawled the country looking for something that we liked, visiting small studios and meeting the artists, discussing what we'd viewed over cosy lunches until we found something just perfect. Now, as Laurence is so tight for time and we usually miss our anniversary, we tend to pick them straight from a catalogue and get the gallery to send one over. It's not quite as romantic, but nevertheless lovely, as it always reminds me of how we used to be. Beyond the silver birches, the wood leads onto a small wild-flower meadow where

16

I have a few beehives; our gardener produces the most wonderful honey from them.

Along the side of the garden there's an oak garage big enough for three cars and behind that is stabling enough for our horses and a large paddock where we can turn them out to grass. Hettie and Hugo both have ponies and I have a highly-strung Appaloosa called Spot. Laurence's polo pony is here too – but he rarely gets to play now unless it's something to do with work. We have someone from the village to come in and groom them and exercise them because, as you can imagine, it's far too much work for us to do on our own.

There's no denying that the Podere Cielo was utterly exquisite, but there's nothing quite like your own bed and your own cup of tea, is there? I hope that I never lose the joy of the simple pleasures in life. Once we're home, I shall unpack the cases and put the laundry on. My cleaner is coming tomorrow so I'd like to have a few loads ready for her to iron.

Glancing behind at the children, I see they are sound asleep, but they both have contented smiles on their faces. I have a few more weeks at home with them before they go back to school and I'm really looking forward to that.

I let my head rest back and close my eyes. It's Sunday afternoon and it's getting late. Not far to go now. Travelling is wonderful, but coming home is even better.

Chapter 4

When we turn from Church Lane and pull into our drive, I sit bolt upright in my seat and gasp out loud. 'What's happened?'

The doors and windows of our house are all boarded up. The front door looks as if it has been jemmied around the lock. The car has barely come to a halt before I jump out, and my husband is hot on my heels.

'My God,' I say. 'Oh, my God!'

Laurence is staring, open-mouthed, at our home.

'What's happened?' I ask again, dazed. 'Has there been a fire? Have we been burgled?'

Peter is out of the car too now and is looking embarrassed. Laurence strides to the front door and tries his key in the lock. For a good five minutes, he jiggles it this way and that, but the door stays firmly shut. 'Changed,' he mutters. 'They've changed the locks.'

'What?' I say. 'Who have? What's wrong?'

'The locks have been changed,' my husband reiterates.

'Who by? Here, let me try.'

Laurence hands over the keys but, as he does so, he says, 'It's no use.'

And, sure enough, despite me nearly snapping it off in the lock, the key is useless.

Then, as I turn round, I notice that the garage too has large metal bars across the front and padlocks that wouldn't look out of place in the Tower of London. The children are now out of the car, rubbing the sleep from their eyes. Then they also stand and look in a perplexed manner at our boarded-up house.

'Go to the stables,' I say. 'Go and say hello to the horses.'

Hugo doesn't need to be told twice and he races off, Hettie following in his wake.

Spinning, I face Laurence. 'Do you know anything about this?' My husband's features are ashen. 'What's going on?'

He opens his mouth but doesn't speak.

'What? Talk to me, Laurence.' I take his arm and shake it.

'It's all gone,' he mumbles eventually. 'It's all gone. All of it.'

'What do you mean?'

Then the children are back, running even faster. 'The stables are all locked up,' Hugo says breathlessly. 'I don't think the horses are there.'

Now Laurence blinks. 'They've taken the horses too.'

'Who have? Laurence, who has done this?'

One of those shuddering breaths again. 'Bailiffs,' he says, flatly. Then, for the first time, he meets my eyes. 'I have, desperately, desperately, been trying to sort this out all the time we've been in Tuscany, Lily. That's why I wanted to fly back. I thought I could . . .' His words trail away. Then, 'Believe me, I never thought it would come to this.'

Peter shuffles uncomfortably. He looks like he would rather be anywhere else in the world – and I know how he feels.

'We've lost our home?' My voice is quieter, less hysterical than I think it should be.

'I thought I could strike a deal, that something would come up at the eleventh hour.' Laurence shakes his head again, shattered. 'I truly never thought it would come to this.' Unhinged laughter breaks from him, and his eyes fill with tears.

'Tell me this isn't real.'

'It is, Lily. We have nothing. Nothing but the clothes we're standing up in.'

'This must be wrong, Laurence. There must be something you can say, something you can do.' I can't believe that we're here in the drive having this discussion, barred from our own

19

home. This doesn't happen to people like us. Laurence must be mistaken. 'Whatever you've done, whatever we owe, they can't put us out on the streets. They can't make us homeless.'

'They can,' he says firmly. 'And they have.'

I lower my voice so that Peter can't hear. My poor husband must be beside himself with humiliation. 'Laurence, we are *wealthy* people. How can this be happening? How can you be taking it so calmly?'

'I'm taking it calmly because, in truth, I knew it would happen. I might have tried to pretend I didn't, but I did. In my heart.' He looks at the house again, but it's as if he's not seeing it at all. 'We're not wealthy, Lily. We haven't got a bean to our name.'

I almost laugh. Now I'm feeling exasperated with him, as if he's hiding a piece of the jigsaw from me. 'Don't be silly.'

'We can't come back here. It isn't ours any more.'

'What about the apartment? If you insist we can't get into the house for the time being, we could go and live there for a while.'

'We can't. That's gone too.'

'Laurence, I have no idea what you're talking about. Why do you keep saying everything's gone? You're starting to scare me.'

This is ridiculous. I'm not going to wait on the drive of my own home all night until Laurence comes to his senses. The children are exhausted. We'll have to sort this all out tomorrow, find out what's gone wrong – as clearly something has.

Laurence puts his hands on my arms and turns me towards him. His eyes are red-rimmed. 'I tried everything I could to prevent this,' he assures me, 'but we've lost everything. It's all gone. I can't say it any plainer. We have nothing left, Lily. Nothing at all.'

'We'll break into the barn. Everything we have is still in there.' At least, I'm assuming it is. 'It's ours.'

'Not any more. How many more ways can I tell you? It no longer belongs to us. The bank has repossessed the house.'

Repossessed. The word strikes at my heart.

'If we break in, we'll be charged with criminal damage on top of everything else.'

Repossessed? I can't quite take this in. 'They only do that if you've fallen behind with your mortgage,' I tell Laurence. 'That can't be us.'

He laughs, but it's obvious that he's not finding this funny. 'Oh Lily. We're behind with the mortgage, our credit cards have been stopped, the bank has cancelled our overdraft. Do I need to go on?'

I can barely find my voice. 'I knew nothing of this.'

'No,' he says. 'No, you didn't.'

'Surely we'll be able to get some of it back?'

'I don't know,' Laurence admits. 'I really don't know.'

Needless to say, this has never happened to me before, to us. The Lamont-Joneses have always paid their bills on time. Or I thought we had. 'You have got us into this mess without telling me?'

'Yes.'

The hysteria is building inside me now as I realise that this nightmare is my new reality. I was sure that there would be a valid explanation. It seems that there isn't one, beyond the fact that somehow, some way, we are broke. Completely broke. 'Where will we go?' My voice is rising now. 'What will we do?'

Laurence pulls the children to him. 'We'll think of something.'

'*We?*' Now it's my turn to pull that card.

'All right – *I'll* think of something.'

'You knew about this,' I say. 'You knew all about this and you never thought to tell me?'

'I didn't want to worry you,' my husband tells me.

'Well, I'm worried now,' I spit.

'If I'd tried to tell you,' Laurence says, 'would you have wanted to listen?'

Peter coughs gently before I can think of an answer. 'Is there somewhere I could take you?' our driver offers kindly. 'Friends that you can stay with till you get sorted?'

'Friends . . .' Laurence looks as if he's considering the idea.

'Who has room for all of us?' I interject. 'I can't think of anyone.' And they'd know, I think. They'd know that our life

21

had just disappeared down a particularly smelly drainhole. We can't let them find out. We need to weather this quietly and get through it as quickly as we can and then no one, beyond Peter, would ever need to know. He's been loyal enough to us over the years and I'm sure, if necessary, a few hundred pounds would buy his silence. 'We need time to think about this. Clearly. Rationally.' But, try as I might, my brain isn't coming up with any solutions at all.

Neither, it seems, is Laurence's. My husband stands there silent, dejected while I'm lost in my own maelstrom of panic, fear, anger and confusion. We have to hold it together for the children's sake. Their faces are white with fear as they know that something is terribly, terribly wrong.

'I could take you to a hotel,' Peter pipes up. 'Perhaps the Travelhotel, Mr Lamont-Jones. They're very basic but . . .'

Cheap is the word that remains unspoken.

'Yes,' Laurence says as if in a dream. 'Yes, Peter, that sounds like a jolly good idea.'

'Mrs Lamont-Jones?' Peter holds his arm out towards me, shepherding me to the people-carrier.

'Thank you, Peter. Back in the car, children,' I say and usher them inside. Our cases, which haven't even been unloaded, now contain all our worldly goods. And we have Laurence's golf clubs too − some good they will do us.

Peter slides into the driver's seat. I turn and take one last look at my home, my beautiful, beautiful home with my Chalon kitchen and my SMEG fridge and my Designer's Guild furnishings.

'Are you okay with this?' my husband wants to know.

'Okay?' I say. But the word is filled with tears. 'Of course, I'm okay.'

Then, before Laurence can catch me, my legs give way and I sink to my knees in the gravel and howl with despair.

Chapter 5

Peter, as he had suggested, drove them straight to the Travelhotel. At the door, while Laurence checked in, their driver unloaded the suitcases still filled with bright holiday clothes.

Before the trip, Lily had kitted out both of the children with new shorts, T-shirts and swimsuits for their summer break. Surely they didn't grow so fast these days that the ones they'd had last year didn't fit? Laurence thought. There had also been a slew of new dresses for her, linen crops and shirts for him. All unnecessary and all designer-labelled. He had been terrified to tell her that they could afford none of it. Not one single scrap. The cost of the holiday had been the straw that had finally broken the camel's back and yet he still hadn't been able to put a stop to it. He still couldn't bring himself to say no to her.

Here, at the Travelhotel, a family room was £29.95 for the night. A bargain by any reckoning. They'd been paying more than that for each of the bottles of vintage wine they'd been swigging as if it was water over the last few weeks. But handing over the money brought the taste of bile to his mouth. It was virtually all he had in his pocket, apart from a handful of euros.

Laurence went back into the car park with the plastic keycard. Lily, Hettie and Hugo stood huddled round their suitcases. They looked like orphans, evacuees, shocked and stunned people who had been made homeless through no fault of their own. It was his doing. His alone.

'We're in,' Laurence said.

'I'll give you a hand with the bags, Mr Lamont-Jones.'

'Thank you, Peter.'

Together they carried the cases and his golf bag into the hotel. He thought of the difference between this and the Podere Cielo and nearly laughed out loud at the absurdity of it. The sublime to the ridiculous.

The room, when they found it along the endless beige corridor, was basic, a bit scuffed, but comfortable enough. It was warm and they had a roof over their heads. That was all that mattered for now.

Peter brought the last of the cases in through the door. 'Will that be all?'

'Yes, thank you, Peter. You've been very kind.'

The driver cleared his throat and lingered awkwardly.

'Oh,' Laurence said, suddenly twigging. It was payment time.

'Can't do this one on account, sir.'

'No, no. Of course not.' Laurence pulled the smattering of euros from his pocket. 'I could go to the cashpoint . . .' The sentence trailed off. It would only spit his card out. What was the point in pretending otherwise? 'Can I owe you, Peter?' Add him to the growing list.

'Of course, sir. No problem. No problem at all.' The man turned towards the door and Laurence followed.

'I really appreciate this, Peter. You've been very good to us.'

In his hand, surreptitiously, Peter held a roll of cash. 'If this will help . . .'

Laurence felt himself flush. How the mighty fall. Peter had been his driver for years, the one who had been offered a wedge of notes for services rendered, and now he was offering him a handout. 'Thank you,' Laurence said. 'That's very thoughtful of you. But we should be fine.'

'Are you sure, sir?'

Then Laurence remembered that they would have to eat tonight and had no means to pay for it. 'Perhaps if you could see your way . . .'

Peter pressed the money into his palm. 'No rush for it back, sir. Whenever you can.'

Reluctantly, Laurence folded his fingers around it. Before,

24

when all this had been hypothetical, when he'd been trying to balance the books, make a sow's ear into a silk purse, he'd never foreseen what it would really be like.

'I'm sorry.' Peter looked uncomfortable. 'I'd better go. My missus will be fretting. If there's anything you need, sir, anything I can help you with, you just give me a call.'

'Thank you, Peter.'

The man nodded to Lily. 'Mrs Lamont-Jones.'

'Thank you, Peter. You've been very kind.' Lily stood hugging herself and Laurence could tell that his wife was only just managing to hold back her tears.

'Well,' he said when the door closed. 'Home, sweet home.'

'Don't,' Lily snapped. 'That's not even funny.'

He put his arm round her and pulled her to him. 'There's nothing I can do about it tonight, darling. But I promise that I'll try to sort something out for us tomorrow. First thing. I'll get onto the building society, the bank, the council. It will all look very different tomorrow.'

'But it won't get us our house back?'

Laurence's throat closed. 'No.'

Perhaps because he'd known this was coming, knew the debts were piling up faster than the money was coming in, he felt a kind of calm resignation, an inevitability. The train crash that had been looming slowly, slowly, slowly over the course of the last year had finally happened; the train had hit the buffers and had ended up in a tangled mess.

Strangely, he felt a relief. Was almost giddy with it. As if a weight had been lifted from his shoulders. He shouldn't feel like this because he had no idea what tomorrow would bring, and all of his life he'd been a man with a plan.

'We'll talk about this later,' he said, glancing towards the children.

Lily nodded.

'I'm hungry,' Hettie complained.

Laurence and Lily exchanged a glance.

'We all need to eat,' his wife said.

So, not knowing quite what else to do, he took his family

25

across the road to the conveniently-sited McDonald's — a place they would normally have avoided like the plague — and the children had Big Macs and fries and milkshakes while he and his wife picked at a soggy carton of fries between them and they spent some more of the money that they didn't now have. Laurence broke into a cold sweat every time he thought that he no longer had the lifeline of a credit card. It had always been so easy to put things on a card; it never felt like spending real money.

His wife looked drawn. Already, the tan that she'd acquired in Tuscany seemed to have drained from her face and left her looking sallow. The children were bickering away, tired and crotchety, but he hadn't the heart to chastise them. How would the seismic change in their circumstances affect them when they realised they wouldn't be going home again? Maybe they were just too young to understand. Laurence hoped so. He'd always wanted to provide a life of ease for them. That's all. He had never viewed their voracious consumerism as greedy or grasping. It was just what people did. He'd wanted to give his children a better start than he'd had — and who didn't want to do that? And it had been going so well. He'd been riding high. He'd been the first person in his family to go to university, the first with a white-collar job. Promotion had come easily and he'd risen through the ranks with no discernible setbacks. A charmed life. For years everything he had touched had turned to gold. He was invincible.

Tears sprang to his eyes.

Lily's hand covered his. 'Okay?' she asked.

Laurence nodded, unable to trust his voice. His family had never seen him cry and he wasn't about to start now.

'We'll get through this,' she said. 'We'll get through this together.'

When the lump in his throat had gone, he said, 'Thank you.'

He could remember the exact moment when it had all started to go horribly, horribly wrong. For the last year it had played out like a video on slow motion in his brain. If only he'd done this differently or done that differently. If only he'd taken more care, had been more cautious, had stepped back from the edge, had convinced himself there was no such thing as a free lunch.

If only he had done these things, then they wouldn't be in this mess now.

Chapter 6

I tuck the children up for the night in their tiny single beds in the cramped room that adjoins our equally minuscule one in our budget 'Family Suite'. But I shouldn't complain – at least we're not sleeping on the street. Not yet.

'Are we still on holiday, Mummy?' Hettie wants to know.

'No, darling.' We're back down to earth with a bump.

'So why aren't we in our house?'

Where do I start? I'm not even sure myself why we're not in our house. My husband still has some pretty nifty explaining to do. 'There's a little problem at the moment,' I tell her. 'Daddy will try to sort it out tomorrow.'

'Is someone else going to live there?'

'I don't know, poppet. I hope not. I hope we'll be back there soon.'

She slips her thumb into her mouth and I kiss her sunbronzed face. What has Laurence done? How could he have compromised his own children's future like this? I want them to sleep sound and untroubled in their beds every night of their lives while they're young enough to be under our protection. I want them to have everything that I never had, and more. How can we have let them down so badly?

I kiss Hugo too. 'What about Boo and Silver?' he asks. Their ponies.

'We'll get them back,' I say. 'Just as soon as we can.' But I think I may be lying to them. If the house has gone and the cars and the apartment in London, then we must be in very, very dire straits indeed.

'Sleep tight.' I close the door behind me and lean against it, sighing.

The contents of the suitcase are scattered on the floor and Laurence is sitting on the bed in a T-shirt and his boxers, head in hands. I wonder why on earth I went to the trouble of bringing back some beautiful balsamic vinegar and the best porcini mushrooms from Tuscany. Fat lot of good they'll do us now.

It's not even eight o'clock yet and already it feels like this has been the longest day of my life.

The room is stifling and I open the window. The noise of the traffic on the adjacent road floods in. I shut the window again. Then I sit down next to Laurence and he takes my hand.

'I'm sorry,' he says again.

'Don't keep saying that.' I feel as if I want to shout and scream, vent some of this roiling anger, but I just don't have the energy. It's as if I've been sucked into the vortex of a black hole and don't have the strength to fight my way out. 'Just tell me what the hell has happened.'

He takes a deep and shuddering breath before he starts. 'This time last year. I invested a lot of my clients' money in a special fund. When everything else was going pear-shaped, the returns on this looked too good to be true. I committed heavily to it.' Laurence runs a hand through his hair and shakes his head as if still bemused. 'Turns out it *was* too good to be true. It was one of these pyramid scams like the Madoff scheme in New York. I lost everything. All of my clients' money has gone.'

'Didn't I read about this? Wasn't it in the papers?'

'Yes.'

'And you were involved in it?'

'Not in the scam. Just in being stupid enough to invest in it.' He turns to me, his eyes bleak. 'The upshot was that I didn't

29

get my bonus last year, and I only hung onto my job by the skin of my teeth.'

My husband's bonus was usually a big six-figure sum and, it seems a stupid thing to say, but we relied on it to fund our lavish lifestyle. The children's school fees alone are more than sixty thousand pounds a year. Add to that a gigantic mortgage, two posh cars, four horses to feed and shoe, and our monthly outgoings were – when I'm forced to think about it – quite unbelievably staggering.

'The whole thing started to unravel then,' Laurence continues. 'I'd gone from being the blue-eyed boy to a liability – literally overnight. When word got out, I became a pariah. No one was investing in my funds. I was watching my career bleed to death. Then the company pulled the plug.'

'Pulled the plug?'

'Yes. After years of being one of their best managers, I found myself out on my ear.'

'You mean that you've no job?' That sets my head reeling again.

Laurence nods. 'I've been gainfully unemployed for over three months now.'

'Oh, Christ.' I think I'm going to be sick, so I gulp in deep breaths. 'How have you managed to keep this from me? Why didn't you tell me? I'm your wife. Does that mean nothing?'

'I didn't want you to know,' my husband explains.

I feel as if I'm listening to a stranger.

'I thought that it would be short-term. That someone, one of my contacts, would come to my rescue. I've been in the industry for years. Have been well-respected. Surely someone out there would throw me a lifeline.' Laurence takes a shuddering breath and then blows it out. He sounds exhausted, as if he's run a marathon or climbed a mountain. 'So I got up every morning, put on my suit, kissed you goodbye and took the train to London. But instead of going to the office, I trawled the head-hunters, met up with long-lost colleagues who I thought might be able to help. Generally, I spent the day knocking on doors.' Laurence laughs and it's a hollow sound. 'I even thought of standing by the side of the road with one of those sandwich boards on, advertising my wares. The only thing that stopped me was thinking that you might see me on the evening news.'

'I can't believe I'm hearing this.'

'I put the apartment in London up for sale the minute I realised that my bonus wasn't going to be there to cover the mortgage. But who's buying places like that now? In the end, I just had to give the keys back. The building society are in the process of selling it and I'm hoping they'll make enough to cover the mortgage, otherwise that will be added to our growing debt too.'

'Why didn't you tell me?' I still can't get my head round the fact that all this has been going on and I knew nothing about it.

'The finances have always been my concern. You've never been involved in the money side of things.'

It's not said as an accusation and, moreover, it's true. I've never really had to budget, not in recent years. When we started out, when it was just the two of us, things were tight as they are for everyone trying to build a home. But latterly, everything I've ever wanted – either for myself or the children – has always been provided and, I feel ashamed to admit this now, but I've grown accustomed to it. The money has always been there and I never questioned too deeply where or how we came by it.

'If you'd told me,' I say, 'if you'd given me any sort of hint that things weren't as they should be, we could have sold the horses, the cars. I'd have never booked the ridiculous holiday we've just come back from.' My stomach rolls at the thought of how much money we've spent that we didn't actually have. 'Why couldn't you have sat me down and told me?'

'I never thought it would come to this. I thought I could fix it all, find another well-paid job and you'd never be any the wiser.'

'Oh, God.' I close my eyes. 'What are we going to do?'

'I don't know.' A sob escapes from my husband's throat.

'Don't,' I say. 'Don't. We can sort this out together.'

'I thought you'd leave me,' Laurence says shakily. 'I thought

31

if you found out about this, that I'd risked everything, then you'd go. You'd pack a bag, take the children and go.'

I smooth his hair down. It breaks my heart to think of him pretending to go into work every day, pounding the streets, looking for work, carrying this alone. 'How can you think that? I love you.'

Then Laurence cries. He cries like a baby. 'I love you too. Promise me that you'll never leave me. Promise me that you'll never take my children away.'

'Never.' I cradle him in my arms and rock him gently as I would Hettie or Hugo if they were ill. 'Promise me that you'll never again keep secrets from me.'

'Never,' he says and, by all that is good, I'll make sure that I hold him to it.

As we lie with our arms round each other, I realise that we haven't shared our emotions together for some time now. In recent years we've gone through life pretending that everything was wonderful when, in truth, it has been far from it. We've both been guilty of papering over the cracks. If we're going to get through this, then we have to start being honest with each other.

Is it true that facing adversity together can bring a couple closer? It looks as if I'm about to find out.

Chapter 7

Laurence and I both lie awake all night, eyes wide open, staring at the ceiling. We hold hands under the thin duvet – not our usual luscious goosedown quilt – gripping onto each other for comfort or to stop us breaking down. If we weren't on the ground floor, I might consider flinging myself out of the window. This situation currently seems insurmountable, but we have to stay strong for the children. Tomorrow, our first priority is to find somewhere for us to live. We can't stay in a hotel forever – even a budget one.

I think of my beautiful barn, cold and dark, empty. I'm terrified of the future and I wonder whether, if Laurence had told me about his troubles sooner – if we'd flogged off all the things we could have done without, sold the horses, the cars, taken the children out of school, cut our costs to the bone, cancelled the holiday – would we have been able to cling onto the house, to our home?

I know he seemed to think that some Superhero might swoop down and save us all from disaster, but that was never likely to happen. Was it? Weren't we in way too deep for that? But why did he wait to tell me until everything had gone?

That was my dream home. Now what will happen to it? Will it be sold off cheaply to someone who won't care about the rose garden or the beehives? Someone who might put a monstrous plastic hot tub in the stables instead of our beautiful boys? And where are they? Who will give our ponies new homes? Especially Spot, who is more highly strung than a

Supermodel and would bite you on the elbow as soon as look at you. Who will love him as I did?

I don't know what terrors are going through Laurence's mind, but I'm sure they're the same as mine.

The grey dawn brings no relief. I get up and visit the cold, functional bathroom, trying not to think of our spacious shower cubicle with rainfall head. Then I open the door to the children's rooms and check on Hettie and Hugo. They're both still fast asleep and I'm sure they will be for hours yet, as they've become accustomed to long lie-ins on our lazy holiday. The holiday that makes me feel sick to my stomach now.

As I come back into the room, Laurence slides out of bed, flicks on the cheap plastic kettle and makes us two cups of tea in hefty mugs that look as if they've been well used. We share the complimentary packet of shortbread biscuits and switch on GMTV.

'We'll have to try to get them into the local state school,' I say flatly. There'll certainly be no more swanky private school for the foreseeable future. How will they cope with that? They were both doing so well at Stonelands. Model pupils. Will all this disruption affect their schooling? It's bound to. We've always tried to give them the best education possible. Laurence and I both went to state schools and came through the system relatively unscathed. We scraped decent degrees in the end. But aren't standards so much worse now? I've seen the advantages and privileges that private education can offer, the doors it opens, and I still want that for my children. Who wouldn't? They have a lovely circle of friends too. Most of the time their social lives are better than ours. They'll miss them like mad. I find that I'm wringing my hands together and force myself to stop. Stop wringing, stop thinking.

'We'll need to know where we'll be living before we can do that,' Laurence reminds me. 'I'll get onto the council first thing and find out where we stand.'

'I don't even know anyone who's been in this situation that I can ask.' Amanda Marquis will probably know someone. She is the fount of all knowledge when it comes to scandal. I realise

34

that's what we'll be now — the subject of dinner-party gossip. People will go quiet when we walk into the room. We'll be the ones who they'll talk about behind our backs. And I'm sure there'll be as much sniggering as there is sympathy.

'What are we going to do about paying Amanda and Anthony?'

'We can't,' Laurence confesses. 'We just can't.'

'Oh, Laurence. They're our friends. We can't *not* pay them.'

'We have no choice, Lily.' My husband rubs his hands over his face. Perhaps reality is finally hitting home. 'I'll call Anthony. Explain. He'll understand.'

'But it's twenty thousand pounds. Would *we* be understanding if someone did that to us?' I don't think so. We'd probably try to sue them. Oh, God. Don't even go there.

'We've had nothing before,' Laurence reminds me. 'We can do it again.'

'That was different,' I say. 'We were young, starting out. No one has anything then.'

When you're first married or living together and get your first home there's a sort of fun in having a spartan existence. Laurence and I started out in a damp flat in Leighton Buzzard with nothing but one deckchair and a bean bag in the lounge and a second-hand futon for a bed. They say that love can keep you warm and it certainly did back then. But then we'd met at university when we were both accustomed to student digs, so our expectations were low. Neither of us had privileged upbringings. We're both from working-class stock. My parents had to work hard to make ends meet, but we always had a roof over our heads, there was always food on the table. I know what it's like not to have money, but I thought those days were far behind us. And I don't want to go back to it now. No, thank you.

There's no doubt that we've been lucky. But we've striven for all that we've got, we've earned it. Laurence has worked ridiculously hard to get to where he is — or where he *was*. In fact, that has been the major bone of contention in our relationship. We might have had all the trappings of wealth, but I could count on one hand the times when Laurence has been able to attend a school sports day, a nativity play, parents' evening. There have been dozens and dozens of cancelled theatre trips, dinner parties we've missed, times when I've had to get on and go to things alone otherwise I would have had no life at all. I can't think of one year since the children were born when Laurence has been around to celebrate their birthdays; more often than not he's been in Frankfurt or Hong Kong or New York, and I've organised their parties alone. My own birthday has become a fluid date, fitted in when convenient around work schedules. Yes, we've had it easy, but there have been sacrifices too. We've had all the creature comforts, there's no denying that, but Laurence's work, I'm pretty sure, has been sucking the heart out of us for years.

While my life as I know it spins out of control, on GMTV they're talking about the fashion trends for the autumn – bright colours from a variety of designer names. Normally, I'd be making a mental note to rush out and buy them. Now I wonder whether I'll ever give a damn about that sort of frippery again.

Chapter 8

Laurence had eventually managed to get through to the council's housing 'hot line'. It had taken over an hour of redialling a constantly engaged phone. Clearly, being suddenly homeless was a problem that was being encountered by many other people.

He had, however, eventually managed to speak to someone and had instantly been redirected to Streetways Housing Association. More calling and more hanging on the line and he'd secured an appointment that morning with a lettings officer at Streetways, and now he was heading to their offices to see what, if anything, they were able to offer in the way of help.

In the absence of a car, he'd walked to the centre of the city. It had taken him half an hour and, despite the coolness of the day, he was now sweating slightly. He wasn't sure if it was from fear or from exertion.

The Streetways offices were plush, furnished stylishly and air-conditioned to arctic temperatures on what was a reasonably miserable summer's day. If worse came to worst, he'd be more than happy to set up camp here.

Despite having an appointed time, he waited for two hours in the small reception area along with a bewildered-looking kid of about sixteen, and a woman with two small suitcases and a toddler; both mother and child cried ceaselessly. Laurence had no idea what to do to comfort either of them, so spent the entire time studying his feet. Perhaps they too wondered what he was doing here in a casual linen shirt, crops and Crocs.

To his relief, he was summoned through to the office.

'Now, what can we do for you?' the lettings officer asked.

And he had poured out his sorry story. As he did, he wondered what the stories of the other people were who came through here.

Despite thinking that he would get little sympathy, the woman behind the desk was so concerned about his plight that it made Laurence's eyes brim with tears.

'We've lots of forms to fill in, love,' she said.

So, for another two hours, together they completed the necessary forms on her computer – the woman with the air of someone who had done it far too many times before, Laurence with a growing sense of desperation.

'You're assessed by a points scoring system,' she explained. 'You get more based on income – or lack of it, whether you've got any assets that can be liquidated, how many children you have, any disabilities or health issues.'

He wondered if you got fewer points for just being plain stupid, for managing to accure so much and then just letting it slip through your fingers.

'You probably see a lot more deserving cases than me.'

She shrugged. 'Battered women, abused teenagers, people living ten to a house. We had one case last week where a sixteen year old had come home from school to find that her parents had moved without telling her.' Her eyebrows were raised. 'There's probably a lot of parents who feel like doing that but, thankfully, few who do. I've seen it all here.'

A previously well-heeled financial whiz down on his luck was the least of her worries. The only thing in his favour – if you could call it that – was that Laurence had three depend-ents, massive debts, absolutely nothing in the bank and no family to fall back on. When she had finished tapping on the computer, she'd informed him that they could, mercifully, be classed as Priority Needs, and told him all the benefits that he was likely to be entitled to.

'We have one house,' the woman said with a world-weary sigh. 'It's all that's available today. This is with a private landlord and we'll arrange for your housing benefit to go direct to him.' They'd filled in the forms for that too. 'It's the best I can offer as there's at least a six-month waiting list for one of our own properties.'

Six months?

'The house isn't great,' she went on. 'Not up to our usual standard. The previous tenant has just been evicted.'

So he got a home at the cost of putting someone else back on the street.

'But if you don't want to accept this,' she continued, 'then we'll have to put you in bed and breakfast accommodation. You could be four to a room with no guarantee of when we could move you.'

The look that she gave him told Laurence that he didn't want to go down that route. But he'd already made his mind up to take the house. He was grateful, just grateful for anything. They could say goodbye to the Travelhotel and they'd have a roof over their heads again. This would give them a fresh start.

After signing a multiplicity of paperwork, he was handed the key to a house. A grubby paper label gave the address. Netherslade Bridge. Not good.

This was the sort of area that frequently featured on the front pages of the local papers for arson attacks and knifings, and it always topped the burglary list.

'Thank you,' he said.

The woman gave him a smile. 'Don't hesitate to contact me if there's anything else you need,' she said. 'Good luck.'

Good luck. He was going to be needing it.

As he left the offices, clutching the key in his hand, Laurence wondered how Lily would feel about this. He couldn't believe that his wife was prepared to stand by him when he had messed up so thoroughly. But then that was Lily. She'd always been strong, efficient, steadfast. He'd been away from home too much over the last few years, missed too many of the children's birthday parties, too many of their anniversaries. His wife had celebrated her own birthday alone more than once. While he was off making deals, bringing home the money, she had tended the children, the home, the horses, so that he'd never had to worry about anything else.

When the money had been pouring in faster than they could spend it, that had been all well and good. Laurence knew that he should have addressed their mounting difficulties earlier, but he had never thought it would come to this. He should have come clean, confessed to Lily when their eviction notice was first served. But he hadn't. He'd kept it all to himself, carried on as if nothing was wrong. Even then he thought there was still something that he could pull out of the bag at the last minute. When he was in court – months ago now – listening alone to the eviction hearing and the details of the order, he'd assumed that somehow he could avert it, that some miracle would occur and that at the eleventh hour all would be saved. Denial at its very deepest.

He walked back to the Travelhotel. Lily was sitting in the bedroom with the children. They were all watching television.

'I didn't know what else to do,' she said as he entered the room.

At home, at their beautiful lost home, she'd probably be baking something, the children would be out riding or playing in the garden or having a game of snooker in the games room if it was raining. Now they all sat glued to the banal daytime shows, faces listless.

'The housing association have given us a place,' he said excitedly. 'It's a three-bedroomed terraced house.'

Lily's face lit up and he could have wept to see it. 'Thank God. We can get out of this place.'

'It's in one of the rougher areas.'

'I wasn't expecting Kensington and Chelsea.'

'Don't get your hopes up,' Laurence warned. 'It was either this or bed and breakfast accommodation, but I have a feeling that it's not going to be great.'

'It has to be better than here.'

And he could only cross his fingers and hope that his wife was right.

Chapter 9

'Oh. My. God.' I never knew that places like this existed. Not here. Not in our town. Not more than a few miles away from the beautiful barn in which we were living.

Laden down with our holiday suitcases and Laurence's wretched golf clubs, we got the bus to Netherslade Bridge – and it's the first time I've been on a bus since I was a student. Hugo and Hettie were quite excited at the prospect, and I'm ashamed to say that it was the first time my children had *ever* been on a bus. I suddenly realise what a very sheltered life we've all led.

Now we stand outside the house, clutching our bags, and terror has gripped my heart.

Laurence has gone white. 'It won't be forever,' he says. 'I promise that I will get us out of here at the very first opportunity.'

I dig my nails into my palms so that I don't cry and, for the sake of Hettie and Hugo, I plaster a smile on my face. 'I'm sure it will be fine.'

Inside, I'm crying, 'We can't possibly stay here!'

'Right,' Laurence says decisively.

But none of us make a move.

The estate looks like the bad side of Beirut. Our new home is in a street of prefabricated terraced houses. They were, I believe, originally built in the seventies to house the builders and labourers who worked on constructing the new city. They should have been pulled down years ago but, instead, they were used as social housing and now the quandary is what to do with them.

41

The houses are long past their sell-by date and there's frequent talk about getting rid of the whole lot and starting again. But where do you put the displaced people while you're doing that? What happens when you smash apart communities even though, on paper, it might be for the good of all in the long run? Do the council buy up the smattering of homes that have been bought by tenants under the Right to Buy scheme, with compulsory purchase orders? It's such a controversial topic and arouses such ferocious opposition from the residents that the council have decided, perhaps prudently, to do nothing. I have read about all this, vaguely, tut-tutting about it in the local paper, never thinking that I would find myself living here, never thinking that it might directly affect *me* one day.

The house is small, flat-roofed – something that is infinitely suitable to sunny climes, but positively ill-advised in this country – and is faced with what appears to be corrugated iron in an attractive shade of grey. Outside on the scrubby area of grass that I hesitate to call a lawn is a stained sofa that looks like it has been there for some considerable time. There's a pile of black plastic rubbish sacks beside it, which the local cats, rats or foxes have had a thorough rummage through. Chicken bones, eggshells and orange juice cartons are strewn around. The front door of the house is white plastic, covered in green mould. There's a piece of plywood where the window should be, and someone has ripped the door off the utilities cupboard next to it.

We also have a shopping trolley on its side, a plastic garden seat with broken slats and the remnants of what was once a motorbike in place of the modern sculptures we're both so keen on. There's a hanging basket by the door filled with faded plastic flowers, and the house name plaque reads *Shangri-La*. Earthly paradise. The optimism of it nearly makes me break down.

I look along the street at a row of identikit houses. The one immediately next door to the right is relatively normal, but the one beyond that still has all of its Christmas decorations pinned to the front of the house. And there are a lot of them

– twenty or more at a quick estimate: a Santa in a sleigh joined to a flying angel by loops of colourful lights, alongside a flush of snowflakes and a twinkle of stars. Below that there's a festive Homer Simpson and Tinkerbell. The tasteful white lights we used to string between our silver birch trees could not begin to compete.

But at least these two are occupied. On the other side, we seem to have no neighbour at all. The windows of the house are boarded up, and so is the door. It looks as if the place may have been burned out inside.

Further down the street there's a rotting caravan outside one house that also has an England flag hanging out of a window, and another has around a dozen motorbikes in various states of disarray. I count at least three vehicles that have been clamped and several more with foreign numberplates. One car is coated with green slime and has flat tyres and no back window. Several basketball hoops are in evidence. There's a Sky satellite dish fixed to the front of every house, including the one that is to be ours.

On the plus side there is a nice public green opposite the house and a lovely silver birch tree that reminds me of the woodland glade we have left behind – except that this solitary specimen has several bike tyres threaded in its branches.

Just then, a man with a ponytail and at least a dozen dogs walks by. The animals range from a Great Dane at one end to a Jack Russell at the other. All manner of sizes and colours make up the rest of the contingent. 'Wotcher, mate,' the man says, his eyes still on the pavement and failing to meet our stunned gaze.

'Good afternoon,' Laurence says politely and the dog-walker looks taken aback and hurries on. Perhaps he thinks that my husband is from the council.

I take a deep breath. Laurence seems to be rooted to the spot, but we can't stand here for the rest of our lives. 'Come on,' I say with a weary sigh. 'Let's go and see what we've got.'

My first impressions might be wrong. I'm hoping to all that is good, that they are.

Chapter 10

The door needs an almighty shove. Laurence nearly has to shoulder it in. The hall is filled with free newspapers, red bills addressed, presumably, to the previous occupant, and flyers for pizza delivery emporiums and Chinese takeways. The overwhelming smell is of damp. We may have no money, but I'm going to spend an awful lot of it on Febreeze.

The floor is bare here and I'm distressed about that until we go through to the living room, where brown, swirly-patterned carpet abounds. That wouldn't be so bad if there wasn't purple, swirly-patterned wallpaper on the walls.

'Oh, God,' Laurence says, taking the words out of my mouth.

The children haven't expressed their opinion at all. I think they are too shell-shocked. It's safe to say that in their rather pampered lives, they've never been in a place like this before.

I realise that this small room constitutes the dining room too, but then I'm not really complaining about that as we have no furniture to fill any of it. There might be hysteria rising inside me but I'm too appalled, too stunned to let it out.

Ratty net curtains are draped at the windows, but the poles are half-hanging out of the walls. I trail through to the kitchen. Laurence and the children follow suit. Most of the units are bereft of doors, and the one on the oven hangs drunkenly on its hinges. I could weep when I think of my cream Aga and who might soon be using it instead of me.

There are piles of rubbish on the floor – newspapers, cereal boxes, used tea bags – and I wonder whether squatters have

44

lived here. Certainly some mice have. The back door is also boarded up with plywood and the broken glass still lies on the lino floor.

'Mind that,' I say to the children and, gingerly, they skirt round it.

I wipe some grime from the window and look out into the back garden. It's sizeable, but a complete wilderness. The over-riding impression is of long grass interspersed with brambles. The back end of a garage juts into one corner and, somewhat unexpectedly, there are two very large concrete eagles situated on the roof. There's a car in the garden too. The colour is of the green slime variety and the grass comes up to the windows. It doesn't look like it's moved in a very long time. In lieu of a patio there are two mattresses with mushrooms growing out of them.

Laurence takes my hand. 'We can't stay here.'

'Where else do you suggest we go?'

He has no answer for that.

Perhaps somewhere in my psyche I'm trying to punish him by making him embrace the full awfulness of our situation. This is what we're reduced to. This is what our reckless spending has brought down on us. Because of our sheer stupidity, this broken hovel is to be our home. Laurence has earned fantastic money for years – money beyond the dreams of most people – and, as fast as it has come in, we've spent it. We've indulged ourselves, denied ourselves no luxury, large or small. And have never saved for a rainy day. Well, that rainy day is well and truly upon us now.

We could have lived in a more modest family home and have been mortgage-free by now. We could have taken up a cheaper hobby than horse-riding, driven family saloons from Ford or Vauxhall or Skoda. The children could have gone to a school that wasn't frequented by the offspring of earls and entrepreneurs. We could still have been happy like that.

Now we're here I realise that we are truly starting again. From rock bottom. We've no clothes – save our cheerful holiday ones which hardly fit the mood – no furniture, no electrical goods and, more importantly, no food. The only way from here, surely, is up.

'We're entitled to some benefits,' my husband assures me. 'I'll get onto that tomorrow.'

A sob catches in my throat. 'Christ,' I say with a ragged huff, 'is that what it's come to? We're the last people in the world who should be drawing benefits. We should be thoroughly ashamed of ourselves.' And there's no doubt that we both are.

Laurence's expression darkens, but before we can launch into a discussion about our circumstances, my mobile phone rings. I wonder how long it will be before the contract on that is cut off.

I look at the caller identify before I answer. 'It's Amanda.'

'You might as well speak to her,' Laurence advises. 'We can't put it off forever. She'll know soon enough.'

I feel like telling him that *he* can speak to her, but he takes the children and heads back into the living room.

I press the green button on my phone. 'Hello, Amanda. Did you get home safely?'

There's a crispness to her voice when she says, 'I was just calling to ask you the same thing.'

She knows, I think. Already, she knows. The phones in the village must have been red hot.

'Have you heard that we've lost the house?' I ask.

'Yes,' she says. 'I'm very sorry to hear it.'

But my friend, someone I've ridden with, gone to the health club with, whose children I've looked after and who has looked after mine, and who I've just come back from holiday with, doesn't sound sorry at all.

'A housing association has given us emergency accommodation.'

She has nothing to say to that.

'We've lost everything.'

'And the twenty thousand pounds that you owe us for the holiday amongst it?' Amanda adds.

'Yes. It looks that way.'

There is silence on the end of the line, but I can feel the

hostility coming from Amanda Marquis in wave after spiked wave.

'We are going to do our very best to get it all back to you.'

'I sincerely hope so,' Amanda says. 'Anthony could see this coming. He'd heard rumours. The only person who was in denial was your husband.'

'So it seems,' I say.

There's more silence and I wonder for a moment if Amanda has put the phone down on me and then she lets out a sigh.

'I'm sorry. So sorry,' I offer. 'We really will try to make it up to you.'

'I sincerely hope so,' my friend repeats. I'm using the term 'friend' loosely now. Then Amanda does hang up.

Laurence is leaning on the doorjamb. I'm not sure he should be doing that as the house might fall down. 'How did she take it?'

'Very badly.' I shrug. 'We would have done as much.'

'Didn't she even ask where we were?'

'No.'

He puffs out a disappointed breath. 'These people are our friends. I would like to think that if they found themselves in this situation, we would have helped them out.'

'But would we?' I ask. 'Would we really have done that?' Or would we have reacted in exactly the same way that Amanda and Anthony have? Talking behind their backs, saying that they only had themselves to blame for their folly and feeling smug about our own good fortune?

But before we can fully explore the subject of whether we possess the Good Samaritan gene in spades or not, we hear the front door swing open and a woman's voice shouts, 'Coo-ee!'

Chapter 11

After the shrill call, a woman pops her head round the kitchen door. 'Hiya,' she says. 'I'm your next-door neighbour. Tracey Smith.' She extends her hand to me and, somewhat dazed, I shake it.

'Lily,' I say as she pumps my fingers vigorously. 'And this is my husband, Laurence.' She shakes his hand too.

The woman is small, on the chubby side, and has dyed black hair that's feathered around her face. She's very pretty, but looks quite hard. I'd guess that she's a good few years younger than me, in her early thirties perhaps, but – if it doesn't sound rude – she looks like she's seen a lot more of life. My new neighbour is dressed as if she's going to a nightclub. There's a tunic in psychedelic print, cropped silver trousers and what Laurence would call 'hooker shoes'. She has a tattoo of a butterfly on her shoulder. Her eye-shadow is glittery and plentiful. Large hooped earrings dangle down the sides of her neck, which is an unnatural shade of orange. 'Came to see if you needed any milk or tea bags.'

We all take in the kitchen.

Tracey grimaces. 'Looks like you need a bit more than that, love.'

With that, all my resolve, my stoicism, my stiff upper lip crumbles and I cry. I cry and cry and can't stop. Loud, wracking sobs shake my core. How can I face this? How can I be strong when I'm hurting so much? How can I live here? How can I do this to my children? How can I be a good mother when I haven't even got a kettle?

Tracey pushes past Laurence, who is standing looking embarrassed by my spontaneous outburst, and comes and puts her arms round me. She's wearing a lot of perfume and I can hardly breathe and I'm not a cuddly sort of person – particularly with strangers – but there's something comforting about being held in her plump arms and having my back patted as I used to do to the children when they were babies.

'Love, love, love,' she croons as she squeezes me tighter. 'It's not as bad as it looks.'

I'm thinking that she has no idea what she's talking about.

'These are sturdy houses,' she says. 'Bit of Cif and some elbow grease and you'll have it fixed up in no time at all.'

I look at the wreck around us and weep again. If she knew where we'd lived before, what we've come from, then she'd realise the extent of our fall.

'It's a really nice area,' Tracey says enthusiastically, then she produces a clean tissue from her pocket and dabs at my tears with it. 'All the people are lovely. You'll fit right in.'

We won't, I think. We so won't. We'll be out of place. Fish out of water.

My neighbour holds me away from her. 'I think you all need a cup of tea. Shall I put the kettle on?'

Laurence and I exchange a wary glance. Then I think, What the hell? There's no need for me to pretend here. She might as well be aware of our circumstances. 'We have no kettle,' I tell her.

'Is your stuff arriving later?'

'We have no stuff.' A wavering breath steadies my nerves. 'We were thrown out of our previous home. Everything we have has been taken. All we've got is what we're standing up in and four suitcases crammed full of nothing more useful than holiday clothes.'

If she's taken aback then it doesn't register on her face.

'Then you need tea and a bloody good brandy down you, girl,' is her conclusion.

The tears spill over my lashes again.

'Ssh, ssh,' my neighbour says. 'Crying is going to get you

nowhere. You need a plan, love. Come next door and I'll put a brew on while we come up with one.'

I look to Laurence and he shrugs his approval. Frankly, what else is there that we can do?

'Come on, kids,' Tracey says. 'You can meet my two. And wait until you see what's in my biscuit tin, you'll think you're in heaven.'

She ushers us all to the door and, like the lost sheep that we are, we let ourselves be herded towards Tracey's house.

'Thank you,' I say meekly.

'Nonsense,' she retorts. 'What are friends for?'

I think of Amanda slamming the phone down on me and I wonder, what indeed?

Chapter 12

Tracey's home is immaculate even if the décor is somewhat . . . creative. In the main room the wallpaper is cheerful pink, red and orange spots, the carpet electric blue. The table is set with a checked tablecloth and spotted crockery and glasses. The sofas are pink leather, and in one corner is the biggest television that I've ever seen.

In the kitchen, the cupboards would seem to be the originals that came with the house, but they're painted a sugared-almond shade of pink. The toaster, kettle and microwave are retro designs in shades of pale blue.

'You have a lovely home,' I say.

'Yours could be just like it,' Tracey encourages me. 'Once you take stock, it won't look so bad. Just one minute.' She squeezes past us and we all stand, not knowing quite what to do in the kitchen. Me, the doyen of charity dinners, is socially inept in my new neighbour's kitchen.

She has a table crammed into the kitchen and Laurence sits down at one of the chairs. I join him, smoothing my skirt over my knees.

Tracey stands at the bottom of the stairs and shouts, 'Charlize! Keanu! Get down here!'

'Charlize is a pretty name,' I offer for lack of anything else to say.

'I was going to call her Chlamydia,' Tracey tells me. 'But I thought it was too posh. No offence to your two.'

'Charlize is much nicer.'

Then a moment later there's the thundering of feet. I wonder whether we'll be able to hear that through the walls which I'm betting are of the paper-thin variety.

'They've got a very big television,' Hugo whispers. 'And a Wii.'

He looks quite excited about that and my heart goes out to him. They both had televisions, computers and Wiis in their bedrooms at home to keep them amused. Now what will they do for entertainment?

Tracey ushers her children in. They look just a little bit older than Hettie and Hugo – a couple of years at the most, which is a relief. At least they will have some friends here. I push my two forwards.

'Hettie and Hugo,' I say when they remain speechless.

The children all eye each other warily.

My neighbour opens one of the high cupboards and pulls out a huge tin. When she takes off the lid, I can see that it's filled with a veritable treasure trove of delights – Penguins, Wagon Wheels, KitKats, Caramel Wafers, Snowballs, Marshmallows. All the things that I don't allow Hettie and Hugo to have at home.

'Tuck in,' Tracey says.

They turn to me with pleading eyes. How can I deny them? I nod and they dive in.

'Just one each,' Tracey says. 'I don't want you spoiling your dinner. Then out you go.'

Their garden is the same size as ours, but it's dominated by an enormous black trampoline with a net that must be six feet high around it. I'm not a big fan of trampolines. They invariably end in visits to A&E.

Tracey must sense my apprehension as she says, 'They'll be fine.'

How will we take them to the hospital on the bus? Oh God, something else to worry about.

'Shouldn't one of us go out to supervise them?'

'You've got enough to think about,' Tracey says. 'Chill for a bit. They'll come to no harm out there. I'll kill them if they do.'

I watch the children head for the arm-breaking trampoline. There's no doubt that the biscuits have been successful ice-breakers as they all troop happily across the garden discussing their favourites.

My neighbour puts on the kettle. Then she pulls three glasses out of the cupboard and a bottle of supermarket own-label brandy. 'I'm not in shock,' she says cheerily, 'but I might as well join you.'

'Sun's over the yard arm,' Laurence says with a forced laugh.

'If you say so.' Tracey hands out the brandy. 'To your new home.' She offers her glass up in a toast.

My husband and I raise our glasses even though I'm not sure I want to be toasting my arrival in Netherslade Bridge.

'To our new home,' Laurence agrees bravely, and we both take a drink of the brandy.

It burns a line down my throat and I set myself off coughing and spluttering.

'Should have warned you it's like rocket fuel,' Tracey grins. 'But it'll do the job.'

Laurence coughs more politely and takes another sip. By the time the tea is ready, we've had our glasses replenished. I'm not sure if I've eaten today, certainly not since breakfast, and the alcohol is going straight to my head.

Even my husband has a flush to his drawn face and I reach out and stroke his cheek.

Tracey brings a tray of tea to the table and plonks her spotty mugs in front of us. Then she sits down too. When we're all nursing our drinks, I say, 'You don't know how much we appreciate this.'

'Go on with you,' she laughs. 'Anyone would do the same thing.'

The look that Laurence and I exchange says that they wouldn't.

Tracey stares at us directly. She has kind eyes with lots of wrinkles round them and I'm sure it must be because she laughs a lot. 'You really have got nothing?'

Laurence and I swap guarded looks again, but he nods that I should fill Tracey in on the picture. 'The bailiffs had been while we were on holiday.' I get another wave of nausea when I think of how much money went on that little jaunt. 'The house was boarded up, the cars gone.' I decide not to mention the horses. 'I don't think we'll get any of it back.'

My husband swigs at his brandy again and it's hard to ignore the broken look on his face. I wonder will he be able to pull himself up again from this.

'We're literally starting from scratch.'

Our neighbour frowns. 'What are you doing for food tonight? Where are you going to sleep?'

Those thoughts have been racing round and round in my brain at such a pace that I haven't managed to snatch at any of them and come up with a sensible answer. I hang my head. 'I don't know.'

Laurence and I are the responsible adults in this family and we're behaving like irresponsible idiots. I turn to my husband. 'Couldn't we go back to the Travelhotel?' I suggest. 'Just for tonight?'

'We can't,' he says. 'We have to watch every penny now.' It's clear that he feels awkward admitting this in front of Tracey, someone we didn't know until an hour ago. 'We have an alternative and we have to make the best of it.'

'When you've had that brew, I'll give you some cleaning stuff,' Tracey says. 'We can go back and set to for an hour or so, then I'll pop back and put some tea on for us all.'

'You can't do that.'

She waves my protest away. 'It's no trouble.'

'Aren't you going out?'

'Me?' She laughs at that. 'Chance would be a fine thing.' Then she sees me looking at her sparkly leggings. 'I just like my bling. Nowhere to wear it, mind, but a girl's gotta try.'

'I just don't want to spoil your plans.'

'*Plans?*' That sets Tracey off laughing again. 'I've no plans. Other than to knock something together out of what I've got in the cupboards. We'll be having nothing fancy,' she says, 'but I've plenty for a few more mouths.'

'I don't know what to say.'

'Say that you like chips and beans and eggs.' We all laugh at that.

So, fortified by too much cheap brandy, I say, 'Let's do it! Let's go and knock that house into shape.'

Chapter 13

When we get back to our own house, armed with bottles of bleach, bathroom scourer, rubber gloves and J-Cloths, I realise that, on reflection, I have not drunk anywhere near enough brandy to be able to face this.

Apart from the lounge, every other room is plastered with wood chip painted in a startling variety of garish shades. And I didn't even know that wood chip still existed.

When she sees me hesitate, Tracey takes my arm. 'Come on,' she says. 'You can do the bathroom. I'll start on one of the bedrooms. Laurence, you take the other one.'

My husband nods and does as he's told. I can't think when Laurence last involved himself with cleaning products. Nor me, if I'm brutally honest about it. We had a cleaner in three mornings a week, so my involvement in domestic chores has, in recent years, been fairly minimal. Laurence, I'm pretty sure, hasn't had a duster in his hand since I said, 'I do.'

Tracey ushers me into the bathroom and gives me Cif, bleach, rubber gloves and a scouring pad. 'Crack on,' she says, and then harries Laurence into one of the bedrooms to set him to his task.

If it wasn't for my neighbour's encouragement, I think I would have laid down on the floor and let myself die.

The bathroom is pink – and pink in a very bad way. Pink that shows that the suite has not been replaced in, possibly, thirty years. Still, it's all intact. The sink is in one piece. The bath might

55

be faded but, as it's plastic, it's not chipped. Let's just hope the loo is functional.

I hold my nose and pour in some bleach. I'll deal with that in a little while when the first stage of fumigation has had time to take hold.

Tracey is singing away tunelessly and loudly; the sounds of 'Don't You Wish Your Girlfriend Was Hot Like Me' drift along the hall and it makes me smile. I'm not the biggest fan of the Pussycat Dolls but my daughter is. Laurence and I prefer more classical music to relax to.

The wood chip in here is the colour of custard. The carpet is red and shagpile, and I dread to think what it's harbouring. Scrubbing at the sink, I try not to think of what the future holds for us. How are we ever going to get ourselves out of here again? Will starting over make us or break us as a family?

While I'm still lost in my own morbid thoughts, Tracey pokes her head round the door. 'Back bedroom's looking better,' she says. 'It wasn't too bad.' Though she seems to have two big black bags filled with rubbish. 'Outside windows need a bit of a wash and the door needs some work, but all in good time.'

'Thank you,' I say. 'Thank you so much.'

'I'll go and put tea on. Give me half an hour?'

'Are you sure?'

'Of course. Can't have you going down the chippy on your first night here.'

I listen to her steps clatter down the stairs and the bang of the front door. Then I down my scrubber and peel off my rubber gloves and go into the main bedroom where Laurence is scraping layers of grime off the windowsill.

'How's it going?'

'She's a force to be reckoned with,' my husband says. 'I could do with her on my team at the office.'

Then he realises what he's said and that there is no team, no office. He comes and takes me in his arms and we hold each other tight. 'I'm so sorry to have put you through this,' he says. 'I'll make it right. I'm determined to. You just see. We'll all be absolutely fine.'

56

I nod and cling to him. Perhaps Tracey's brash brand of optimism has worked its magic on him and I'm glad of that. For me, I can't see how this is going to work out all right at all.

Chapter 14

An hour later and we're back in our neighbour's home. Tracey has put the small kitchen table alongside the one in the living room and now all seven of us are squeezed around them both.

'It's a bit cosy,' our neighbour says, 'but I thought it would help us to get to know each other better.'

The children already look as if they're getting on famously. They're currently tucking into eggs, beans and Smiley Faces. We're eating the same, but Tracey has substituted oven chips for Smiley Faces. Hettie and Hugo's own smiley faces are studies in delight. They love this sort of food – much to my dismay. I spent a great part of my day as a housewife and mother preparing nutrition-ally balanced and healthy meals – couscous, polenta and brown rice featured heavily on our menus. Along with white fish and plenty of vegetables. Every mealtime was a nightmare and I was convinced that they'd be back to eating rubbish the minute they returned to school where I couldn't keep my eye on them.

But that's unfair, I'm not calling this rubbish. It might be basic and there's not a green vegetable in sight but, at the moment, it tastes like one of the best meals I've ever had. I think that's because it was so unexpected and thoughtful. Tracey might not have much, but she's chosen to share it all with us – strangers who are down on their luck and down in the dumps. At the thought, tears spring fresh to my eyes.

'Enough of that,' Tracey warns. 'Have more chips.' She puts another lavish spoonful on my plate and I eat them without argument.

When we've finished the meal, Tracey orders the children to clear the table and take the dishes into the kitchen, which they do without protest.

'Laurence,' she says, 'you put your feet up in front of the television. I want to take Lily upstairs for a minute.'

My husband obeys too – surprise, surprise – also without any resistance.

In Tracey's bedroom, which is as brightly coloured as the living room, she flings open a cupboard and pulls out a selection of bedding. 'Some of it's past its best now,' she says apologetically, 'but if you can use it to tide you over, then you're more than welcome.' She tosses the duvets and pillowcases onto the bed for my inspection.

'That's very kind of you,' I say, and mean it.

She squeezes my hand. 'I think you and I are going to become firm friends.'

I've never known anyone like this before. In all of my previous relationships – certainly beyond university – I feel as if I've always been kept at arm's length by friends. But then I tend to keep people at arm's length too. I'm not one for confiding, opening up. We've had appearances to keep up and have done that very well. I think of how long it took me to break into the inner circle of Amanda's friends, to be accepted by them. Tracey probably knows more about me than any of my other friends and we only met a few hours ago. She has an open and sunny nature and how I wish that I did.

As she rummages through another cupboard, I pick at the corner of a faded pink duvet and ask, 'Is there a Mr Jones?'

Tracey shakes her head. 'I've had two husbands,' she says. 'That's more than enough for one lifetime. I've become allergic to wedding cake. No one else is getting their feet under the table here. It's just me and the kids from now on. All men have ever done for me is promise me the world and then clear off leaving me up to the eyeballs in debt. I've been a mug twice. No more.'

She piles some duvets up next to me. 'Winter weight. Fifteen tog. These houses can be a bugger to heat. You might swelter

59

tonight, but you can use them to lie on top of until we can find you some proper beds. I'll put the word out tomorrow, see what we can do about rustling up some furniture.'

'We're up to the eyeballs in debt too,' I remind her.

'Yeah, but you've got a good one there,' she says, flicking her head towards downstairs and in Laurence's general direction. 'At least you're trying to sort it out together. He didn't just clear off and leave you with the mess.'

It's unthinkable. How would I have coped then? What would have happened to us if Laurence had done that?

'Will that be okay to get you through the night?'

'You're so kind. I don't know what we would have done without you.'

'We're going to have fun, you and me, Lily. You wait and see.'

Despite my pain and despair, I find myself laughing. And, for the first time since my lovely life crumbled around me, I don't feel quite so frightened of the future.

Chapter 15

'She's very nice,' Laurence says as we lay out the duvet on the floor. We spread the cover on top and slide under it. Our suitcase is open on the floor. Welcome to our humble abode.

'Tracey?'

'Yes,' he says. 'I feel quite positive.'

'Me too.'

The children are settled together in one of the other two rooms, sleeping on similar borrowed duvets, and seem to be viewing it as an adventure rather than the catastrophe that it is.

Our bedroom is at the front of the house and is certainly cleaner than it was, but it still feels dusty in here. I borrowed Tracey's vacuum cleaner and ran it round before we made up our temporary beds, but it could really do with a serious deep clean. I've opened the windows to try to let out the whiff of the cleaning products and to let some fresh air in. There are no curtains in here and the moon is streaming in, highlighting the tree outside and picking out the bike tyres looped over its branches.

The duvet on the threadbare carpet isn't quite a match for the interior sprung mattress that we're used to, but then I shall be eternally grateful to Tracey as, otherwise, we'd be sleeping on the floor without even a modicum of comfort. Under the cover, Laurence reaches for my hand and laces his fingers in mine.

I wonder what we would have done if our bouncy and bubbly new neighbour hadn't come in and taken control of our lives. Would our introduction to Netherslade Bridge have ended in an argument of recrimination and resentment? Would Laurence and I now be sleeping in separate rooms? (If there were any others clean.) Would Laurence be on the sofa if we had one? It's very peculiar because I have never felt more close to him and, at the same time, so far away.

How could he have been going through all this and for me to be completely unaware of it? Was I so wrapped up in my own little life? I thought I was doing a great job for the family. Clearly I wasn't, after all.

A car alarm starts up outside and, for one mad moment, I wonder if it's ours — and then I remember with a sinking feeling that we don't have a car any more.

When it goes off we can hear a couple of likely lads running down the street laughing and swearing. I saw a pub at the end of the road which looked like a real den of iniquity and I wonder whether this is what we have to look forward to every night.

'Shall I go out to check if I can see anything?' Laurence asks.

'No,' I snap. 'I don't want you getting stabbed.'

So we lie there in the dark, bodies tense. Instead of the sounds of the countryside that I'm so used to, the familiar comforting creaks of the barn as it settled down for the night, the hooting of an owl in a nearby tree, the rustle of leaves in the breeze, I am trying to become accustomed to my new surroundings, new clunks and thunks, the sounds from the street, the muted murmur of the television coming through the walls from next door. I get up and close the window. It feels safer, somehow.

In our old home, if I couldn't sleep, sometimes I used to pull on my dressing-gown and wander out into the garden. I loved to see the roses bathed in moonlight and I used to marvel at the sanctuary we'd created. Very rarely, I'd hear the badgers snuffle out of their sett and wander into the wood; even more rarely, if I stood stock still, I'd catch a glimpse of them. I sigh to myself. Don't think I'll be doing that here.

'We'll get used to it,' I say into the darkness as I crawl back into our makeshift bed.

Laurence strokes my fingers tenderly. 'My positivity is slipping away.'

'Mine too.' I snuggle up next to my husband.

'First thing tomorrow, I'll get out and look for a job, Lily. Now that I'm not tied to London, I can go round all the local agencies too. Some of them already have my details, but I've heard nothing. I'll go and chivvy them all up.'

I try not to think about the fact that he has been looking for another job for months and has, as yet, found nothing. In the paper, just the other day, I read that now at least ten people are applying for every single job vacancy. The daughter of one of Amanda's friends recently applied for a post as an editorial assistant in London. Hers was one of two hundred CVs they received. She had a first-class honours degree and still failed to get the job. How can one hope to stand out from the crowd with so many people chasing work? People with strings of qualifications and years of valuable experience are taking on menial posts just to get employment at all. Maybe Laurence will have to lower his sights for a while until the economy picks up. We, like the rest of the country, will have to cut our cloth accordingly.

'Everything will be all right.'

Then we hear Hettie crying.

'I'll go to her,' I say and slip, once more, out of bed. Sleep, I think, could well be an optional extra tonight.

I make my way along the unfamiliar territory of the landing and into the bedroom that Hugo and Hettie are sharing. When we clear out the box room, Hettie can have that.

'There, there,' I whisper as I sit down beside her and pull her onto my lap. 'What's wrong?'

'I don't like it here,' she says, sobbing. 'When can we go home?' The adventure, it appears, is already starting to pale.

'This *is* home, poppet. At least for a little while.'

'Why?' she says. 'I want to go to our real home and see Boo and Silver. Who will be looking after them?'

'Someone else is looking after the ponies now,' I tell my daughter.

'Boo is *mine*,' she complains. 'Will another little girl love him like I do? Will she know all of his favourite things?'

'I'm sure she will. And Boo will let her know – just like he did with you.' I have my fingers crossed behind my back so that I'm not really lying. I'm also hoping that Boo isn't currently on his way to the glue factory. Do they still do that to unwanted horses?

Hettie sobs into my lap while Hugo, thankfully, sleeps on. How I wish that she didn't have to deal with this sort of thing. I always wanted to give her the most idyllic childhood that one could imagine. I wanted her to look back when she was older and think of nothing but long, hot, trouble-free summers, me drifting about in a floaty summer dress oozing earth mother vibes, pandering to her every desire. Now she's having to cope with all this upheaval.

'Mummy and Daddy are having a little bit of trouble at the moment,' I say as I stroke her hair from her forehead, 'but we're trying to sort it all out. Everything will be back to normal before you know it.'

And I can only hope again that I'm not lying.

Chapter 16

We're all awake. I can hear the children arguing in the back bedroom. There's a knock on the door and I'm the one who plods down to open it. Tracey is standing there with two cups of tea, two glasses of orange squash, a box of Sugar Puffs, a pint of milk, four bowls and four spoons. It serves to remind me that we really do have nothing at all.

I would normally feel very conspicuous answering the door in my dressing-gown at the barn but here, I don't think anyone will give a damn. Tracey, even at this hour, is in full make-up and nightclub gear – white crop top, pink leggings, five-inch heels, earrings like chandeliers.

'It's not much,' she says, 'but it'll keep you going until you can get to the shops.'

'You're a lifesaver.' I hadn't even considered what we might do for breakfast.

'What are you up to for the rest of the day?'

'I don't know,' I admit. My brain seems to have gone into shut-down mode.

'I can come round and give you a hand with the cleaning,' Tracey says. 'If you'd like.'

'That would be wonderful, but I don't want to impose. Don't you have other arrangements?'

Tracey laughs. 'Lily, did anyone ever tell you that you talk like the Queen?' Then, 'No, I don't have "other arrangements".'

'Then a hand with the cleaning would be very much appreciated.'

'I'll give you time to get yourselves together,' she says, 'then I'll be round.' My neighbour waves as she totters away and shouts over her shoulder, 'Laters!'

I take our room service breakfast tray inside. Laurence is already dressed and downstairs. 'No hot water,' he says with a mock shiver. 'Didn't think to switch the boiler on. I'll do it now.'

'Tracey brought us breakfast.'

My husband examines the tray. 'Sugar Puffs? I didn't know they still made them.'

His usual breakfast consists of muesli, blueberries, fresh yoghurt and a homemade fruit smoothie – mango and passion fruit was his favourite.

'It's very thoughtful of her,' I reproach him.

'I'm not complaining,' Laurence says defensively. 'I used to love these as a kid. Why do you never buy them?'

He pours out four bowls and tips some milk into his own. 'Thought I'd go round the recruitment agencies today,' he says. 'Get them fired up again.'

'Like that?' I take in his white linen shirt, cropped combats and black Crocs.

'Oh, shit.' His shoulders sag. 'No suit.'

'You can't manage without a suit,' I say. Then a wave of grief washes over me. 'This is ridiculous. How can they have done this to us? Even criminals aren't treated like this. What would we be doing for food, for crockery, for cutlery if Tracey hadn't taken us under her wing?'

'I don't know,' Laurence admits. 'It doesn't bear thinking about.'

I hand him a mug of tea. 'You'll have to get a suit. Whatever it costs. How are you going to get a job if you turn up looking as if you've just wandered in from a beach in the Bahamas?'

'I'll go to a charity shop,' my husband says. His chin juts bravely. 'See what they've got.'

Laurence has never been near a charity shop in his life. The only time I ever go there is to make donations. When I think of all the clothes that I've blithely discarded over the years, I could weep at the waste of it. I think of Laurence's rows of Hugo Boss suits hanging in the wardrobe. Who needs a dozen suits at nigh

66

on a thousand pounds a pop? My husband, it seems. Now what will happen to them? Where will they go? Perhaps they will be already waiting patiently at the charity shop when Laurence arrives. If we'd been at home when the bailiffs arrived, would we have been given a chance to take some of our personal possessions with us? If I'd let him fly back from Tuscany for the day as he'd asked, would this have turned out differently for us?

The children appear, rubbing sleep from their eyes. At least they got some. I lay awake all night, wide-eyed and worrying. And so did Laurence.

I give them their Sugar Puffs which they eye suspiciously. 'That's all there is,' I say. 'Mummy will go to the shops later.'

'There's nowhere to sit,' Hettie whines.

'Go into the living room and sit on the floor,' I tell her. 'That's what God gave you a bottom for.'

'You don't allow us to eat in the living room.'

'That was in our old house. Things are different now.'

'You're telling me,' Hugo complains.

Scowling, they both go and sit down in the living room. The absence of a kitchen door means that I can keep my eye on them. They tuck into their Sugar Puffs.

'At least we're getting better breakfast cereal here,' Hettie mutters to her brother. 'I hate muesli.'

Laurence glances at his watch. 'I'll be going in a minute. Want to make the most of the day. What are you going to do?'

'Tracey's coming round. We're going to carry on cleaning.'

'Have a good day.' My husband comes to me and wraps his arms round my waist.

I love Laurence, I really do, but part of me wants to pull away from him too. He has put us in the most terrible situation and I want him to suffer. I'm pleased that he's feeling chipper and ready to face the day but, on the other hand, I want him to be depressed too – as I am.

'We *will* be okay,' he assures me as he kisses me. I turn to avoid his mouth and he kisses my cheek instead. 'Trust me.'

'I've always trusted you, Laurence,' I remind him. 'And look what's happened.'

Chapter 17

Laurence caught the bus into the city centre. In the modern, airy public library, he signed up as a user and headed off to the computer area to log in to Google to find out where in the city the nearest charity shops might be.

When the children had been toddlers, Lily used to take them both along to the story-time sessions every week. In the last five years, however, they'd just popped into Waterstones and had bought whatever books they needed without a second thought. How ridiculous, when they had this fabulous resource right on their doorstep!

As he surfed the net, he thought about Lily and what a good wife and mother she'd been. Perhaps that was why he'd never been able to deny her anything. It wasn't that she'd been overly demanding. If he was honest, they'd both had expectations, aspirations. It was what they did, what their friends did. There was never a conscious decision to accumulate the designer labels, go for the very best of everything – somehow it just happened.

Every year, without really noticing it, the stakes had gradually got higher and higher, the spending ratcheting ever upwards until it was spiralling out of control. When the money had been there, it hadn't been a problem – though sometimes he used to look at the sums that went out of their account every month and would break into a cold sweat. When the money had started to dry up, it had been easier not to open the bills, not to check the bank statements, not to admit – either to himself or to Lily – that the mortgage payments were being missed. Why hadn't he raised it with his wife? Perhaps together they could have come up with a rescue package, made cutbacks. In their marriage, he'd always been the one to make the decisions, look after things. Lily's job had been to keep the house and family ticking over. He simply hadn't raised it with her because he thought – *knew* – that he would be able to pull it off on his own. He'd been wrong.

Half an hour later and, armed with the information he needed, Laurence headed off to the nearest charity shop. As he stepped in through the door, the smell of unwashed clothes hit him. Like most men, he hated shopping at the best of times and this certainly wasn't the Bond Street experience he was used to.

Trying only to exhale, Laurence flicked through the rails looking for a thirty-eight regular suit in a dark colour.

'Can I help you, dearie?' an elderly lady asked him.

'I'm looking for a business suit,' he said. 'Thirty-eight jacket. Thirty-two waist trousers, preferably something dark.'

The woman took over the flicking and he was happy to let her. Minutes later she produced an inoffensive navy number. 'What about this one? This is nice.'

'Can I try it on somewhere?'

She looked round. 'We don't really have a changing room.' More puzzling. 'We could pull some of the rails together. If you don't mind that.'

'I'll need a shirt and tie too,' Laurence said. 'And some shoes.'

Together they manoeuvred three of the clothes rails together until they made a makeshift area of privacy for him. Behind them Laurence stripped off his holiday crops and tried on the navy suit trousers. A bit snug – too much pasta and wine on holiday – but they'd do fine. They were way too long, but surely he could do something about that.

His new dresser handed him a pale blue shirt. 'That looks about your size,' she said. 'And here's a tie too.'

A navy and red diagonal stripe in 100 per cent polyester. Not bad. He suspected Lily would hate it. But beggars couldn't be choosers.

He tugged off his shirt and slipped the blue one on his shoulders. It smelled of cigarettes and cheap aftershave.

'What size shoes are you, dearie?'

'A nine, please.'

A moment later, she held up two pairs of reasonable brogues. 'Black or brown?'

'I'll try the black ones.' She handed them over the rail.

A bit neat but perfectly serviceable. Shrugging on the suit jacket, Laurence emerged from behind the rails. 'What do you think?' He did a twirl for his elderly style adviser.

'Lovely,' she said. 'You look like a proper businessman.'

For a moment his *joie de vivre*, his bluff confidence faltered. A proper businessman. If only she knew.

'I'll take it,' he said. Some more of Peter's money gone. 'Can I leave it all on?'

'Now?'

He nodded.

'The trousers are a bit long.' She was frowning at him and the small concern of a stranger nearly had him undone. 'Shall I pin them up for you?'

'That would be very kind,' he said, ridiculously choked.

And while he stood still, the woman knelt on the floor in front of him and turned the hems on his ten-pound charity shop suit with safety pins.

Chapter 18

A knock on the door and a 'Coo-ee!' heralds Tracey's arrival just after Laurence has left the house.

'Come in,' I shout. Already, I'm hitting the kitchen with the bleach.

My neighbour totters in on the hooker heels. 'Look what I found in my loft.' Tracey is carrying a cardboard box containing a kettle and a toaster which she puts down on the work surface. Also inside are four plates, bowls, knives, forks and spoons, plus a saucepan and large frying pan, both of which have been well used.

My mind drifts and I wonder where my Wedgwood dinner service is now. Twelve full place settings, it consisted of. Who is having the pleasure of using them now? Will they turn up on *Bargain Hunt* or *Flog It* one day? Will I ever have the money again to buy them back if they do? I pull myself together and take the box from my neighbour. 'Thank you,' I say. Words that don't even begin to cover how I feel.

The box seems like a treasure trove to me and it looks, thanks to my neighbour's good grace, as if we are fully operational on the crockery, cutlery and cooking front again.

'That's a bit more civilised, girl. We'll get you back in the land of the living yet.' Tracey rubs her hands together. 'What do you want me to do then?'

'I think our first job should be to test out one of my new electrical appliances. What do you say to a cup of tea?'

Then I remember that I have no tea bags.

71

On cue, Tracey pulls a supply of tea bags out of the depths of the box she carried in.

'You think of everything,' I say.

I find the milk that she brought for our breakfast cereal. While the kettle is boiling, the children come in. 'We're bored,' they chorus.

I'm sure the Famous Five never kicked round the house whining that they were bored.

'Can we play outside?'

I gaze out at the wilderness that is our garden with the mattresses and the broken-down car.

'Why don't you go and give that car a good wash?' Tracey suggests. 'Then you can play in it.'

'I don't think so . . .' I start to say.

'It's not going anywhere,' my neighbour counters. 'They'll be all right.'

And then I think that I let them ride horses from when they were knee-high, so how dangerous can a clapped-out car be? It's hardly likely to jump into life even if they had an ignition key.

'Be careful,' I tell them. 'Don't shut your fingers in the doors. Don't cut yourself on the glass. Just watch what you're doing. I can't cope with any accidents today.'

While I make the tea using Tracey's kettle and Tracey's mugs and Tracey's tea bags and Tracey's milk, my neighbour kits them out with a bucket and hot soapy water – Laurence having eventually managed to light the boiler – and two sponges. Smiling broadly, the children heave their bucket between them and weave out towards the car. Perhaps I ought to go out there and check for syringes or mantraps or something. But then I take a deep breath and try to leave them to it.

I hand over a mug of tea. 'Where are Charlize and Keanu today?'

'At their nan's. She takes them for me quite a bit in the holidays. I love 'em to bits but sometimes I just need a break. My mum's brilliant and they both idolise her, which makes my life easier. It's not much fun bringing up a couple of livewires on your own.'

'I can imagine.'

Tracey jumps up and sits on the work surface and, breaking every rule I've ever had about kitchen hygiene, I hoist myself up so that we're sitting next to each other.

'This is going to be rough for you, Lily. I can tell that you're used to better. But whatever life throws at you, try to stick together.'

I turn to my new friend. 'I had the perfect life, Tracey. It's only now that I realise just how lucky I was. We've lost everything. Mostly through our own stupidity.' It's hard to admit this. 'I don't know if either of us will have the strength to start all over again.'

'Of course you will.' She digs me in the ribs. 'And I'll help you out all I can.'

'Why are you doing this for us? You don't know us from Adam.'

She shrugs. 'That's what mates are for.'

'I think most of my mates will be turning their back on me when they find out what's happened to us.'

'Then they're not really mates at all.'

'No.'

'You've just got to keep going,' Tracey says. 'Do your best for those two.' She nods at Hettie and Hugo, already hard at work, washing the car in the garden.

'That's what we were trying to do.'

'It's not all about money,' Tracey says. 'Though God only knows that I could always do with some more. You love them. That's what matters more than having the latest trainers, the latest computer game.'

'Do your two buy into that?'

'No!' Tracey giggles. 'Of course they don't. They want the latest this, the latest that, but you can tell that it's a speech I've given many times before.' My neighbour jumps down. 'Come on,' she says. 'Let's get going before Laurence comes home and thinks that we've done nothing but gossip all day. First, I'm going to give that manky front door a good scrub then I'm going to hit that oven.'

Tracey hands me the bleach. This woman lightens my heart. She makes me feel as if I can be myself with her, can achieve anything. She doesn't care that I haven't got ten pence to my name. But, the sad thing is, *I* do.

Chapter 19

An hour later, the front door scrubbed and shining, Tracey retracts her head from the depths of my dirty oven and straightens up. 'You can't live with this. It's gross.' She peels off her rubber gloves.

'I'm not sure that we have a choice.' I've been on my hands and knees for most of the day and, after a night spent on the floor, my back is aching.

She waggles the hinges. They're very loose. When she closes the door, it drops straight open again. My neighbour tuts. 'There's not even a proper door on it. You'll give yourself salmonella poisoning if you use this. I'll give Freddie the Fixer a call,' she says, reaching for her phone. 'He can sort out anything. He'll get his hands on a cooker for you. Not new, secondhand. But it will be better than this heap of crap.'

She speed-dials a number. 'Want him to give you a quote on some other furniture too?'

I nod, unsure what else to do. We might not have any money, but we can't spend forever sleeping on the floor and eating borrowed food off borrowed plates.

'Hi, Freddie,' Tracey says brightly. 'Wonder if you can help out a friend of mine?'

I feel a rush of pathetic gratefulness that Tracey refers to me as a friend.

'She's in a bit of a fix and needs some cheap stuff.' There's some muttering from the other end of the phone line. 'Cooker. Sofa. Three beds – one double, two singles.' My neighbour casts her beady eye round the kitchen. 'Fridge.'

My goodness, it hadn't even occurred to me that there wasn't one here.

'What about a washing machine?'

Tracey covers the mouthpiece. 'There's a laundrette up by the shops.'

A laundrette? I've never been in one before. Even in my student days we had the use of a washing machine. Still, I'm getting used to the idea of washing my dirty laundry in public so a laundrette should be a doddle.

'Think you can do that for me, Fred?'

More muttering.

'I want a good price, mind.' And with a chirpy, 'Laters!' she hangs up.

Folding my arms round me, I say, 'It will need to be a really good price, Tracey, because we have no cash at all. Laurence has even had to go to the charity shop this morning to buy a suit before he could go round the recruitment agencies.'

'He shouldn't have done that. I've got a wardrobe full of clothes from the last Mr Jones – who just walked out and left his stuff behind. It's been two years. Don't suppose he's coming back for it now.' Tracey manages her trademark laugh, but it's the first time that I've heard bitterness behind it. 'Laurence looks about the same size as him. He's more than welcome to try them on. Can't say that there'll be a suit in there though. My ex only ever wore one if he went to court.'

'How would you go about raising some emergency cash?'

Tracey shrugs. 'Flog something off or pawn it.'

I'd heard that pawn shops were a thriving business again but, of course, have never had to use one.

'They'll take anything,' she tells me.

'The bailiffs came while we were on holiday. All we have is our suitcases and an entirely useless selection of shorts and sandals. And Laurence's golf clubs.'

'He might be interested in those, I suppose. But you must have some jewellery. Anything – watches, rings?'

I think of my silk wrap of jewellery in my suitcase. Of course! 'Yes,' I say. 'Yes, I do.'

'Freddie'll give you a price on it.'

'Is he a pawnbroker?'

She gives me a sideways glance. 'It's probably best not to ask too many questions about Freddie's credentials, but he's a sound guy. He's helped me out a time or two.' There's a wistful look in her eye. 'And he's hot too!'

We share a giggle at that.

'When you're ready he can fix you up with all sorts of things – cheap paint, carpet, Broadband, dodgy Sky telly. He can get your gas and electric meters fiddled if you want. That's what he does. Fixes stuff.'

And, as I reach for the Cif once more, I wonder if Freddie the Fixer is a good enough fixer to be able to fix our lives.

Chapter 20

Laurence left the charity shop with a spring in his step. In a used carrier bag, he toted his Crocs, crops and shirt. That hadn't been nearly as painful as he'd imagined. Then he caught sight of himself in the window of the shop opposite and he looked like a worn-down, middle-aged man in a cheap, ill-fitting suit.

Out of the shop and the general smell of stale clothes, the suit had an unwashed whiff to it, and before his spirits sank too much, Laurence headed to the supermarket across the street. He found the aisle that contained the air fresheners and sprayed himself liberally with the 'fresh grass' scent of Spring Glade.

Surreptitiously, he sniffed himself. Better. Not perfect, but infinitely better. He headed next into the city and, in the same Bureau de Change that he'd used before they went to Tuscany, he exchanged the remaining euros he had for sterling. At least he had a bit more cash in his pocket now. That would see them through this week, and after that . . . he didn't want to think that far ahead.

For the rest of the morning, Laurence trawled round the recruitment agencies either introducing himself to those he hadn't yet contacted or refreshing the memories of those who already had his details on file and had failed to contact him with anything. He wanted to remind them that he was still alive, still looking, still hungry. It was likely that he'd be better off going into London to look for a job, but there was the cost to consider. Thirty pounds or more for the train and Tube alone, with no promise of anything at the end of it. The best they could probably find him locally was a stop-gap, but that would certainly do for now. This had been a terrible blow to his confidence and he wasn't sure that he had the balls to cut it in the City right now.

Trawling job agencies was a depressing way to spend a day. No matter how much enthusiasm one started out with – and he'd tried to be upbeat about this for months – they always managed to grind you down. The fact of the matter was that currently there were nearly three million people unemployed in Britain. A startling figure and one statistic he'd never in his wildest dreams expected to be included in.

He'd always assumed that people were unemployed because they didn't want to work – not because they tried and tried and tried to find a job and just couldn't get one, couldn't make anyone see what a fabulous employee they'd make. There was still a part of him – a part that was probably too large – that didn't want to believe that their situation was real. He kept thinking that his boss, Gordon Wolff from Helston Field – the company he had done his very best for over the last ten years – would call him up, tell him that it was all a big mistake, that he was in the clear, that his fraudulent investments had somehow come good. But the people whose money he had so catastrophically lost in his last great deal would, if they could see him brought so low, probably be thinking that he'd got his just deserts.

He could sign on the dole, draw benefits. They'd told him that at the housing office. He was entitled to Job Seekers Allowance, for one. But was he the sort of person who could go down to the Job Centre and stand in line for charity? He'd thought that he'd be able to claim the benefits that were on offer. Goodness knows he'd paid in enough over the years in tax to deserve something back in hard times, but the look on Lily's face had brought him to his senses. Accepting help to pay the rent and keep a roof over their heads was difficult enough to bear. There was no way that he could rely on handouts. If he was that sort of person then he'd have done it long before now. When push came to shove, he'd rather starve first. Then he

79

thought of Hugo and Hettie – could he let them starve too? He moved the thought to the back of his mind.

He'd take any job that was on offer over the alternative. Christ, he still had some pride left. He'd always provided well for his family and he could do it again. He'd renew his efforts tomorrow, phone some old contacts – again – and see what a new day would bring.

It was getting late into the afternoon now. His 'new' shoes were pinching and he hadn't eaten any lunch. He just wanted to go home and see Lily, but the thought of returning to that house, that estate, made his stomach roll. Until they'd been forced to give it up, he hadn't realised how much his heart had lifted at the sight of the barn as he swung into the lane. That was what a homecoming should feel like. Going home shouldn't give you a heartsink moment. But then Lily and the children had been stuck there all day. At least he'd managed to escape for a few hours.

Looming ahead of him were the doors of the last recruitment agency on his list and it took him all his strength to pin on a smile and breeze in.

The woman behind the desk was, thank heavens, very helpful even though she didn't have much good news to offer him.

She scrolled through the list on her computer while Laurence sat waiting patiently. Every now and again, she shook her head. 'I'm sorry,' she said. 'There's not much about at the moment. And certainly nothing in the salary bracket that you're used to.'

'I don't mind about that,' Laurence said. 'I'll consider anything.'

She pushed her keyboard away from her which he knew was a bad sign. 'Nothing today, I'm afraid.'

'Thanks.' He stood to leave.

'I'll keep looking for you,' she assured him. 'Don't you worry.'

But that's exactly was what he was doing. Worrying.

Chapter 21

Freddie the Fixer phones Tracey back later that afternoon just as we're both wiping down the grimy paintwork in the living room. It will, he tells her, cost £300 for a job lot of furniture that will meet all of our immediate needs.

Three hundred pounds. A couple of months ago, a couple of *days* ago, I would have thought nothing about spending that on a blouse or a handbag or a pair of trousers. We'd spend three hundred pounds on a night out – a meal at a decent restaurant in London, throw in a bottle of champagne and we'd see little change from that. Now it seems like an insurmountable sum of money to find. All I've got to my name is twenty pounds in cash and some euros.

'Want it?' Tracey asks. 'He can bring it round in an hour.'

'I've no money,' I admit, feeling helpless.

'I'm strapped too,' my new friend says, 'otherwise you could borrow it off me.'

'Do you think he'd buy or pawn some of my jewellery to pay for it?'

She talks again to the mysterious Freddie, and tells me, 'He'll come round in an hour.'

When she hangs up, I say, 'I'd better go and sort out my jewellery then.'

'Want me to come with you?'

I nod. Strangely, it's not a task that I want to do alone.

'I'll make another brew,' Tracey says. 'We deserve one.'

It's fair to say that we've worked wonders on this house

today. It's also fair to say that it's never going to feature on the cover of an issue of *Beautiful Homes*, but it looks marginally less like it should be condemned or that we're going to catch a communicable disease in it.

'You've been a marvel,' I say with sincerity.

'I'll bring this up. You go and get your jewellery out. If Freddie says an hour, he means an hour.'

In the bedroom, I lift my silk jewellery wrap out of my suit-case. Laurence always complains that I take too much jewellery on holiday with me. He'd prefer for me to leave it in the little safe we have set into the back of the wardrobe in our bedroom and just take some of my costume jewellery. But my jewellery is amongst my most prized possessions and I think that you should wear it, not hide it away. They've never been pieces purely for investment purposes, they all have sentimental value attached. Now I'm so glad that I have them with me.

My heart sinks when I think of all the other irreplaceable possessions we've left behind. Photographs of the children, my parents who are no longer with us. I still have a case of baby clothes that Hettie and Hugo wore tucked away in the attic. Their matinée coats are in there, their first shoes, locks of their hair. What will happen to them now? It will mean nothing to anyone else and I wonder why I can't be allowed to have my cherished mementos back.

Sitting on the duvet-cum-bed, I undo the ties on the wrap and spread it out. Tracey comes in with the tea. She puts the mugs on the floor and we sit opposite each other, legs crossed.

'That is a *serious* jewellery collection,' she says, giving a low whistle.

'Laurence has always been a good jewellery buyer.'

'You're lucky.'

'Yes.' Now I'm beginning to realise quite how lucky.

Today, I'm only wearing my wedding ring which I never take off. My wrap contains my engagement ring. It's a single carat, emerald-cut diamond set in platinum which was last valued at ten thousand pounds and I absolutely adore it.

'Oh my word,' Tracey says, eyes widening. 'Can I try it on?'

I hand it over.

When we were first engaged, my ring was the best we could afford. Not this one, of course. My ring then was more setting than diamond and cost us less than I'm planning to pay for a job lot of someone's cast-off furniture. We'd both just started work and money was tight; expensive jewellery was the last thing on our minds. Keeping a roof over our heads had been our priority, which seems like a salutary tale now. How did we forget that so easily? My husband bought me this infinitely more lavish replacement on our tenth anniversary from Tiffany when we thought the roof over our head was . . . well – as safe as houses.

'It's beautiful.' Tracey turns her hand this way and that to admire it. The diamond catches the light even through the dirty windows and captures a rainbow prism of sunlight that brightens the grubby bedroom. 'You can't let this go, Lily.'

I sigh. 'I might not have any choice.' What's the decision? Selfishly hang on to my jewellery or live in penury?

Tracey slips of the ring and hands it back with an expression of extreme reluctance on her face. 'Let's see what else you've got.'

'Laurence bought me rings when both of the children were born.' I hold up the pretty twist of dark blue sapphires that he bought me for Hugo. Blue for a boy, he said.

'Oh, Lily.' Tracey tries that one too. 'It's gorgeous.'

'Laurence has impeccable taste.'

'You're telling me.' She grins at me. 'Has he got a brother?'

''Fraid not.' I pass over the trio of pink sapphires set into white gold that marked my beautiful daughter's arrival into the world. I hoped that the children would inherit these – Hettie for herself, Hugo for his own wife.

'Good job you didn't have half a dozen kids, otherwise you'd have been broke long before now.'

I laugh, even though I want to cry. How can I part with any of this? The jewellery is more than just trinkets to me. They map the story of my life. If I pawn it – even some of it – with Freddie the Fixer, am I ever going to be able to afford to get it back?

83

Each birthday over the years has been marked with a luxury present – brooches, bracelets, earrings, pendants – and most of it is back in the safe. Just my most treasured jewellery, the pieces that I'm most emotionally attached to, travel everywhere with me.

There are diamond earrings that were for my thirtieth birthday. A particularly good year. I have two gold bracelets with me, but they only cost a few hundred pounds each – what they'll raise now won't go very far towards buying the furniture. I have a princess-cut diamond on a pendant, also one carat and worth about six thousand pounds. That was for Christmas one year and, that's probably the piece I'm least attached to. I let the chain slip through my fingers.

'What shall I do?' I ask Tracey. 'Have you done this before?'

She snorts. 'More times than I care to remember. I've no jewellery left to pawn – all mine went years ago. Now my bling is firmly fake from New Look. I've even pawned the telly before now *and* my kids' computer.' Despite her bravado, she avoids my eyes. 'I'll flog anything I can lay my hands on.'

'Do you think Freddie will be interested in any of this?'

'Might be a bit out of his league,' Tracey says. 'Best thing is to get him to have a look at it, see what he thinks.'

'Right,' I say. 'I'll do that.' Tears spring to my eyes.

'Oh, love.' Tracey hugs me tightly. 'Don't cry.'

But I do.

Chapter 22

An hour later and, true to his word, Freddie the Fixer arrives. His BMW pulls up outside our house followed by a large white van driven by a shaven-headed and much-tattooed man with his mate beside him. And to think that all our furniture previously came from Heals. I have a quick glance to check the children are still happily entertaining themselves in the garden wasteland, then Tracey and I head out to the street to greet them.

The famous Freddie is not quite as I imagined when Tracey said he was hot. Hot to me means men who could be in Il Divo or, if I'm going for the populist vote, George Clooney.

Freddie the Fixer has the air of aging rock legend about him. His spiky hair is dyed blond and he's wearing sunglasses which I suspect he'd still be wearing even if it was dark. His ensemble consists of jeans, a cream suit jacket and a pale blue shirt. Round his neck there are three gold chains, and a small crucifix hangs from one pierced ear. Freddie is of an indeterminate age.

Tracey nudges me. 'Fit, eh?'

'Dodgy' is the word that first springs to my mind. The man with the dozen or more dogs wanders past. The dogs wag their tails at me. He holds up a hand but doesn't make eye-contact. 'Wotcher,' he says.

'Hello,' I say politely, and he sidles off again.

Freddie the Fixer strides towards us. 'Ladies, ladies, ladies,' he says, which sends Tracey into raptures of giggles. 'Want to see what I've got for you today?'

More giggling. I try to join in so that I don't look stuck-up.

He jerks a thumb towards the van behind him. 'Stick your head in there before I get them to unload it. See if you like what I've got.'

From behind his sunglasses, I just about see that Freddie winks at me. Obligingly, Tracey and I go to the van. Inside, there's the result of the shopping list my neighbour reeled off to him – a cooker, a fridge, a sofa, three beds and a table and chairs.

I look at Tracey for her approval and she nods. 'It looks fine,' I say. 'Thank you.'

'I'll want five hundred quid for the lot.'

I gasp.

'Three hundred,' Tracey says.

'I've brought all you asked for and a table and chairs too,' Freddie counters.

'Three fifty,' my neighbour concedes.

'Four fifty.'

Tracey's hands are on her hips. 'Three fifty.'

'You're supposed to say four hundred, if we're going to haggle properly.'

'Three fifty.'

Freddie holds out his hand. 'Done.'

'We'll want to check it all out first,' Tracey says.

'It's all in lovely working order.'

'It had better be,' she warns.

I'm feeling slightly redundant to the proceedings and even more so as we stand and watch while Freddie's two henchmen unload the furniture and take it to the house.

I follow them inside and watch as they dump the sofa in the living room. It's blue velour and a bit shabby, but it's perfectly serviceable. The table and chairs are varnished orange pine but, again, sturdy and fit for purpose. The cooker looks almost new and is certainly a vast improvement on what we've got. And it's great to have a fridge.

The men dump the old oven in the garden and heave my new one into place. To my relief, the kitchen looks fit for cooking in once more.

Freddie comes in to supervise the delivery, followed by Tracey.

86

The sunglasses do, indeed, stay in place. 'She's got no cash,' my neighbour says.

'I haven't,' I agree.

Freddie frowns. 'Not the time to tell me, now it's all offloaded.'

'I told you on the phone,' my neighbour reminds him. 'Lily's got some lovely jewellery. I'm sure you'll be interested in doing a deal.'

Freddie shrugs and I get a momentary panic-attack. What will I do if he doesn't want any of my jewellery? How will I pay? Will everything have to go back on the van again?

'Want to bring it down, Lily?' Tracey says.

'Yes. Yes.' Upstairs the men are hauling the mattress for the double bed onto the landing.

'In here, love?'

'Please.'

They exchange a glance and then follow me as I slip in before them and, once again, retrieve my jewellery wrap from my suitcase. Then I pull the duvet out of the way on the floor and they let the mattress crash down on to the base that's now in situ.

On our newly acquired dining-room table, I spread out my jewellery.

Freddie purses his lips. 'Nice.' He picks through it all and I really don't want him to. His fingernails are longer than a man's should be and are suspiciously well-manicured.

'It's all of sentimental value,' I tell him, my voice wavering.

'What do you want to get rid of?'

None of it, I think. I want to get rid of none of it. I want it all to become heirlooms that I can pass on to my children.

'How much would you give me for the diamond pendant?'

He picks it up and lifts his sunglasses momentarily. Their absence reveals muddy brown eyes.

'It's one carat,' I supply, 'and a very high clarity. Virtually flawless.'

More pursing.

'I'll give you five hundred quid for it.'

'Five hundred? But it's worth thousands.'

'Not to me,' Freddie says.

I look to Tracey for help. I've never had to sell my jewellery before so I've no idea what a good second-hand value would be. I feel as if I'm being ripped off, but what can I do? We can't manage for much longer without any furniture at all.

'Would you do it on a pledge?' Tracey asks.

'I'll give you the three fifty,' Freddie says, addressing my neighbour not me. 'Which makes us quits on the furniture. And a month to get it back.'

Tracey looks at me. 'Is that do-able?'

'I don't know.' I feel massively out of my depth. I wish Laurence was here. He is the one that handles any negotiations. 'What does it mean?'

'That you need to find three-fifty plus commission, within the next four weeks or Freddie keeps the necklace.'

Oh. Is that better than selling it outright for five hundred?

Freddie glances at his watch. 'I have to be going, babe. People to see, deals to do.' He nods to his two guys who have rejoined us. They head towards my newly acquired sofa.

'I'll take it,' I say in a rush.

'Done,' my pawnbroker says. I think I have been.

Perhaps Laurence should go into the dodgy dealing business because Freddie's business certainly seems to be thriving – but then some would say my husband *was* in the dodgy dealing business before.

Freddie spits on his hand and holds it out to me. Somewhat reluctantly, I shake it, and I feel pathetically grateful even though I realise that I've probably been fleeced.

'Pleasure doing business with you, ladies.' Freddie pockets my beautiful pendant. 'A month,' he says to me over his sunglasses. 'You've got a month to get this back.'

After we've watched him drive off, my friend scans the living room and says, 'That looks better now. More like home.'

Having some furniture here doesn't exactly make it feel like home, but it does feel like less of a squat.

'Do you think I'll ever see my pendant again?'

'Depends how much you want it back,' Tracey advises.

And I think that, like my old life, I want it back very much.

Chapter 23

When Laurence comes home, he's wearing the world's nastiest suit and a dejected expression. My expression, conversely, is one of surprise as it's only five o'clock and I don't think I've ever seen him come through the front door before eight in all our years of marriage. But then I remember he's only here early because he doesn't have a job – something else that hasn't happened in all our years of marriage either.

'What's this?' He looks aghast at the velour sofa and the pine table.

'Beggars cannot be choosers,' I say defensively. 'Tracey organised this for us and we should be very grateful. At least I can make us dinner tonight,' or I would be able to if I'd bought any food, 'and we don't have to sit on the floor like animals.'

Laurence runs his fingers through his hair, cowed. 'How did we pay for it?'

I take a deep breath. 'I pawned a piece of my jewellery.'

There's a shocked gasp from my husband. 'You did *what?*'

'An odious man called Freddie the Fixer gave me three hundred and fifty pounds for my diamond pendant so that I could pay him for the furniture he'd supplied.'

Laurence slumps onto the velour. 'It was worth a fortune. That sounds like a scam to me.'

'He knew that we were desperate. What else could I do?' I sit beside him. The sofa's not very comfortable, but I'm not planning on voicing that fact. 'We have a month to raise the money to buy my necklace back.' I decide to omit the commission part as I realise I have no idea how much that might be.

'What happens if we don't?'

'Then Freddie is a very happy man and I lose one of my favourite pieces of jewellery.'

'We could have got much more for it than that.'

'But we didn't,' I say. 'I did the best that I could, given the circumstances.' If my husband starts lecturing me about my housekeeping skills, then I just might become hysterical.

Seeing my expression, Laurence wisely backs down. His excuse for getting us in this mess is that he was doing his best and that's mine too. I would never have had the confidence to do this before – my husband has always been the strong one – but now I'm fighting for the survival of my family.

'I've had no luck today,' he says with a weary sigh.

At this point we'd normally crack open a decent bottle of red, sit down to a meal of crayfish risotto and rocket salad and then we'd pick at some fresh fruit and I'd flick on the Delonghi cappuccino-maker and all would be well with our world. Tonight, I'll be heading down to the local cheapo supermarket to buy something frozen to heat up until I can get to the shops tomorrow. But, at least, thanks to Freddie the Fixer, we now have a cooker that works. And, thanks to Tracey, something to serve it on and to eat it with.

'I changed the euros today,' Laurence says and he hands over twenty pounds. 'That makes a bit of extra cash to keep us going.'

Twenty pounds isn't going to get us very far at all, I think, but I take the money gratefully and slip it into my pocket.

The children rush in and, to be perfectly frank, I've been so wrapped up in my own troubles that I've hardly given them a passing thought today. They've kept themselves entertained for the best part of the day by washing down the old car in the garden, both inside and outside. It doesn't exactly shine like a new pin, but it looks less like a deathtrap now.

'Daddy, come and look what we've been doing,' Hugo says.

'Give me five minutes to get changed,' Laurence says, 'and I'll be right with you.'

Hugo and Hettie run back outside. Laurence loosens his tie. 'I like the suit.'

'A very nice old lady at the charity shop kitted me out.'

'If I can borrow a needle and cotton from Tracey, I'll hem the trousers later.' I hope that no one else has noticed that they're held up with pins.

'There's not a lot out there,' my husband tells me. 'I trawled round just about every agency. *Nada*.'

'Something will turn up.'

'What if it doesn't?' he says bleakly. 'What if this is it?'

'We can't think like that. We have to be positive.'

'I've been positive for three months,' Laurence reminds me. 'It lost us the house, everything.'

'That was being blindly optimistic,' I point out. 'Being positive is different and, this time, we're doing it together.'

He comes and takes me in his arms. 'What would I do without you?'

'Keep any more secrets from me and you might just find out.'

'No more secrets,' he agrees.

'Go and play with your children,' I say. 'They need you.'

'More than you?'

'Just as much.'

'The funny thing is,' Laurence says, 'even though we're in this scabrous place, it's still nice to come home.'

'Yes,' I say. Though what I think is, I hope to God that it's not for too long.

Chapter 24

I clean the new cooker – not that it looks like it needs it, but you can never be too careful. Then I gaze out of the window for a while, wondering what I would have been doing today if I had been in my own home and not trying to fumigate this one. Riding would have been involved – probably with my former friend, Amanda. Coffee somewhere with the rest of our friends. We'd become quite a tight-knit group, the four of us, and I wonder if Amanda has called the other girls already to spread the news of our misfortune. I'm sure she has and it's disappointing that I haven't heard a single thing from either one of them. I pick up my phone and check that I haven't missed any calls or texts. I haven't.

Crushed, I return to my reverie. Then, back at home, in my former life, I might have flicked through some recipe books to find some marvellous creation to rustle up for dinner. Tomorrow, I'd be doing pretty much the same thing.

Somehow, it sounds quite dull, now that I come to think of it.

In my new life, tomorrow will be spent trying to get the children into one of the local schools as term is due to start next week and I don't even need to ask whether Laurence has paid for their old school. Goodness only knows how much they're going to miss Stonelands.

Out in the garden I can see my husband and Hettie and Hugo clambering all over and in and out of the old heap of a car. Who'd have thought that it would prove to be such a resounding hit? I should ask Laurence to look it over to make sure that it hasn't got any sharp bits or isn't likely to jump into life on its own and run one of them over. But if I'm truthful, the car doesn't look like it's going anywhere in a hurry. Hopefully, it has distracted them from the direness of our situation. I know that children are adaptable, but mine have been so cosseted that I hope they cope with the drastic change in their lifestyles without having to go into therapy later in life.

When Laurence picks Hettie up and swings her round, my daughter laughs with sheer, unadulterated joy. It makes me smile too and my heart lifts. I haven't seen my husband play with the children like this in a long time. When they're away at school we don't see them until they come home for week- ends, and then Laurence is usually too tired to think about running around with them. He might go and stand on the sideline of a rugby pitch and make enthusiastic noises if pressed, but he's not really been that involved with them, that hands- on. Still, we're all fit and well and healthy, and that's really all that matters.

I watch as Hugo rugby tackles Laurence, grabbing him around the thighs, and they both disappear into the waist-high grass. Hettie jumps on top. I hope to goodness that there's no broken glass or needles or anything else dangerous lurking in there, but all I hear is giggling and no shrieks of pain and no spurts of blood. Always a good sign.

'Laurence,' I shout. 'I'm going to the shop. I won't be long.'

'See you in a while,' he says and is pulled, laughing, into the grass again.

I take the key and close the door behind me and, circum- navigating the detritus that litters our garden, I head towards the row of shops. It's only a five-minute walk away from the house and I'm grateful for that. To be honest, if it was dark there's no way I'd venture out here on my own.

At the end of the street, there's a man using an axle grinder to remove a yellow clamp from the wheel of his vehicle. The car doesn't look in much better condition than the one that my children have commandeered in our garden.

I'm thinking about crossing the road to avoid him when he says, 'Hiya, darlin',' and gives me a gappy smile.

'Hello.' I move to the outside of the pavement.

'I hear you're the posh new folk,' he says. 'Settling in?'

'Yes. Thank you.' He has more tattoos than bare skin showing and has a shaved head with an ink-red dragon curling around it.

He nods towards our house. 'If your old man wants to borrow a mower to run over that garden then just give us a shout.'

'Thank you,' I say. 'That's very kind of you.'

'No worries.' He returns to vandalising the clamp.

I hurry on towards the shop. The man with the multiple dogs is outside. Now the dogs want to be my best friends. They wag their tails and bark delightedly when they see me.

'Wotcher,' he says to me again, still failing to make eye-contact, as I nod a 'hello'. I thread through them all and duck inside.

Grabbing a basket, I throw in a dozen eggs – not organic – figuring that omelettes will be cheap, quick and nutritious, and a sliced white loaf – no granary – and a couple of pints of milk. To liven up the omelettes I chuck in a packet of cheddar cheese which is on offer at half-price as it's reached its sell-by date. Then my brain won't think beyond that. I'm going to have to work out how much money we've got to last us for the rest of the week and budget accordingly.

The woman behind the counter eyes me up cautiously as I pay for my goods – I wonder if she's heard about the posh new folk – and I put them in a carrier bag.

The estate is bleak, I think as I walk home, and the overall impression is one of rundown decay. But, as I look closer, I can see that it's only one or two houses that pull each street down – Chez Lamont-Jones being one of the main culprits in our particular row of terraces. Some people have tried really hard to keep their houses neat when they don't have much to work with to start off. Whoever designed these places should have been shot.

As I'm ruminating on the lack of imagination in architects, a car pulls up beside me and makes me jump. I turn to see who it might be and automatically expect to get mugged for my eggs and cheese and milk. What shall I do if they leap out and grab me? Run? Scream? Drop the food that I need so much and let them have it?

I'm so scared and so wrapped up in considering my options, that I don't immediately recognise the black Mercedes, and it's not until the window slides silently down that I realise who the occupant is.

'Want a lift?'

I nearly drop my meagre groceries anyway. 'Amanda!' I say. 'What are *you* doing here?'

Chapter 25

'I was coming to see how you are,' my former friend says over the top of her sunglasses. But her mouth is tight, no smile.

'We're fine.' Then I sag. 'No. Not fine. We're coping.'

'Hop in.'

'The house is literally two minutes away,' I tell her as I open the door and slip into the luxurious leather seat. It's the same car as I used to drive and I wonder where my Merc is now. I direct her round the corner.

Amanda's eyes widen when we pull up and she doesn't even try to hide the horror on her face as she takes in our new abode. 'You're living *here*?'

'This is what happens when the bank forecloses on you.'

'It's a hovel,' she says.

'Yes.' But it's my home now, I think, surprising myself by how territorial I feel. It's a bit like when you criticise your own husband/mother/children, but no one else is allowed to do it.

'You can't live here.' I wonder if she's about to offer us the use of one of their rental homes, perhaps at mates' rates.

'There weren't a lot of options open to us.'

And there still aren't, as the offer of a cheap place to stay doesn't come. But then I remember that we're already seriously in Amanda and Anthony's debt.

'How the mighty fall,' she says.

'Yes. And "there but for fortune", to use another cliché,' I counter. 'Would you like to see how awful it is inside?'

She looks undecided, as if she too will be contaminated by setting foot in our skanky house.

'Don't worry,' I say crisply. 'We don't have fleas.' That is, primarily, because I've been cleaning it vigorously all day.

Amanda looks slightly shamefaced and gets out of her car. She follows me into the house. I knew this wasn't an olive branch visit as she'd have brought something entirely inappropriate as a present – an orchid or something equally useless. No, my one-time friend has simply come to check out where we're living. Clearly, she can't believe the gossip and has to see it with her own eyes.

In my new abode, her mouth drops open again as she takes in the full horror of our surroundings.

'Amanda,' Laurence says when he sees her. He looks dishevelled from running around in the wilderness of the garden. 'You're the last person I expected to come calling.'

My friend doesn't know what to say and I wonder why she's felt the need to come and see for herself whether it was all true.

'About the money we owe you,' my husband says next. 'I will do my level best to get it all back to you, every single penny.'

'I do hope so, Laurence. That's an awful lot of money in anyone's book.'

'You may need to be patient with us as it might take some time.' He gestures around him. 'You can see how we're fixed.'

'Have you got work yet?' she asks.

'Not yet,' Laurence admits. 'But I'm trying very hard.'

'Will you stay for a cup of tea?' Amanda might have forgotten her manners, but I haven't forgotten mine.

'No,' she says, eyeing my blue velour disdainfully. 'I won't.' And adds, a bit too late, 'Thank you.' She folds her arms around her. 'I take it the children won't be returning to Stonelands?'

'Of course not,' I tell her. 'We can't possibly afford the fees now. I'm hoping that they'll go to the local school. You'll have to bring Arthur and Amelia round to play. I'd hate for the children to lose touch with each other simply because they're not at the same school.'

My friend looks like she might have an attack of the vapours. There's no way that she'd let her precious children set foot in here. It seems there's a fair chance that Hettie and Hugo will be erased from their playdate list. I bristle for my children more than me.

'I don't know that I'll be able to come to the next lunch,' I say. 'Please pass on my apologies to Charlotte and Lucinda. I'm sure they'll understand. Then, hopefully, when we're on our feet again . . .'

'I think it's for the best that you don't come,' Amanda says curtly. 'We don't want it to be embarrassing.'

'No,' I agree, but I wonder who it would be most embarrassing for. Me, that I now can't keep up with them, or them, for having a poor friend. As soon as you don't have the cash to flash, you clearly become a social pariah. I should have expected that but, somehow, it still hurts.

'I should be going,' Amanda says, and she backs towards the door.

'Call again any time,' I say with false brightness. 'If you're passing.' When would Amanda ever need to darken the door of Netherslade Bridge?

'Yes, yes,' she says and, in my heart, I know that I'm never likely to see her again.

I knew that Amanda was unlikely to embrace me with open arms, but I didn't think that I'd become *persona non grata* quite so quickly or quite so completely. We have been shunned by our own set in an instant – and that's a painful lesson to learn.

'Good luck,' my one-time friend says as she leaves, hurrying towards the sanctuary of her Mercedes, Jimmy Choo heels click, click, clicking on the broken paving slabs.

As she drives away, I think that we're going to need it.

Chapter 26

I make the omelettes for dinner, eke the cheese out over the four of them and we fill up on stodgy white bread, the like of which I haven't eaten since the 1970s. My budget domestic goddess will kick in soon, I'm sure of it. I just can't quite get my head together at the moment.

Later Hugo and Hettie each take showers under the dribble of warm water it supplies and, when they've gone to bed, Laurence turns to me and says, 'Shall we share a bath?'

It's something that we haven't done together for a long time. Before the children came along we used to linger in a deep, hot bubble bath, wine to hand, candles galore. It was always a precursor to making love. My husband, I think, is trying to be romantic, but I can only see the practicalities of sharing as I'm now acutely aware of how much it costs to heat water. We're on a pre-payment meter and I watch in amazement as the clock whizzes round, faster and faster as you turn each appliance on. I might well take Tracey up on her offer to get Freddie the Fixer to fiddle the meter.

At home our bath fitted us both in easily, but Shangri-La's tub is a tight squeeze and I'm sure it's not because we are both heading towards middle-aged spread. This is a small bath and the bottom of it is worryingly scratchy. We can't lie full length but have to sit knees up, which is about as unromantic as it sounds.

Still, we make the best of it, and Laurence's toes toy with mine under the water. A glass of wine would go down a treat right now and, again, I didn't realise how we took our nightly bottle for granted.

'I'll take my jewellery to a proper jeweller tomorrow,' I say. 'See what sort of price I can get for it.'

'I don't want you to do that,' my husband says. 'I bought you all that with love. I don't want you to part with it.'

'We have no choice, Laurence.' There's a little place in Woburn Sands where I bought a lot of my jewellery from and I'm thinking that I'll try there first.

'Then I'll give you my watch too.' My husband's watch is a Tag Heuer Aquaracer – a watch that he coveted and that I bought him for his last birthday. It's water-resistant to a depth of 300 metres. Not entirely necessary for a man who never goes deeper than a relaxing bath. He's wearing it now and strokes it lovingly. His other watches, a Rolex and Rado, are in the safe at our former home and I can't help thinking that they would have come in very handy now.

'There's a clock on my phone,' he goes on. 'I can use that.'

'How long will we have the phones for?'

'I don't know,' he admits. 'The company are still paying my bill, but someone is bound to realise that I no longer work there before too long. Yours is on a credit card that's completely maxed. It will probably be cut off at the end of the month.'

I shudder at the thought of it.

Laurence shrugs. 'We can prepay one. Put a fiver on at a time. That's the cheapest way. We can manage without mobile phones if we have to.'

That's probably true enough. We'll have no one who wants to call us.

'Let's just make the best of it while we can,' Laurence adds.

Afterwards we lie in bed for the second night in our new home. I thought that I'd be more relaxed after my bath and happier that I'm not spending another night on the floor, but the bed is lumpy and I can't help but wonder who has slept in it before me, plus my nerves are swiftly shredded by the sirens and the shouting and the speeding traffic on the main road beyond the ragged green. I can't settle and eventually say to Laurence, who is also still awake, 'I'm going to get up for a while.'

'Don't sit downstairs alone,' Laurence says, pushing himself up on his elbow. 'Bring a cup of tea back. I'm going to have a look through the local free paper.' He reaches down for the newspaper by his side. 'The jobs section looks quite healthy.'

So, I do just as my husband suggests. I pad into the gloomy kitchen and with just the light of the moon illuminating the room, I put the kettle on. The house doesn't look quite so rancid in twilight. We're nearly at the end of Tracey's tea bags and I must go out and shop for some store cupboard staples tomorrow. If I can sell a couple of pieces of my jewellery at a decent price and maybe Laurence's watch, then that should keep us in food for a few weeks. Perhaps even longer now that I'm born-again frugal.

I take two mugs of tea back to bed and hop in beside Laurence and snuggle into his side. In a bizarre way this does seem to have brought us closer together. Seeing a more vulnerable side to my husband has reminded me what he was like when we first met – before he became the self-assured – arrogant even – wheeler-dealer of recent years.

'Anything in there?'

'Not much,' he says as he sips his tea. 'Unless I want to be a classroom assistant or a carer in an old people's home on minimum wage.'

'Perhaps I could do something like that?'

'You'd consider going out to work?'

'The children will be at school all day. From next week, hopefully. I could try to find something that would fit in with their hours. I know that I could ask Tracey to help us out.'

'We hardly know her.'

'Already she's been a far better friend to me than my own supposed "friends". I trust her.'

'Let's hope it doesn't come to that. Surely something will turn up for me.'

Laurence has been used to providing everything for us, but

this has shown me that I'm capable of more. I went straight from home to a cosseted life at university and then into a comfortable marriage. I've never really had to struggle or stand up for myself. Somehow this 'catastrophe' has shown me that I have more to offer than that. I'm not a helpless victim in this. I can do something to help my family to get back on our feet.

'I'll take the jewellery in tomorrow.' I cast my eyes over the wrap on the floor by my bed.

'Only if you really want to,' Laurence says. 'We should leave it as a last resort.'

'It *is* a last resort, Laurence. I have nothing to buy food with.' My husband has no other suggestions to remedy that. A siren wails by outside again and I sigh.

He unclips his watch and hands it to me. 'Then take this too.'

'Are you sure?'

My husband nods. I put the watch down on top of my jewellery wrap. 'We should try to settle down, get some sleep.'

Laurence folds the paper and tosses it onto the floor, then he takes me in his arms and I curl into him.

'We will get through this,' he says, his breath warm against my neck. 'Tomorrow is another day.'

'Yes.' And I hope to all that is good that it's not another miserable one.

Chapter 27

In the dead of the night, I hear a crash, but feel as if I'm drugged and can't open my eyes. After a few days of insomnia, sleep has now overtaken me with a vengeance and I sink back into it.

The next thing I know, there's a shadow moving beside me. I try to rouse myself. 'Hugo,' I say sleepily. 'Is that you, darling?'

But there's no reply and, suddenly, all the hairs on the back of my neck stand up. Even in my confused state, I register that the fuzzy outline is way too tall to be my son. Then the shadow retreats, somewhat hastily, and there's another thump, this time against the bedroom door.

I go to reach for the bedside light, then remember that I don't have one. My heart pounds in my chest as I lie there immobilised with terror. Eventually, my brain convinces my body that I can't just lie there and do nothing, so I manage to force myself to scramble out of bed. 'Laurence,' I urge, 'wake up.'

Crossing the room, I fumble for the light switch and, before my husband is properly awake, flood the bedroom with the bright glare from the single bare light bulb in the middle of the room.

'What on earth . . . ?' Laurence mumbles, putting his hand above his eyes.

I fly along to the children's rooms, but they are – thank God! – safely tucked in their beds, sound asleep.

Back in our own bedroom, I give a quick scan to check whether anything is missing. And, as we have very little in the room, it doesn't take me long to realise what has gone.

Laurence is sitting up now, but still looking bleary-eyed.

'My jewellery,' I say. 'My jewellery has gone.'

'What?' My husband is immediately wide awake.

'It's gone.' I'm staring, frozen, at the patch on the floor where my jewellery wrap was only an hour or two ago. 'All of it. And your watch too.'

Laurence is out of bed in an instant and races down the stairs. I shake myself into action and follow him.

Sure enough in the kitchen, the back door is open. If it had a curtain, it would be flapping in the breeze. One of the plywood panels has been kicked or punched in, taking the few remaining remnants of glass with it. Down at the bottom of the garden, there's a dull thud and we both see a figure vault over the fence there.

'I'll have that bastard,' my husband says, and he shoots out of the back door.

'Laurence! Come back.' He's wearing boxer shorts and a T-shirt and has nothing on his feet. 'He'll be long gone by now.'

My husband hits the long grass, running, and then shouts out: 'Damn it!'

Then he hops about, clutching his toes.

'Come in,' I say wearily. 'He's got away.'

Laurence trails back to the door. 'I'm going to get dressed and look for him.'

'Is there any point?'

'I have to do something.'

'Be careful.' I put my hand on his chest and he clutches it to him. 'He could have a knife or anything. There might be more than one of them. I'll call the police.'

'What have we done to deserve this?' he asks. His voice is bitter, wearied. 'We're not bad people.'

Then he goes upstairs and, a few minutes later, the front door closes behind him.

I call the police who are distinctly disinterested it seems in yet another burglary in Netherslade Bridge. I'm assured that an officer will call round tomorrow, despite my pleas that the man might still be in the area and he's taken all that we have, but I'm sure we'll no more see the police here than we will Amanda and Anthony Marquis.

Back in the bedroom, I check our suitcases to see if anything else has gone missing. After a cursory rummage, it seems that everything is still there. And, in the depths of the case, I discover the video camera – something that I'd forgotten was even there. Why didn't they take that? But then, I feel that the thief who came in here knew exactly what he was looking for.

With shaking hands, I put the kettle on again. In the corner of the room, I see Laurence's golf clubs. At least they didn't steal those, I suppose – though he'll not be able to afford a round of golf for some time. I should have offered those to Freddie the Fixer but, somehow, in all the wheeling and dealing, I forgot all about them. Turning Freddie's name over in my brain, I wonder just how much he had to do with this. I'll admit that I'm not very au fait with the ways of the world, but this doesn't feel like a coincidence to me.

Ten minutes later, Laurence returns. He's out of breath and he's empty-handed.

In the kitchen, he bends double while he pants out, 'I've been everywhere. Not a sign of him . . . them.'

'I telephoned the police,' I say, 'but they're not interested.'

'If we'd still been in the barn, they'd have been there in five minutes,' my husband notes sourly.

That's true enough, I think. But burglars at the barn would have struggled to get past the state-of-the-art alarm and CCTV cameras. Now we have nothing but a bit of cheap glass or flimsy plywood to protect us. The thought makes me shiver.

'What will we do now?' Laurence wants to know.

'I'll have a word with Tracey in the morning,' I say. 'I bet she'll know who the rogues are around here.'

There's one of them that even I can readily name who was well aware that I had a silk wrap of expensive jewellery in my bedroom.

Chapter 28

We stagger back to bed just before dawn, and when we wake up the next morning – late, late, late – by some terrible irony of fate, we're all covered in flea-bites. The children are positively eaten alive. They look like they've both got chickenpox or maybe just the pox. It gives me the opportunity for a bitter smile. In some perverse way, I'm hoping that my dear ex-friend, Amanda – after hovering near our lousy sofa – has woken up covered in them too. I hope she looks like she's got the pox too. See if *that* matches her Jimmy Choos.

Then I remember that during the night, while we lay sleeping, someone stole into our room and robbed us of all our worldly goods. The thought is like a body blow and I feel bile rise in my throat.

In my dressing-gown, I go next door to Tracey on the pretext of borrowing some antihistamine or antiseptic cream or anti-flea potion. But my main reason, of course, is to see if I can get any information from her about the criminal activities in Netherslade Bridge and who would be the most likely candidate for 'lifting' my jewellery, as I believe it's called.

My neighbour is still in her dressing-gown too as I somehow knew she would be.

'Flea-bites,' I say, showing her my arms.

'After we've done all that cleaning? Bloody persistent sods.'

'I think it might be the sofa.'

Tracey has calamine lotion and cotton wool in the cupboard

and hands it over. 'You can get stuff for them. Little swines,' she commiserates. 'You just spray it round.'

'I'll get some today,' I promise. But I wonder what with.

'That bloody Freddie,' she says with a cross tut. 'You wait till I see him. He told me that was good stuff.'

'It doesn't matter,' I say, scratching. Perhaps I deserve to be covered in flea-bites. 'Something even worse happened in the night.'

My friend raises an eyebrow.

'Someone broke into the house and took all of my jewellery.'

'Last night?'

I nod. 'Every last scrap of it. About four in the morning.'

'Ohmigod,' Tracey says. 'Everything?'

'The lot.' I let the information sink in before I say tentatively, 'Think I can lay that one at Freddie's door too?'

Tracey looks mortally offended. 'Freddie?' She shakes her head. 'He's a wide boy, all right. But he's not a crook. No way.'

'Do you think that he could have told someone else about my jewellery then? Tipped them off?'

'He wouldn't do that,' she says vehemently. 'Not Freddie. I'd trust him with my life.'

Personally, I think Tracey is misguided in that. I wouldn't trust him as far as I could throw him and I feel really stupid that I let someone like that come over my threshold. But I was desperate, in need and he knew that, and I wouldn't be at all surprised that he took advantage of it. 'It just seems a bit suspicious. That's all I'm saying.'

Tracey's face darkens. 'All you're saying is that we're a bunch of crooks and lowlifes round here.'

'I'm not saying that at all,' I counter. 'But it must have been someone who knew. Surely?'

'Why?' she asks. 'It could have been an opportunist thief who got lucky.'

'He knew exactly what he was looking for. He came straight to my side of the bed. Nothing else is missing.'

'You haven't got anything else worth pinching,' Tracey points out crisply. Which stings even though it's true.

'Someone must have known. You wouldn't look at that house and think, as you so rightly said, that there was anything of value in there.'

'I think you've got a nerve,' Tracey spits. She folds her arms across her chest defensively. 'I've done all I can to help you out since you arrived and now you're accusing my friends of robbing you.'

'It's not that.'

'I think it is.'

'Don't you view it as suspicious?'

'No, I don't. This is life now, Lily. You're not in your gilded cage any longer. Get used to it.' She turns away from me. 'You'd better leave now.'

'Tracey, I'm not saying that it's in any way your fault.'

'I think you are.' Her lips are pursed. 'I think you're blaming me for bringing Freddie to your place. But it's not like that round here. We look after our own.' Then she says, 'I should have known that you'd never be one of us.'

This is not how I expected Tracey to react and I'm wounded. 'I don't want us to fall out.'

'I think we already have,' she says tartly.

My shoulders sag. I don't have any fight. I should have realised that it was silly to consider this woman a friend so easily. When all our true friends have deserted us so quickly, should I have stopped and wondered what was in it for her? She might even be Freddie the Fixer's accomplice, for all I know. All this friend-ship act and she might have just been setting me up. I'm too trusting. Too easily led. And now I'm paying the price. Well, it's them and us from now on. I'm never going to trust anyone again.

Chapter 29

Taking the calamine lotion, I douse us all liberally in it. I probably rub harder than I need to, as mums do, but then I'm cross. Cross that someone has had the nerve to help themselves to my jewellery when it's all that we had to keep our heads above water. Cross that Tracey thinks I was somehow accusing her of being party to this thievery. Cross that our lives have descended to this and at such an alarming rate. Cross that after having everything we have so very little left.

'Ouch,' Laurence says.

'Ouch,' Hugo says.

'Ouch,' Hettie says.

'Stop complaining,' I snap at them all. And, when they start to scratch: 'Don't scratch.'

Then, when I've finished scratching myself, I lather my bites in the pale pink chalky fluid and put on a linen blouse with long sleeves so that I don't look as if I've been chewed alive by the little blighters.

'I want to keep the fleas as pets,' Hettie whines.

'You can't keep fleas as pets.'

'Why not? We haven't got pets any more. I miss my pony.'

'A flea is hardly the same. You can't ride a flea.'

This makes my daughter pause to consider her logic and, during the pause, I swoop in with, 'The discussion is closed. We are not keeping fleas as pets.'

Laurence is about to leave the house in his cheap suit and ill-fitting brogues to go and knock on doors for another day and I kiss him lightly on the cheek in what I know is a distracted manner.

'What are you going to do today?' he asks.

'I suppose I should wait in just in case the police do deign to turn up.'

He nods his agreement. 'I'll see you later. Wish me luck.'

'Good luck,' I say flatly.

'Chin up,' Laurence says.

I don't want to keep my chin up. I want to let it trail along the floor. I want everyone to know the extent of my misery.

My husband leaves and now I'm not sure what to do with myself. Normally, the children would be away at school or, if at home, would be entertaining themselves on their computers or the Playstation or the Wii or in the games room. Now they have nothing to do, none of their things with them and I realise how heavily we relied on technological distractions to keep them amused while they were with us.

'What can we do?' Hugo wants to know. 'We're bored.'

A good question. 'Would you like to play out in your car?'

They both nod and rush off for their shoes.

Thank goodness for that old wreck, I think gratefully. What would they be able to do otherwise? There is a kids' playground just down the road, but the equipment looks as if it is mostly vandalised and, when I passed by yesterday, going to the shop, it was populated by teenagers with bottles of cider rather than the children it was intended for. I wouldn't be able to let my two out of my sight here. Wherever they went, I'd have to go with them. How different from when they had all the land they needed behind the barn to play in. Now they're restricted to the overgrown mess that's classed as our garden.

I gaze out of the window. What would I be doing at home now? If the children were away, I'd be going to the gym with Amanda or, in the summer, we'd ride out on our horses through the leafy green lanes around the village. Perhaps there'd be a cake to bake for a charity fund-raiser or a lunch to organise. I'd shop for something wonderful to cook for dinner – never eaten before nine due to Laurence's hours. Then we'd relax together with a glass of wine and some light jazz or classical music on the iPod, before falling into our sumptuous bed, safe behind our state-of-the-art security system. Good grief, what a truly pampered existence I had. But then I remember that some days I didn't see another living soul from dawn to dusk. No chance of that now we are living cheek-by-jowl with our neighbours.

'Come and see our car, Mummy,' Hugo says when he returns, breaking into my musing. 'It's most excellent.'

'Be careful of any sharp bits,' I warn.

I should actually go out there and also check that there's nothing terrible lurking in the grass that could harm either of them. I shouldn't be at all surprised to find a stash of used syringes somewhere.

So, I slip on my own shoes and follow them into the garden. The grass is past my knees. Perhaps we could take up the tattooed man's offer from down the street and Laurence could borrow some tools to make a start on getting this under control. I can't see us making our escape from here imminently. The children go to the car and Hettie gets into the passenger seat and Hugo is the driver.

'I want to drive later,' Hettie says. 'But you can do it for now.'

'Girls are all rubbish drivers,' he says, and I know he's got this politically incorrect information from his father, but I'm too weary to challenge him.

I make my way further down the garden, treading carefully. I've only got light sandals from my holiday – what will I do when the weather turns cooler and I need something more substantial? I push the thought to the back of my mind. Frankly, I have more things to worry about than appropriate footwear.

How do people manage, I wonder, who live like this all the time? People who are permanently dragged down by grinding poverty. I need to go and get some sort of chemical cocktail to eradicate our flea colony, but I have to weigh up how much the bus fare will cost me for just that journey and know that I'll have to wait until I've got several errands to do simply to make it cost-effective. Before, I'd think nothing of jumping in the car and driving thirty miles to a nice little deli I know just for a special herb that I wanted for supper, or a particular kind of olive. I feel nauseous at the waste of it now.

How did it get like this, I wonder? My parents didn't bring me up to embrace profligate waste. They had to watch the pennies. They made do and mended. They managed perfectly well with one car for all of their married life. When did that all end? Why did we think we needed two cars when one of them used to spend all of its life on the drive? With a bit of juggling of the diary we could have managed perfectly well with one vehicle. As a child I had one holiday a year in Bournemouth or Wales – usually involving dawn to dusk torrential rain, if I remember. Why do we now think our children are deprived if their passports aren't full by the time they're ten? Hugo and Hettie have seen more places than most folks will go to in a lifetime. Does that make them better people? Or are we just breeding the next generation to have unrealistically high expectations of what life will bring them? I really don't know and I'm too tired to think any more about it.

There's all kinds of junk buried in the depths of the garden. A few bits from the car, some discarded and rusty tools, a tyre – all long since consumed by the grass. And then, as I get to the bottom of the garden near the fence, something catches my eye. There's a vague hint of a glint in the wilderness and, I don't know why, but my heart skips a beat. I bend down, my breath stops in my chest, and I part the fronds, digging down to the earth. Sure enough, there – deep, deep down in the grass – is a ring. How I spotted it, I'll never know.

Picking it up, I nestle it in my palm. It must have fallen from my silk jewellery wrap as the burglar vaulted the fence. That's the only thing I can think of. It's the pink sapphire ring I was given for Hettie's birth. I sit back on my heels and study it. Hot tears spring to my eyes. I feel somehow that we've been given a reprieve. I cry with relief, hugging myself, careful not to lose my grip on the precious find clutched in my fingers.

There *is* a God. Even though most of the time He seems to be an inconsiderate bastard, occasionally He comes through.

This is my lifeline. If I can only sell this, I think, then we can start to get back on our feet again.

Chapter 30

Laurence did another round of the recruitment agencies, even the ones that seemed particularly useless. He worked on the theory that if he made enough of a nuisance of himself then they'd find him a job just to get rid of him.

Gone were the days when his phone was red hot with head-hunters bandying about high six-figure salaries to lure him from his current employer. These all kept telling him that he was over-qualified – but the world for which he *was* qualified didn't want him any more. Those who knew him now associated him with the pyramid scam that he'd been foolish enough to invest in. Those who didn't, wondered why he hadn't already been snapped up by a rival organisation. Also, times had moved on. Recruitment in the City had pretty much ground to a halt; cutbacks, natural wastage and golden handshakes were much more common now. But it didn't matter to him about getting back into the City – he'd resigned himself to that already. Now he felt that he'd work at anything, so long as it gave him his dignity back.

He'd exhausted his list of contacts, a few of their old friends in the industry, colleagues with whom he'd worked happily for many years. Hadn't he always been one of the most popular members of the team? Everyone knew that. Now, it seemed, he was about as welcome as a fart in a spacesuit. His calls had gone unanswered and, if he'd summoned up his courage to leave a voice message, invariably they had not been returned. The word would be out that the bailiffs had been and that he owed Anthony Marquis a small fortune. No one dropped a mate in it and got away with it.

Lily, bless her, was optimistic about her chances of getting a job. But, by anyone's standards, she'd had a half-hearted attempt at working when they'd first been married and had just left university. She temped part-time in a solicitor's office despite achieving a first-class degree in History. Even in this enlightened age, she'd been brought up to expect to be a wife and mother, nothing more. She'd gone to university because she'd been the cleverest in her class, but it had never been much more than a stop-gap for her before marriage and starting a family. And that was one of the many things that had attracted him to her. Unlike most of the women at uni, Lily had strong traditional values and he'd bought right into it. The fact that she was a stunner with her soft red hair and dazzling green eyes had done nothing to dissuade him. There'd never been a discussion about it but, from day one, it had always been an unspoken expectation that he'd be the breadwinner and she would stay at home. The minute she was pregnant with Hugo, she had given up work and had never made any suggestion about returning to it since.

If he was struggling for work, he wondered how Lily would fare with no office skills, no experience and over a decade at home as a pampered housewife. He couldn't see her trailing around like this, like some sort of desperate door-to-door salesman. Three months felt like an eternity to be out of work, but ten years . . .

Laurence longed for a coffee, but even the joy of a simple Starbucks latte was staggeringly out of reach at the moment. His throat was parched and, in his poorly fitting shoes, his feet were aching. But even they didn't ache as much as his heart. It wasn't until the fourth agency he visited that there was a glimmer of hope.

'There's one here,' the woman behind the desk said, chewing on her pen. 'Assistant manager at an organic farm shop.' Then she looked up at him, apologetic. 'Not really your thing.'

'It could be.' At this point, he'd consider anything. 'We're

115

very keen on organic food at home.' He thought of the Sugar Puffs they'd eaten for breakfast. No more homemade muesli rich with exotic fruits and nuts.

'The salary's pretty low.'

He'd already resigned himself to that fact.

She printed out the details and pushed them across the desk to him. Laurence scanned the job description and took in the figure.

'Surely there are some noughts missing,' he said.

The woman laughed. 'Unfortunately not.'

'Wow,' Laurence said.

'Want me to set up an interview?'

Laurence sighed inwardly. Was it worth it? It couldn't be considered remotely in his field and the salary was truly dreadful. He would have spent that kind of sum in one evening entertaining a few clients.

'There are quite a few applicants,' the woman said as she let her eyes wander over the listings on her computer. 'And not much else on the horizon.' She pursed her lips at him. 'Sign of the times, I'm afraid.'

He might as well pitch his lot in with the other applicants even though his heart wasn't in it. It was all well and good saying that he'd take anything but, when push came to shove, it seemed there were limits.

'I'd like an interview, if possible.'

'I'll call the owner, Mr Cherry, now,' she said. 'Let me get you a coffee while you wait. Sugar?'

'One, please.' The woman went to get him a coffee from the nearby machine.

It wasn't the frothy Starbucks' creation he'd envisaged, but he was very grateful for it nevertheless.

While he sipped at the lukewarm, bitter fluid, she called to set up an interview for him. 'Tomorrow at eleven o'clock,' she said when she hung up. 'Does that suit?'

There was nothing else pressing that he had to do. 'Sounds fine.'

'I hope you do well,' she said, then glanced at the clock to indicate that it was time for him to leave.

116

And despite it not being his dream job and despite it not carrying the sort of salary that would keep them in the style to which they'd become accustomed, Laurence left the recruitment office with a definite spring in his step.

Chapter 31

Just after noon, Laurence comes back to the house. 'I have an interview arranged for tomorrow morning,' he says with a relieved smile.

'Thank goodness.'

'It's not what I'm used to,' my husband admits. 'Assistant manager at an organic farm shop called Cherry's out in Great Brickhill.'

I know it well. The village is a pretty little place where the children and I used to go hacking sometimes. The farm shop is popular, always busy. I've been there myself often enough and I have to say that I wouldn't have considered it a place where I could see Laurence working. I don't voice that opinion, however.

'But I thought I might as well give it a go,' he continues. 'Get back into the swing of interviews. It could well do to tide us over.'

'Absolutely.' I kiss him on the cheek. 'Well done.'

My husband shrugs. 'I couldn't face knocking on doors this afternoon, so I thought I'd come home and do something to this place.'

'Torch it?'

'I was thinking something slightly more constructive.'

'There's a man who lives down the road – scary-looking character . . .'

'That description could encompass *all* of our new neighbours.'

'More scary than the others. Lots of tattoos. Lots and lots. Shaved head.'

'Again, that could describe many of our neighbours,' Laurence notes. 'Particularly the women.'

I laugh at that, but can hear the weary tone underneath it.

'This one has a red dragon tattoo on his bald head. He offered to lend us his lawnmower.'

'That's very decent of him.'

'I thought so. Perhaps we could take him up on his offer.'

'I'll take a wander down there when we've had some lunch.'

'Lunch?' I say. 'I hadn't even thought about that.'

'I bought some rolls and ham from the shop at the end of the road. It's a bit plasticy, but it will keep us going.'

'I found this in the garden.' I hold up my treasure. 'Looks like the burglar must have dropped it. I'll take it to the jewellers this afternoon while you're here to watch the children.'

'Do you have to do that?'

'It will keep us going, Laurence.' Believe me, if I didn't think it was necessary then I wouldn't dream of parting with my ring. 'Lunch might be organised but we haven't got any food for supper.'

'I might get this job tomorrow.'

'Even if you do, it will take time to get paid, and we need money to keep us going now. It's the right thing to do.'

'If you're sure.' Then he comes to me and wraps his arms round my waist. 'I don't deserve you.'

'You don't,' I tease.

'I will make this up to you,' he says against my neck. 'I promise.'

Then the children burst in through the plywood back door and any glimmer of romance that might have been stirring is immediately thwarted. Laurence and I pull away from each other.

Hettie giggled, embarrassed. 'Mummy and Daddy! You were cuddling!'

'Yuk,' Hugo says.

'You *never* cuddle,' my daughter points out. And I wonder if she's right. Laurence and I aren't particularly touchy-feely people, that's true enough. Isn't that another thing that goes out of the window, the longer you're married? Laurence and I have, more often than not, been like ships in the night and we don't often have time for that sort of business. Yet another thing to worry about.

'We'll sit in the garden and eat the rolls,' I say. So we take them outside – no plates, no napkins, no patio table or chairs. No patio, in fact. We avoid the mattresses with the mushroom crop and stamp down a bit of the long grass near the children's car and all sit together there. I hand out the rolls and at the bottom of the carrier bag find four apples that Laurence has bought too.

'This is fun,' Hattie says excitedly. 'Like a picnic in a wild place.'

I think of the time when we dragged them all the way to the Seychelles for a holiday and they were bored out of their heads after a week.

The sun beats down on us, the birds are busy in the trees, their song blending with the sound of traffic. The stone eagles keep their beady eyes on us from their eyrie on the garage roof. We haven't even been round to the back of the property yet, nor have we checked if there's anything in the garage. It's probably chock-full of more rubbish, but I must definitely check the access road there to see if our fumble-fingered burglar has fortuitously dropped anything else.

Laurence is smiling.

'What's wrong?' I want to know.

'Nothing.' He shrugs. 'This is rather nice. I quite like the garden in this untamed state.'

I look at the shabby grass round my ears, the abandoned car, the mattresses – the dumped cooker I've added to it – and think of my previous rose-scented sanctuary and want to weep.

'It feels very rustic,' he continues. A motorbike roars past and somewhat shatters that illusion.

'I'm just going to check down the road at the back for any stray jewellery and then I'll be off.'

'Excellent idea.' Laurence's eyes are heavy and he looks like he might just lie down and have a sleep.

Well, good for him. A wave of irritation prickles over me.

We both had a virtually sleepless night and here I am trying to do the best for us while my dear husband is thinking about having a nice nap in this excuse for a garden.

Then I watch as Hettie snuggles up next to him and puts her head in his lap and Laurence strokes her hair. Not wanting to be left out, Hugo shuffles towards them and, self-consciously, takes the other side of his lap. This is all too rare a moment in the Lamont-Jones household, and it hurts to acknowledge that. I think about going to get the video camera I've just rediscovered to record the moment – start collecting a new set of memories – but they all look so peaceful that I don't want to disturb them.

Instead, I take one last glance at my family, then tiptoe out of the garden and go in search of more of my jewellery to sell.

Chapter 32

Sadly, only my pink sapphire ring has escaped the clutches of our night-time thief. So, with it safely tucked into my handbag, my flea-bites and I wait for the bus to take me into the city centre and then for another one to take me out to the little jewellery shop that I know in the High Street in Woburn village.

The young woman who owns it, Anya Collinge, is a contemporary designer of some note and Laurence has bought me a few pieces from her in the past. I know that she also buys and sells some second-hand items if they're good enough quality. This isn't one of her designs, but she's always admired this ring of mine, so I'm hoping that she'll give me a good price. I'm even more anxious to part with it when I realise that the bus fare alone takes nearly all of my remaining money.

The shop is called Ornato and the bell chimes pleasantly when I push open the door. Inside it's unbelievably stylish and stark in its whiteness. I look longingly at the glittering baubles displayed temptingly beneath the glass counter, but with a heavy heart I acknowledge that my days of impulse jewellery-buying are long gone and may never be seen again.

A man comes out to greet me. 'May I help you?'

'I was looking for Anya,' I tell him. 'I've bought a number of pieces from here in the past.'

'Anya's moved into London,' he says. 'I'm Seymour Chapman.' He holds out his hand and I grasp it. His fingers are long, tapered, artistic. 'I took over the shop just a few months ago. But we're still selling Anya's designs and I'm planning to offer pieces by other upcoming designers too.'

Seymour Chapman is tall and gangly. His brown hair is swept back and is receding slightly at the temples. It's too long at the back, curling over his collar, and, if I was his wife, I'd make him have it cut. Yet he has one of the warmest smiles I've ever seen and his pale blue eyes twinkle with kindness. He's wearing a brown linen suit with a shirt beneath it which matches his eyes perfectly. And, I don't know why, but I wonder if he's chosen it himself or whether that is down to his wife too.

'Are you looking for something specific today? For a particular occasion?'

I shake my head and my face grows warm. 'I'm not looking to buy today,' I confess. I'm failing to meet this man's eyes. 'I was hoping to sell.' My voice breaks on the last word and I could kick myself for my weakness.

'I see,' Seymour says.

But I don't think he does see. He doesn't see how desperate I am, how much I need this money now.

'I hadn't planned to buy jewellery,' he tells me.

'Oh,' I say. Now I don't know what to do. I've spent virtually every penny I had on this wild-goose chase and have absolutely nothing to show for it. 'I'd better go then. I'm sorry to have troubled you.'

Tears spill over my lashes as I turn to leave.

'Wait.' Seymour gives a little sigh. 'Would you like me to take a look at what you've brought in? It can't do any harm,' he says gently, and that makes my throat close up completely.

I don't think that I've ever felt so humiliated in all my life. I don't feel as if I'm selling something fair and square, I feel as if I'm begging, holding out my bowl for a few scraps and I never in my whole life expected to feel like this.

Blinking back the tears, I nod then dig deep into my handbag to find my cherished ring. The bag's worth a few pounds of anyone's money too – perhaps I could sell it on eBay if I could get access to a computer.

Seymour lays a black cloth on top of the counter and, with a shuddering breath, I place the ring in the centre of it.

'This is the ring I had when my daughter, Hettie, was born,' I say, the words wavering. 'Pink sapphires set in eighteen-carat white gold.' I can hardly get the sentence out and I try to convince myself that selling it doesn't matter to me; it's a bauble, nothing more. I stop to bite hard on my lip which has started to tremble.

Seymour studies me intently and I do wish he wouldn't. I'm currently struggling to hold it all together. 'It's a very fine ring,' he says.

I push it forward on the black velvet and, as Seymour reaches for it, another telltale tear escapes from beneath my lowered lashes and splashes onto the cloth.

'Oh, dear.' Seymour looks up from the ring and to me.

'I'm sorry,' I say. 'This is very difficult for me. I'm more used to being a buyer rather than a seller.'

'I can tell that,' Seymour says.

Now I can't stop the tears at all and I let them fall, splashing onto his immaculate black cloth and the immaculate glass counter.

'Oh, dear. Oh, dear,' he says again.

And I can't help myself, but I laugh – somewhat hysterically – and want to sag to the floor. This poor man doesn't deserve me breaking down in his nice, shiny shop.

'I have an idea,' Seymour says. 'Let's have a cup of tea.'

I laugh the laugh of the unhinged again. 'I couldn't possibly.'

'Nonsense. I was just about to make one for myself.'

I try to sniff away my tears, but fail. 'Then that would be very kind of you.'

Seymour hands me back my ring and then strides to the door, his long frame covering the distance in seconds. He flips the Closed sign and turns back to me. 'Come this way.'

Keeping hold of my ring, I follow him, easing behind the counter and into the small room at the back of the shop. It's quite sparsely decorated in here; more functional than stylish. There's a desk, a computer, a filing cabinet and, fortunately, two armchairs in a Cath Kidston floral print.

Seymour indicates that I should take one and I do, gratefully.

In the corner, on another cabinet, there's a kettle and a tray with cups, a bottle of milk and tea bags. While Seymour gets on with the business of making tea, I find my handkerchief and wipe my silly, silly tears away as quickly as I can.

'I have only builder's tea,' he says over his shoulder. 'Nothing fancy.'

'That would be lovely.'

'I didn't get your name,' Seymour says.

'Lily,' I supply. 'Lily Lamont-Jones.'

'Well, I'm very pleased to make your acquaintance, Lily. Even though I wish it had been in more auspicious circumstances.'

I can only nod in agreement.

Chapter 33

Seymour Chapman hands me a mug of tea. A fine bone china mug.

'Thank you.' The tea burns my throat as I swallow it. 'This is much appreciated.' I give him a rueful smile. 'Life hasn't been very kind just recently.'

'Perhaps I should have put a couple of spoonfuls of sugar into it for you. It looks like you've had a bit of a shock.'

'Yes,' I agree. 'I've had a shock.'

Seymour lowers himself into the chair opposite me and nurses his tea. 'Want to talk about it?'

I shake my head. 'It's nothing,' I tell him. I remember the flea-bites beneath my designer blouse and think how low we've sunk. 'And I've already taken up too much of your valuable time.'

'Business is slow today,' he assures me with a lazy shrug. 'I was only doing tedious paperwork. You'd be doing me a favour.'

'It's really nothing.'

'I don't think you'd be bringing me one of your most loved pieces of jewellery, if there was nothing wrong.'

'No.' Then it all seems too much to hold it all in, to pretend that everything is all right when it patently isn't. 'My husband has lost his job,' I blurt out. 'He was working in the City but somehow got into a dubious scheme too deeply and had his fingers burned.'

'Ah.' Seymour frowns. 'I'm sorry to hear it.'

The stupid, stupid thought goes through my addled mind

that he looks just as attractive when he's frowning as when he's smiling.

'We've lost everything,' I continue shakily. 'Our homes, our cars, our horses. All I had of value was my jewellery. Then some rogue came in and stole it all. The ring is all I have left.' I glance at the ring in my fingers and fight back the tears. 'The burglar dropped it in the garden.'

'And now you want to sell it?'

'*Want to* is perhaps overstating the situation. *Have to* is more accurate.' I sigh into my teacup. 'I don't have any choice.'

'Are you sure?'

I nod, unable to trust my voice.

Seymour leans back in his chair. 'Then I'll give you a good price for it,' he says. 'A fair price.'

'Thank you.'

He shrugs. 'If that's what you really want.'

I sit forwards in my chair. 'I do.'

Seymour reaches out a hand. 'Let me have a closer look at it again.'

I go to hand him the ring and, as I do, our fingers touch. I jerk my hand back in embarrassment while Seymour merely parts with another one of his languid smiles.

He reaches for an eyeglass and studies the stones. 'Very nice,' he says, half to himself. Then looks back at me.

'Seven hundred pounds,' he says. 'I can't be fairer than that.'

'Seven hundred?'

'No more.'

I nod with relief. 'I'll take it.' At one time, a few short weeks ago, I would have thought nothing about spending that in a week, a day even; now it sounds like a life-saving amount of money. If we're frugal, that could last us for a good few weeks, months perhaps. Surely, Laurence will have found a job by then.

'Thank you so much,' I say to Seymour. 'You have no idea what this means to me.'

'It's my pleasure, Mrs Lamont-Jones.'

'Lily, please,' I say to him sheepishly.

He puts down his mug and goes to open a small safe. Seymour

counts out the money into my hand. Then he slips my ring into the safe.

'I hope to see you again,' he says.

'I'm sure you will,' I reply.

But now that my jewellery-buying days are at an end, I'm absolutely sure that he won't.

Chapter 34

As I take the bus, joggling all the way back to Netherslade Bridge, the seven hundred pounds that Seymour Chapman gave me for my beautiful pink sapphire ring is burning a hole in my pocket. I don't know if it was a good price or not for a second-hand sale, but I know that Seymour had a kind and honest face and I'd rather trust him than Freddie the Flaming Fixer any day.

My first purchase from my bounty was flea spray from the ironmonger's store. Not an exciting way to spend my newly acquired cash, but I'm sure that my family will be grateful for it. I scratch at my arms self-consciously.

Outside the local shop, the bus stops and I get off. Inside, I buy supper for tonight. If I shop on a daily basis then there will be less waste. At home our fridge was always overflowing with all manner of delights and I think of all the expensive food I used to throw in the bin without a second thought and it makes me feel ashamed.

Putting some spaghetti in my basket – no wholewheat pasta here – I eschew the minced beef as being too expensive to buy and too cheap in quality to eat. I throw in some tinned tomatoes, an onion and a glass jar of dried herbs – something I've never ever used in my life before. But it will be another inexpensive and filling meal and that will have to do us for now. Then I throw caution to the wind and buy a bouquet of flowers to give to my next-door neighbour as an olive branch. They're a little past their best and are reduced to £2.99. In my previous social circle this would have been seen as poor etiquette. I would have gone to a high-end florist and had a bouquet specially made, but I'm sure that Tracey will appreciate my gesture. I only hope that she does. I also realise that I would normally have done this because it was expected of me, because it was seen to be the right thing to do, not because I'm trying to be a nice person and really want to.

I walk back towards our new home. The man with the million dogs is out walking them. They wag their tails as they see me and I stop to pet them, sending them into a frenzy of joy. The man nods his head to me and says, 'Wotcher.'

'They're lovely dogs,' I tell him. Every one of them is groomed and healthy-looking. Which is more than I can say for the owner.

'Thank you, madam,' he says, embarrassed, and then he's off again with his multiple canine charges in tow.

There's no sign of the man with the tattoos and the axle grinder and I wonder whether Laurence borrowed his lawn-mower or whether my husband fell asleep in the wilderness garden.

I let myself into the house, now used to having to shoulder the warped door as I do.

'Hello,' I shout, but there's no reply. In the kitchen, I dump my carrier bag on the work surface and look out of the window. The back door is open and when I poke my head outside all I can see is Laurence's jean-clad bottom sticking in the air.

Next to him is the tattooed man and it looks suspiciously like they are laying a patio.

Laurence straightens up. 'Hello,' he says. 'Had a good afternoon, darling?'

'Yes.'

'This is Mr Skull,' he says, and the tattooed man nods at me and continues to put a slab in place and hit it with a mallet wielded like a club. Rather forcefully.

'Just Skull,' he corrects.

'Skull and I have already met,' I remind my husband. And that slab is never going to move.

'Oh, yes. Of course.' Laurence looks in admiration at his own handiwork. 'Never done this sort of thing before.' He wipes the sweat from his brow. It's fair to say that my husband would never win an award for his handyman skills. I can't think when he last troubled himself with power tools or any form of manual labour. 'Damn fine fun.'

Skull raises his eyebrows at that but says nothing.

'Mr Skull . . . Skull . . . had some paving slabs going begging and I thought "why not?". We've been very busy since you left.'

'I can see.'

'Do you like it?'

I look down the garden. The lawnmower is standing there and my husband has mown a wide meandering strip down the middle of the garden so that we can walk to the end unencumbered by foliage. He's also mown a strip to lead to the door of the children's car.

The two mushroomed mattresses are stacked beside the garage next to the cooker, and there's a veritable pile of rusty old metal on top and a tyre that has clearly been pulled out of the grass.

'It looks a million per cent better,' I say. And it does. In a hideously unkempt way. Not that we're ever going to be able to show our garden at Chelsea, but it's a start.

'Last slab,' Skull says with a grunt. He browbeats it into place.

Both he and my husband stand back and regard their work. A tidy rectangle of grey concrete paving now borders the rear of the house.

'I'll come round tomorrow and point it,' Skull says.

'This is my first patio,' Laurence says excitedly. 'It deserves a toast. A beer or something.'

'We haven't got anything,' I remind him. 'I could walk back to the shop for some.' I can hardly begrudge them a beer or two after the work they've put in to smarten this up.

'I've got a six-pack in the fridge,' Skull says. 'I'll get it.' He stabs a tattooed finger at the just-laid slabs. 'Don't stand on those.'

'No, no,' Laurence says. 'Absolutely not.'

131

Skull disappears into the house and, a moment later, we hear the front door reverberate on its hinges.

'Impressed?'

'I don't know what to say.' The bleakness of it all still breaks my heart, but for Laurence's sake, I plaster on a smile.

'Perhaps we could put some wild flowers in the grass. That would be very fetching in the spring.'

I fold my arms and hug myself. 'Looks like you're planning to be here a while.'

'No,' he says. 'Not at all.' Laurence pulls me to him and I sink into his embrace. 'We'll be out of here just as soon as we can. But while we are stuck with this, we might as well make the best of it.'

'I sold my ring,' I say sadly. 'But I think I got a good price for it. The jeweller gave me seven hundred pounds.'

The relief on my husband's face is palpable. 'That will certainly help us out.'

'I bought flea spray.'

We both laugh.

'That's a very good start,' Laurence concurs.

'Where are the children?'

'Next door,' Laurence says. 'They went off to play with . . .'

'Charlize and Keanu,' I supply.

'Good God,' Laurence says with a sigh. Then, 'I said it was all right.'

'It's fine.' More than that. I'm hoping that this means that Tracey's forgiven me for my awful faux pas earlier today. 'I'll go and check on them.' I kiss my husband, patio-layer extraordinaire, on the cheek.

Then I pick up the bouquet of flowers from the kitchen and brace myself to make my apology.

Chapter 35

On the short journey to my neighbour's door, I hatch a plan. I could use half of the money I've just received from Seymour Chapman to buy back my jewellery from Freddie the Fixer. I'm sure if I then re-sold it to Seymour – if he'd have it – then I'd get a much more decent price and the Lamont-Jones Benevolent Fund would be better off. Goodness only knows, my poor jewellery must be dizzy with all this to-ing and fro-ing. I know that I am.

Heart in mouth, I knock tentatively at Tracey's door. A moment later she answers it. When my neighbour sees it's me her lips tighten. I hold out my flowers. 'I brought these. To say that I'm very sorry.'

Immediately, her face softens and she opens the door wider. It seems as if my neighbour can't stay cross for long.

'I can't take the flowers as I'm having my nails done.' She holds up a set of formidable fake talons. 'Come in.'

'I won't stay if you're busy.' I start to back away. 'I'll come back another time.' It was never socially acceptable in my former life to call on someone unannounced. I don't know why I thought to do it now.

'Come in, you silly cow,' Tracey insists. 'We don't stand on ceremony here. Besides, we've just cracked open a bottle.'

So I follow her into the kitchen and see that her table has been turned into a temporary beauty salon. A very pretty young black girl in extraordinarily tight leather trousers and a one-shoulder cropped top is sitting waiting with a bottle of nail varnish in her hands. She's also wearing very large sunglasses – indoors.

'This is Jamelia,' Tracey says by way of introduction.

'Yo,' she says to me.

'Hello.' I give a self-conscious wave.

'This is the best nail lady around,' my neighbour assures me. 'This is my good friend and neighbour, Lily Jones.' Tracey and I exchange a glance and I see that I'm already forgiven. 'Lily's lovely, even though she talks like the Queen.'

I give her a self-deprecating look.

'Jamelia does great spray tans too,' Tracey continues. 'Brings all the stuff with her. You're looking a bit pasty.'

After our holiday in Tuscany – the benefits of which have long since been obliterated – this is tanned for me. But it's fair to say that I'm not the deep shade of orange that Tracey is.

'Pop the flowers in the sink,' my neighbour says. 'I'll sort them later.'

'I could do it for you, if you have a vase handy.'

'Have a rummage in those bottom cupboards. I've only got one and it'll be near the back. It's a long time since anyone bought me flowers. But before you do that, get a glass of this down your neck. Looks like you could do with one.' She points to a bottle of white wine on the table. 'There's a glass on the drainer.'

I get the wine glass and do as instructed. The wine is very cold and sharp. But, you know, it hits the right spot and I give an involuntary sigh of appreciation.

'Good girl,' Tracey says. 'Have some more.'

And I think, sod it, and take another swig before topping up my glass again.

'Do you want more, Jamelia?'

The beautician holds up a hand. 'I'm good, man.'

Tracey turns her attention back to Jamelia's ministrations.

In the garden, I can see my children bouncing up and down like mad things on the giant trampoline with Tracey's two. I wave to them and they ignore me completely. Clearly all is well in their world.

So, I find the appointed vase and give it a rinse to wash off the dust. It certainly looks like it has been a long time since it's been used. I think of my own selection of vases that I had at the barn – one suitable for every possible occasion. On the drainer are a pair of kitchen scissors. Filling the vase with water, I take it over to the table with the scissors and the shop-bought bouquet and set out my stall next to Jamelia.

While the beautician paints Tracey's nails an alarming shade of bright blue, I start to turn this borderline wilted bunch of mixed blessings into a creation that would be worthy of the WI.

'I've got the word out on your jewellery,' Tracey says. 'Someone somewhere will know about it.'

'Thank you. I really appreciate it.' I snip the dry bottom off the stems. Despite being in a bucket, I don't think these have seen water for days. Poor things will be just grateful for a drink. A bit like me, really. I take another gulp at my wine and the chilled, acidic liquid works its magic once again.

'Sorry about this morning,' Tracey says. 'You just caught me at a bad time.'

'No, no,' I counter. 'It was entirely my fault.'

Tracey waves a painted finger at me, dismissively. 'Let's not mention it again.' Then, 'You should see the jewellery Lily has,' Tracey tells Jamelia, who is now sticking transfers of tiny butterflies over the blue nail varnish. 'Phew. I bet Paris Hilton hasn't got as much. It was to die for.'

'No jazzin'?' is Jamelia's conclusion.

'I do need to speak to Freddie again.' I start my arrangement, using the meagre wisps of foliage to create a frame. 'The burglar had dropped one of my rings in the garden and, goodness knows how, but I found it. I managed to sell it today for quite a good price. It means that I can buy that diamond pendant back from Freddie.'

'Fabulous,' Tracey says. 'I'll give him a call.' With the hand that's finished, she calls him on her mobile. 'Freddie. It's Tracey. Get back to me.'

She clicks off and shrugs. 'Not like him. Our Freddie doesn't like to miss a call.'

135

I make my best stab with the pale pink carnations and white chrysanthemums, snipping away any drooping petals. When I'm done, I'm pleased to say that it looks quite pretty.

'That looks fab,' my neighbour says. 'You should do this professionally.'

'I just tinker with it,' I say modestly. Even though I was, at one time, a leading light on the church flower committee. Not perhaps a marvellous achievement for a woman with a degree in History, but it makes me happy nevertheless.

'Fancy having your nails done to say thank you?'

'I can't possibly,' I say.

'I'm paying,' Tracey tells me.

'No, no. It's very nice of you, but—'

'Got time, Jamelia?'

'No worries,' Jamelia says.

I look at my short, neat nails. I'm the sort of person who paints one coat of pale pink polish on them on high days and holidays. 'No, really, I—'

'No arguments,' Tracey says and ushers me into her seat.

While Tracey tops my glass up again, I submit my nails to Jamelia's tender touch.

Within minutes my own dear, uninteresting nails have been transformed into inch-long acrylic wonders.

'You might not have any money,' Tracey says, 'but it doesn't mean that your nails have to suffer.'

I feel that my nails are suffering now. Jamelia brandishes a plum-coloured polish. 'Bare cool,' she tells me.

'Bare?'

'Very.' Tracey supplies the translation. At least I know what 'cool' means though, clearly, I'm not it.

'Right.' Plum it is. I know that Hettie will adore it.

An hour later, I'm half cut, I have fingernails so long that I'm struggling to pick anything up and Jamelia is now my new best friend. She's packing up her stuff ready to go. 'Have this one on me, Lily,' she says. 'To welcome you to the 'hood.'

'That's very kind of you.'

Tracey calls Freddie again. 'Still no reply,' she tuts. 'Have you got the money now?'

'Yes.'

'Then let's go straight round there.'

So, staggering somewhat, we all head to the door. Much kissing ensues as Jamelia prepares to leave in her exceedingly pink RAV4.

I throw my arms round her. 'I love you,' I slur. 'I love my new nails.'

'Coolio,' she says as she sets off. Tracey and I wave like loons.

Then, completely forgetting that our four children are entirely unattended in the back garden, we weave off down the street to find out where on earth Freddie the Fixer might be.

Chapter 36

Wobbly of foot, we wander through the tangle of streets of Netherslade Bridge. Streets that all look identical to our own. We pick our way through abandoned bikes, sofas, cars, Tracey's arm through mine for support.

We see the dog man in the distance and Tracey waves to him. He raises a hand in return and carries on his way, dogs scampering behind.

'That's Len,' my tipsy neighbour tells me. 'Len Eleven Dogs. Though I think there are more than that now. All he's got is those dogs. His son was stabbed a few years ago on the estate while he was trying to break up a fight. His daughter turned to drugs and she overdosed on heroin a year later. Then his wife topped herself.'

'God, that's tragic.'

My heart goes out to him and his sad little procession. All we've lost is our possessions and that's bad enough. How does anyone cope with loss like that? We might not have the flash cars in the drive or, indeed, any money in the bank, but we all have our health and, relatively speaking, our happiness.

'He takes in any dog that's abandoned around here,' Tracey continues. 'And we all kind of look out for him. I'll take him a casserole or something once a week. So do a couple of the other neighbours. He doesn't stint on food for the dogs, but he's not that good at looking after himself.'

I'd suspected as much. 'That's very kind of you.'

She shrugs. 'You have to do it, don't you? Everyone looks out for each other.'

I think of the world that I've come from and I don't think that everyone looks out for each other at all. I think they very much look after themselves and, I'm ashamed to say it now, but I would have counted myself among them. I would have looked at people like Tracey and Jamelia and Len Eleven Dogs and thought myself better than them because I had money and they didn't. It just goes to show that one can be very wrong.

Halfway along the street – I have no idea where I am now – there's a house with the world's largest satellite dish attached to the front. In the drive is a shiny BMW which I take to be Freddie the Fixer's.

Still propped up against each other for support, we totter in tandem up to Freddie's door and Tracey presses the doorbell. A few tinny notes of 'God Save the Queen' trill out and a moment later the great man himself opens the door.

The sunglasses are still in evidence. But today's attire consists of skin-tight jeans and a white shirt with multiple gold chains. He gives a quick check down either side of the street and, for some reason, we do the same.

'I've been phoning you,' Tracey says. 'Why aren't you picking up?'

'Busy, love,' Freddie says. 'What can I do you for?'

Much laughing at his own joke. Just Freddie.

'My friend, Lily, has come to buy her jewellery back,' she tells him.

'This is not a good time,' Freddie says shiftily.

'It's good for us,' Tracey says, and pushes her way past him, yanking me in behind her.

'You'd better come in,' Freddie says, and he follows us into his house.

The outside of the house may be unprepossessing, but inside it's clear that Freddie likes his luxuries. We pass the kitchen, which features glossy black units and more spotlights than the stage at the Sydney Opera House. The living room is dominated by a television that is big enough to be seen from space, which could go to explain why the satellite dish is so enormous. It's even bigger than Tracey's, if that's possible. There's a plush black leather suite and a glass-topped coffee table supported by elaborate gilt fish. There seems to be a surplus of remote control devices.

'I have the money here,' I tell him.

'I think you owe us some discount,' Tracey says. 'That sofa you got her was full of fleas. Look at this.' She pulls up the sleeve of my blouse to reveal my reddened nibbles.

It's hard to read Freddie's eyes behind the sunglasses. But that, I guess, is the point.

'Sorry, darlin',' he says. 'I got that furniture in good faith.'

'Fifty quid should do it,' my neighbour says.

Freddie reels at that.

'I just need my jewellery back,' I say. 'That's all I want.' I open my bag and pull out the wad of cash that Seymour Chapman gave me. 'Three hundred and fifty pounds.'

Freddie sucks on his teeth. 'Bit of a problem, darlin'.'

The hairs stand up on the back of my neck.

'Sold it on,' he admits.

'You've what?' Tracey is furious.

'Sold it on. Never thought you'd get the money for it.'

'But you've never let me down like this before, Freddie.'

'Times are tough,' he says by way of explanation.

'This was done on a pledge,' Tracey reminds him.

He shrugs.

'You need to get this back from whoever you sold it to.'

'No can do,' Freddie says.

'I brought my friend to you because I thought I could trust you, Freddie Fulway.' Tracey's face is as black as Freddie's kitchen cupboards with mounting fury. 'We had a deal and you've welched on it. You gave Lily a month to buy it back. Barely a week has gone by and she's here with the cash and you're telling us she can't have her necklace back.'

'That's right.'

'That is a completely shitty thing to do,' Tracey rails on my behalf while I'm too stunned to speak.

'So sue me,' Freddie says.

'Your reputation will be mud round here if you start doing business like this, Freddie.'

I can only think that Freddie perhaps realised the true value of my diamond pendant and decided he could do a lot better with it than keep a promise to sell it back to its owner. After all, what comeback do I have? I can hardly go to the police. It's entirely my own fault for consenting to deal with such a dodgy bloke. In my former life, I would have run a mile from someone like Freddie the Flaming Fixer, but those type of people prey on the desperate – and desperate I was. I have to walk away and chalk this down to yet another character-building experience. He's probably fenced my necklace – if that's the correct term – to someone else and netted himself a few thousand in the process. A few thousand pounds that, by rights, should have been mine.

'Let's go,' I say to Tracey.

Freddie looks like he thinks that's a jolly good idea.

'You haven't heard the last of this, mate,' Tracey warns.

'Afternoon, ladies,' our fraudster replies. 'I'm sure you can see yourselves out.'

And we do.

'I feel like bricking his windows in,' Tracey says as she stomps down his drive.

'Me too.'

'Somehow, I'll get that necklace back for you, Lily,' she says. 'I promise you.'

But I don't think my friend can promise that at all, and in a cold, hard place in my heart, I'm resigned to the fact that I've been taken for a mug.

Then we walk back down the street to Tracey's house with a lot less enthusiasm and a lot more sobriety than we had on our journey here.

Chapter 37

'Dat was a bustin' ting,' Hugo says as we leave Tracey's house later.

'I beg your pardon?'

'Dat was . . .' he begins. My son is holding his fingers up in some sort of Hoodie salute. The sort of thing you see thugs doing on *Panorama* or *Newsnight* as they're hauled into court.

'I know what you said,' I tell him. 'I'm just wondering why you're speaking in a West Indian accent.'

'It's how Charlize and Keanu talk,' Hettie informs me. 'They said we were too posh.'

'There's no such thing as being too posh.' I usher them to the front door and shoulder it in. 'You were both brought up to speak nicely, and speak nicely you will.'

'But this is how people here speak.'

'Not you,' I say. 'This is not how *you* speak.'

'They're going to teach us,' Hugo protests.

'I don't think so.' We may be down on our luck, but it doesn't mean that standards have to slip. Then I remember that I have spent the latter part of the afternoon having my nails painted purple, getting drunk and trying to get my jewellery out of hock.

Hettie slips her hand into mine. It's so small and soft, and it reminds me of how vulnerable our children are and how they need our protection. We will only be in Netherslade Bridge for a short while and, though they're coping well with the upheaval, I must do more to shield them from the harshness of the world.

All the things I had most feared for them, and for myself — poverty, poor education, poor diet, even poor elocution, for heaven's sake — are now what we are living slapbang in the middle of.

'Your nails look blinging, Mummy,' my daughter says, and I have no answer for that as they probably do.

In the back garden, Laurence and the Skull are sprawled out on the mowed strip of grass swigging beer from cans and laughing as if they're old mates. If I had another bottle of wine, I'd open it. All in all, it has been another traumatic day in the Lamont-Jones household. And to think that my lovely, lovely life used to run like clockwork.

'Better be going,' Skull says. He and my husband stand up. 'Catch you both later. I'll be back to point that patio tomorrow.'

Laurence claps him on the back. 'Sterling work.'

Skull returns the affection and nearly sends my husband across the garden with the force of it. 'No worries, Lozzer.'

We follow him into the kitchen then watch him weave through our house and out of the front door.

'Lozzer?' I query in the wake of our departing guest.

'When in Rome,' Laurence suggests. 'He's a fine fellow.' Then he notices my newly-painted nails. 'Good Christ! What's happened to your fingers? You look like one of the living dead.'

I hold out my hands for inspection. 'Jamelia, the nail lady, gave me a complimentary introduction to the joys of false nails,' I tell him. 'How could I refuse?'

'How indeed?' Laurence smiles at them.

'Our daughter says that they're blinging.'

'Is that a good or a bad thing?'

'I'm not sure. They're learning a whole new vocabulary here and it terrifies me.'

'They'll be fine,' my husband reassures me. 'I'm quite enjoying bonding with our new neighbours. There are some interesting characters here.'

'Yes.' I decide not to tell him about being twisted by Freddie the Fixer. Not yet.

143

'I could do with my shirt washing and ironing for tomorrow's interview, Lily. What if I make dinner while you do that?'

This is the first time in his life that my husband has ever offered to cook, and whilst I don't want to look a gift-horse in the mouth, I say, 'There could be a slight problem with that.'

He waits to hear what it is.

'We have food, but no washing powder, no iron, no ironing board. So I couldn't uphold my part of the deal.'

'Right.' Laurence scratches his head.

'There's pasta and tomato sauce for tonight. The best I could rustle up. What I need to do is go and spend some of our newly acquired cash at the supermarket and stock up the cupboards.' Though I wonder how I'll struggle back from the supermarket if I'm loaded down with bags and on the bus. Like a million other people do every day, I suppose. And I think, once again, how cosseted we've been from the harsh realities of life.

'Wait until I know if I've got this job tomorrow before we do that,' Laurence says. 'Let's manage with what they've got in the local shop for now.'

And there's the rub too. If you can't get to the supermarket easily, then you have to pay the prices in the local shop which are much higher and the choice is much more limited.

'I'll ask Tracey if I can borrow her iron.' And a pinch of washing powder. I wonder for the umpteenth time what on earth we would have done without Tracey's help and, at the same time, baulk at how quickly we've come to rely on her selfless generosity.

'We could look at selling those too.' He glances at his beloved bag of golf clubs stacked in the corner of the kitchen.

They, so far, had escaped my commercial attentions.

'Are you still a member at the club?' My husband, of course, belonged to one of the most exclusive golf clubs in the area with fees that would make your eyes water.

Laurence shakes his head. 'I didn't renew the annual subscription when it ran out. I couldn't.'

'So all those Saturday mornings when I thought you were playing golf?'

'I was sitting in the car in a lay-by somewhere wondering how I was going to get out of this mess.'

'Then, yes, we could definitely sell the clubs. If you can.' The chances are that it will be a long time before Laurence is able to play golf again.

'I'll text a few people, see if they're interested. Perhaps Anthony knows someone . . .' Then my husband lets the sentence tail off.

'I don't think it's a good idea to contact Anthony or Amanda any more,' I say quietly.

'No,' Laurence agrees. His voice sounds choked. 'That guy was the closest I had to a best friend.'

'Then we should have been straight with them,' I remind him. 'We owe them a lot of money. I wouldn't blame them if they never forgive us.'

'We will pay them back,' he promises. 'Every last penny. If it takes till my dying day.'

I go and lean against my husband. The numbing effect of the alcohol is wearing off now and, with it, comes a feeling of crashing depression. 'We are going to be all right, aren't we?'

'I do hope so,' Laurence says. He holds me tightly. 'Let's see what tomorrow brings.'

And, once again, I can only pray that it doesn't bring another big pile of poo.

Chapter 38

Laurence caught the bus to Great Brickhill. There was only one and that ran every hour starting at eight-thirty in the morning. It took over an hour to get to the village – a ridiculous amount of time for the distance of the journey. It was perfectly fine for the purposes of this interview, but absolutely no use at all if he used the bus every day, as he'd have a nine o'clock start. He could hardly make a good impression by being tardy every morning. There was only one thing for it. He'd have to get a bike. Years ago he'd ridden one and, if the old adage was right, he'd be able to ride one again now. It would take him about half an hour to cycle here which, at this rate, would be considerably quicker than the bus. The distance was definitely do-able, it was just all the stops that the bus made and its slightly circuitous route that slowed it down. The cost was appalling too and he'd have to take that into consideration now that every penny counted.

He settled back into his seat for the journey. Soon they'd bounced beyond the city limits and out into the countryside. It was one of the reasons that had attracted them to this area; there was the convenience of the city, the proximity to London and the gentle rolling green spaces that surrounded them on all sides. Not that he'd ever had much chance to explore the country-side. What spare time he'd had at the weekends had always been spent on the golf course. Pretty in its own way, but it could hardly be considered getting back to nature. He wondered how Lily had put up with it now. Him away all week and then rarely around at the weekends, indulging himself in his own pastimes. Perhaps she appreciated that he needed time to himself to cope with the stresses he was under. But then, if he was honest with himself, it had been the one bone of contention in their marriage and, effectively, Lily had been left to her own devices while he slipped in and out of family life as he chose.

It was only in the last few days when they'd all been thrown together in this small, neglected house that he realised how little in the last few years he'd really been involved with his wife and children.

The hard lines of the dual carriageways gave way to meandering country lanes and the bus trundled beneath a canopy of trees. Laurence's eyes began to roll. It was quite a pleasant journey. How different from the daily squash into the City – crammed onto the overflowing express train, then pressed up against someone's armpit on the rattling Tube. This was infinitely preferable. The route took them over a small, humped-back bridge across the Grand Union Canal, then wound its way along to the village itself.

Laurence pulled himself together and took the folded job description out of his pocket, feeling somewhat naked without his usual briefcase. He would have to visit the charity shop to look for one of those too. The job was as an assistant manager for a small open-farm complex which had its own organic shop supplying local produce. There was a café too and a children's play area outside. According to the sheet of paper he had in front of him there was also an interactive area for the kids featuring rabbits, lambs and chickens. A petting zoo, by the sound of it. The job was as far outside his area of expertise as it was possible to be.

The bus dropped him at the end of the lane which led to the farm and Laurence felt conspicuous walking down through the pleasant scenery trussed up in his suit and his pinching shoes. Eventually, he swung in through the gate and there was a good smattering of cars and 4x4s parked up already. All high-end. All probably carrying yummy mummies and their spoiled offspring. Envy pinched at him just like his shoes.

Sure enough, a dozen or more small children were busy on the wooden climbing frames and swings in the play area. Right next to that was the big main barn. This looked like where the shop and the café would be housed and Laurence made his way inside.

The barn was big, bright and homely. To one side, there was the organic shop with a small butcher's counter, colourful displays of plump fruit and vegetables, an area selling locally-made cheeses and a large wooden rack of fat, brown loaves. What he wouldn't give now for a slice of thickly buttered bread and some fragrant, crumbling cheese, with a soupçon of Lily's homemade onion marmalade on the side. Laurence's stomach rumbled in response. In his previous working life, he'd either be on his way to an extravagant business lunch or eating a plastic sandwich at his desk.

At the back of the barn, with huge windows overlooking the countryside beyond, there was a scattering of tables and a glass counter containing a range of dishes made from local produce. The café offered a farmhouse breakfast at a good price and was already bustling. Opposite the shop was a small customer information desk and Laurence headed straight to it, checking his sheet as he did so. 'I have an interview,' he said. 'With Christopher Cherry.'

'I'll let him know that you're here,' the woman behind the desk said.

Suddenly, Laurence was suffused with nerves. He, a man who'd handled millions of pounds' worth of investments – badly, as it turned out – was as nervous of this interview as if he was fresh out of school, a green youngster and not someone with a wealth of business experience under his belt. Perhaps it was because this was the first interview that he'd managed to secure – and that was something he never thought would trouble him – that made it so important for him to do well. He felt as if he'd been out of the world of commerce for years rather than months, and was only just beginning to understand what a serious blow to his confidence this whole damn mess had been.

Before he could dwell on it further, a stocky man came

striding out of the office behind the customer services desk. His face was ruddy from years of outdoor life. He was about ten years older than Laurence and wore the uniform of a country gentleman of leisure – checked shirt, corduroy trousers and a big, broad smile. It could only be Mr Cherry.

The man clasped Laurence's hand. 'Welcome to Cherry's.'

His enthusiastic handshake nearly crushed Laurence's fingers. 'Laurence Lamont-Jones.'

'Aye. I know that. Let's show you round, lad, and then we can see what you're made of. I can't for the life of me think what you're doing here.'

To be honest, Laurence was thinking pretty much the same thing.

Chapter 39

I have an appointment with the Head Teacher of the local school, so I smarten myself up and walk down there. Soon, I'm going to have to confront the fact that holiday-style clothing will not be appropriate. Already the tips of the leaves are turning brown and before we know it, autumn will be upon us. I'm going to have to find the money from somewhere to buy us all a winter wardrobe.

Fortunately, all this school requires in the way of uniform is a sweatshirt – so different from Stonelands, which had a list of 'essential equipment' as long as my arm. I wonder where it is now and think how it's going to waste. We also had to buy from one specialist supplier at the children's former school but now, Tracey tells me, I can just pop along to Tesco or Asda and get what I need from there. I'm just hoping against hope that Laurence gets this job today. I have everything crossed for him. This morning, I think I was even more nervous than he was.

Now, I stand outside the school and sigh deeply. It looks as if everything will be different from Stonelands, not just the uniform.

Netherslade Bridge School isn't set in acres of privately-owned rolling countryside. It doesn't look as though the National Trust maintain their gardens for them as they do at Stonelands. I take in the scrubby, muddy playing-fields and anonymous concrete monstrosity which can't quite match the palatial Grade I Listed house that was built in the eighteenth century in the Palladian style. Netherslade Bridge School seems to have been thrown up in the 1970s with more of an eye on budget than any aesthetic consideration. My heart goes out to my children. Not only have they lost their ponies, but there'll be no more lacrosse, no heated pool, no school cinema, no luxury of any kind. Hugo was in the under elevens rugby team and they were due to be coached by England players next term in preparation for a mini-tour of South Africa. Hettie was a leading light in the Theatre Club and her chess was shaping up very well. She had a best-selling children's novelist come in once a week to tutor their creative writing.

I wonder what extra-curricular activities will be on offer here for my babies. Already, I know that the class sizes here are up to forty pupils, whereas Stonelands never had more than ten. The adage that you get what you pay for has never seemed truer and I can only hope that Hettie and Hugo, who were doing so, so well at their previous school, will cope with the transition.

Then, my heart goes out to all the other children who are educated here. Doesn't every pupil deserve to have a school environment that's comfortable and clean and is conducive to study? Being cooped up in a building like this all day can't be good for the soul. We should all expect better for our children, not just those who can pay for it.

I have my tour with the Head Teacher, Mr Clarke, and I can't, unfortunately, say that the inside of the school is any better than the outside. To be fair, Mr Clarke seems to be doing his best in difficult circumstances and clearly has his heart in the right place. He's only been here a year and maybe he will be able to turn this place around. Perhaps Laurence and I should apply to join the Board of Governors when the children are settled in. One thing that I'm still undeniably good at is fund-raising, and Netherslade Bridge School certainly looks like it could do with a bit of extra cash.

When we've agreed that the children can be admitted to the school at the start of the new term next week, I walk home and call into Tracey's house on the way to collect Hugo and Hettie.

My new – and only – friend makes me a welcome cup of tea and we sit on a plastic bench outside her back door and watch our four children bounce their insides up and down. And, despite teaching them some colourful vocabulary, Charlize and Keanu seem to be looking after my two quite nicely.

'I'd offer to pass on some hand-me-downs of school uniform, but my kids shred it,' Tracey offers. 'God only knows what they do to it. The knees in Keanu's trousers last a week at the most.'

'Thanks for the thought. I'm hoping that Laurence gets this job today and then we won't be quite so strapped for cash.' In fact I'm pinning all my hopes on it. I glance at my watch and think that he might be coming home soon.

'Cheer up,' she says. 'It's not a bad school.'

Once again, I'm not sure that Tracey really appreciates what I'm comparing it to.

'They have a Dance Club afterwards for the girls and the boys can do boxing.'

I can't stand the thought of anyone hitting Hugo though, strangely, I was quite happy to see him bashed about on the rugby pitch.

'Aren't you glad to have them home?' she says. 'They were telling me that they used to go away to school and they hated it.'

That pulls me up short. Did they hate it? They never said. 'They loved it,' I protest.

Tracey shrugs. It's clear that she finds that difficult to believe. 'Didn't they miss their mum? Mine would be lost without me.'

Were mine lost without me? I always thought they did so well. Now I wonder whether it's just because they had to. Sometimes Hettie used to cry when we took her back, but doesn't every child go through that?

'I could never do that to Charlize and Keanu,' she adds, racking up my guilt quotient.

Until this moment, I'd never truly considered what an odd thing it is to do, to send your children off in their tender years when they need you most to be brought up by total strangers. In my heart, whenever I'd had doubts or had wanted to keep them at home, I comforted myself with the thought that everyone else did this, all of our friends boarded their children. I tried to make myself believe that we were doing the best for them and that I should put my own feelings aside for their long-term benefit. I'd always felt quite ashamed when I had the urge to pull them out of Stonelands and have them at a school close by. Now part of me is secretly pleased that they'll only be round the corner from me every day, that they'll both be in their own beds every night where they should be. They might not get top class tuition in the arts or sports as they did at Stonelands, but aren't they actually better off at home, wherever that may be, with us – with their mum and dad?

I start to laugh as if a cloud has lifted from over my head.

'What?' Tracey says.

'I'm just laughing at how funny life is,' I tell her.

'Yeah, hilarious. All these lines are because I've spent my life laughing my head off.'

Then Hettie comes over. My daughter is breathless, flushed and looks like a ragamuffin. Her grin is from ear to ear. 'This trampoline is slammin'!'

I'm taking it that's a good thing. 'Lovely, darling.'

'Come on it, Mummy. It's fun.'

'No, no.' I smooth my skirt down. 'Mummy can't do that.'

'It is fun,' Tracey says with a nod towards the monstrous contraption. 'Just kick your shoes off.'

'I don't think so.' I have never been on a trampoline in my life and have no desire to start now.

'Go on!' My friend takes my cup of tea from my hand. 'Let your hair down. You might enjoy it.'

It looks like I'm going to have no choice. So I kick off my shoes and walk across to the trampoline and, with as much dignity as I can muster and just the very slightest of 'ouffs', haul myself on.

The others get off so that I'm left with just my daughter. Hettie holds my hands. 'Take little bounces at first,' she instructs with her serious face on. 'Like this.'

Hettie shows me what bouncing entails. I take a tentative bounce, my feet showing a reluctance to leave the surface.

I've always hated making a show of myself. I'm more of a sit-in-the-background-and-applaud-politely kind of woman. An exhibitionist, I'm most definitely not.

'A bit harder,' my child urges.

I do as she says. I try to relax my rigid knees and go with the motion. When I do, I start to bounce. My hair flies out around me. Actually, it feels quite nice. Liberating.

'Mummy's bouncing,' Hettie shouts with glee.

I laugh with my daughter.

Then I see Tracey kick off her shoes and she climbs on the trampoline to join us and takes my hand.

With my friend bouncing too, I start to go higher. My skirt starts to flare up, showing my legs and my underwear. I struggle to hold it down.

'Tuck it in your pants,' Tracey says.

'What?'

'Come here.' My friend grabs hold of the hem of my skirt and jams it into the sides of my knicker legs. 'That'll hold it.'

Then, before I can protest, she grabs my hand again and we're off bouncing once more.

'Higher!' Hettie shouts. 'Higher!'

And, for once, I let my natural caution go with the wind. Forgetting my troubles for a moment, I just enjoy the sensation of being with my darling daughter and my good friend as we're all catapulted into the air, laughter ringing in my ears, breeze in my hair.

Chapter 40

Laurence fell into step next to Christopher Cherry as the latter took him through the various operations of the business. 'I used to run the whole farm,' Mr Cherry told him. 'Five hundred acres. We had a pick-your-own business even then – strawberries, mainly. But it was hard work. I never stopped. Seven years ago, I decided I'd worked hard enough. So I sold off some of the farm, rented out the majority of the other fields and set up this lot.' He swept an arm round the barn. 'Much more manageable. Ticks over nicely, even in these difficult times.'

'The produce looks fabulous.'

'We grow some of our own veg, but we buy most of it in from other local farms,' Mr Cherry said. 'The recruitment agency told me that you know a lot about organic food.'

'No,' Laurence admitted with a self-deprecating laugh. 'Nothing other than eating it, and my wife is the one who is the stickler for that.'

Christopher Cherry took that in with a good-humoured laugh. 'Then she'll be pleased to know that we have a good stable of suppliers – pork, beef, good local lamb. Some excellent small cheesemakers. Most have been with us from the start. I believe in treating people fair,' he said. 'They do the same back. Mostly. If they don't, they're out.'

Laurence tried to imagine himself working here and struggled with the image. Would he be comfortable in this genteel environment after being used to the cut and thrust of the City? 'What would my role be?'

'I've just acquired two new grandkiddies,' Mr Cherry confided. 'Can't believe my own kids are old enough.' He gave Laurence a bewildered smile. 'You'd be taking the weight off me. I want to spend more time with them. When my own were growing up, I was always out in the fields, working all hours. I never saw them. The farm was more important to me than family life. I reckon I've got the balance right now – or near enough.'

Laurence could empathise with that. 'Can't say that I've managed that myself.'

'It didn't happen overnight,' Christopher Cherry admitted. 'Right – come and see what we've got out here.' Leading the way out through the glass doors, he picked up a bag of feed from the desk.

Together they walked past the terrace where there were a few more tables and chairs – all full, Laurence was pleased to note – and out towards the small 'interactive' area as it had stated on the job description.

A range of soundly constructed pens housed a selection of cute and appealing animals. There were a few dozen fine-looking chickens and a handful of tiny lambs and what Laurence assumed were their mothers. Beyond that was an enclosure with a clutch of adorable pygmy goats. He would have to bring Hettie here – his daughter would be in her element.

The two men stood and leaned on the fence, the sun beating down on Laurence's neck. In the City, he was sometimes hard-pressed to step out of the office for five minutes' fresh air. It could be 70 degrees outside and he'd never have known, as all he experienced was the artificial chill of the air-conditioned office from one end of the day to the next.

'I feel a little overdressed,' Laurence said with a laugh, indicating his suit jacket.

'Take it off, lad. Get rid of that bloody tie too. Be comfortable. It's a glorious day,' Mr Cherry said. 'If you come here, you can leave your suit behind. Cherry's is not a suit sort of place.'

Laurence slipped off his jacket and put it over the top of the fence, being careful to avoid the inquisitive nuzzlings of the goats.

You didn't want to go to a job interview where the livestock took a shine to one's clothing. He bent down and offered the goats a handful of feed instead; they gobbled it up greedily. As a job interview it was also bordering on the surreal. He'd always prided himself on being able to charm the birds out of the trees when it came to business matters. He'd always thought that he'd be able to talk himself into any job that he fancied. Now the glib words, the easy chat, seemed to fail him.

Christopher Cherry leaned on the fence next to him. 'What would you bring to the table, lad?'

Six months ago he would have been bragging that he could run this place with his eyes closed, that it was beneath him even. Now he was so desperate for a job, any job, that he didn't want to bullshit any more.

'My experience is all in the City,' Laurence explained. Honesty, he decided, was the best policy. Christopher Cherry didn't look like the type of man who wanted to employ some flash, City wide-boy. 'I'm used to dealing with multi-million-pound companies, handling multi-million-pound contracts, and I had it all kicked out from under me.' He took a deep breath. 'I lost my job three months ago. I've lost everything. The bailiffs have taken my house and I'm living in a rented place in Netherslade Bridge.'

'I saw the address on your CV and wondered why a posh lad like you was living there.'

'I am at the very bottom of the pile and starting out again.' Laurence's voice threatened to jam in his throat. He couldn't meet Mr Cherry's eyes and, instead, focused on the goats. 'If you take me on I'd be eternally grateful and I'd work damn hard for your business.'

'But would you stay?' Christopher Cherry asked. 'If it all turns round and the economy picks up? What would you do if something more in your line of work came up? What if someone offered you the mega-bucks again? Would you drop old Cherry's Farm like a hot brick?'

It was a fair question and demanded a fair answer.

'I'd have to do what was best for my family,' Laurence answered.

157

Mr Cherry nodded. 'Them goats are greedy little blighters,' he said with a laugh. 'They've eaten all you brung.'

Laurence looked down to see that his hand was empty, outstretched, but the goats still nuzzled hungrily.

'I've got other people to see,' Christopher Cherry said. 'Eighty people have applied. *Eighty.*' Mr Cherry shook his head. 'Jobs are hard to come by.'

'No one appreciates that more than me,' Laurence said.

Both men then walked back towards the barn, Laurence with his jacket slung over his shoulder. 'Like what you see?' asked Christopher Cherry.

'Yes, I do.' Strangely, he did. This wasn't what he'd imagined himself doing at all. But even after this short time, he could see himself working here at Cherry's. The owner was a good, solid man whom he could respect, and there was a quietness and a calm here that had been sadly missing in his life.

Mr Cherry shook his hand. 'I'll be in touch then, lad.'

Laurence found himself hoping, very much, that Christopher Cherry would.

Chapter 41

As a family we're all sitting round our new dining-room table for the first time. Dinner consists of tinned tuna – rather too redolent of cat food for my liking – along with jacket potatoes and a cos lettuce salad which came from Skull's allotment. He very kindly dropped the veg off when he came to point up the patio. I wouldn't have had Skull down as a grower of his own organic fruit and vegetables, but it goes to show that one should never judge a book by its cover. Also, Mr Cherry sent Laurence home from his interview with some tiny plum tomatoes still on the vine and I've livened up the potatoes with a dab of real butter.

'So you think it went well at Cherry's?' I say to my husband.

He shrugs. 'It's hard to tell. My judgement is so skewed at the moment that I'm thinking of a million things that I should have said that I didn't. But I tried to be straight with him. He's that kind of man. Wouldn't take any . . . *bullshit*.' My husband mouths the last word.

'I know what you said, Daddy,' Hettie observes.

'I'm sorry, darling,' Laurence says to our sharp-eared child.

'We'll just have to keep our fingers crossed.'

'And everything else,' he agrees.

'I know a rude joke,' my daughter announces, and before we can censor her she launches into, 'Why did Tigger put his head down the toilet?'

'I don't know,' her father obliges. 'Why did Tigger put his head down the toilet?'

'Because he was looking for Pooh.' Hugo and Hettie fall about with laughter.

'Hettie,' I say, 'that's not very ladylike.'

'But it's very funny,' she insists. 'Charlize told me,' she adds, not hesitating to put her new friend in the firing line.

Laurence rolls his eyes and says under his breath, 'What are we going to do with her when she's fifteen?'

'I have no idea,' is my honest answer.

We finish dinner, such as it is, and I ask the children to clear the table. As I'm starting to wash the dishes, I hear the front door open and Tracey's familiar 'Coo-ee!' comes down the hall.

A second later, she bursts into the kitchen. My friend is flushed in the face and looks furious. I peel off my rubber gloves. I might be consigned to handwashing rather than a dishwasher but I'm not going to ruin my 'blingin' nails to boot.

'Is everything all right?' I ask her.

'You need to come with me.' Tracey clutches at my damp hand. 'Now.'

'Right now?'

She tugs me towards the door. 'This minute.'

'Laurence,' I shout. 'I'm popping out for a moment. Can you keep your eye on the children, please? They've gone out in the garden to play in their car.'

'Yes,' I hear my husband mumble.

So, without further ado, I allow myself to be led by Tracey – at speed – out of the door. 'What's the matter?'

'You won't believe this,' she says crisply as we cross the well-trodden grass to her door.

I note that Jamelia's pink RAV is parked outside my neighbour's house and wonder if it's anything to do with her.

Inside and the exquisitely-painted beautician is sitting at the kitchen table. She's tapping her nails against the top in an agitated drumming rhythm.

'Show her,' Tracey instructs.

Jamelia holds out her long, slender fingers. Her nails today are orange with pink tips. They have diamanté stones encrusted in them. She waggles one finger, inviting closer inspection.

My hands fly to my mouth. 'Oh my goodness me!'

Tracey folds her arms. 'Thought so.'

On Jamelia's uniquely manicured digit, my beautiful engagement ring is sitting.

My knees will hardly support me and I hold onto the table to steady myself. 'Where did you get this?'

'Freddie the Fixer is sellin' it down The Nut, man.'

'The local pub,' Tracey translates. 'It's called the Acorn and Squirrel.'

Jamelia admires her purchase. 'I paid fifty notes for this.'

My ten-thousand-pound diamond ring has been flogged off for fifty pounds. I gasp in horror.

'I knew it was no ordinary knock-off bling,' Jamelia continues. 'Then I remembered that Tracey said you'd been robbed. That's when the alarm bells they started ringin'.'

'We'd better get down there.' Tracey's face is like thunder.

'Plenty of other dudes were buyin',' Jamelia tells us. 'If you're gonna have a chance, you'd better get your skinny white asses movin', sisters.'

'Come on.' My neighbour grabs my hand again. 'We'll have to hurry if we're going to stop him.'

We rush to the door.

'You coming too, Jamelia?'

'You think I'm gonna miss this?' She totters behind us as fast as her heels will carry her. 'We'll take my car. It will be quicker.'

So we all jump into Jamelia's pink RAV and race to The Nut to see if we can stop Freddie the Fixer in his tracks.

Chapter 42

Jamelia slews the car into the car park in the style of that Stig person on *Top Gear* that Laurence and Hugo are so keen on. Then she parks it across three spaces in the style of an old-age pensioner. Simultaneously, we jump out and race into The Nut.

Sure enough, Freddie the Fixer is there, as large as life. The one good thing about his distinctive style of clothing – tonight he's wearing a white *Saturday Night Fever* suit – is that you can spot him a mile away. He's bent over a table in the corner and, even from here, it's clear to see that he's offering the punters some hookey wares. Oh, my goodness. I didn't even know I had this kind of terminology in my vocabulary.

Tracey, flanked by my good self and Jamelia, marches up to him, grabs hold of his shoulder and spins him round. 'Can I have a word, Fred?'

'I'm busy, love,' he says, brushing her off.

'Not now you're not,' she informs him. Then she pushes her face close to his. 'We can do this nicely,' she says under her breath, 'or I can call the Old Bill and see what they have to say about your new jewellery business.'

'Dunno what you're talking about,' Freddie says, grinning with an attempt at false bravado. It doesn't quite hide the panic in his eyes.

'I think you do.' Tracey grips Jamelia's finger and yanks it forward. She brandishes the ring for Freddie to see. 'That's so bloody hot, it's still smoking.'

Now the smile has been well and truly wiped off his face.

'That jewellery belongs to Lily,' she says. 'As well you know.'

'It's similar,' Freddie tries.

'I have photographs of all of it,' I pipe up. Even though I haven't. 'And it's all ID marked.' Even though it isn't. 'For insurance purposes.'

Beneath his sunglasses, I think I see our jewellery dealer blanch.

'Don't come with the five-finger discount so close to your own turf, Freddie,' Tracey says. 'Now I want you to go round the whole pub, get the jewellery back from whoever you sold it to and return the money to the nice people. Then you can give Lily all her goods back too.' She darts a black look at Freddie. 'And I mean *all* of them.'

When he hesitates, Tracey pulls her mobile phone out and lets her fingers wander over the keypad. 'I'll count to three.'

Our little jewellery thief sighs. 'All right. Keep your hair on, girl,' he says. 'Give me ten minutes.'

'You can buy us a drink while we wait,' she says.

'Don't push it, love,' Freddie warns and he slouches off, scowling, to the table he's just come from.

'We'll have three dry white wines,' Tracey tells the barman. 'Put them on Freddie's account.'

The barman does as he's told without speaking. He pushes the glasses towards us and we all go to sit at the nearest table and down them. I notice that Tracey's hands are shaking. My knees are too. Only Jamelia looks as cool as she normally does.

We keep our eye on Freddie as he moves round the pub from table to table, doing deals, doling out cash to complaining customers.

'I don't want that bastard making a bolt for it,' Tracey mutters.

A good fifteen minutes later, Freddie reluctantly makes his way back to us. He tosses my things onto the table with a clatter, as if they are cheap baubles. 'All there?'

I do a quick check, trying to remember everything that I had. The diamond pendant is there. My bracelets. My precious sapphire ring to mark Hugo's birth is there. Laurence's watch. 'Yes,' I say breathlessly. 'It's all there.'

163

'And you owe Jamelia fifty quid for the sparkler,' Tracey reminds him.

Freddie fishes the great roll of money out of his pocket, peels off five ten-pound notes and throws them in the general direction of Jamelia.

'Have you done?' he demands.

'Yeah,' Tracey says. 'Have you?'

'Don't come running to me, lady, next time you're up shit creek and want something hocked,' Freddie warns. He thrusts a threatening finger at her. 'Your card is marked.'

'So is yours,' Tracey counters. 'Do that again and I'll make sure everyone and his brother knows. This gets out and you're finished round here. Who'll deal with you when you've got that kind of reputation. We look after our own. You know that.'

'*She's* not one of us,' he says, casting an accusatory glance at me. 'Never will be.'

'She is.' My friend is on the defensive. 'She's down on her luck. Helping yourself to her gear when she's trusted you? That's no way to welcome someone to our neighbourhood.'

Freddie shrugs. 'Take my number off speed-dial. That's all I'm saying.'

'It's done.'

Business concluded, Freddie stomps out, slamming the door behind him. There's a scandalised rash of muttering in his wake.

'Thank you,' I say, close to tears. The relief that washes through me as I scoop my jewellery into my palms and secrete it deep in my skirt pocket leaves me feeling as weak as a kitten. 'Thank you so much. Thank you both so much.' I hug them both to me.

Tracey knocks back her wine. 'That's what friends are for.'

'Shame about the ring,' Jamelia says, admiring her newly acquired rock again. 'It looks well fine.'

With a rueful smile, she slips it from her finger and hands it over.

'I owe you a big drink,' I say. I'm touched at Jamelia's honesty and the way she's helped me to get this precious haul back. 'A *very* big drink.' I wonder if they will have champagne here?

'Right on, girl. I'm gonna have to leave my wheels in the car park,' Jamelia says. 'I'm gonna get wasted.'

'I'll get them in.' I stand up and then something hits me. 'Oh. I haven't got any money.'

We all burst out laughing.

'Nice one, Lily. Ten grands' worth of bling in your pocket and not a penny on you. Maybe I could give you a loan, darlin'.'

Ten grand, I think. What we couldn't do with that amount of money. Wait until I tell Laurence. And wait until I can get back to Seymour Chapman and sell it all again.

Chapter 43

Later – much, much later – we walk Jamelia home. By this time we've all had more than enough to drink, and in the deep dark recesses of my brain I somehow recall that three hours ago I told my husband that I was just popping out for a moment.

The three of us are strung out across the pavement, arms linked. I think we might be singing. If it's not us then someone else very close by is doing a terrible rendition of 'Dancing Queen'.

Once Jamelia is safely delivered into the arms of her boyfriend, Tracey and I turn on our heels and weave our way back home. I see my friend safely into her place and then stagger back to my own house.

Unlocking the door, I shoulder it to gain entry and then manage to lose my balance and fall in an undignified heap in the hall. I know that I shouldn't find it funny, but I do. In fact, I think it's hilarious and lie on the floor, looking up at the ceiling, chuckling to myself.

Next thing, I see Laurence looking down at me. His face is all blurry and I don't think that he's finding the fact that I'm lying on the floor as funny as I do. Hugo and Hettie's worried and equally blurry faces appear next to his. That makes me laugh even more.

'You're drunk,' my husband accuses.

'Yeth,' I slur. I can't remember last when I've had too much to drink. 'A lickle bit tipthy.' I let my body melt into the floor. For the first time in weeks, I have no pain anywhere. None at all. I hear myself sigh contentedly. 'I had a very nithe time.'

'I wondered where the hell you were,' Laurence snaps. 'I was out of my mind with worry.'

'You could have called.'

'I have been ringing your mobile phone all night.'

I prop myself up on my elbows. With some difficulty. 'Have you?' I pull my phone out of my pocket. Twenty-two missed calls. Hmm. 'Thorry. Thorry. Tho thorry.'

'I think we'd better get Mummy to bed,' my husband says crisply.

'Oo, er!' I giggle.

Laurence takes my hands and tries to get me to stand up, but my knees collapse again and I'm down on the floor once more laughing like a drain.

Now my husband yanks me up by my underams and tosses me over his shoulder. 'I'll be back in a minute, children,' he says. 'Just watch television.'

'We haven't got a television,' Hugo points out helpfully.

'Just watch the walls then,' I offer from over his shoulder.

Laurence hauls me up the stairs, still laughing hysterically. And, in the bedroom, dumps me down on the bed with an 'ouff' that might be from me or him or both. The room is helicoptering around me.

'We might be living in a dump,' he says tightly, 'but we don't have to stoop to their level.'

He tugs off my sandals and then starts to pull at my clothes and I'm suddenly sober. I force myself to sit up.

'Stooping to *their* level has meant that I've got all of our stolen jewellery back,' I retort. The noise makes my head hurt and I put it gingerly in my hands.

'What?' Laurence says.

'You heard. Due to Jamelia and Tracey's thoughtfulness and bravery, we've got our valuables back. My jewellery and your watch.' I fumble in my pocket and, for one horrible minute, can't feel anything. Then I realise that being drunk and being

167

focused are not necessarily bedfellows. The jewellery is safe and sound in my other pocket. I spread it out on the bed.

'Good Christ,' Laurence gasps.

'Precisely.'

'I thought it had gone for good.'

'Me too.' I stare up at him, bleary-eyed. 'So if I've had a few too many drinks in celebration of that fact then I think I deserve them.'

'Of course, of course.' My husband is instantly repentant. 'I must thank them both myself. This is wonderful.'

'We hardly know these people,' I remind him, 'and they've done their very best to help us out. Where are our old "friends"? We haven't had one word from any of them. If this is how "their kind" behave, then I'm all for it. They've been nothing but helpful, generous and friendly. The most tattooed and shaven-headed man I've ever met helped to put food on our table tonight. Jamelia handed over a ring that she'd given fifty quid for that she knew was worth thousands without a second thought. How many people would have done that?'

My husband, quite rightly, looks shamefaced.

'I, for one, am eternally grateful that we landed up here. I don't know how we would have managed without them.'

Then, when I've finished my oration in defence of the good people of Netherslade Bridge, I dash to the bathroom and am promptly and heartily sick.

Chapter 44

I wake up, groggy and with a thumping head, to the sound of my dear husband whistling in the kitchen.

Dragging myself out of bed, I pad gingerly down the stairs. The children are at the table eating their Sugar Puffs and Laurence has progressed to singing 'Un Bel Di' in a mock falsetto – and yet I never previously had him down as a fan of *Madame Butterfly*. How I wish we had a radio and could tune it to Classic FM instead of being subjected to his rendition of opera. I think he is doing this just to torture me. It's working.

'How are we feeling this morning?' he says brightly when he sees me.

'We are feeling fairly awful,' I supply.

'If we had any bacon or eggs I would offer them to you, just to see what shade of green you turned.'

'Very amusing.'

'Tea?'

'Yes. Black, please.' Even the thought of milk is making my stomach roil. Downing more than half a dozen glasses of cheap wine – I lost count after that – seemed like such a good idea last night. Less so this morning.

'I can't believe you got the jewellery back.' Laurence is hideously chipper and, although I'm delighted that this has cheered him up so much, I just wish that he could share it with the volume turned down.

I slide into a chair opposite the children.

'You look sick,' Hugo says.

'That is one of the perils of strong alcohol,' I tell him. 'You must never in your entire life touch a drop of the stuff.'

'I like you drunk,' Hettie says. 'You're funny.'

'Thank you, darling.'

'In fact,' my daughter continues, 'I like my new mummy better than the old one. My old mummy would never go on a trampoline or have pretty fingernails. It's much better fun now we live here.'

'Except for the television,' Hugo contributes.

'Except for the television,' Hettie agrees.

Laurence comes up behind me. He puts a cup of tea on the table and two slices of lightly buttered toast. I can cope with that. I just hope that the toast doesn't crunch too much.

My husband massages my shoulders. And, while the sentiment is wonderful, he's jiggling my head about more than is currently desirable.

'I feel this is a turning point for us,' he says 'We're back on the road up.'

'Yes.'

'I should hear about the position at Cherry's Farm today. I can't wait to get back out to work again. Whatever kind of job it is.'

Then, on cue, Laurence's mobile phone rings. 'Laurence Lamont-Jones.' He walks away from the table and I hear him saying, 'Yes. No. Yes. No,' until he's out of earshot.

A moment later, he comes back into the living room. His face is white, and all the merriness and cheery banter of a few minutes ago has completely gone.

'I didn't get it,' he says, and slumps into the chair next to me. 'I thought I did so well. The agency said that Christopher Cherry has offered someone else the job. How could he not give it to me?'

'You said yourself that he'd had an enormous amount applications.'

Laurence's countenance darkens. 'What do these damn people want? Blood?'

'Perhaps they thought you were over-qualified.'

'Of course I'm over-qualified! All he wanted was someone to do little more than a bit of book-keeping and organise the chicken-feeding rota!'

I decide to keep any other opinions I might have to myself.

'Looks like I'm going to have another day knocking on doors,' Laurence says. 'Just when I thought things might be improving.' He slams out of the kitchen and his feet thunder up the stairs.

Again, I think that it's better if I don't say that I believe it will be a rather long time before our life is anything like back to normal again.

'Why is Daddy so cross?' Hettie wants to know.

'He hasn't got a job to go to at the moment, darling,' I tell her. 'And Daddy finds that a bit difficult.'

'Perhaps he could go on *The Apprentice*,' Hugo suggests. 'I heard him telling Uncle Anthony that they were all wankers on that show and that he could do better than any of them.'

'Yes, yes. That's a good idea. But I don't ever want you to use that word again.'

'What, wankers?'

'Enough, Hugo.'

'Wanker, wankers, wankers,' Hettie trills.

'Why don't you tell *her* off?' Hugo wants to know.

But I can't think of a valid explanation other than that their mother is a faint-hearted drunk. So I drink my black tea and eat my cold toast – which does crunch – and then go upstairs to get myself ready for the day.

Laurence is in the bedroom in the nasty suit. Perhaps that was why he didn't get the job. If he still had his Hugo Boss, would people take him more seriously?

'I thought I'd take the jewellery back to the nice shop in Woburn, see what the chap will give me for it.'

'I don't want you selling it,' my husband says crisply. 'Now we've got it back, I don't want it to go again.'

'We have no choice.' It would have been a different story if Laurence had been given the job at Cherry's Farm. But he

171

wasn't and we still have the slight problem of having no money. 'Unless you want to sign on.'

'That would be the ultimate insult,' Laurence counters.

I don't mention that the 'ultimate insult' might put some food on the table. We can't rely on contributions from Skull's allotment to supplement our meagre expenditure on groceries.

'I would roll over and die rather than do that.' He straightens his nasty tie and puts on his nasty shoes. 'I'll see you later.' With that, he thumps down the stairs again like a recalcitrant teenager and bangs out of the front door.

I sit on the bed, head in hands, and decide that whether Laurence likes it or not, I'm going to take the jewellery to Seymour Chapman. That's the only option I can see that is open to us.

Chapter 45

I rely on Tracey's good nature again and throw the children in with hers. Hugo and Hettie don't complain. They love to be round at Tracey's house as she's considerably more lenient on the chocolate biscuit front than I am. In these new days of frugality, the biscuit barrel – if, indeed, we had one – would be bare.

'We gave that Freddie what-for,' Tracey says. 'Didn't we?'

I have to admit that I am rather gratified to see that my friend is also suffering with a hangover.

'*You* did,' I correct. I think I may have just stood there being pathetically grateful that she was taking charge.

'We won't see him round here for a while,' she continues. 'Stupid twit. Doesn't he know that you don't crap on your own front door?'

I can only agree with the sentiment. 'But if he hadn't,' I point out, 'then I wouldn't have got my valuables back.'

'Now you're off to sell them?'

'It seems criminal,' I say, realising my pun, 'but I have to. We can't eat diamonds.'

'Good luck,' my friend says, and then she stands at the door and waves me goodbye until I'm out of sight.

Now I'm on the bus heading to Woburn. I don't know why, but I've taken an inordinate amount of care with my outfit and my make-up this morning. I washed my hair and took time to straighten it – thank God for the travel-size GHDs which were tucked in my suitcase. For some reason, it's important for me to show Seymour Chapman that I once was a woman of substance – even if I'm not any more. I check my appearance in my handbag mirror and touch up my lipstick.

Once again, the bell over the shop door at Ornato heralds my arrival and as I wait, momentarily, for him to appear, my stomach flutters with nerves.

His smile is wide as he comes out of the office and, thankfully, it widens even more when he recognises me. 'Mrs Lamont-Jones,' he says brightly. 'How lovely to see you again.'

'Thank you, Mr Chapman.' He seems more handsome than when I first met him. But perhaps I simply wasn't in the mood to notice then. I didn't think that I was in the mood to notice today. His face is gentle, kind, as is his manner.

'I hope all is well with you.'

'Fine, fine.' I have already decided not to tell him about my hangover as I don't want to give him the wrong impression.

'You do look a little peaky.'

I have to laugh at that. 'A tiny hangover,' I am forced to admit. 'I had some good fortune last night, Mr Chapman.'

'Please,' he says, 'Seymour.'

'I was celebrating the return of my jewellery . . . Se-Seymour.' For some reason, I stumble on his name.

'Oh, that is good news, Mrs Lamont-Jones.'

'Lily, please.' It can't hurt to return the favour, in the circumstances. Then I'm serious again. 'But my joy is rather short-lived. I have to sell another piece,' I tell him. 'If you're interested.'

'Come through.'

For the second time in our meetings, he flips the Open sign on the door to Closed and waves me through to the back of the shop. I follow him into the now familiar office. This time, I'm not offered a cup of tea or coffee. Instead, Seymour Chapman gets straight down to business.

I hand over my plastic bag filled with jewellery and he produces a black velvet cloth and lays it out on his desk. Then he gently spreads my jewellery out too.

'What would be your choice?' he asks.

'One of the bracelets, perhaps? I have less sentimental attachment to those. After that, possibly the gold pendant.'

'The watch?'

'That's my husband's. I have absolutely *no* sentimental attachment to that.'

We laugh together.

'As much as I like it, perhaps I'd better steer clear of it. I don't want your husband down here chasing me.'

'Probably wise,' I agree.

'A bracelet it is then.' He studies the items again. 'I can offer you two hundred pounds for this one.'

Two hundred pounds it is then. Enough to keep us going for a bit longer. 'Thank you.' Then I wonder how long this will last us if Laurence continues to be unable to find work. 'Thank you very much. I can't tell you how much I appreciate this.'

Seymour opens the safe and counts out the money for me. The first time, I found this most difficult. Now, I have no trouble at all pocketing the cash.

'Could I ask you a favour?' I chew at my lip. 'Is it possible for you to keep the rest of it in the safe for me? I feel quite vulnerable having it in the house. We have no burglar alarm and I'd hate for this to go missing again.'

A lot of people in the area will, I'm sure, know all about our escapades in The Nut last night. I should hate for Freddie the Fixer to come and try to 'borrow' it again.

'Absolutely,' Seymour says. 'No problem at all.' He pulls a large brown envelope from his desk and puts the rest of my jewellery in it. Then he seals it. 'Sign it across here,' he instructs, and I do as I'm told. 'Better pop a contact number on there too. Just in case.'

As I scribble down the number of my mobile, I wonder how long the phone will continue to be active. He writes out a receipt for me and hands it over. I tuck it into my pocket.

'Anytime you need it, you can just pop by.'

'If I'm honest, I think it will all have to be sold in the next few months.' I pat the envelope fondly. 'This will help to buy us some time, but we're not out of the woods yet.'

175

'Husband having no luck on the job front?' He takes my jewellery from me and puts it into his safe.

'No, not yet.' I shake my head. 'The children start at their new school next week. As soon as they do then I'm going to be looking for a job too.'

Seymour's eyebrows rise. 'Really?'

'Just something part-time. I still want to be at home for them.' After having them away at Stonelands, I realise how much I love having them around in the evenings and not just occasional weekends and holidays.

Seymour glances at his watch.

'I'd better be going.' I stand up and the world tilts just a little bit. I am never, ever going to drink to excess again.

'I was thinking that it was just about lunchtime,' Seymour says rather quickly. 'Fancy having a bite to eat with me?'

I think I do a bad job at hiding my surprise.

'We could go across the road,' he suggests. 'The Little Café is very nice.'

It's one of my favourite lunch haunts. Back in the day, I was there at least once or even twice a week. Now, it's so beyond my budget that I want to jump at the chance to go there again and, for reasons best known to himself, Seymour is providing it. Without thinking futher, I say, 'That would be lovely.'

'Excellent.' A smile lights up his face. 'Lunch it is.'

Then he closes up the shop, takes my arm in his and we walk across the road in the sunshine to the Little Café.

Chapter 46

Laurence trawled round all the recruitment agencies again, but nothing had changed. No new jobs, no fabulous opportunities. No one clamouring to snap up his skills.

He sat in the square by the shopping centre and called everyone again who had failed to call him back last time and left another raft of voice messages. His tone was closer to begging than he'd have liked to admit.

The only glimmer of hope he'd had was the opportunity at Cherry's Farm and someone, some lucky bastard, had pipped him to the post and he was finding it impossible to accept defeat.

Without knowing what he was doing and with no particular plan, minutes later he found himself on a bus heading out to Cherry's farm shop complex once more. His mind was in turmoil as he was jolted along the country lanes for the second time in as many days. He had to know why he'd been rejected once again. Hadn't he got on famously with Christopher Cherry? Didn't the man think he had enough to offer?

He found Mr Cherry in the farm shop, arms folded, chatting genially with one of his customers who was poring over a selection of homemade chutneys. When he saw Laurence, he subtly broke away from his conversation and walked towards him.

'Why?' Laurence said without preamble. 'What did I do wrong?' He sounded desperate but, at that moment, he didn't care.

Christopher Cherry sighed. 'You heard that I gave the job to someone else?'

Laurence nodded.

'Come and sit in the sunshine, lad,' Mr Cherry said, and steered him towards the open doors at the back of the barn. Then to one of the women behind the counter in the café area as they passed, 'Bring us a couple of coffees outside will you, Mary, love.'

They found a picnic bench and sat down, both on one side so that they could take in the view down the fields to the canal that meandered at the far end. To the left of them the little petting zoo was doing great business; a crush of excited children were thrusting feed at the chickens and the goats with outstretched hands.

'I could do great things with this place,' Laurence said. 'You've got a terrific base that we could build on. We could brand a whole range of products with the Cherry name. Organic ready-made meals, cakes, herbal teas.'

The coffees were brought out for them.

'Was I not enthusiastic enough?' Laurence continued. Perhaps he hadn't been. Perhaps he'd given the impression that the job was below him. Now he realised that he really wanted to be here, that he could make a difference.

'Aye, lad. It wasn't that what I questioned,' Christopher told him as he stirred his coffee.

'Then what?'

The other man sucked up the froth with an appreciative lip-smacking noise.

'Thought you wouldn't stay the distance,' he said frankly. 'I want someone here that I can rely on. Long-term. I thought that you'd be off to the bright lights again when things turn round and the offers come rolling in again. And they will.'

'I wish I had your faith.'

'You're too canny a lad to stay out of work for long.'

'I would have stayed,' Laurence said. 'I would have stayed and worked wonders with this place for you.'

Christopher Cherry shrugged. 'Then maybe I've picked the wrong man,' he admitted. 'What will be, will be. If we're meant to work together, young Laurence, then it will all come out in the wash. I'm a firm believer that everything in life happens for a reason.'

For the last three months, Laurence felt like he'd continually had his legs kicked out from under him and couldn't see any good reason for that at all. He was trying his best, that's all he was doing, and it didn't seem to be anywhere near enough for anyone.

The older man drained his cup. 'Now, I'd better get on.' He held out his hand.

Laurence shook it. 'Thanks.'

'Remember when you're tempted to run back to London that you've a young family to look after and watch grow up.' Christopher Cherry ambled towards the door. 'It's not all about money, lad.'

It was easy to say that when you had money.

'Things will work out,' Mr Cherry said. 'You see if they don't.'

And Laurence, as he walked, dejected and discouraged, back to the bus stop, wished that he had that kind of optimism.

Chapter 47

Seymour and I are given a nice table in the window of the Little Café. He pulls my chair out for me to sit down. As he does so, I notice that two of my old acquaintances are seated in another part of the restaurant. They're friends of Amanda's rather than mine, but usually they would come over, offer air kisses and say hello. Now Karin Williams and Freya Turner both blank me. They catch my eye, sure enough, and then they both turn away from me, pointedly, without acknowledgement.

'Someone you know?' Seymour asks as he feeds his tall frame into the chair opposite me.

'Yes,' I sigh. 'Looks like I'm *persona non grata* now that I'm no longer eligible to mix in their social circles.'

'I'm sure that it will all come right for you in the end,' Seymour says.

'Yes.' But in my heart, I'm not so sure.

When the waitress comes to take our order, Seymour says to me, 'Champagne?'

I hesitate. There's no way I can even offer to go Dutch on this if we have fizz.

'Lunch is my treat,' Seymour adds casually, but I can tell that he's anxious to avoid any embarrassment on my part. 'To seal our latest business deal.'

And, suddenly, I long for the taste of bubbles bursting on my tongue. The vestiges of my hangover are already forgotten when I say, 'Oh yes, please.'

We select our food and the waitress brings the champagne.

'What shall we toast?' Seymour asks as we hold up our exquis-itely slender glasses. He touches the rim of his glass against mine.

I feel myself flush. 'I don't know.'

'To better times,' he says.

I can agree with that. 'To better times,' I echo.

Our food comes – smoked trout and crayfish salad with horseradish dressing for me and baked goats cheese and roasted fresh figs for Seymour. This is so civilised. In so short a time I had forgotten this is how my life used to be. I glance at my old acquaintances in the corner and they can hardly concen-trate on their own food for looking at me and my companion. Let them gossip. Let it get back to Amanda that I was having lunch with a handsome young man who wasn't my husband.

It might be my glass of champagne or it might be my new 'fuck it' attitude to my lowered social status – I giggle to myself at the unaccustomed swearword – but I start to relax and enjoy myself. Seymour is pleasant and entertaining company and it's nice to have some luxury in my life once more, however short-lived.

I tell Seymour how we came to be in this mess, about my nice new neighbours and our home on the sink estate with one of the worst reputations in the area.

Seymour Chapman is a most attentive host. He laughs in all the right places, commiserates when he should and for a brief time makes me forget what desperate trouble we're in.

'Are you married, Seymour?' I can see no evidence of a ring – for a jeweller, he's not adorned at all – but what does that mean these days?

He shakes his head. 'I was. For ten years. It ended some time ago now.'

'Children?'

'Sadly no.' Seymour sips at his champagne again. 'We wanted different things in life. I'm lazy and want a quiet time in the country. Izzy was – still is – ambitious, driven and much happier living the city life. We lived apart within our marriage for many years, so it was inevitable really when we eventually divorced. We'd each been doing our own thing for so long, that there was very little animosity when we made it permanent.' He shrugs. 'I'm on good terms with Izzy – as well as one can be with an ex-wife – but we have no real cause to see each other now. She contacts me every so often for advice or a good deal when she's buying jewellery for herself or for a gift. Nothing more.'

I can feel the alcohol making my cheeks glow.

'One of the benefits of not having children is that we have nothing to tie us together – other than the memories of a few good times. It's much easier to move on.'

'Yes.' I think of Laurence and me and wonder if we will manage to weather this storm together. Couples split for less, I think. And despite trying to put a brave face on it all – mainly for the children's sake – there is a part of me that, deep down inside, feels betrayed by my husband's deceptions. If he had come to me as soon as he'd known we were in trouble, then maybe I'd feel differently. 'Perhaps if we didn't have children,' I muse out loud, 'then I wouldn't be standing by Laurence.'

'Really?'

'I don't know.' I try to shake off the feeling. 'It's a hard one to call. Sometimes doing the right thing doesn't come easily.' To start with it was just a matter of survival, when one's natural instincts kick in. Now that the worst of it is over – I hope – I'm having time to process my feelings more. Not all of them are positive.

Without warning, Seymour places his hand gently over mine. 'Did anyone ever tell you that you are the most extraordinary woman, Lily Lamont-Jones?'

My eyes fill with tears. 'Not recently.'

'Well, you are,' Seymour tells me. 'You truly are a wonderful woman.'

'I don't think so.'

'You're resourceful, determined . . .'

'I've done nothing but cry,' I protest.

'A few tears,' he says dismissively. 'Who wouldn't shed some in your situation? Underneath it all I can tell that you're a very strong person. You'll come out of this on top.'

'I do hope that you're right, Seymour.'

Then I notice his watch and realise what the time is.

'I'm keeping you,' I say. 'And I, too, must get back. My bus will be along shortly.'

'You don't look like the sort of woman who should have to resort to taking public transport.'

'Needs must.' I do miss my car. Every journey has to be planned so meticulously, no just jumping into the Merc spontaneously and going where I will.

Seymour Chapman's fingers squeeze mine. 'Will you do this again with me?'

'Have lunch?'

'Yes,' he says.

'It's been lovely.'

'Sometime soon then?'

'I don't know. It's very difficult.'

'I enjoy your company.'

'And I've enjoyed yours.' How could I not? He's charming, witty, easy on the eye.

'You know where I am, Lily. I'd like to see you. As friends.'

I glance across the room. My old acquaintances are talking behind their hands. Oh, let them get an eyeful of that, I think. This has been a welcome and momentary escape from the bleak nightmare that my life has become and I sorely needed it. Now it's back to the grindstone.

'I'm hoping to be working soon,' I remind him. 'It may not be possible.'

'I'm sure we'll find a way,' he says and winks at me.

And I laugh because I really have no idea how.

Chapter 48

When I get home, Amanda Marquis calls me. I'm taken aback to see her name on my caller ID. But perhaps I shouldn't be.

'Karin and Freya said they saw you today in the Little Café,' she coos after the most cursory of hellos.

'Did they?'

'Having lunch with Laurence . . .' She tails away meaningfully. 'It was Laurence, wasn't it?'

So Karin and Freya were pretty sure that it wasn't my husband, but weren't sufficiently in the know to identify just who it was.

I could just say yes, it was Laurence, but what do I care what they're saying about me. 'It was Seymour Chapman,' I tell Amanda. 'The new owner of Ornato.'

'Oh.' Amanda sounds taken aback. 'I've met him. He's divine.'

Yes, I think. He is.

There's a sour note in her voice when she continues, 'Been buying jewellery then?'

'Hardly.' I suppress a sigh. 'I was selling some.'

Amanda goes, 'Oh,' again, but in a much more contrite tone.

'We're just about managing to keep our heads above water,' I tell my one-time friend.

'I have been meaning to call.' Now she's defensive and I think, My arse you have.

'I know that it's the charity swishing party at Brasserie Bleue next week,' I continue. I caught sight of the date on my phone's calendar this morning on the bus while I was idling the time away.

The swishing parties are Amanda's brainchild and we used to do it once or even twice a year. Everyone would get their designer gear together and sell it for Amanda's chosen charity. They were always a wonderful opportunity to bitch about your friends' taste in clothes and I shudder to think of how shallow that version of me was. Still, amid the back-stabbing, you could pick up a Ben de Lisi or little Stella McCartney number for a few pounds. How I could do with that now! I'm going to need a couple of outfits for when I start my job hunting. All I have is sundresses and pretty soon we're going to run out of sun.

'Cancelled,' she says too quickly. 'It's not only you who's feeling the pinch.'

Feeling the pinch? I have had my home, my possessions, my life taken from me. A tad more than 'feeling the pinch', I think bitterly. Does Amanda really have so little appreciation of our situation? 'Perhaps you could let me know when the next one is.'

'I've pulled the plug on it for now as we're all tight for money. Speaking of which . . .' she says.

'I can't pay you anything yet,' I tell her honestly. 'Not until Laurence is back in work. But we haven't given up hope.'

'Me neither,' Amanda says. Then, 'I'd better dash. Nice to chat.'

Before I can say anything more, my ex-friend hangs up. All my warm and lovely feelings from my lunch with Seymour are dashed against the rocks of disappointment.

Heart in boots, I trail round to Tracey's house to find my children. The front door is wide open, as is the back one, so I let myself in shouting the required 'Coo-ee!' and go through to the garden where I find Tracey in a deckchair, feet up and reading an ancient and battered Jackie Collins novel that has clearly been in and out of the charity shops several times. There's a glass of white wine in her hand.

She jumps up when I stick my head round the door and gives me a hug.

'Have the children been good?'

'Didn't know I had them.' From the depths of the adored

trampoline, my two give me a cursory wave. Clearly they haven't missed me as much as I missed them.

Tracey's wearing a baggy T-shirt with a psychedelic print, leggings and beaded flip-flops. I feel over-dressed in my prim linen shift. 'How's your day been, darlin'?' she asks.

'Mixed,' I say, throat tight with tears. I can't even bring myself to tell her how my old friends have deserted me and that I feel more lonely than I ever have in my entire life.

'Sit yourself down.' She gives me her chair. 'Wine box in the fridge. I'll get you a glass.'

I'm too weary to protest and gratefully take the glass she hands over to me. If I'm being truthful, the wine is sharp, but tastes every bit as good as my lunchtime champagne as it was offered with friendship and kindness.

'You look like you need that,' Tracey observes when she sits down.

'Laurence didn't get the job he was hoping for,' I tell her.

'There'll be others.'

I hold the cold glass against my cheek. 'I don't know. Wonderful offers of work seem to be a bit thin on the ground at the moment. As soon as the children go back to school, I'm going to look for something – even if it's only part-time.'

'Have you ever worked?' Tracey asks.

'Not really,' I admit. 'I made a cursory effort when I finished at Uni, but all I ever wanted was to settle down and have children.'

'Me too,' my new friend says. 'I trained and worked as a nursery nurse when I left school and really enjoyed it, but I fell pregnant with Keanu – complete accident – and didn't go back to work. Even though money was tight I wanted to be at home with him.'

I think of how much I'm enjoying my own children being at home with us rather than doing what we thought was the right thing and sending them away to a boarding school.

'Then we had Charlize and her dad walked out pretty soon after that, leaving me right in the lurch.' Tracey swigs her wine.

'I've never had a bloke who could really look after all of us, and now I'm stuck in a rut. I could only get a menial job so it makes more sense financially for me to stay at home and on benefits than to go out to work. It's a crazy system, but that's the way it is. By the time I've paid for childcare in the holidays, I'd be out of pocket.'

'Doesn't your mother have them for you?'

'A lot of the time, but she still works to make ends meet too. She tries to take the pressure off, but she can't have them every day.'

'It seems such a shame. You're so good with people and with children. Don't you want more than this for yourself?'

'Yeah,' she says. 'Now the kids are older. I'm bored all day waiting around for them to come home from school. They don't need me so much now.'

'Then perhaps it's time to do something for yourself.'

'What could I do?' Tracey shrugs. 'I've got no confidence now. No skills that anyone wants.'

'Perhaps you could go back to college, take a training course of some kind. Try to get some work in a nursery?'

'Yeah,' she says. 'Maybe.'

I squeeze her arm. 'Let's see how I get on first. I'm dreading putting myself back onto the job market after all these years of a life of leisure, so I've no idea why I'm encouraging you to go through it too!'

We both laugh at that.

'Thankfully, I sold some more jewellery today,' I tell Tracey. 'At least I can buy myself some clothes. All we've got is what we took on holiday with us.'

'You're more than welcome to have some of my stuff if you'd like,' she offers. 'Some of it's a bit neat on me now but it would definitely fit you.'

'I couldn't, Tracey. You've already done so much for us.'

'Nonsense.' She bats away my protest. 'They're only cluttering up the place. I'll look some things out for you tomorrow.' My neighbour gives me a hearty nudge and laughs. 'You and me, we'll have a girly trying-on session.'

I think of how I've been cut out of the swishing-party circle for the misdemeanour of being poor, and yet here is this woman whom I barely know who has so little and is still offering to share it with me.

Chapter 49

When I get home there are some freshly-dug carrots on the doorstep – another welcome donation from the abundant allotment of Skull.

We'll have them tonight with the cut-price chicken pieces I bought from the local shop and some potatoes I've still got left over from yesterday's food parcel.

Laurence is sitting in the back garden when I walk through to the kitchen. I go and sit next to him on the paving – also courtesy of Skull.

'I went to see Christopher Cherry,' he says before I have a chance to speak. 'Practically begged him for a job.'

'Oh, Laurence.'

'I didn't know what else to do. I had to find out why he turned me down.'

'And?'

'He thought I wouldn't stay there.' Laurence takes my hand. 'I never thought it would be this hard,' he admits. 'I thought I'd just fall into another job – if not in the City, then some-where else. I never realised how easy life was for us.'

'It wasn't *easy*,' I point out. 'You worked ridiculous hours, you never saw the children – or me. Yes, we had money, we had a comfortable lifestyle but I'm realising now that we've paid a price for it.' I slip my arm through his and lean against him.

'That's what you have to do,' he says crisply. 'It's the way of the world if you want to get on.'

Is that all it's about – getting on? Wouldn't the world be a better place if everyone could just stop believing that they should have what they perceive everyone else has? I want to tell him that I've discovered that there might be a different way of doing things. We were shallow, self-centred people, and it's only since I've been forced to take a step back away from our previous life that I can see that. But it's not what Laurence wants to hear now. He's so wrapped up in his own despair, I decide that now isn't the time to try for a philosophical discussion about the meaning of life. Instead, I say, 'I'll go inside and get supper ready.' I leave him staring vacantly at the rusted car and the overgrown grass.

An hour later and we're all seated round the table. I've grilled the chicken and boiled the potatoes and there's a bowl of Skull's buttered carrots which I know will be sweet and delicious.

'Tracey is a brilliant cook,' Hettie tells me. 'She gave us fish finger batties and chips for lunch.'

'Butties,' Hugo corrects.

'It was wicked.'

I think of all the cous-cous I've rammed down my children's throats for years and all they want to do is eat like kids do.

Given a choice between alfalfa sprouts and chocolate, what would *you* choose?

After dinner we all clear the table together and then Hettie produces a board game – Cluedo. A game I remember playing with my own parents.

'Charlize gave me this to borrow because I told her we had no television.' She plonks the game on the table. 'She says we must be really poor if we haven't even got *one* television. Are we?'

Laurence and I exchange a glance. Yes, we are really poor, I want to tell her. Instead her parents both fail to answer the direct question.

Picking up the Cludeo box, I say, 'Let's have a look at this, shall we? What fun!'

How long has it been since we all played a board game as a family? Not since Nintendo DSs were invented or since their bedrooms had laptops and their own televisions and Wiis.

I banned the children from taking their DSs on holiday because I knew that all they'd want to do was bury their noses in them. Now I wish I hadn't been so harsh as they'd still have them.

'They don't use it because *they've* got their own television,' she announces. 'One each.' In case I failed to miss the point first time.

'Well, they're very lucky,' I observe. I take the lid off the Cluedo. 'I used to love this game as a little girl. It was my favourite.'

Hettie doesn't look as if she's buying into it.

This was obviously once a much-loved set. The box lid is broken at all corners and is now held on by an elastic band. Inside, the player pieces – Colonel Mustard, Miss Scarlet, Reverend Green *et al* – are, mostly, the original brightly-coloured cones with a ball for a head. Only Mrs White has been replaced by a piece of square white Lego. The murder weapons haven't fared so well though. The lead piping is still intact, but the dagger – always my favourite – has been replaced by a cocktail stick. The rope is a bit of twisted pink wool which doesn't look very deadly at all and the candlestick is now a spent tea-light – vanilla fragrance. I'm not sure that anyone has ever been bludgeoned to death with a tea-light.

As the instructions have long since gone, Laurence and I trawl our brains to remember how to play it. I think we make most of it up, but soon enough we have the children squabbling over who they want to be and then play commences.

The game ends hours and many bitter arguments later when my daughter, Miss Scarlet – I do hope that's not an omen – shrieks with delight at having discovered that the murderer is my husband, Mrs White the Lego piece, with the tea-light in the dining room.

We pack the pieces safely away and the children, still hyperactive, are dispatched to bed. I sit on Hettie's bed as I kiss her goodnight.

'That was brilliant,' she says. 'Not as brilliant as having a television in my own room, but *quite* brilliant.'

'Good,' I say, as I wonder if Tracey has some other board

games we could borrow, or perhaps I could find a couple in one of the charity shops. I'm sure the murderous delights of Cluedo will soon wane.

Hugo is already asleep when I go into his room. At home he would have to be cajoled to log off from chatting with his friends on MSN every night. I hope my child survives this ordeal unscathed and, judging by the way he's sleeping soundly, arm thrown carelessly above his tousled head, then I have every right to hope.

In our room, Laurence is also already in bed. He's lying with his hands behind his head, staring at the ceiling.

'That was fun, wasn't it?' I say.

He nods. 'Yes. We should do it more often.'

I don't like to tell him that I'm planning on doing it again tomorrow night – and every night for the foreseeable future. Instead, I kiss his forehead and say, 'I'll be back in a minute.'

In the dilapidated bathroom, I take a quick shower and try not to let the mildewed curtain spoil my mood. I dry myself and brush my hair in the mirror. I'm sure I've developed new wrinkles in the last few weeks and I pull my skin this way and that to try to ascertain whether it's all just in my imagination. I'm on the very last scrapings of my Crème de Mer facial cream. I can't believe now that I paid so much money for a beauty product. How ridiculous of me. I could feed us for a month now on the price of a single pot.

It's not that I want to become completely haggard. I'll just have to ask Tracey what she uses. As young as she looks, I could bet you, sure as eggs are eggs, that she doesn't spend more than a fiver on her face cream. And, if it's good enough for her, then it's good enough for me.

I take another look at myself in the mirror. Does Laurence still fancy me any more, I wonder? It's been months since we made love. Even the sultry nights in Tuscany didn't manage to stir any sexual desire in us. Ending up in Netherslade Bridge hasn't improved the situation any. Perhaps I could rectify it now?

I leave my nightdress off and, slipping my dressing-gown on,

I pad along the landing and back to the bedroom. Laurence is still awake, still looking very depressed.

Standing by the bed, self-consciously I let my dressing-gown slide from my shoulders and fall to the floor.

'Won't you be cold?' is my husband's response to my naked state.

Easing into the bed next to him, I say, 'Not if you keep me warm.' I press my body against his. How long is it since we've done this? Kissing my husband's neck, I intertwine my legs with his. Laurence lies stock-still while I murmur, 'Mmm,' and work my way lower.

His hands move in stilted circles across my back, more irritating than arousing, but I don't give up. I travel down his stomach with butterfly kisses, nipping with my teeth. When I reach the parts where it should get more interesting, there's nothing much going on down there either.

'Lily,' Laurence says, holding my arms so that I can't move. 'This isn't really working for me.'

I can see that much. Giving up on my quest towards his nether regions, I join him again at the other end of the bed and prop myself up on my elbow. 'Want to talk about it?'

My husband shakes his head. In the dark I can see that his eyes are glittering with unshed tears. We might not be love's young dream but this has never happened to us before. One more thing for Laurence to mark down as a failure and, in his current state of mind, I know that he will.

I rest my head on his shoulder and stroke his chest softly. 'It'll be fine,' I say. 'It will all be fine.'

And I wonder if I say it often enough, whether it will be.

Chapter 50

A week later and the children are starting their new school. They are both kitted out from the supermarket at less than twenty pounds apiece.

Hettie has her hand in mine. My children have coped remarkably well so far with the prospect of going from world-class public school to without-class local middle school. My daughter has, more or less without complaint, accepted that she no longer has a horse or drama lessons, and in return for that I have given in to her more base desire for fish fingers and pizza, and no longer try to force-feed her Parma-ham-wrapped quail or asparagus risotto.

We are accompanied on our short walk to the school by Tracey and her two children, Charlize and Keanu, who have proved to be remarkably good replacement playmates for Amanda's Arthur and Amelia. The hope is that my two will find it easier to integrate into their new surroundings if they can prove that they're already 'in'.

Only Hugo is quiet and perhaps, as he sees the school, he realises that life will never be quite the same for him again. There'll be no rugby coaches of international standard, no school swimming pool that any health spa would be jealous of, no individual tennis coaching. My heart goes out to my boy and I know that he'll bear this all stoically because he is his father's son.

At the school gates, I'm horrified to see the rag-tag of assorted children that will be their classmates. I thought that Stonelands was quite a multi-cultural school – they prided themselves that there were pupils from all corners of the globe – but I can see quite clearly now that it wasn't. Half a dozen ethnic minority children in a school doesn't make it inclusive, whereas half a dozen white children in a school probably does.

Hugo pulls away from me straight away and goes off on his own to find his class with Keanu. Hettie hangs back and I go with her to find her new class teacher. Ms Davy is a Goth and has multiple piercings. My child, instantly forgetting her good manners, stares at her open-mouthed.

Reluctantly, I leave her in Ms Davy's tender loving care. At the gates, Tracey is waiting for me. I sit on the wall and cry. Cry that we have come to this. Cry that so many people never have a chance to experience what else is available if only you have money.

'Come back to mine,' Tracey says. 'We can have a root through my wardrobe as I promised.'

I nod mutely, unable to form words that would adequately describe my misery. The only thing I am thankful for is that at half-past three, Hugo and Hettie will be released from their concrete prison into my care once more. Then I wonder why it didn't seem so bad sending my children away for a whole term, just because the building was ivy-clad?

Back at my friend's house and Tracey makes a cup of tea. We take it upstairs into her bedroom. I sit on the bed and nurse my tea while she flings her wardrobe doors open. 'Mi wardrobe e tu wardrobe!' she declares in an approximation of a well-known saying. 'Try on anything you want. If it doesn't fit me, you can have it. If it still fits me, you can borrow it.'

I don't know where to start. Everything is more brightly-coloured, more sparkly than I'd normally wear. I've always tended to go for classic clothes, simply-cut in expensive fabrics. Tracey, it's fair to say, has none of those.

'I'm not sure what suits me,' I say honestly.

'Let's pretend I'm Gok Wan,' she says.

'Who?'

'I sometimes wonder whether you have lived on the same

planet as us,' my friend tuts. 'He's a style guru. The best. And I'm going to be him. So trust me – I'll find something in here that suits you.'

'Okay. Let's go for it.'

'Get your kit off then, girl.' And, not that I have much choice, I strip down to my underwear while Tracey rummages through her clothes.

After a few moments of thought, she tugs out a silver Lurex tunic and some black leggings. I back away. 'Oh. I'm not really sure that's me.'

'I'm Gok,' she insists. 'Get them on.'

I get them on.

'What do you reckon?' She pulls the other wardrobe door open as far as it will go and turns me towards it. 'Suit you or not?'

I'm stunned at the woman who's looking back at me.

'You need some heels,' Tracey decides. 'These look fab, but they're crippling. I bought them a size too small, hoping that I'd slim into them.'

Four-inch stilettos are produced and I slip my feet into them. I don't think I have ever had shoes this high or this tarty.

'They look great,' she says.

They do. I'm staring at me looking ten years younger instantly.

'How did you do that?'

'What?'

'Make me look like that?'

'If you don't mind me saying, Lily, you wear clothes that are far too dowdy. Even my mother wouldn't wear clothes as old-fashioned as yours.'

'They're classic,' I object, almost speechless.

'Classically old,' she points out. 'You can do clothes like that when you're sixty. You're forty years old, girl. In your prime. A yummy mummy. Dress like it.'

'A yummy mummy,' I repeat like a mantra as I admire myself from all directions. I certainly feel like a yummy mummy. I feel like a yummy everything! 'Bring it on, Tracey. What else have you got?'

An A-line skirt is the answer, complete with patchwork pockets and embroidery all round the bottom. My new stylist teams it with biker boots, a plain black tee and a cropped cardigan. I don't look like me at all.

'I always thought you needed a bit of livening up,' my neighbour says. 'You're a pretty woman, Lily, but you looked like you were stuck in a time warp.'

I might have spent hundreds – and hundreds – of pounds on my clothes, but perhaps Tracey is right – I was dressing much older than my age. I don't want to turn into a WAG but there's nothing wrong with me looking young and funky, is there?

'I need something for an interview,' I remind her.

'Hmm. That's going to be a bit more tricky.' She stands back and eyes me up and down. 'Keep the T-shirt on and the boots.'

She rummages in her wardrobe some more until she produces a cream knee-length jersey sleeveless dress with a 'Ta-da!'

I slip it on over the tee and Tracey puts a slender patent belt under my bust in the empire style.

'That will do the job!'

'Trendy secretary,' I say, swishing this way and that.

'Trendy whatever you want to be,' is her view. 'The world is your oyster.'

'It is,' I say, pouting and posing in her mirror. 'I'm going out there and I'm going to be fabulous!'

Chapter 51

And my new-found confidence lasts for – oh, nearly an hour. I go home in the biker boots and embroidered skirt feeling like some sort of cool chick for the first time in my life. Then, with a flash of bravado, I pick up the local newspaper and start bashing my mobile phone, calling the numbers of any of the jobs advertised that I think might suit a yummy mummy with a feisty attitude and, as quickly transpires, zero skills.

I call about a job in media sales – whatever that is – which says in the advertisement that all training will be provided. As soon as they ask me about computer experience I am stumped, found out and quickly discarded. You can't even, it seems, answer phones these days without a degree in computing. And all training is provided, except for the bit that I really need.

The next one I try is for a receptionist in a doctor's surgery; they too require a raft of previous experience in a similar role. When I enquire after the job as a school secretary, I'm told that they've had over 100 applicants so I don't even ask them to send me a form. Even the popular sandwich bar in Woburn that I contact – the Brunch Bunch – who want part-time staff ask if I've had any catering experience or have a 'food handling certificate'. I don't know what a 'food handling certificate' is, but I tell them that I've single-handedly fed my family for fifteen years and that I've cut more sandwiches and baked more cakes for the WI than I care to remember. They take my number and say they'll call me back. I don't hold out much hope.

Then there's a company asking for female escorts and, to be

honest, I'd even consider that, but I'd probably be too old. And I'm not sure that Laurence would be that impressed if I chose 'escort' as my new career. It might pay better than the others though.

Soon, so very soon, and all my enthusiasm has been drained out of me by a variety of people who don't care whether or not I need a job, let alone how much. I want to scream at them, 'Don't you know how difficult this is for me?' but then, I guess it is just the same for anyone else seeking work with nothing much to offer. My skill with flower arranging and cake decoration means little in the cruel world of commerce.

I'm just putting on the kettle to make myself a cup of tea as consolation when Laurence comes downstairs. To be honest, he makes me jump. I'd forgotten that he was still at home and unhappy. 'Not going out today?'

'Can't face it,' Laurence says flatly. 'Not again.' He's unshaven, his hair unkempt. 'Besides, what's the point?'

After my futile hour on the phone, I can't really argue with him. He has been hounding the job agencies for months now and nothing. He was at the top of his tree in the City and has years of experience behind him. If Laurence can't get a job, then what hope do I have?

I make him tea and put two slices of bread in Tracey's toaster. 'I'm going into the city centre today. See what I can find.'

'I'd rather you didn't,' Laurence says. 'I don't want you working.'

'What choice do we have? It will do me good. I can't sit around here all day.'

His face darkens.

'I didn't mean anything by that,' I say hurriedly. 'I know how hard you've been trying. It's fine to take a day or two off, recharge the batteries.'

Laurence snorts. Then suddenly his eyes bulge wide and he stares at me. 'Where did you get the clothes?'

'Tracey,' I admit. 'Where else?' I give him a twirl. 'What do you think?'

'You look fantastic. Amazing.'

199

'Thanks. She sent some clothes for you too. One of her old boyfriends had left them behind.'

I indicate the pile on the edge of the worktop. My husband holds them up for inspection. There's a pair of jeans, trendier than Laurence would normally wear, a couple of striped shirts, a black V-neck sweater, a particularly smart dark grey Harrington jacket and a pair of Skechers trainers that look as if they've never been worn. If I'd previously brought these home – not that I would have – Laurence would have simply refused to wear them. Now he just looks immensely grateful that he has a choice between the nasty suit and holiday clothes.

'Hmm. I hope this little lot will make me look ten years younger too.' Then he goes all glum again. 'I hope they make me *feel* ten years younger too.'

'It will all come right,' I say, not for the first time. But even I'm beginning to think that there's a hollow ring to it.

Chapter 52

Another two weeks have gone by and still there's no change in our circumstances. The job offers haven't flooded in for Laurence or for me. Our meagre stash of money continues to dwindle away. Since our aborted attempt at making love, we haven't tried again.

I'm in the kitchen, tidying up after breakfast and ushering the children to get ready for school.

'No fighting today,' I tell Hugo. Virtually every day my son has come home from his new school having been involved either in a minor skirmish or a full-out brawl that results in a torn shirt or a split lip or a handful of his hair missing.

'I can't help it,' Hugo says as he puts his cereal bowl in the sink. 'They all pick on me. They call us the posh kids. But we're not posh any more.'

How true is that.

'I have to fight back,' he insists.

I think my son is actually relishing his new action-packed, fight-club school. He always seems very cheerful about his wounds and I wonder how the other poor child has fared in the battle. This is why I haven't been to the Head Teacher to complain. I'm waiting for *him* to come to *me* to complain about Hugo.

'You like it,' Hettie pipes up. As I suspected.

'No, I don't.' I ignore the pinch he gives her as she stamps on his foot in return. That's my girl.

'Stop squabbling. Are you ready? Go and knock for next

door.' Tracey and I have fallen into the habit of walking the children to school together every day. Then, invariably, I go back to her house for a coffee.

Laurence has given up his daily quest to search for work. Worryingly, he's spending virtually all of his days at home and he's getting up later and later. Today, he hasn't put in an appearance at all yet. With us both mooching round the house all day we're starting to grate on each other, so I do my best to push him out for a few hours to go to the library and get online or I disappear to Tracey's house for some solace.

I gather up the children and their school bags – more welcome cast-offs from next door – and my friend is already coming out of the door with Charlize and Keanu as we emerge.

She kisses my cheek. 'Morning, darlin'.' I kiss her back. We fall in step together. 'Another day in paradise,' Tracey says.

'Yes. Beautiful.'

The morning air is spiked with the freshness of autumn. Normally we chatter so much that I don't notice the rusting cars and the litter, the constantly refreshed supply of abandoned tyres and shopping trolleys. Who brings them here? Why do we never see anyone dumping them? Or hear them clattering along the street? This morning, however, we're both quiet.

We drop off the kids and I renew my threat to Hugo. 'No fighting,' I say. 'This is your last warning.'

He grins and it's clear that he's paying no attention to me at all. It's easier, I think, to control your children when you can take things off them as a punishment. When they have nothing, what can you confiscate? An hour without her Nintendo would have previously sent Hettie into a flat spin. Hugo at ten years old used to be permanently welded to his mobile phone and we thought nothing of having a contract for him that cost forty pounds a month. For a child!

It's funny, though; now they're not away at Stonelands and are at home with us every night, the children seem freer, more themselves. No doubt they're naughtier, feistier, but somehow I don't mind that. They're not so constrained, so stressed; they're more like children should be and not like robotic, miniature adults.

My friend and I watch them disappear into the school and then turn for home. 'You're quiet today,' I observe. 'Everything all right?'

Tracey shrugs. 'Oh, you know.'

I notice that there are dark shadows under her eyes and wonder if she's sleeping well. I might moan about Laurence being around and under my feet all day, but at least I have him to talk to and we have each other. Tracey has to manage all of her troubles on her own. Although she has her mum, I know that she doesn't like to bother her if possible.

'Anything I can help with?' I ask gently.

'A few money worries,' she admits.

That's the one thing I probably *can't* help her with.

'It's all bills, bills, bills,' she complains. 'Don't get me wrong, I wouldn't be without my kids. But they cost more and more as they get older. Keanu is eating me out of house and home.' At twelve, her son is already taller than Tracey and despite his prodigious eating habits is whip-thin. 'No wonder they all end up like giants these days.' She shakes her head. 'I'm worried about the fuel bills now that it's getting colder too. These houses are a pig to heat. It'll soon be time to turn on the heating and that costs a king's ransom now.'

We're all on pre-paid meters here and, stupidly, the tariff for that is even higher than normal, hitting the people who can least afford it. No wonder they call it the poverty trap. Once you have no money, it is dastardly difficult to claw yourself out of that situation. It's exactly like being trapped.

I link my arm through hers. 'How short are you?'

Tracey shrugs, but her face colours up. 'I could do with a couple of hundred quid to tide me over.'

As my friend managed to retrieve my jewellery for me the least I can do is sell a piece for her.

'I could help you out you know.'

'You've got enough on your plate,' she says. 'I'll be all right. I'd normally go to Freddie for a bit of extra cash, but I'm out of favour with him.'

'Not surprisingly.' We both laugh as we think of our night

203

in The Nut with Tracey strong-arming Freddie. I am so grateful for that.

'I'll be fine,' my friend says. 'I've got through worse than this.'

I feel drained because we've been living like this – hand-to-mouth – for a few weeks, but Tracey has had a lifetime of this with little or no respite. And, as she's been so good to me when I needed a friend, I resolve that if there's any way that I can help her out, then I will.

Chapter 53

Mid-morning I get a surprise phone call. The manager of the sandwich bar in Woburn that I spoke to weeks ago is on the other end of the line. He asks me to go in for an interview that afternoon at two o'clock, which sends me into a blind panic. I don't think I've had an interview since the late 1980s.

Irrationally, I feel the need to practise my sandwich skills and make Laurence and me a ham and cheese with mayo on brown for our lunch. My husband is distinctly less excited about my interview than I am.

'But you'll have to get the bus there.'

'I'll have to get the bus to any job,' I point out.

'What are the hours?'

'It's part-time,' I tell him, in between mouthfuls. 'But I don't know the exact hours yet.'

'Humph,' he says, and doesn't comment on the delights of his sandwich – which makes me even more nervous.

After lunch, I take the bus and gently bump my way out to Woburn. The sandwich bar, the Brunch Bunch, is in the High Street just a few doors down from Ornato. I glance in the window as I pass, but there's no sign of Seymour inside the shop and I don't have enough time to pop in.

The Brunch Bunch shop is bright and airy. All the assistants wear green checked aprons and matching baseball caps. In all my years on this earth, I never envisaged myself doing a job that involved wearing a baseball cap. To be honest, me doing a job *at all* never featured that heavily.

I put on my best smile and step inside. The owner greets me. I'm assuming he's the owner because he's the only one not wearing a baseball cap. He also has sandy-coloured thinning hair and a tummy that speaks of too many sandwiches. 'You must be Lily.'

'Yes.'

'Alan Green.' He shakes my hand and then he goes on to show me around the tiny space which effectively holds nothing more than a long glass counter in which all the various sandwich fillings are spread out. The lunchtime rush has just died down, he tells me, and the afternoons are quieter, but they sell a lot of homemade cakes just before three.

I could see myself working here. Despite a lack of formal qualifications, I think I could manage making sandwiches on a commercial basis.

'The hours are ten till four,' Alan says. 'Five days a week, Monday to Friday. Some Saturdays for holiday cover. How would that suit?'

'Marvellous.' I could take the children to school and still be at home shortly afterwards. I'm sure Tracey would keep an eye on them until I can get back. Alan tells me the hourly rate and I have to admit that it shocks me. This must be the minimum wage. I'm going to work all day for less than I used to spend on a lunch.

But then I think that beggars can't be choosers and if the job is on offer then I'll bite the man's arm off.

'Can you start next week?'

'Yes,' I say before he's fully completed the sentence. 'Yes, I can.'

He holds out his hand again and grasps mine. 'Then welcome on board, Lily.'

I'm in a daze. Minutes after arriving here, I have the offer of a job. This calls for a celebration. I buy two éclairs oozing with fresh cream and topped with a tempting glaze of dark chocolate, and Mr Green even takes off my staff discount even though I'm not yet officially employed. My next bus isn't due for half an hour and I'm thinking that I'll call in to see Seymour, perhaps have one of these cakes with him to thank him for his kindness and to kill some time. While I'm there, I'm also going to ask him if he will buy another piece of my jewellery so that I can help Tracey out with a little bit of cash. She has done so much for me and the rest of the family since we arrived unceremoniously in Netherslade Bridge that I would love to do something in return for her.

Chapter 54

'I come bearing gifts,' I say when Seymour Chapman appears behind the counter of his cool, calm jewellery boutique.

'Lily!' His face lights up when he sees me and he takes my free hand in his and lifts my fingers to brush his lips.

My heart starts to race and the only thing that has made my heart race in recent weeks is the thought of any bills dropping on the doormat.

Then, as I struggle to appear unruffled, Seymour inspects the box in my other hand. 'My favourite,' he declares. 'Time for tea?'

'Only if you have.'

'Lily . . .' There's a wistful sigh in his voice and I don't know many men over the years who have spoken to me whilst sighing wistfully. I find it most endearing – in a worrying way. 'I will *always* make time for you.'

So, once again, I find myself in the back of Seymour's shop waiting for the kettle to boil. I hand an éclair over to my host, take one for myself, then, as my nerves subside, I settle back in his armchair and cross my legs.

'What brings you out this way?' he asks.

'I've just had some good news,' I tell him.

He studies me intently as he waits for me to spill the beans, his eyes crinkling softly at the corners.

'I've just been offered a job at the Brunch Bunch.'

'A job?'

I nod, still delighted with my little self. Seymour busies himself making tea, then hands me a cup.

When he sits down opposite me again he rests his chin on his hand and fixes me with his soft blue eyes and says, 'What about if I offer you a job too?'

'Here?'

'I can't see you spending your days in a sandwich shop, Lily,' he says with a laugh. 'You can do better than that.'

'I haven't worked in years,' I remind him. 'Years and years. I have no experience. I don't know one end of the computer from another. What do I have to offer?' Other than I can do marvellous bread buttering.

'You're charming, stylish, wear jewellery well,' he says. 'I think you'd make a wonderful assistant for Ornato.'

I get a brief heartsink moment. Suddenly my new job doesn't look so wonderful. I bet I wouldn't have to wear a baseball cap here. 'I wish you'd said so before.'

'I didn't know that you were really serious about looking, but I have been thinking about employing an assistant for a while. It would free me up to search out new designers, possibly open another branch.'

'Oh. I don't know what to say.'

'How much is Alan paying you?'

'The bare minimum, I think.'

Seymour shrugs as if money is no matter. 'Then I'll pay you more.'

'You can't do that!'

Now he has a glint in those oh so appealing eyes. 'I'll double what he's offered and you can have ten per cent commission on everything that you sell.'

I start to laugh. 'Seymour, that's insane.'

'I want you here at any price, Mrs Lamont-Jones.'

'The Brunch Bunch only wanted me part-time.'

'Name your hours.'

'Ten until three.' Then I could be home in time for my children every day and wouldn't have to rely on Tracey at all.

'Done.'

'It can't be that easy!'

'Why make life difficult? I couldn't stand for you to be in

a shop just a few doors away and not be able to gaze on you all day.'

That makes me flush and my insides go all of a fluster again. I know I might be looking a gift-horse in the mouth, but I ask, 'Are you really sure that there's a job for me here?'

'Of course,' my new boss says. 'There's plenty to do that just gets left undone now.'

'If you're sure.'

'I'm sure.'

'What will I tell Alan at the Brunch Bunch? I feel terrible.' Not fifteen minutes ago we shook on a deal, and he seems such a nice man. 'How can I let him down?'

Seymour bats away my anxieties with a flick of his hand. 'Tell him that his loss is my gain. Surely all's fair in love and war and, this time, the best man won.'

I chew at my lip.

'There'll be a dozen other candidates for him to choose from, Lily,' Seymour stresses. 'Alan's an amiable sort. He won't bear you any ill-will.'

I have to say that I'd rather be in a beautiful shop like this all day, surrounded by wonderful things, than doling out tuna mayonnaise on brown and, with the offer of twice the amount I'd earn at the sandwich bar, how can I really refuse? This is, after all, about getting in as much money as we can, otherwise we'll be stuck in Netherslade Bridge forever.

'Do we have a deal?'

'We do.' My heart's thumping faster again just thinking about it. This beats making sandwiches hands down, doesn't it? Perhaps I might even get to wear some of the jewellery while I'm here.

Even though my fingers are sticky from the éclair, I reach out and shake Seymour's hand. Disconcertingly, he grasps my fingers tightly and doesn't let go.

The sandwich bar isn't half so attractive, but it might just be the safer option. There are too many temptations on offer at Ornato and I don't just mean the jewellery.

Chapter 55

'I must dash,' I tell my new employer when we've lingered a little too long over shaking hands, 'otherwise I'll miss my bus home.' I hesitate before I make my exit. 'But I wondered if you'd buy another piece of jewellery from me before I go.'

Seymour Chapman looks puzzled. 'If you really want to sell it.'

'This is to help out a friend,' I say. 'Someone who's been very good to me.'

He opens the safe and removes the brown envelope that bears my signature.

'Just something small. I only need a few hundred pounds.'

'This?' Seymour holds up a pendant with a swirl of gold studded with a pearl.

Selling off my jewellery gets easier every time, but I'm still hoping that Laurence gets a job before we've worked our way through it all. Just wait until I tell him that I've managed to bag myself a smashing position!

Seymour counts the money out and hands it over to me.

'Thank you,' I say. 'Now I really must dash.'

'Don't. I'll run you home. Stay and have another cup of tea. I have a little bit of work to do, but why not take some time to acquaint yourself with the stock?'

'We haven't even discussed when you want me to start.'

'Now,' Seymour says. 'Start now.'

I laugh again. 'This is madness.'

'If it is, then it feels rather pleasant.'

'Rather pleasant,' I echo. Then I realise that if Seymour runs me home then he'll see where I live. 'I can't let you take me home.'

'Whyever not?'

'I don't want you to see where I live.' I feel guilty for saying that, but the truth is that, despite all the people being so lovely to us, the place is still a terrible eyesore. 'It's awful.'

'Then I'll drop you wherever you think is suitable,' he offers. 'I'm not trying to make trouble for you, Lily. I just want to help.'

'Then, thank you. I'd like that. As long as it's not taking you out of your way.'

'Of course not.' Seymour drains his tea and places his hands on his desk. 'Now, I have to tend to some paperwork. Please, browse through the stock and, if you have any questions, we can talk them through on the way home.'

I leave him in peace and wander through to the shop. If I weren't a coward, I could go back to see the man in the sandwich bar and tell him that I've accepted another offer. But I am a coward and, instead, will call him in the morning to let him know that he was gazumped.

In the shop, I stand behind the counter trying to view it as my new domain. I pick up and try on various rings and bracelets, checking the discreet price tags. Gone are the days when I could come in here and leave fifteen minutes later with my credit card several hundred pounds lighter. Who would have thought that one day I would be on the other side of the counter – gamekeeper turned poacher, as it were?

The baubles sparkle on my wrist and fingers. Who would have thought that I'd be working in a shop and yet wouldn't mind? Suddenly, I realise that while my days were perfectly pleasant in my former life, they had no purpose and a lot of the pastimes I had were to simply fill the hours that I spent alone and that, strangely, I'm really relishing the thought of coming to work here. I slip the jewellery off and arrange the pieces back in their proper place in the display. Already, I feel quite proprietorial about them.

A moment later and Seymour is at my shoulder. 'Ready to go?' he says.

'Yes. Whenever you are.'

'I've already set the alarm and I'll show you how to do that tomorrow.'

'I think I'm really going to enjoy working here,' I tell him.

'And I'm going to enjoy having you here.'

Outside, there's a sleek silver Jaguar parked and Seymour holds open the door while I ease myself inside. When he joins me, we purr out into the road and head towards Milton Keynes. I settle back into my seat, enjoying the comfort and luxury while Seymour drives and we listen to the light classical music on the stereo.

A short while later, the country lanes give way to dual carriageways, and then the traffic becomes busier as we get within striking distance of Netherslade Bridge. When I see the first sign to show that we're approaching our estate, I rouse myself from my contented stupor and say to Seymour, 'You can drop me anywhere here.'

He turns to me. 'It doesn't matter to me where you live.'

'It does to me,' I tell him.

With a soft sigh, he pulls over to the side of the road before the turn-off to Netherslade Bridge.

'Thank you.'

'I'll see you in the morning,' Seymour says.

'I'm looking forward to it.'

'Me too. Sure that you're okay here?'

'It will take me five minutes to walk.'

At that he nods and I slip out of the car. Then I stand and watch as Seymour, my new and unexpected employer, drives away.

With a spring in my step, I head home. But as I turn into Netherslade Bridge and am assaulted by the litter and the dumped cars and sofas and the graffiti, my stride slows and the reality of my life starts to weigh down on me once more.

Chapter 56

When I get home, shouldering in the warped door, I find Laurence sitting on the patio in the overgrown garden while the children play in the car which is now barely visible, the grass is so high. He's drinking a cup of tea and staring vacantly into space.

'Kettle's just boiled,' he says when I poke my head outside.

So I go back in and make a cup for myself even though I really don't want another one.

It's six o'clock now and I know that I've not done very much today in comparison with some, but I feel quite drained. Perhaps it's the emotion of finding that I'm not on the job scrapheap and that not one but two people wanted me today – one possibly more than the other. Or perhaps it's the relief of knowing that there will be some sort of money coming in next week, even though it's not a fortune. I sit down on the slabs next to my husband and sip my tea. My stomach growls and I remember that I've eaten nothing today but an éclair. 'Did you think about anything for dinner?'

'Me?' He looks blankly in my direction.

'I thought as I'd been gone so long that you might have started preparation for supper.'

'No,' he admits. 'Though I did wonder where you'd got to.' He glances at where his watch should be to check the time, and we both silently note that it isn't there any more. Perhaps I should have got it out of Seymour's safe for him now that we're not in imminent need of selling it.

Still, at least Laurence had noticed that *I* wasn't here, so I should be thankful for small mercies. And to be fair to my husband, he has never before troubled himself with the minutiae of domestic chores, so perhaps it's unrealistic of me to expect him to pick up the baton now without some cajoling. However, it does mean that my little bubble of joy is now completely and utterly burst and, instead, a prickle of irritation rubs over me.

'What *have* you been doing today?' I ask.

'Nothing much,' he says.

'That's not going to pay the bills, is it?'

'No.' Then Laurence turns to me and his expression is black. 'But it's how you've spent the last fifteen years or more, Lily, so I thought I'd see what it felt like.'

That stings. Yes, I've had a cosseted life, a life of leisure. I'd be the first to admit that I was a lady who lunched. 'But that's because we could afford it,' I point out. 'Now we can't.'

'Don't you think I'm aware of that?' Laurence snaps. 'I have tried everything. I have phoned every single person that I know begging for work, the same with the recruitment agencies. I feel as if I am banging my head against a brick wall. No one wants me, Lily. No one. Just what more do you want me to do?'

The answer is that I don't know. Instead, trying to defuse the argument, I change tack. 'I got a job today.'

'Well, bully for you,' is my husband's crisp response.

'I thought it would help.'

'What are you bringing in? A hundred? A hundred and fifty grand a year?'

'Of course not. I've got a part-time job in a jewellery boutique in Woburn.'

'That's hardly going to get us out of this dump, is it?'

'No,' I concede. 'But it's a start. We can perhaps feed ourselves and pay our bills without having to sell off our valuables.'

'As I said, good for you.' Then he returns to staring into the middle distance.

I didn't expect Laurence to run round the excuse of a garden waving a flag, but I did think he would be pleased for me.

215

I thought he would see it as me striking a blow for Team Lamont-Jones, but clearly this is me against him. My employment is a threat to his stupid manhood or something. I can't be doing with that now. I'm pleased with myself and Laurence will have to lump it. I stand, wearily. 'I'll find something for supper. Is pasta all right?'

'Again?'

'It's cheap and cheerful.'

'Count me out,' Laurence says. Then he gets up and pushes past me. 'I'll be back later.'

I watch him stomp away, sulking, and to be honest, at this moment I really don't care whether he comes back at all.

Chapter 57

Laurence, hands deep in pockets, walked up to the local pub. He tried to close his eyes to the squalor around him, but it wasn't easy. Being at home with no immediate prospects was sending him into a deep depression and he had to do something to snap out of it.

Of course, he should have been pleased that Lily had landed herself a job and was trying her best to help them out. God only knows she'd been a saint in standing by him at all. If Anthony Marquis had messed up like this, would Amanda be happy living in a place like Netherslade Bridge? Well, perhaps 'happy' was stretching it a bit, but Lily did very little in the way of complaining.

He'd been going stir crazy at home all day. There was nothing to do. He couldn't watch television, they had no books, no internet and he had played more Cluedo in the last few weeks than a man should be required to do in a lifetime. He felt like clubbing himself to death with the tea-light or strangling himself with the pink wool. He'd just needed to get out of the house; going to the pub wasn't perhaps the ideal answer, but he had no idea what else to do.

When he looked up, he realised that he'd walked in completely the wrong direction for the pub. Instead, he'd reached the far side of the estate – somewhere that he hadn't ventured before. If possible, it was even more bleak here. The houses looked more rundown and there was a sour scent to the air.

The Grand Union Canal ran through here – a scruffy,

litter-strewn section, totally lacking in charm. The pretty, tourist canal boats that hit this stretch must have thought that they'd accidentally sailed into Hades.

He walked down to the side of the canal and stood on the bank. A slick of oil floated on the water, creating a delightful rainbow pattern that looked completely out of place. Laurence thrust his hands into his pockets. What if he jumped in here, he thought. Wouldn't it be better to let the water close over his head and stop this feeling of uselessness. Would anyone care? Would anyone miss him? Would the world miss one more washed-up, out-of-work, middle-aged man? Would it make it easier for Lily if he just wasn't around? Financially, it would be hard as all the insurance policies he'd thought would ensure their future in the event of a tragedy were courtesy of his company, and now that his services had been dispensed with, his family had no security at all. He was a waste of space.

Laurence leaned forward, testing how far he could go without falling. Would he spread his arms wide or just fall forwards and let the dirty water swallow him? His heart throbbed with pain in his chest. His mouth went dry. It would be easy. So, so easy. No more worry; no more humiliation; no more struggle. This would be an end to it all.

While he was lost in thought, contemplating, he'd failed to hear the man with all the dogs come walking by until he was right upon him. One of the dogs nuzzled his leg and made Laurence jump out of his trance.

'Wotcher mate,' the man said.

'Hello,' Laurence responded on auto-pilot.

'You don't want to do that.'

'No?'

'Life's not that bad.'

'Isn't it?'

The man shrugged. 'Come to the pub.'

'That's where I meant to go.'

'Come on then.' He gave a flick of his head.

Laurence wasn't sure whether the man was addressing him or the dogs, but, nevertheless, when they set off again he fell into step with the motley pack. They walked along the canal bank in silence, Laurence still brooding.

'I'm Len,' the man said eventually.

'Laurence.'

Then another few hundred metres without speaking.

'It's the people you leave behind that you hurt the most,' Len said. 'They never recover.'

'No.'

Laurence thought of Lily and Hettie and Hugo and knew that he couldn't leave them behind to sort out the mess alone. He was a husband, a father, and he had a duty to care for those who relied on him.

'Thanks,' he said.

Len shrugged.

Laurence looked at the man with the dirty face and the dirty coat and the mouth that had few teeth, the dogs that clearly adored him, and wondered what his story might be. Then they fell silent again as Laurence didn't know what else to say without seeming impolite. The man just might have saved his life, after all.

Chapter 58

They tied the dogs up outside the pub and they all, as if it was their usual routine, lay quietly on the pavement. While Laurence stood and watched, Len patted their heads, each in turn.

It was the first time he'd been in the Acorn and Squirrel – or 'The Nut' as the locals preferred to call it; in fact, it was the first time he'd been in a pub like this since he'd been a student. But it was clear from the abundance of the clientèle on a week night that The Nut was the social centre for the estate. The place was buzzing. Everyone seemed to know everyone else – except him.

The carpet probably used to be brightly coloured, but now it was black with years of wear and sticky with the residue of a million spilled drinks. The seats were red plastic and, after a quick scan, he saw that most were torn.

Many heads swivelled when he walked across the floor trailing after Len and, feeling self-conscious, Laurence was mightily relieved to see that Skull was propping up the bar. Another friendly face. Laurence and Len went and took up places next to him.

'All right, Lozzer?' Skull said with a welcoming nod. 'Len.' He clapped the dog man on the back. Then to the barman: 'Get these gentlemen a beer, Brian.'

It probably wasn't the right place to be ordering a glass of decent red or a gin and tonic, which were Laurence's usual drinks of choice, so a pint of beer it was.

'Thank you.' In his haste to depart, Laurence hadn't thought to check how much cash he had in his pocket. In the places he used to frequent, he would have simply put a credit card behind the bar and would have started a tab. He guessed that wouldn't be so easy in The Nut. It wouldn't be easy anywhere now, he remembered, as all of his cards had been cancelled.

'What brings you here?' his one and only friend in Netherslade Bridge asked.

'Had to get out,' Laurence told him. 'Being unemployed isn't suiting me at all. I've got nothing to do all day.'

Thankfully, Len was drinking his beer silently and gratefully beside them and said nothing about finding him standing at the edge of the canal considering his mortality.

'You need to come down the allotment with me,' Skull said. 'I'd find plenty to keep you busy.'

'I might just do that.' Laurence sank his pint, suppressing a relieved and somehow contented sigh. What had he been thinking of? Nothing was so bad that he had to consider ending it all. They could get through this, come out the other side as survivors. 'Do you work?'

'Cash in hand,' Skull said. 'A bit of this and that. Some labouring, some garden maintenance. I'm on the sick, down to my bad back.'

'Oh.' Was it only he who found the thought of claiming benefits completely abhorrent? Perhaps he should swallow his pride and get everything he could out of the state. Goodness only knows, he'd paid enough in tax over the years to be due a little bit back.

Two more burly men joined them at the bar. Skull conducted the introductions. 'Digger and Danny,' he said to Laurence. 'Lozzer,' he said to Digger and Danny. 'Beer?'

Five more pints appeared. One was handed to Len who stood at the bar, but didn't contribute further to the conversation. He learned that Digger and Danny were brothers, that Digger drove JCBs and that Danny did 'door work' – whatever that was. Then five more pints appeared and they were joined by Metal Mick who had his own garage and by Greek John who had a kebab van that was constantly being raided for selling drugs.

Then Len said he was going and headed outside back to the dogs. Laurence felt that he should say something, perhaps go after the man, thank him. But he felt ridiculously tongue-tied and just plain ridiculous, so he watched the man leave, vowing that one day he would make it up to him.

Their now rather merry band decamped from the bar to the pool table and soon, too soon, Laurence lost count of how many games of pool he had played and against whom and how many pints he had drunk. He thought that he might have won more games than he lost, but couldn't be sure. If he had, it was more by good luck than good management. There was much back-slapping and joshing and Laurence was included in all of it.

At one point he looked up from the pool table and Skull winked at him. 'You're all right, Lozzer,' he said. 'A top bloke.'

But after that everything went very cloudy and Laurence remembered little else.

Chapter 59

In my husband's absence, the children and I have risotto made from Skull's vegetables, since even I am tiring of pasta and tinned tomatoes. I'm also glad to see that my culinary skills are making a resurgence as I'd started to wonder whether my children would get rickets or scurvy as we weren't eating nearly so much fresh fruit and veg as before. It seems to be so much more expensive to have the kind of diet that we used to, and as soon as I'm working I'm not going to have hours to spend preparing a meal every day as I once did. Thank goodness our new friend has kindly taken to supplementing our diet with his homegrown produce. I don't know what I'd do without him. I'm thinking that I might start growing some herbs of my own on the kitchen windowsill to add flavour to our food.

I have to bear in mind that Hettie and Hugo, on the other hand, love their new temporary diet of chips and chicken nuggets and frozen pizza, and don't have to have food coaxed down them as they did before. Again I wonder if I was doing everything wrong when I thought I was doing everything right. I will try to strive for balance in my new phase of cooking. I'm sure my children won't care if they never set eyes on grilled sea bass ever again.

'Hugo used the "c" word today,' my daughter kindly informs me as she spoons in her risotto in a languorous way.

After I splutter on my own risotto, I turn to my son. 'Hugo?'

'Everyone uses it,' he says with a shrug. 'It's no biggie.'

'Well, I think it *is* "a biggie",' I tell him. 'I won't have you using language like that.' Just because they're now being educated by the state there's no need for standards to slip. Stonelands would never have put up with this.

'But they *are* chavs at my new school,' he insists.

'Oh,' I say. 'That was the "c" word?'

'What else?' My child rolls his eyes.

What else, indeed?

'How are you liking your new school?' I ask tentatively.

'Great,' Hugo says with a big grin. 'We don't have to do anywhere near as much work and we can text each other all the time. It's really easy.'

I am just very glad that I'm not paying for this.

'I like my teacher,' Hettie says. I think of the Gothic and multi-pierced Ms Davy with a shudder. 'When I grow up I'm going to wear black lipstick and get a silver thing in my tongue.' My daughter shows me her tongue in case I'm unsure what one is.

God help me, I think. God help me when they are teenagers.

When we've finished supper and have cleared away, we troupe round en masse to Tracey's house. It's no hardship for my children as next door has television and computer games. In fact, I struggle to get them *out* of the place, if I'm honest.

On the way, Len Eleven Dogs greets us with a wave and his usual 'Wotcher', and we all stop and fuss the animals.

The minute we're inside Tracey's front door, all four children disappear upstairs together and the two of us sit at the kitchen table. My neighbour opens a bottle of wine. Another thing that I've realised in the last few weeks is that a bottle of £2.99 plonk from the local supermarket does the job just as well as a fifteen-pound bottle of fine French wine.

'I got a job today,' I tell her.

'That's fab,' she says. 'Then we really deserve a drink.' My friend raises her glass to mine. 'To your new job.'

'I'm nervous,' I admit. 'I start tomorrow. It all seems a bit sudden.'

'You'll be fine.' Tracey swigs at her wine. 'Tell me all about it.'

'It's at the little jewellery shop in Woburn – Ornato. I'm just going to be a sales assistant and do a bit of paperwork.' At least, I think so. 'I'll be working for the chap who's been buying my jewellery from me.'

224

'Then here's to him.'

We toast Seymour Chapman and as we do I wonder if I'm more nervous about starting work again after all these years of idle pursuits or whether I'm more worried about spending my days in close proximity to someone as attractive as Seymour.

I push the thought away from my mind and instead, dig into my handbag. 'Here,' I say to Tracey. 'I want you to have this.' Pulling out the two hundred pounds that Seymour gave me today, I slide it across the table to my friend.

My friend gapes at the cash. 'What's this?'

'I sold a pendant. I want you to have the money. You said you were a bit strapped.'

'So are you,' she reminds me. 'I can't take this.' She pushes it back to me.

I do the same in reverse. 'Tracey, I don't know how we would have managed without you. At least let me help you while I can. If this job works out then I'll have some regular money coming in.'

'I can't take it, Lily. It's too much.' She pushes the money back towards me again. Then she looks a bit shifty. 'Besides, I contacted another loan shark today.'

'Oh, Tracey.'

'He's okay. I think. He's a bit more dodgy than Freddie . . .'

That's pretty dodgy, I'd say.

'. . . but I was able to get five hundred off him straight away, no questions asked. That'll see me right.'

I sigh. 'I wish you'd let me help.'

'It'll be cool.' She waves away my fears. 'I can handle it. This is how I've always lived, Lily. You get used to it.'

But I don't want to get used to it. I don't want to have a hand-to-mouth existence. I don't want to dread the postman coming as I do now. I don't want to have to resort to using dodgy dealers and loan sharks. I want to have money in the bank again. I want to sleep through the night once more and not wake up in a cold sweat at three o'clock in the morning wondering how we're going to pay our bills.

Chapter 60

At two o'clock in the morning, I am still pacing the floor. Of Laurence, my dear husband, there is no sign.

I came home from Tracey's house feeling rather more mellow than when I left the house at about eight o'clock. Laurence still hadn't reappeared. The children had a bath, went to bed. I had a cup of tea and followed them at about ten o'clock. It's so much easier to get plenty of sleep when there are no other distractions. At midnight, however, I woke up and realised that Laurence still hadn't come home and then I started to worry.

Now I'm panicking. I am a hair's breadth away from phoning the police. What if he's so down and depressed about our situation that he's done something stupid? How could I live with myself if our last few words together on this earth were harsh ones? I've tried his mobile a million times, but it goes straight to voicemail and Laurence is the sort of man who's spent the last ten years with it permanently clamped to his ear. It's a wonder he hasn't got a brain tumour. But then I think perhaps he has. What if he's blacked out somewhere, unable to call for help? He could be in a ditch, have fallen into the river – Furzton Lake isn't far from here and the canal runs along the back of the estate – or he could have stumbled onto one of the many busy dual carriageways that intersect the city.

Pacing some more, I think that I can't just stay here. I'm going to have to go out and look for him at least in the immediate vicinity of the house. I'll go and knock up Tracey and see if she can keep an eye on the children. I'd take them

226

with me, but they have school tomorrow and I don't want them trailing round Netherslade Bridge in the middle of the night looking for their father.

Just as I resolve to do that, I hear a commotion outside the house and rush to the bedroom window to look out. I can't see anything, but there's definitely someone outside my front door. I hope to goodness that this is Laurence and that we're not about to be burgled again while I'm alone in the house.

Then I hear a burst of uncontrolled giggling and lots of shushing, so I fling on my dressing-gown and fly down the stairs. Through the glass in the door – the one door that has been repaired and now has glass rather than plywood – I can see a bunch of burly shapes. Oh, heaven help me. What if it's the burglar come back as I'd feared, this time with associates? My stomach drops as if I'm on a rollercoaster. What can I do? I can't hide. It would be pointless phoning the police. By the time they arrived – even if they bothered to come out – the heavies would be long gone. I have to face this and face this alone. Perhaps if I confront them and the element of surprise is on my side, then they might scarper before they can do me any harm.

My heart hammering in my chest, I wrest the door open and standing before me are four men the size of brick outhouses all tittering like silly schoolgirls. Between them they're bearing a wheelbarrow and in it, giggling the loudest, is my husband.

When I appear, the men pushing the wheelbarrow fall silent and do their level best to appear sober. They fail. Only Laurence is left chuckling like a loon.

So not burglars come to murder us in our beds after all. Just a bunch of half-cut, silly men. As the red mist clears from my eyes, I recognise Skull.

'Lozzer,' he says in a stage whisper. 'Loz! You're home, mate.'

At that my husband rouses himself from his stupor and leers at me. His clothes are all dishevelled and, in his hand, he's still clutching a pint glass – albeit now empty, the contents either in Laurence's stomach or on the path on his way home.

'He's feeling a bit crook,' Skull informs me.

'Thank you,' I say tightly as I remember my manners. 'Thank you for bringing him home.'

'No worries.' Skull holds up a hand to me and grins like a madman.

Laurence's gaze roves towards me. 'I love you,' he says without entirely focusing. 'I bloody love you. You're the best wife. The *best*.'

My husband tries to push himself out of the wheelbarrow and fails, falling backwards into it once again. His cohorts all splutter again and double up with laughter.

'I love these guys too,' he sighs. 'I love you. I love you all.'

I also sigh. 'I think we'd better try to get him inside.'

Two of the blokes who I don't know from Adam come forward and start to heave my husband unceremoniously from his wheelbarrow. They all, as I could have predicted, find this hilarious and convulse with laughter again. I'm tired now. Bone tired. I just need to go to bed.

'I have had the *very* best night of my life,' Laurence 'Lozzer' Lamont-Jones informs me expansively. 'The *very* best!'

And I veer between wanting to kill my husband and being so relieved that he's not lying dead somewhere and has come home to me.

Chapter 61

Of course, Laurence spent the rest of the night being sick in the bathroom while I sponged his face and made sympathetic cooing noises while trying not to give in to the temptation to club him to death with the toilet brush.

He did also tell me a hundred times more that he loved me. The feeling, this morning, is not reciprocated. Relief at him being safe very quickly morphed into irritation at how he could behave like such an idiot when he knew that it was my first day back at work in more years than I care to admit.

Now he's still comatose in the bed while I am stomping around the bedroom getting ready. The children and I rush down our breakfast. They squabble incessantly and I can't summon up the energy to stop them. When they were away at Stonelands they seemed to develop some sort of reverence for each other and even looked forward to the times they spent together in the holidays. Now they are at home and together all the time they fight like cat and dog. What's the saying about familiarity breeding contempt?

I wanted a gentle, quiet start to today, but it seems that isn't to be. To punish Laurence further, I don't even kiss him goodbye. Not that he'll notice. When we emerge from the house, me nagging the kids like a shrew and them dragging their heels, I notice that Skull is still fast asleep on the skanky sofa outside our house. Of the other drunkards there is, thankfully, no sign. I decide to leave our neighbour sleeping peacefully as he seems to be coming to no harm and the weather is mild. One day I will get all of the rubbish cleared from here, including the sofa-cum-flophouse.

As we pass, Tracey comes out of her house with Charlize and Keanu and we fall into step together. I complain to Tracey about my disturbed night and my ridiculously drunk husband and she coos sympathetically in all the right places. We walk to school, me grumbling to Tracey, and Hugo and Hettie grumbling tiredly between themselves. Then, when all the children are safely inside, Tracey escorts me until I reach the bus stop.

'I'm terrified,' I admit as we wait for the bus to arrive.

'You'll be fine,' my friend assures me.

But when it does arrive, she hugs me tightly. And, as I mount the step, I turn to see her wiping a tear from her eye. She is clearly as worried as I am.

On the journey, I struggle to keep my eyes open after just a few hours of sleep, and my palms are damp with nerves. At ten o'clock – the duly appointed time – I enter the calm world of Ornato where there are no puking husbands and no squabbling children, no wood-chip wallpaper and no winos in the front garden.

I almost sigh out loud with relief. The cool white walls, the glittering glass cases of jewellery, the soft, smiling welcome from Seymour seem a world away from my life and offer a glimpse of sanity when I was beginning to think that all had turned to madness. I want to lie on the tasteful oak flooring and stroke it.

'I'm here,' I say unnecessarily.

'So you are,' Seymour reciprocates. He helps me out of my jacket and I hang it up behind the office door. A sure sign that I've arrived. 'We'll start with a cup of tea,' my boss says. 'Then I can show you how the computer works and how to enter the sales figures into Excel.'

Now I really am worried.

'You'll be fine,' he says, when he sees my concerned frown. 'I'm a very patient teacher.'

So with the promised cup of tea, we sit side-by-side as he takes me through the basics of computing. And, to be honest,

I realise that I do actually know much more than I thought. I can send email, open Word documents and so Excel doesn't look too complicated at all when Seymour shows me that. I have done a lot of these things in connection with my voluntary work and with the Women's Institute, and somehow I just thought business systems would be so much more complicated. I'm relieved to find that they're not.

I have my first two customers in the shop mid-morning and they make all the right noises about the jewellery and buy two pieces each. Seymour seems pleased with my progress.

It's one o'clock, lunchtime, before I come up for air and I realise that I haven't thought of my husband or my children at all.

In a small, sunny courtyard just behind the shop, Seymour and I sit quietly and eat sandwiches that he kindly collected for us from the Brunch Bunch. He also told Alan Green, the manager, of my change of heart and, thankfully, he was very understanding. Though I feel terrible letting Seymour do my dirty work for me, I'm also very relieved that he did.

The courtyard has a set of white wrought-iron furniture in the middle, surrounded by a dozen potted red geraniums. It's like a little slice of the Mediterranean and very welcome indeed.

'My first morning at work has been very civilised,' I say to Seymour.

He gives me one of his languid smiles. 'I hope there'll be many more of them to come.'

And, if it carries on like this, I feel the same way too.

Chapter 62

Laurence woke with a stonking hangover. He peered through a half-open eye at his phone. It was already ten-thirty. The house was empty, both Lily and the children gone and he hadn't heard a thing. He went to move and the room spun lazily round his head so he flopped back on the pillow.

Oh my goodness. It was all coming back to him now. The heavy drinking, the pool games, the trip home in the wheelbarrow. It had seemed such fun at the time. Now it was clear he was paying the price for it. Lily had every right to be furious.

A rap on the door raised him from his reverie. Pulling on a T-shirt with his boxers, he staggered down to open it.

Standing there was Skull. 'I've spent the night on your sofa, Lozzer.' His new friend indicated the sofa in the garden. 'Can I use the lav?'

'Yes, yes,' Laurence said, trying not to nod his head. 'Come in.'

'You're a lifesaver,' Skull said.

While Skull used the facilities, Laurence put the kettle on and flicked on the grill to warm.

'There's only one thing for a hangover,' Laurence said as Skull joined him. 'Bacon sarnies.'

'Now you're talking.'

Laurence made two mugs of tea and piled sugar in them both. He followed that with two rounds of bacon sandwiches each – a pile of bacon, plenty of tomato sauce (thank God they'd got proper bottled ketchup and not the organic, real tomato purée that Lily used to buy that cost a fortune and tasted like crap).

He left the fat on the bacon, slathered the bread with butter and cut the sandwiches in two halves rather than the four triangles that Lily insisted on. Having bonded quite heavily with Skull and his mates last night, he didn't want him thinking that he was some sort of city poof who didn't know how to eat man's food.

Laurence found them both napkins in the cupboard, realising that this might not be in keeping with his new macho image, but old habits die hard – and they went to sit out on the small patio they'd constructed together in the weak sunshine. They polished off the sandwiches and the sweet tea without speaking.

When they were done, Skull smacked his lips in appreciation. 'Have to be off, Lozzer,' he said. 'Gotta get down the allotment.'

'Oh, right.'

They both stood up.

'What are you up to today, mate?' Skull enquired.

Laurence shrugged. 'Nothing much.' Nothing at all, in fact. A day of kicking his heels loomed ahead of him. He couldn't face going back to the recruitment agencies. The children were at school. Even Lily had found herself a job to go to. What on earth was he going to do with himself all day?

'Digging's just the thing to clear your head,' Skull advised. 'I've got some potatoes and carrots to lift and I'd like to get some spring cabbages in. Plus I've got some winter salad to sow today.'

'Sounds good,' Laurence concurred. After years of being cooped up in a office the thought of getting his hands dirty and doing some physical work was quite appealing.

Skull lifted his heavy shoulders. 'Come with me.'

Laurence brightened. 'Can I?'

'Always happy with an extra pair of hands,' his new friend said.

Laurence clapped his hand against Skull's shoulder and tried not to wince as his fingers reverberated against the immovable muscle. 'Then let's do it.'

They both strode, fortified, towards the door. Then Skull pulled up short. 'Just one thing,' he said. 'I wonder what the hell happened to my wheelbarrow?'

233

Chapter 63

Laurence had stripped off his shirt and the sun was beating down on his back. It felt good to be getting some exercise, to be doing something constructive. He'd never previously considered himself an allotment type of man. Weren't the people who had allotments all new-age, hippy types? He glanced over at Skull. Def Leppard – so he'd been told – pumped out of the ghetto blaster in his shed, and Laurence thought perhaps not. The shed was made of assorted planks of wood and old doors. There was a set of motorbike handles attached high on the front. Below it was a reasonably skilled painting of a skull and crossbones with flames coming from it.

'Did you do that?'

Skull shrugged. 'Yeah. I like to dabble. Studied Fine Art at college, but dropped out. Well, it was hard to carry on the course while I was banged up.'

Laurence felt his throat go tight. 'I see.'

With no further explanation as to why he had found himself residing at Her Majesty's Pleasure, Skull had given him a spade and set him to work on digging up the potatoes and carrots that were ready. It was the first time that Laurence had involved himself with vegetables, particularly the growing of them. Eating them was about as far as he'd previously got. He couldn't even recall the last time he'd peeled a potato or anything else for that matter. Now, as he pulled a bunch of vibrant orange carrots from the ground, still dusted with black earth, he could appreciate the joy of growing your own food, lifting it from the land and taking it to your own table.

Surely this was the sort of work that men were meant to do, not sit number-crunching in offices all day long.

Laurence stood up and stretched his back. He and Skull had worked side by side in quiet companionship for the last few hours. 'Do you think that I could get one of these?'

Skull, who was planting cabbages in another bed, raised his head. 'An allotment?'

'Yes.'

'There's a waiting list,' Skull informed him, 'but there's nothing to stop you from putting your name down. Might take a while. In the meantime you can help me out here if you like. There's plenty of produce to share.'

'I'd like that.'

Skull spat on his hand and held it out. After a moment's reluctance, Laurence shook it.

'A deal,' Skull intoned. 'A solemn bond. Till death us do part.'

Laurence felt the horror register on his face. What had he agreed to?

'Just joking, Lozzer,' Skull grinned. 'You take life too seriously.'

He laughed. Perhaps he did. But the stakes had been so high in his former life that it had left little time for fun. He wondered at all the money he had made over the years and, yet, had never really had any time to kick back and enjoy.

After the carrots and potatoes had been lifted and the cabbages and salad were in the ground and Laurence's hangover had long since disappeared, his friend leaned on his spade and wiped his brow. 'What about we call it a day?' Skull suggested.

Laurence checked the clock on his phone. 'Is that the time already? I don't know where the day has gone.'

'Nothing like hard labour to take your mind off your worries.'

Also leaning on his spade, Laurence agreed with a nod. 'You're right.'

'I suggest that we cement our new partnership by cracking a few tins open.'

'I'm all for that,' Laurence said.

235

So they downed tools and decamped to the shed. Inside, Skull shook out two striped deckchairs and set them out in front of the door in a narrow band of shade. Bobbing in a bucket of water, there was a six-pack of lager. Skull removed two cans, flipped the openers and handed one to Laurence.

'To vegetables,' Laurence proposed.

'And all who grow them,' Skull added.

They sat in the two deckchairs and relaxed.

'This is the life,' Laurence said, eyes closed against the sinking sun. It wasn't likely to earn him much money, but he could think of a lot worse ways to spend his days.

Then his mobile rang. He thought that it might be Lily, but he didn't recognise the number on the caller ID. Standing up, he flicked open the phone.

'Laurence Lamont-Jones,' he said.

'The other bloke turned down the job, lad,' Christopher Cherry's booming tones announced. 'Are you still up for it?'

'Yes.' Laurence fell to his knees in the dirt. 'Oh yes.'

'Can you start Monday?'

'I can start tomorrow.'

'Fair enough,' Mr Cherry said. 'I'll see you tomorrow then, lad. Nine o'clock.'

'Thank you,' Laurence said. 'Thank you so much.' He hung up and stared up at Skull. There were tears in his eyes when he told his friend, 'I've got a job.'

The shaven-headed, tattooed man pulled him to his feet and grasped him in a bear hug. 'Well done, Lozzer!'

'I've got a job,' Laurence shouted. He wanted everyone to know. On the allotments a variety of people poked their heads out of their sheds to see what the noise was. 'I've got a job,' he shouted again. 'A bloody job!'

His audience burst into spontaneous applause as Skull grabbed him by the waist and together they waltzed around the allotment to Def Leppard, Laurence shouting out his joy to anyone who'd listen.

Chapter 64

Laurence had bought two bottles of red wine at the local shop and had lashed out on some chicken breast fillets. He could barely contain his excitement.

Skull, next to him, sipped at his glass of extraordinarily cheap Merlot as he leaned against the kitchen cupboards. 'Now fry the chicken breasts in the oil.'

Laurence did as he was told. On the chopping board there were carrots, onions, potatoes, all peeled, sliced and diced. And all, of course, provided by Skull.

There were sliced green beans, courtesy of the allotment too, waiting to be blanched as a side dish. He'd bought a dessert too – a frozen one, admittedly – some sort of berry and meringue concoction that Skull assured him would be the perfect accompaniment to his main course. That was currently thawing out on the windowsill, the dying sun helping to speed the progress.

'Just until they're golden brown,' Skull instructed solicitously. 'Then add the veggies.'

'Veggies. Right.' Laurence tipped them into the pan and stirred anxiously. He didn't think he'd ever cooked dinner for Lily before. Not really. Maybe he'd opened some cheese, a box of crackers, but nothing more strenuous. That had always been his wife's domain. Very rarely had he arrived home before nine o'clock and you could hardly start in the kitchen at that time of night.

'Why don't you stay for dinner?' Laurence suggested to his culinary adviser. 'Help us to celebrate.'

'You should have a romantic meal with your missus,' Skull advised. 'You both deserve it.'

'You're right,' he said. 'I should have bought some candles.'

'Tracey next door will have some. She'll give you a lend.'

'Yes, yes. She seems to have everything.' And always seemed willing for them to borrow whatever they needed.

Sighing to himself, Laurence felt as if a cloud had lifted from him, a weight had gone from his shoulders. Lily would be delighted to learn that he'd got a job. At long last! This was a good way to put the past behind them and start out on a new track.

He felt bad that he'd reacted negatively to Lily's announcement of her new job; he'd put that right straight away. Hopefully, she'd enjoyed her first day and would see tonight's dinner as a suitable apology.

'Now stir the flour in, cook for a minute. Then add the stock.'

Flour. Cook for a minute. Add stock. There was more to this cooking lark than he'd imagined. But then for the last ten years or more his meals had appeared in front of him on a regular basis without him ever having to think about the effort it had required for them to do so. He should have said thank you to Lily more often. It didn't stop there either. There was a lot that he'd done over the last few years that he wished he'd done differently.

He poured the wishy-washy-looking liquid into the pan and immediately it bubbled and started to thicken. Laurence was quite pleased with himself.

'Turn it right down and put the lid on. It'll be done in about an hour,' Skull said. 'Don't let it dry out.'

'Don't let it dry out,' Laurence repeated.

'The beans will take five minutes. Don't overcook them. There's nothing worse than soggy beans.'

Laurence hardly dared take his eye off the pan. 'Nothing worse than soggy beans.'

'Serve them with a nice dob of butter and plenty of seasoning.'

He nodded vehemently. 'Dob of butter. Plenty of seasoning.'

Skull drained his glass. 'See you later for a beer with the boys?'

'One,' Laurence said, risking taking an eye off his dish to glance at his friend. 'One beer. If you bring me home in a wheelbarrow again, Lily won't let me in.'

Skull chuckled. 'Plus you have a new job to go to in the morning.'

They high-fived each other and Laurence clasped his friend, laughing out loud. 'Yes.' He liked the sound of that. 'And I have a new job to start in the morning.'

Chapter 65

My first day at work is going well until late afternoon. I've stayed past my allotted time to show willing and now I'm just thinking about tidying up and heading for home, when the door chime rings and in walks Amanda Marquis.

She slips off her sunglasses and we both start in alarm as we make eye-contact. Of course, I should have seen this coming. Ornato is the place where people like Amanda, my former friends, would do their jewellery shopping, and I'd mentioned that I'd been selling my own jewellery here which may have brought it to the forefront of her mind again. But I didn't give a moment's thought to the possibility that she might well breeze in through the door while I was behind the counter when I accepted Seymour's offer.

My former friend is the first to recover her composure and speak. 'Well, well,' she says, eyeing me up and down as if she's never seen me before in her life. 'I didn't expect to see *you* here.'

I bite down the uncharitable retorts that spring first to mind. 'No,' I say softly. 'I just started here today.'

'Having to work now?'

'Yes,' I say to her, fighting down the bile that's rising. 'Things aren't getting any better yet.'

'Laurence has become a bit of a pariah in the City.' There's a smirk behind the condescending smile.

How I would like to wipe it off her face. 'So I believe.' *No doubt helped by your husband, Anthony, spreading the story of the debt that we owe to him.* But I'm going to be professional about this. I don't want to be rude to one of Seymour's customers, no matter how much I long to be. Business is business. 'Can I show you something?'

'I've been looking at this.' She points a manicured finger at the display case.

One of my favourites too. Amanda has her beady eye on a Lisa Perona open-heart pendant in eighteen-carat gold, set with pavé diamonds. It's beautiful.

'Would you like to try it on?'

Amanda nods.

I slip it out of the glass cabinet, surreptitiously removing the price tag of over five thousand pounds. Amanda recoils slightly when she sees the purple paint job on my acrylic talons. I think at that moment I start to really like them. It shows how used to them I've become as I have no trouble opening the tiny loop of the fastening. My old friend leans in towards me, offering her slender neck. 'I must say,' she giggles. 'This seems very strange – you *serving* me.'

I don't rise to the bait. 'It looks absolutely lovely,' I say, offering her the mirror to admire herself in. And it does, there's no denying it. I just think now how much more I could do with five thousand pounds rather than wear it round my neck. But I mustn't think like that. Amanda has the money to buy this necklace and I shouldn't begrudge her that. Not a few months ago this could have easily been me preening in here.

'I'll take it,' she says.

At that moment, Seymour swans in from the back. 'Mrs Marquis,' he says. 'A pleasure to see you again.'

'Thank you.' Amanda goes all girlish.

'I'll take over, Lily,' Seymour says. 'You'll want to be going home.'

'I . . . er . . . yes,' I agree.

'Would you like it gift-wrapped?' he asks.

'No,' Amanda answers with a self-deprecating laugh, hand on her chest. 'It's just a little present for me.'

'How lovely.' Seymour slips the necklace into Ornato's trademark white and silver box. 'That will be seven thousand, five hundred pounds.'

I step forward, going to correct the price. Seymour winks at me.

Amanda produces her platinum credit card with a flourish and Seymour processes it efficiently, smiling all the while. He gives her the credit card, slips the box into an exquisite carrier bag and hands it over. 'I look forward to the next time,' he says.

Amanda flushes. 'Thank you.' Then, without saying anything else to me, she breezes out.

We both watch her go, bouncing down the high street, swinging the Ornato bag.

'You naughty, naughty man,' I say without looking at him.

'Until she can play nicely, she's going to pay over the odds in here.'

'There's bad blood between us,' I admit.

'You handled her very professionally,' my boss says. 'Well done.'

'I wanted to choke her.'

'I'm not surprised.' He drapes an arm casually round my shoulder and hugs me gently. The heat of his body is disconcerting. The scent of his aftershave divine. 'The one thing you should learn about wealth is never to flaunt it. That's unforgivably vulgar.'

I ease myself from Seymour's embrace as it feels too comforting, too reassuring, and the temptation is to melt into his body, lean against him for support – emotionally as well as physically. Busying myself by tidying the counter, I say, 'I think I've been equally guilty of that in the past.'

'Then I'm sure, given your current circumstances, you've learned from that.'

'I have indeed.'

I don't ever want to be like Amanda again. I don't ever want to forget the value of money. I don't ever want to think that I'm better than others just because I have more cash in the bank or a bigger house or a flashier car.

Netherslade Bridge might be one of the worst estates in the area, but the people there have taught me the value of friendship and caring once more, and it's a lesson that I don't want to forget.

Chapter 66

The bus was late so it's nearly six o'clock when I get off at the Netherslade Bridge stop. When I do get home I'm pleased to see that Skull has vacated the sofa in my front garden. I'm only halfway down our path when the door bursts open and Laurence sprints to meet me, lifting me into his arms and twirling me round. I feel like the Prodigal Daughter come home. If I'd known that my going out to work would have this effect on my husband, I would have done it years ago.

'I've got a job,' Laurence breathes in my ear. 'A job!'

'Where? When?'

'The one at Cherry's Farm. I start tomorrow.'

'Oh, Laurence.' My heart soars. 'That's wonderful news.'

He kisses me hard. Len and his dozen or more dogs walk by; he's looking embarrassed. 'Wotcher.'

'My husband's got a job,' I tell him.

His careworn face splits into a toothless smile. 'Nice one.' He pauses on the pavement and the dogs curl round his legs. 'Everything okay then?'

His comment is clearly directed to my husband. The men exchange a glance that I don't understand.

'Yes,' Laurence says, lowering his eyes. 'Everything's fine, thanks. Thanks very much.'

And Len continues on his way.

'What was all that about?'

'Nothing.' Then my husband lowers me to the ground. 'How did your day go?'

'Fine,' I say. 'Absolutely fine. The only hiccup was that Amanda came in to buy something.'

'Was she okay with you?'

'Just about,' I admit. 'She clearly quite enjoyed seeing me behind the counter.'

'It won't be for long,' Laurence swears. 'I promise you. The Lamont-Joneses are on our way back up.'

'I think I'm going to enjoy it,' I say honestly. Better than I did staying at home all day. But let's see if I still feel like that when the novelty wears off.

It's just nice to think that Laurence will be earning again and that it will take the pressure off us. We can start to clear our debts and get back on our feet again.

Arm-in-arm we go inside. There's a wonderful aroma coming from the kitchen. 'Dinner?'

'Ha, ha!' Laurence says. 'I am a man of many talents.'

So it seems. In the living room the table has been set for two. There's even a candelabra with two pink candles in the middle. 'From Tracey?'

'Who else?' Laurence laughs. 'I told her that I wanted to cook you a romantic dinner and she insisted on taking the children for the evening.'

'And they couldn't resist the lure of the huge television?'

'Of course.'

'Did you tell her your news?'

'She was delighted.'

I'm in the kitchen now, lifting the lid on Laurence's bubbling pan. 'So? What's cooking?'

'You'll have to wait and see,' he says. 'I confess that this is Skull's recipe. In the absence of any cookery books, he came to my rescue. Most of the produce is from his allotment too. I spent the afternoon there with him. I think we should get one.'

This is the most animated I've seen my husband in years. 'An allotment?'

'It's the most marvellous fun,' he assures me. 'And excellent physical exercise.' He flexes a muscle at me.

I raise an eyebrow.

Laurence stirs his pot. 'I was getting worried that it would burn. I thought you'd be home earlier.'

'I thought I'd stay a bit later while you were here for the children. Show willing.' I think of all the dinners that I've juggled with to keep them from burning when Laurence's return home was somewhat irregular.

'Ready for me to serve?' he asks.

'I'll just wash my hands.'

As I go to leave the kitchen, he sweeps me into his arms again. 'This is going to be wonderful for us,' he says. 'Everything is coming up roses.'

I close my eyes and sigh to myself. Thank God, I think. *Thank God.*

Chapter 67

The chicken casserole, Laurence's first culinary adventure, is excellent – helped, surely, by the freshness of the ingredients. In our borrowed candlelight even this shabby room looks romantic. While my husband put the finishing touches to supper, I slipped into one of my strappy holiday dresses and sexy sandals. I wish I'd had time to repaint my purple nails in a more tender shade and do something with my hair.

'This is wonderful,' I say.

His fingers find mine. 'Thank you.'

'I'm just so thrilled that you've got the job.'

Laurence's smile is pensive. 'It's the first time I've ever been second choice,' he says. 'I only got it because someone else turned it down.'

'You mustn't think like that. It's fate,' I assure him. 'You were meant to get this job.'

'The salary's nothing like we were used to.'

'We'll manage.' Let's face it, our overheads have dropped considerably.

Then Laurence tells me exactly how much he'll be earning now.

'How much?' I feel my mouth drop open. The momentary relief I felt dissipates just as quickly as it came.

'It's a normal wage,' Laurence stresses. 'This is what normal people live on.'

'How?'

'We'll find out soon enough,' my husband points out.

'We'll budget tightly. Keep our expenses as low as possible. Put some away if we can, to pay off our debts. Not fall into the same trap as we did before. We used to manage, Lily. When we were first together we had very little.'

But that was then, I think. As you get older, you get used to a certain level of comfort that's so hard to give up. How will we ever leave Netherslade Bridge, have our own home again if our joint income is less than what Laurence used to spend on wine in a year?

I push my plate away from me.

'Finished?'

'Thank you.' I inject as much enthusiasm as I can into my voice. I should be glad, just glad that Laurence has got something. I should be glad that he's not going to be flogging himself to death in the City every day, never around to see us. But, in my heart, I realise that it won't completely take the pressure off us. We won't be miraculously whisked back to the barn, have high-end cars, horses, all the trappings that we did have. The children will still stay at the local school. I will still work, and scrimping and saving, mending and making do will become the way our lives are led. 'That was lovely.'

I appreciate it even more that Laurence has tried so hard to make this a nice evening for us. When did we last spend some quality time together? When will we ever be able to go away for a romantic weekend, just the two of us?

'The children won't be back for some time yet,' Laurence says. 'Fancy a little lie-down after dinner?' There's a twinkle in his eye that's been missing for a long, long time. And I think it's true that a man's testosterone is directly linked to his status in life. We haven't made love in months – if you don't count one faltering attempt – and it's easy to see why. His self-esteem has been at rock bottom and this failure has struck him to the very core.

Laurence takes my hand and leads me up the stairs and I try not to notice the peeling wood chip and the worn carpet.

In the bedroom, my husband slips my straps from my shoulders and replaces them with hot, tender kisses. My body shivers delightfully in response.

'Cold?' he queries.

'No,' I whisper. 'Not cold. *Hot.*' I unzip my dress and let it fall to the floor.

Laurence lowers me to the bed, showering me with kisses, and I hear myself moan with pent-up pleasure. It has been so long, so long waiting for this. I fumble with Laurence's belt, his zip and ease down his trousers. My husband moves above me and then . . . and then . . . and then . . . Nothing.

'Is everything okay?'

Laurence rolls off me and flops onto his back on the bed. 'No,' he says tightly. 'It's not.'

I sit myself up and edge into his side. 'Here,' I say jokily, 'let me have a go.'

He stays my hands. 'Don't,' he says. 'Just don't.'

'It's all right, Laurence. These things happen.'

'Not to me they don't.' He zips himself up and buckles his belt with jerky movements.

'It's the pressure. It's everything we've been through. It's just a temporary thing.'

'What if it isn't? What if I'm permanently . . . affected?'

'You won't be, darling. Of course you won't. Let's just lie down together and have a cuddle.'

'I should get up,' Laurence says, sitting bolt upright. 'I have things to do to prepare for tomorrow.'

'Lie down for a minute,' I cajole. 'I'll help you do whatever it is you need to do.'

But Laurence is already off the bed. 'I said I'd see Skull at the pub for a celebratory drink.'

'Now?'

'I won't be long.' And before I can protest further, my husband is out of the door.

Chapter 68

Laurence had to organise a taxi to take him to work that first morning. It seemed like a ridiculous expense in the circumstances, but it was the only way to get him to Cherry's Farm before nine when he was due to start work – but such were the trials of being reliant on public transport. He could get the bus home, but the sooner he organised a bike the better. Skull would know someone who had one for sale and he'd put feelers out last night while they were in the pub.

Lily was in the kitchen too, having got out of bed to make him breakfast, even though he was quite capable of pouring a bowl of cereal for himself. Gone were the days when breakfast had consisted of freshly baked muffins, homemade smoothies and Lily's own brand of muesli studded with nuts and fruit.

'Okay?' she said to him, twining her arms round him.

Of course, one beer had turned in to three or four and he'd tiptoed his way into the bed just before midnight. If Lily wasn't fast asleep, she was feigning it well. And he was relieved at that. He was tired, needed to grab as many hours as he could before starting his new job, and was anxious to avoid a difficult or emotional discussion. It seemed that Lily was too.

'Fine,' Laurence answered. Then he sighed. 'Actually, not fine. I'm nervous. Nervous as hell.' He turned to her, concern on his face. 'I feel like it's my first day at school.'

She came and smoothed his collar down, straightened his tie – even though he was wearing his nasty charity-shop suit. 'You're bound to feel like that.'

'I'm a seasoned businessman. A City high-flyer. I'm used to handling millions of pounds. I could do this job standing on my head.'

'I know that you could.'

'I'm terrified, Lily,' he admitted.

'You'll be fine,' she assured him. 'Just be yourself. Ease into it. From what you've told me about Christopher Cherry, he seems like a lovely man. He won't be expecting you to hit the ground running, darling. This is completely new territory for you. He knows that you'll have to learn the ropes. And he still chose you.'

'Second choice,' Laurence reminded her.

'Don't dwell on that. As soon as you're there, he'll know that he's made the *right* choice.'

'I'd better be going in a few minutes.'

'Can I make you a sandwich or anything?'

'No. The contract states that I can have a free lunch at the café.' He, the man who'd come to learn the hard way that there was no such thing as a free lunch, was now entitled to one every day.

'That'll be a big help.'

'Yes. I'll just have something light this evening.'

Lily hugged him tightly. Despite all they'd been through, Laurence thought, there were moments when they seemed closer, when his wife – who had always been cool and collected – seemed warmer, more affectionate and more vulnerable than she had ever been before. He was so disappointed about last night's disaster on the love-making front. It wasn't that he didn't want her. She was still a highly desirable woman. It was just . . . Frankly, he didn't know what it was. Why, after all these years, he suddenly couldn't make love to his wife.

Anyway, that would have to wait. Now he had to go and throw himself back into the world of work. On one hand, he simply couldn't wait and, on the other, he would have liked to have frozen this moment in time, him here in his wife's arms, the children upstairs sleeping soundly in their beds. But it had to be done. He prised himself away from Lily. 'I'll see you later.'

251

'I love you,' she said.
'I love you too.'
'I'll be thinking of you today.'
'So will I.'
Now he had to go and earn some money.

Chapter 69

The taxi whisked him to Great Brickhill much quicker than he'd expected. So as the driver trundled up the country lane leading to Cherry's Farm, Laurence asked the man to stop short. He paid the eye-watering fare and then took the opportunity to walk along the path at the side of the Grand Union Canal and up to the farm that way. Skull had assured him that he'd be able to 'come by' a bike for him, and Laurence hoped that his friend would have been able to acquire one for him by the time he got home this evening. There were only so many days that he could support this expenditure on transport to get him to work on time.

Despite the pain in his wallet, it was actually a beautiful time of day. The sun was not long fully risen, bringing a welcome warmth. There was no one else around and the sound of bird-song was all that disturbed the peace. A whisper of mist sat over the canal and, to his delight, the stunning blue flash of a busy kingfisher darted along the bank beside him. This was the way to start the day, not pressed up against a thousand other sweaty, suited people on the London Underground.

He sat on a wall by the bridge and breathed in the air – clean and cool. Apart from the slight headache brought on by the beer he'd had with Skull, Laurence felt lighter than he had in years. He softened his gaze and let the countryside fill his senses while he waited for his new place of work to open. Shortly before nine, he pushed himself from the wall and walked the last few minutes up to the field behind Cherry's

Farm. The big barn that made up the bulk of the property loomed ahead and he walked through the rough ankle-deep grass to get there. A cock crowed and in the farmyard the chickens were being fed and were also clearly happy to make some noise about it. The doors to the café were thrown open to embrace the day. By the time Laurence put his head inside, tentatively, there was a broad smile on his face.

Christopher Cherry was already there, sitting at one of the tables, paper open, sipping a cup of coffee. 'All right, lad?' he said. 'Don't be shy.'

He stood up and shook Laurence's hand. 'Welcome on board.'

'Good to be here,' Laurence replied. And it was – so very good.

'Don't just stand there. Get yourself a brew and pull up a chair.'

Laurence did as he was told.

'You don't need to stand on ceremony here,' Christopher Cherry said when he sat down. 'You're not working at Lloyds of London now, lad. You won't be needing a suit tomorrow either.' He took in Laurence's stiff appearance. Mr Cherry was in an open-necked checked shirt and corduroy trousers. 'Just a shirt and jeans will be fine. Something like that. I like the atmosphere to be laid-back at Cherry's. You might as well take your tie off now.'

Laurence loosened his tie and removed it. He rolled it up and put it in his pocket. Then he shrugged off his jacket and slung it over the chair. Thank goodness he had some jeans in his suitcase from holiday and another pair that one of Tracey's exes had unwittingly donated to the cause.

'Better already,' Christopher Cherry decided. 'We'll have this brew, get to know each other a bit and then I'll show you round the office, get you set with passwords and all that.'

'I'm really grateful for this chance, Christopher. Really very grateful.'

'Then do a good job for me, lad,' he said simply. 'And don't go running off to London the minute someone clicks their fingers – as they will.'

Laurence wasn't so sure about that. Mr Cherry didn't quite realise the full extent of his downfall from grace if he thought the job offers were suddenly going to come flooding in. Several months of being gainfully unemployed had confirmed that.

'I won't, he said. 'I can promise that.'

'I'll hold you to it, lad,' Mr Cherry said, then proceeded to give him a rundown on the situation of the business. 'Now. Ready to start the day?'

'Ready and raring to go,' Laurence said. It was nearly ten o'clock.

'We'll do this every morning,' Christopher told him. 'Set ourselves up with a coffee. You can have breakfast here if you want. Edna there makes a mean bacon sandwich. It'll give us a chance to catch up with any outstanding business matters before the hordes arrive.'

The hordes currently consisted of a smattering of elderly ladies and their husbands.

'Don't let that fool you,' Christopher said, following his gaze. 'We've got a coach party of women golfers from a local club coming in for lunch. Twenty-five of the buggers. That'll keep us on our toes. I hope it doesn't rain because some of them will have to go outside.' He chuckled. 'I might leave you in charge of them. See how you manage with *that.*'

It was a world away from his job in the City but, despite the daunting prospect of looking after twenty-five golfing ladies, Laurence thought that he was really going to enjoy it.

Chapter 70

My second day at work starts with Seymour giving me a gift. 'What's this for?'

'To celebrate surviving your first day, Lily,' he says.

'I hardly *survived* it. I loved it.' Nevertheless, I open the small and exquisitely wrapped box. It contains six beautiful chocolates, all handmade, from the lovely chocolate boutique further down the High Street that was always one of my first ports of call when a present was required for a person who was tricky to buy for. 'Oh, Seymour. Thank you. These look wonderful.'

I'm not sure how to express my thanks – whether to shake his hand or kiss his cheek. What's the etiquette for receiving a thoughtful present from your employer? I throw caution to the wind and take the kissing option. My lips brush his cheek, which is as smooth as silk.

'Hmm,' he says, as his fingers go to touch the spot. 'Remind me to buy you chocolates more often.'

'I'm going to fly in the face of expert opinion,' I tell him, 'and put these in the fridge. Chocolate, in my book, should always be served chilled. We'll have them with our lunch.' As I clear a space in the small fridge, I say, 'Actually, I'm celebrating today.'

Seymour raises an eyebrow.

'My husband has finally got a job.' The relief in my voice as I say it is tangible. 'He's going to be working at Cherry's Farm.'

'I know the place. Very popular,' Seymour says. 'That is good news.'

'Yes. It's not his usual line of work.' That's somewhat under-stating it. 'But he's really looking forward to it.'

Then Seymour frowns. 'That doesn't mean you'll be leaving me?'

'No, no.' I laugh. 'It's hardly his usual salary range either,' I explain. 'This doesn't bring us anywhere close to be able to return to our former lifestyle. All it will do is help us to keep our heads above water.' I close the fridge door. 'You've got me here for the foreseeable future, I'm afraid.'

Our eyes meet and the intensity of Seymour's gaze makes my mouth go dry. He smiles. 'I'm glad to hear it.'

I'm the first one to look away and, feeling the flush to my cheeks, say, 'I'd better get some work done or you'll be *asking* me to leave.'

Then, as flustered as I am, I settle down to do some paper-work in the office while the shop is quiet. Seymour, sitting in the armchair behind me, uses his mobile phone to catch up with calls to suppliers and designers. It's clear that he has a comfortable and relaxed relationship with all the people he deals with and I feel that I'm very lucky to have found such a sympathetic and kind man as my first boss. There is just a part of me that wishes he wasn't so damn nice or so damn handsome! If he was grumpy or pot-bellied perhaps he wouldn't be quite so distracting.

In between updating the accounts, I serve a handful of customers before noon and I'm gratified to see that they all leave with expensive purchases in the boxy Ornato carrier bags.

'You're a marvellous salesperson,' Seymour says, as the door signals the exit of another satisfied customer.

'Hardly. These pieces are so beautiful that they sell themselves.'

Seymour toys with a row of delicate gold bracelet watches, their faces studded with diamonds.

'There's one thing I wanted to suggest to you,' he says, looking up. 'Would you consider coming with me when I go on my next buying trip to London? I'd like to introduce you to some of the people you'll be dealing with. I'm sure they'd love to meet you too.'

257

'What about the shop? Who would look after it?'

'If we went on a Monday we could close up for the day,' he says. 'That's what I used to do before. I don't have to do it very often, so I'm sure the good ladies and gentlemen of Woburn won't mind waiting for their jewellery requirements until the next day.'

Spoken like a person who is in business because he *can* be, rather than because he *needs* to be.

'It means an early start and we won't be back until late. Would Laurence mind?'

'No, no.' I feel quite excited at the prospect of a day out in London. When was the last time I hit the capital with a vengeance? So long ago that I can't even remember. 'If it's part of my job, then I need to do it. I'm sure my husband will understand.' When I think of all the years that Laurence arrived home late, I'm sure that I'm owed some latitude.

I clap my hands together. 'I can't wait.'

'Me neither,' Seymour says.

Chapter 71

Employing a will of iron, I manage to save three of my delicious chocolates – one for Tracey and one for my husband and just one more for me. These are definitely grown-up treats and I don't want my children anywhere near them.

When I get home, I invite my friend in for a cup of coffee. Charlize and Keanu come with her and, immediately, they both disappear into the overgrown garden to play with Hugo and Hettie in the rusting car. It's strange, but I'm pleased to see that this dilapidated vehicle has given them so much pleasure. I'm sure that it's firing their imagination much more than sitting playing a computer game ever did. Now I'm glad that I didn't get rid of it as my instinct dictated.

I make two coffees, grab the chocolates and we sit outside on Skull's patio and enjoy the final remants of the sunshine. I stretch out my legs and press my back against the brick wall. Perhaps now that we're both working, I could try to find some cheap furniture for here. Nothing fancy. Just a plastic table and chairs would serve us fine. Tracey, as befitting of a guest, has first choice of chocolate.

'Wow,' she says. 'These are yum. And your boss bought them?'

'Hmm.' I tuck into my own. A cherry smothered in thick dark chocolate. Divine.

'Does he need another assistant?'

'I'll ask him,' I say with a laugh.

'Tell him there's a lot of things I'm willing to do for chocolate.'

We both grin at that. 'I will.'

'Is he nice?'

I feel my face suffuse with colour.

Tracey, who rarely misses a trick, spots it immediately. 'Oh yes, Mrs Jones! Tell all.'

I giggle and lower my voice. 'He's very nice,' I confide. 'Charming.'

'Not too shabby in the looks department?'

'He's lovely.' I manage to suppress the sigh that threatens to escape. 'Just a very nice man all round.'

'I don't really need to ask if you're enjoying being back at work then?'

'I'm loving it,' I tell her honestly. 'I wish I'd got myself a job years ago. I know that it's only been two days, but I feel as if I have so much more purpose.'

'I have to do something too,' Tracey says. 'I'm going nuts at home. All I ever see is my own four walls. I'm missing you like mad, now that you're not here during the day.'

'We'll think of something for you to do,' I promise her.

'I need some fun,' Tracey complains. 'I haven't had a night out in living memory.'

'Money's tight,' I remind her.

'Money's always tight,' she counters. 'I can't spend another night watching television by myself. Why don't we get the girls together and go out on the town?'

I'm not sure who constitutes 'the girls'. I only know Tracey and Jamelia. Despite that, I offer, 'It's my birthday next week. Perhaps we could do something then.'

Tracey brightens. 'We could hit the clubs!'

I was thinking of something more low-key. Scampi and chips at The Nut, perhaps. 'I'm on a budget now. I'm not sure . . .'

'Laurence is earning again,' she points out. 'You too. Oh, let's celebrate. You deserve a night out. We both do.'

'Well . . .'

'Come on,' Tracey urges. 'Let's go mad for once.'

'I'll have to see what Laurence says.'

'How can he say no?'

I think of how I would normally spend my birthday. Laurence, when he was next home, would book a romantic restaurant, there would be a piece of jewellery and then we'd make love.

This year there'll be no romantic restaurant, no jewellery and certainly no making love if things don't . . . perk up . . . pretty quickly. I might as well do something completely different. It wouldn't hurt to ring the changes.

'How much do you think it will cost?' It's shameful but I've never had to consider this before, whether a girls' night out is feasible or not.

'Not much,' Tracey assures me. 'Fifty quid? No more. We'll put some bottles of vodka and Coke in our handbags so we don't have to shell out for too many drinks.'

That makes me chuckle. 'Do people still do that? I remember some of the other girls doing that at our annual school disco.'

'School disco! What a great idea!' she says, suddenly animated. 'There's a place in the city that does fancy-dress school disco nights. Let's go to that.'

'Oh, Tracey. I'm not sure that it's my kind of thing.'

'You never know until you try,' she says dismissively. 'It's your birthday. We need to let our hair down. I'm sure the others will be up for it. We'll have a great night!'

'But what would we wear?' I've always tried to avoid fancy dress like the plague. Not that I've often been invited to partake in it. Our friends weren't really the fancy-dress type of people.

'Leave that to me,' she says, rubbing her hands. 'I'll hit the charity shops.'

My friend is well away now and I'm not sure anything I could say would dissuade her. And, to be honest, part of me wants to do whatever Tracey wants to do because she has been so good to me and to my family – and she's absolutely right when she says that she deserves to have some fun.

Whilst our ideas of what is fun might differ, for my birthday it looks very much like I'll be donning a gymslip and going out with a bottle or two of vodka and Coke in my handbag.

Chapter 72

'I'll have to get a bike,' Laurence says enthusiastically. 'I was there early enough in the taxi, but what a price. Then, coming home, I got to the bus stop on time but then had to wait nearly half an hour for the damn thing to arrive. I could have cycled there and back in half the time.'

He's brought home a link of organic pork and leek sausages from one of Cherry's suppliers for us to try and I could weep with joy. Apparently, Christopher wants us to try all of their produce and give him our opinion. I don't think there'll be any hardship in that.

I've teamed the fat, juicy sausages with some of Skull's potatoes and an onion gravy. The children have their elbows out, their heads down and haven't spoken for ten minutes. I do wonder why I spent all those years trying to force quinoa down their throats.

'It will save me a fortune in taxi and bus fares too,' my husband adds. 'Who had any idea that public transport was so expensive? I'm sure it was cheaper to run my Merc than go everywhere by bus or taxi. I'm going to pop to The Nut later, if that's all right, to see if Skull has managed to source me a second-hand bike.'

Seeing an opportunity, I don't want to waste it. This is a good time for me to drop my proposed night out with Tracey into the conversation. 'It's my birthday next week,' I say.

'I haven't forgotten.' Laurence is defensive.

'I know. It's just that we've nothing planned and I've sort of promised that I'll go out for the evening with Tracey. She wants to organise a girls' night out for me. Is that okay with you?'

Laurence hesitates momentarily and then says, 'Of course,' in a very magnanimous way. 'Of course you must enjoy yourself. It will do you good.'

I'm not sure how much good dressing up as a schoolgirl will do me, but I'm prepared to give it a go.

He takes my hand. 'No jewellery this year.'

'I didn't expect any. We'll just have a quiet family meal the next night. Now that I've passed the big four-oh, I'm not so keen to mark off the passing years.'

'I'll cook,' Laurence offers. 'I can bring something nice home from work.'

'So you think that you'll be happy at Cherry's?' There's a knot of anxiety in my stomach as I ask the question, even though Laurence breezed in just before seven o'clock full of the joys of spring.

'It just felt so good to be doing something useful again,' he says with a relieved expiration of breath. 'So good. Christopher is very easy to work with.' I wonder idly if he's as easy as Seymour. 'I think we're going to get on like a house on fire and I believe I can make a difference there.'

'That's good. I'm so pleased.'

'I want to take you all there at the weekend, so that you can see what it's like.'

I don't remind my husband that we've been there before – on several occasions, but all without him. I'll pack a picnic and we can all go along together as a family. It will do us the world of good to get out and about and off the rather grotty environs of Netherslade Bridge for the day. I'm looking forward to it already.

'Now that you're working, Daddy,' Hettie says, 'can we get a television again? I'm fed up of being Miss Scarlet.'

Laurence looks at me for approval.

'We'll have to think about that,' I say.

'When you say that it means no,' Hettie whines. 'Everyone at school is talking about *Britain's Got Talent* and we don't know anything about it.'

'They think we're freaks.' Hugo backs her up.

'We'll *definitely* think about it,' I reiterate. 'Now go upstairs and do your homework while Daddy and I talk.'

'We don't have any homework,' Hugo crows.

'None?' Me.

'That's what's so fine about our new school. Can we go next door?'

'Yes,' I say. 'But only if you're not in Tracey's way. Make sure to ask her nicely.'

They're up and out of the door before I can offer any more wise parental advice.

'We could get a television,' Laurence says. 'The children deserve a little joy too.'

'What I don't want to do is spend money that we haven't got. We've managed perfectly well up until now.'

'Cluedo is losing its appeal somewhat,' he says with a laugh.

I have to agree. What I'm frightened of, I suppose, is starting to recreate our old life so that we have to bring in a certain level of income. 'We have so much else to buy and pay out for.'

'At least we can finally start chipping away at our debts,' Laurence says. Our outgoings compared to those at the barn are minimal, but they still take some finding when your income is minimal too.

I stand up to clear the plates and my husband slips his arm round my waist. 'Thank you for standing by me,' he says.

'I wouldn't dream of doing anything else.'

'I know,' he says. 'But I'm very grateful for that nevertheless.'

I kiss the top of his head. 'Go and put your feet up. I'll bring us some coffee.'

'What have I done to deserve you?' he sighs.

I make two cups of borderline bitter coffee from supermarket own-brand instant powder and don't even long for the rich, smooth taste of freshly-brewed Sumatra Lintong as I used to. Popping the chocolate I saved for Laurence on the saucer, I carry it through to him. He's sitting on the blue velour sofa that I've managed to de-flea.

'A chocolate for you,' I announce as I hand it over.

'This is a bit of luxury.'

'I didn't buy them,' I confess. 'They're from my boss.'

'Hmm,' Laurence says as he bites into the chocolate ganache appreciatively. 'I thought Christopher Cherry was a good chap, but your . . .'

'Seymour Chapman,' I supply as the colour rises, once again, to my face

'Well, he's going to take some beating.'

'Yes.'

Laurence pulls me onto his lap and I twine my arms round his neck. If I risked a kiss, would my husband respond? I wonder. The children will be out of the house for another hour or two yet. Perhaps I won't risk it while all is well at the moment. While he's feeling upbeat, I don't want to remind him of disappointment, so I leave it be.

'Thank you for getting this little job,' he says against my neck. 'I'm sure it will help no end.'

I think of the calm atmosphere of the shop, the joy of sliding a purchase into the stylish bags, the easy routine that Seymour and I are already slipping into. 'I'm enjoying it.'

'I'm glad,' my husband says. 'I'm very glad.'

But I don't add that I might be enjoying it a bit too much.

Chapter 73

At the weekend, as planned, I pack up some sandwiches and we take the bus out to Great Brickhill and Cherry's Farm. The forecast rain has held off, so far, and even though the weather is cool, the farm is busy. Laurence is thrilled to show us around and I can tell that he's itching to get involved. He's going to work alternate weekends with Mr Cherry, and his first official shift is next weekend, but I know my husband too well and am aware that he's struggling to stay away.

During the week, Laurence disappeared to The Nut for what has become his regular pint of beer. He goes two or three times a week and has just the one, mind. I think it is worth the expense to foster community relations and Laurence seems to have found in Skull a close friend, the like of which he's never had before.

Later that evening, he reappeared with a bike that Skull had found for him for ten pounds. It needed cleaning and oiling, but other than that it was in good working condition and, at the end of the week, Laurence surprised both me and himself by riding all the way to work and back and loving every minute of it. Any weight that he's put on through the last few months of enforced inactivity and the previous years of extravagant business lunches will soon be shed, I'm sure.

At Cherry's, I coo over the wonderful produce – fine cheeses, organic meats, wonderful chutneys, freshly-baked bread. Hettie is in her element feeding the chickens and the rabbits and lambs and is running around, her mad red hair flying behind her.

Hugo, trying out his newly-developed attitude, is playing it cool but I can tell that he's dying to cuddle one of the guinea pigs. I decide to give him a get-out clause. 'Darling,' I say to him, 'can you possibly cuddle one of those little things so that you can show Hettie what to do?'

My son pounces on the opportunity and the guinea pig. 'This is how you do it, Hettie,' he says, almost squeezing the life out of the poor creature in his excitement.

'I think we could put a couple of alpacas in there,' my husband muses as he nods towards an empty pen. 'Pretty little things. They'd go down a storm.'

I smile indulgently at him. I'm sure he'll be a great asset to this business as he seems to be quite immersed in it already.

When we've given the animals in the petting area a run for their money, we borrow a football from the basket by the café that contains a variety of plastic play equipment – cricket stumps and ball, a couple of Frisbees, a few skipping ropes and some bats – and play an impromptu game of football in the field that borders the canal, keeping well away from the water. Laurence is charging about looking light-hearted and carefree. I'll swear that some of the grey haggard look that has dogged his handsome face these past months has melted away in the sunshine. It's as if a great weight has been lifted from his shoulders and I feel so glad about that.

When we've all run our legs off, we sit by the canal bank and I unwrap the sandwiches and hand them out. We catch our breath while we eat and I lean against my husband.

'I don't ever think I've seen you so relaxed,' I tell him.

'This is the life,' he says. 'I'm trying very hard to do things differently this time.'

'Then you're making a very good start.'

'The weekends that I'm not working we should make the effort to go out as a family. We have some marvellous places right on our doorstep. We could trawl the local newspaper to see if we could find some bikes. There's bound to be some in there. Or Skull might be able to help us out again. Would you like that, darling?'

267

I haven't been on a bike since I was Hugo or Hettie's age, but I'm prepared to give it a go. 'That sounds lovely. As long as they're not too expensive.'

'I'll have a word with Skull. I'm sure he'll see us right,' he says confidently.

'He should come round to dinner,' I say. 'Is there a Mrs Skull?'

'No,' Laurence says. 'He lives alone. That's probably why we get so many vegetables.'

'Then he should definitely come.'

'I'll speak to him later.' The other benefit of us both earning is that we can now be assured of paying our mobile phone bills and can stay in contact with the world.

We spend the entire day at the farm, taking a walk along the canal after our picnic, Hettie and Hugo racing ahead of us as we stroll hand-in-hand behind them. We wander along all the hedgerows that border the field and fill the plastic bags our sandwiches came out of with fat, juicy blackberries. We'll have a homemade crumble later and then I'll see if my old jam-making skills can be revived.

Then, as the crowds are thinning, and the shadows are lengthening, we walk back up to the café. Christopher Cherry buys us both a coffee and gets some orange juice for the children and we sit outside and listen to his plans for the future.

'Don't let this man of yours work too hard,' Mr Cherry tells me. 'I might be his boss, but I'm not a slave-driver. I want my staff to be happy at work and happy at home.'

I take to this affable man instantly. 'We're certainly a lot happier now that Laurence is working again,' I confide.

'Then that's all that matters,' he says. He claps my husband on the back. 'I'm off home myself in a minute. Looking after the grandkiddies tonight. Got to keep my strength up for that. They run me ragged and then expect me to be up to do it all again at five o'clock the next morning.'

So we say our goodbyes and then walk along the driveway and out of the lane, tired and contented as we clutch our bags of blackberries and head back towards the bus stop.

As we get to the corner of the lane, a car swerves by us and blasts its horn. Inside are Amanda and Anthony Marquis with their two children. That stops Laurence and me in our tracks.

We stare after the rapidly disappearing car.

'Do you think they even realised it was us?' I want to know.

'Yes,' he says sadly. 'I think they did.'

'I'm guessing that we're off their Christmas card list,' I say.

That starts Laurence giggling. 'Yes,' he agrees. 'We probably are.'

And soon we're both clutching at each other, tears rolling down our cheeks.

'Parents,' Hugo says disdainfully to his sister. 'They're so lame.'

Chapter 74

Before I know where I am, the night of my birthday is upon us. I give the children supper early and leave a salad out on a plate for Laurence for when he gets home. He's never late back from Cherry's, it's unheard of. Every night he's home by six o'clock – even though he cycles all the way. Christopher Cherry, he says, chivvies him out of the door as soon as the last customer is gone and won't hear of him staying any later. I think I like the work ethics of this man.

Still, I've been ordered around to Tracey's by six o'clock. Before we go out there is, apparently, wine to be drunk and preparations to be made. As I'm getting ready to leave, Laurence arrives. He's red in the face and sweating from the exertion of his bike ride.

'I'm about to go,' I tell him. 'Will you be all right?'

'Fine,' he says. 'I'm looking forward to my last evening of Cluedo.'

We have decided to bite the bullet and buy a small television so that our children don't go insane or become social outcasts because they don't watch *How To Look Good Naked* or *Hollyoaks*. It's coming tomorrow via contacts from The Nut. Laurence assures me that it's all above board. If it's stolen, then frankly, I don't want to know about it. Gone are the days of John Lewis accounts and black American Express cards.

'Tracey says that I can sleep over at her place,' I tell my husband.

'Why?'

'Our neighbour is planning a late one,' I say. 'I don't want to wake you.'

That statement isn't strictly true. Tracey has booked for us to go to Bistro Live to one of their school disco nights. Or SKOOL DISCO NITE! as our tickets say. I am extremely anxious about this already and what I don't want is for Laurence to see me dressed up as a schoolgirl and, potentially, roaring drunk. I think it's better for all concerned that the fewer people who witness this spectacle the better.

'It doesn't matter. We both have to be up for work in the morning.'

'I'll be back in time for breakfast,' I counter. 'I'm sure you can manage for one night without me.'

Then Laurence flushes even redder and I remember that we still haven't made love since our last aborted attempt. Perhaps absence will make the heart grow fonder.

I kiss him on the cheek and leave him to the children and his salad and a wild night of Cluedo.

When I push Tracey's front door open, Jamelia is already in full flow. There's white tissue paper spread out over the kitchen table and my friend is peeling off her clothes.

'Here's the birthday girl!' she trills. 'Close the kitchen door behind you, love. Thank goodness the kids have gone to my mum's. Don't want them witnessing this. It could scar them for life.'

'What are you having done?'

'Brazilian,' she says. 'Hurts like stink but makes you feel a million dollars. You should try it.'

I hold up my hands. 'No thanks.' I'm already trying to keep my fake nails painted pale colours to detract attention from them. I'm not sure I'm ready for more than that.

'Don't know who I'm having it done for,' Tracey remarks. 'I'm not planning on showing it to anyone.'

Raucous giggling ensues.

'Who else is coming?' I ask.

'Three others – Sarah, Marcia and Ayesha – all old friends of mine from school. You'll love them.' Tracey, in just her bra and

271

pants, climbs up onto the kitchen table. 'You could have invited some of your friends too.'

I decide not to tell my neighbour that I now have no friends other than her and Jamelia. And that my former friends' idea of a good night out would be a few hands of bridge, a glass – or two at the most – of dry white wine or champagne and some canapés.

'This could get messy. You might want to take the head end,' she advises, 'or busy yourself pouring us some wine.'

I do as I'm told, happy to be away from the treatment area.

Jamelia sets to with a pot of wax and some strips. My friend shrieks hysterically whenever a strip is briskly pulled off and I wince along with her. It does sound particularly painful.

'I'll treat you to one for your birthday,' Tracey says through gritted teeth.

'No, no, no.' I hold up a hand. 'No, thanks.'

'Have a look at our costumes then,' Tracey says, waving her arm about vaguely. 'They're over there.'

When I see what she's pointing at, I recoil in horror. 'I can't wear that!'

'Oh yes, my friend,' she says. 'I think you can.'

I look at the outfits with mounting trepidation. Normally, I wouldn't be seen dead in anything like that – never mind go outside in it! But this isn't a normal occasion. It's my birthday and my friend has been so good to me that I want to make sure that we have a truly brilliant time tonight. And if this is her idea of a brilliant time, then I will go along with it.

So I throw my wine down my neck and, with shaking hands, refill my glass immediately. If I am going to go out in *that*, then I'm going to need lots and lots of *this*.

Chapter 75

Perhaps I have too much wine too soon. I've always been proud of being able to 'pace myself', but this time it seems to have gone somewhat awry.

Next thing, I'm climbing up onto Tracey's kitchen table on fresh white tissue preparing to have all my pubic hair removed by a woman that I barely know.

'I can do this,' I intone solemnly. 'I can do this.' Just to be sure, I take another swig from my glass.

Tracey is at the head end this time – oh, and I forgot to mention that Sarah, Marcia and Ayesha are here to join in the fun.

'Lily! Lily! Lily!' they chant.

I don't know that you should ever have a Brazilian – unless you're planning on being a porn star – or that you should ever have hair in a very personal place removed with an audience on hand.

Handing over my glass for safe-keeping, I lie on the table and let my head fall back. I feel dizzy as Tracey, Sarah, Marcia and Ayesha, in my eyes, all flip upside down.

'Ready, girl?' Jamelia asks.

'As I'll ever be,' I tell her.

Then she applies the first strip of wax and it's hotter than I imagined and I can hear myself shrieking before she's done anything else. When she rips the first strip off, taking my precious pubic hair with it, we're all laughing hysterically and my eyes are running with water.

'Good job we've not done our make-up yet, Lily,' Tracey cackles, 'or you'd have mascara tracks down your cheeks.'

'How did I persuade you to make me do this?' I cry out. 'It's worse than childbirth. This is a birthday present?'

'Maybe I should have bought chocolates,' Tracey agrees, and we all fall about laughing again.

'Chill,' Jamelia instructs. 'Laurence will love it.'

It's just as well that my husband and I aren't being intimate at the moment as I'm not going to let him see this!

My torturer tears off another strip and I scream again.

'It sounds like we're murdering you,' Tracey admonishes. 'You'll have him coming round here any minute now to see what's going on. Remember, these walls are paper-thin.'

I laugh again and try to muffle my cries by stuffing my fist in my mouth. Oh, this is excruciating! I'll never be able to stand up again, let alone go out partying tonight.

But, not half an hour later, I get high fives all round for my courage in the face of beauty adversity. Then, before I have time to catch my breath, I'm sitting in a chair while Jamelia applies make-up to my face and Tracey is slapping fake tan over my arms and legs 'because I look a bit pasty' according to my friend. I can't remember the last time I got ready to go out with a group of girls – probably when I was about fourteen and I'd forgotten, torture aside, what fun it could be.

The other girls are applying fake tan, in a more measured style than Tracey did, and make-up too, and soon it's time to don our clothing.

'I thought I'd go down the slut route,' my friend says.

And she certainly has.

Tracey has chosen short grey skirts for the three of us – so short that they barely cover our bottoms. We have black over-the-knee socks and tight white blouses to complement the look. My friend insists that we tie them up, baring our midriffs to the world. I don't think I've ever bared so much skin when I've not been on a beach. While I try to pull my skirt down to my knees, Jamelia works my hair into two short pigtails that stick out at wild angles from my head.

The other girls are also now slipping into their costumes. Ayesha has chosen to be a dominatrix headmistress, Marcia – quite sensibly in my opinion – is dressed as a schoolboy, complete with shorts and school cap, and Sarah, who is the only bona fide schoolteacher amongst us, has plumped for ripped tights and plimsolls.

More wine is poured. 'We're gonna have fun tonight, ladies!' Tracey proposes a toast. 'To us!'

'Happy birthday, Lily,' they all shout as we down our booze. My friend hands round sizeable plastic bottles of vodka and Coke that are to go in our handbags. 'That should keep us going for a while.'

I have no idea how much I've already drunk, but my head is spinning. The only good thing is that it is numbing the throbbing coming from my private parts.

Then, just as we're all ready, the door bell rings.

'That'll be the taxi.' Tracey shoots across the kitchen to open the front door.

Oh, my good Lord. Here we go. I wish we were wearing the kind of fancy dress that could be utilised as a disguise as I still have to get out of here without my husband catching sight of me. After all we've been through, I don't want to add a heart attack to the list.

'Come on, ladies.' Tracey herds us all towards the door. The cab is waiting at the end of the path. There's much giggling and shouting and I'm praying that Laurence doesn't hear us. 'Ready, Birthday Girl?'

Taking a deep breath, I make a bolt for the taxi. At that moment, Len Eleven Dogs and his canine entourage walk past.

'Wotcher,' Len says, and averts his eyes as he hurries past. The dogs try to lick my fake tan.

Then Tracey decides to reorganise the order of who's going with whom and I'm left standing on the pavement, clutching my alcohol-laden handbag and glancing nervously back at my own front door. As it is, I'm last in the taxi.

'Bistro Live,' Tracey instructs the driver.

I close the door behind me. As I do, I see the curtains

twitch in our living-room window and Laurence peers out. But he's too late. He missed the sight of his staid wife dressed as one of St Trinian's finest. And, for that, I am truly, truly grateful.

Chapter 76

The Skool Disco Nite sees Bistro Live packed to the rafters. There must be 500 people here, maybe more, all similarly attired. We eat a passable dinner of sausage and mash followed by spotted dick and custard and much giggling.

The tables are cleared, and then the disco beat ratchets up several notches, making conversation impossible. The music is from the 1970s and it's sad to say that in that decade – even with Slade, The Osmonds and David Cassidy as distractions – I largely listened to classic music as I was studying for my music exams, the cello being my instrument of choice. Or rather my parents' choice. I'd won a scholarship to the local grammar school and they were anxious that I sampled all that it had to offer, whether I wanted to or not.

Now I realise that my youth was misspent – but for all the wrong reasons. I was an only child and tried to be such a good daughter, always doing what was required of me, seeking only parental approval. It's fair to say that I never gave my mother and father a moment's trouble. I did my homework on time and without cajoling, similarly my music practice, and I didn't date until I left home at eighteen. And I've lived all of my life like that, firmly in the bounds of convention. At university I never took drugs, never had an inappropriate one-night stand, never slipped behind with my studies. As a wife I have been a model homemaker and nurturer. I have never been the one to let my hair down or yearn to break free. Appearances have always been important to me. If I behaved well and did the right thing, then surely I would have the perfect life.

Now look at me. I'm up on the table as encouraged at Bistro Live next to Tracey, Jamelia and my new friends, arms slung round each other, singing with all my heart to Alice Cooper's 'School's Out'. I wonder, has it taken until I've reached my forties and when I'm down and out to be shrugging off my restraints for the evening, dressed as a schoolgirl and with a handbag full of vodka.

There's no pretence in my life now. I have nothing. Nothing but my health, my husband and my children. I've no façade to maintain. No one I need to keep up with or in with. This is me. With my bald private parts and my cheap schoolgirl slut fancy dress, throwing vodka down my neck, I feel more at home with myself than I have done in years. Take me or leave me.

At midnight, I launch myself off the table and into the waiting arms of my very best friends. Never in my life have I had such a great night out. I've danced until my feet are sore and blistered, sung until my throat is hoarse, and drunk until I can barely stand.

Arm-in-arm we stagger outside and, when the fresh air hits me, my knees buckle and I find myself giggling on the pavement. Tracey hauls me up.

'We need to go and find a taxi,' she says.

'Can't move,' I slur. '*So* can't move.'

'Then you'll need a bit of help.' With that she wanders off leaving me propped up against Jamelia who, herself, is swaying like a galleon in full sail. Moments later, my friend returns with a shopping trolley.

'Noooo, noooo, noooo,' I say.

But, still protesting, I am loaded into the shopping trolley. It's all hands to the pump and, legs akimbo over the edge of the trolley, I'm speeded through the night-time streets of Milton Keynes shrieking at the top of my voice. With my friends pushing the trolley, we whiz through The Hub – a ritzy area of bars and restaurants – and head towards the taxi rank. I have never, ever been pushed drunk in a shopping trolley before and I feel that I have missed a vital part of growing up as I'm really quite enjoying it. Tracey sets up a chorus of 'Mamma Mia' and I lie back, waving my legs in the air and shout, 'Woo, hoo!' as we round the corner to the poshest of posh restaurants, Brasserie Bleue.

As we do, there is a group of women emerging from the restaurant. They're not staggering, they're not in saucy fancy dress, and not one of them is lying in a shopping trolley. I also know that every single one of them is likely to have their full complement of pubic hair.

My pushers manage to pull up short before we hurtle into them. Collectively, the other women let out a horrified gasp.

'Helloooo!' I giggle.

Amanda Marquis is open-mouthed. As are her henchwomen, Karin Williams and Freya Turner.

'Lily,' my former friend says hesitantly. 'It can't be you?'

'Oh yes. It's me,' I assure her. They're all coming out of Brasserie Bleue with armfuls of clothing – from the swishing party that they told me had been cancelled. And I know that they will have been gossiping about my downfall and how low I've sunk. Now they have it confirmed.

'It's my birthday,' I slur happily. 'I've been out with my friends.'

'Happy birthday,' Amanda says reluctantly, and I see her and Karin and Freya exchange a glance and then eye my friends with disdain. Bitches. I might get out of my trolley and punch them. In fact, I definitely would. If I could.

'Did you enjoy the swishing party?' I ask.

'Yes,' she says tightly, knowing that I've caught her out in her lie.

Hey, but then she's caught me out drunk and incapable in a shopping trolley so I'm not sure who has the upper hand here. And, do you know what, I don't care. I've had a fabulous evening. My birthday has been well and truly celebrated. There's been no bitching, no gossiping, no trying to outdo the people whom you call your friends. It's just been great fun. Really great fun.

'I hope I run into you again sometime, Amanda.'

She opens her mouth to speak, but I don't care in the slightest what she has to say to me.

'Ladies,' I say to my pushers. 'Take me home!' They do as instructed and we all weave off down the street again, resuming our raucous rendition of 'Mamma Mia'.

'Are they friends of yours, Lily?' Tracey says as soon as we're out of earshot.

'They were,' I sigh. 'They were. At one time.'

'Stuck-up bitches,' she mutters.

Yes, I think, you're right. And I am so, so glad that I'm not one of them any more.

Chapter 77

As Laurence heard the taxi pull up, he jumped out of bed and pulled back the curtain to peep out. He hadn't been able to sleep until he knew that Lily was safely home. Milton Keynes was hardly the Wild West but anything could happen to a group of ladies on their own, couldn't it? It was one o'clock in the morning now and he was beginning to get anxious.

Now they were home and he was relieved. He could go and tell Lily that he was wide awake and that there was no need for her to sleep at Tracey's house. Laurence padded down the stairs in his T-shirt and boxers and flung open the front door.

He was halfway across the grass to the taxi when the door swung open and Tracey fell out onto the pavement. Much pulling, pushing and giggling ensued and next to spill out was . . . was that *Lily*?

Oh my good Christ! What was his wife wearing? She hadn't gone out of the house looking like that? Lily − *his* Lily − was crawling along the pavement on all fours. He couldn't believe what he was seeing. He could count on one hand the number of times he'd seen Lily tipsy throughout their entire marriage: one of them being in recent weeks. She was normally the model of decorum, never having more than two or three glasses of wine. Now look at her.

He swept forward and pulled her to her feet. 'Laurence,' she chuckled. 'My husband!' She threw her arms round his neck.

Tracey was on her back on the grass also laughing hysterically.

'Are you all right?' Laurence said.

'Lovely,' Tracey said. 'Bloody lovely.'

He couldn't leave her to go home by herself like this. She could fall downstairs and break her neck and then it would be on his conscience. No, Tracey had to come to their place too.

'I'll be back,' he said to their neighbour. 'Don't move.' Not that she was likely to.

'Mate,' the taxi driver said. 'There's the small issue of the fare.'

'Give me a hand with these two,' Laurence begged, 'and I'll see you right.'

The driver sighed and climbed out of his cab. Laurence picked up Lily and steered her wobbly form towards their front door while the cabbie hauled Tracey up and did the same.

'On there,' Laurence panted as they went into the living room.

Tracey was unceremoniously deposited on the blue velour sofa. She let out a small 'ouff' and slumped comfortably sideways into the seat.

Still trying to prop Lily up, Laurence dug into his pocket and pulled out a twenty-pound note. One of a dwindling number. Thank goodness that he'd be getting paid soon. 'Will that cover it?'

'Thanks, mate,' the driver said. 'Good luck with these two.'

Laurence was thinking that he was going to need it. 'Come on, Lily,' he said. 'One foot in front of the other.'

He tried to make his wife's legs do the walking. Not a hope in hell. So, instead, he hoisted her over his shoulder and carried her up the stairs, hoping against hope that she wouldn't throw up all down his back. He'd return in a minute and make sure that Tracey was all right. It wouldn't be good to have her choke on her own vomit either. Thank goodness that this wasn't a regular occurrence.

In the bedroom, he tried to lower his wife gently to the bed, but it came out more like a toss and Lily laughed hysterically.

'Sssh, sssh,' Laurence instructed. 'You'll wake the children.'

'Sssh,' Lily echoed.

This was all he needed. He stood up and raked his fingers through his hair, looking in amazement at his wife. Was this really the woman who'd been the pillar of society, chairperson of a dozen different superbly run charities, the highly capable mother of his children?

He'd never seen Lily roaring drunk before – or dressed as a schoolgirl, for that matter. Laurence smiled down at her semi-comatose form. She looked very appealing in a tarty sort of way. He should get her undressed and into bed and let her sleep off the worst of her excesses before she had to get up for work in the morning. His poor wife was going to have one humdinger of a hangover.

While she lay there moaning and groaning to herself, Laurence tugged off her shoes and then the black socks that went up to her knees. He grinned to himself. Very fetching, actually. He undid her blouse revealing the black lacy bra beneath it and, unbidden, felt himself stirring. No, he thought, not now! Not when his wife was almost unconscious. Not when it was the middle of the night and they had to get up early. Not when it had been weeks, months since he had felt so turned on by her. And what did that say about him? Did it make him some kind of pervert?

He tried not to think about it and instead turned Lily over to find the zip for the ridiculously short skirt she was wearing and saw that there were angry red marks on the back of her legs.

'What are these, darling?' he said.

'Fell out of shopping trolley,' she muttered and then burped.

A shopping trolley? Laurence shook his head. Now he knew how Lily had felt when he'd been brought home in a wheelbarrow. He thought that the score definitely stood at one all now.

Running his finger along the marks, he thought that she probably needed some antiseptic cream or something on them, but was sure they didn't have any. That was the sort of thing that they would borrow from Tracey. But she was no use to him. Their neighbour was currently passed out on the sofa downstairs.

'Ouch,' Lily complained sleepily.

He found her nightdress and then pulled down her skirt and

her underwear which was no mean feat with her dead weight of a body. Laurence recoiled as he stripped off the clothes. His wife had no pubic hair! He stared again, blinking rapidly. Not that he'd looked, but he was absolutely sure that she'd had some when she'd left home. Where had it gone?

Why would she do that? It wasn't like Lily at all.

Laurence sat on the bed next to her, bemused, and tried to gather his thoughts. Lily had changed so much since they'd come to Netherslade Bridge. Mostly out of necessity. But now this?

Despite not wanting to, he had to admit that it looked very sexy. If only she was halfway awake he would have liked to . . . No, it was out of the question.

'Don't even go there, Laurence,' he instructed himself.

Frowning, he tugged his wife to him and wrestled her into her nightie. Then he heaved her up again and slid her under the duvet.

Before he went to check on Tracey, he looked down at his wife. Already she was sleeping soundly. Dead to the world. The rasping snores were a bit of a giveaway.

They should be back on track now. They had hit the bottom, now they were on their way back up. By some miracle, they'd both managed to find jobs. It might not be anything like he was doing before or earning before, but he thought that he was going to enjoy it at Cherry's and Lily seemed to enjoy her work. So why did it feel sometimes like their life was still in freefall?

He stroked her hair tenderly, then kissed her forehead and said, 'Are we going to be all right, Lily?'

But the only answer he got was his wife grunting in her sleep.

Chapter 78

I have a monumental hangover. My head is throbbing and every bone in my body aches. I wonder why, until I remember that my chariot drivers overturned the shopping trolley as we reached the taxi rank last night and I spilled out onto the pavement in an unseemly hump. Thank goodness that Amanda Marquis didn't see that. Then I remember what she did see and my hearts sinks.

Oh, well. Too late for regrets now. The three of them – her, Karin and Freya – will be able to dine out for weeks on recounting the tale of the sorry state of Lily Lamont-Jones.

I smile to myself and even my teeth hurt. Still it was worth it. What fun we had.

There's a lump on the back of my skull the size of a golf ball. I don't mention this to Laurence and I don't think he noticed the scratches on my arms and legs as I rushed into the bathroom this morning – to be sick, of course.

I'm never going to drink again. Never. And certainly not vodka and Coke.

The gentle tinkling of the shop door chime at Ornato seems to clang like Big Ben this morning. Laurence tried to persuade me not to come into work today, but how could I stay at home? I've barely started here. How would it look if I telephoned in sick so soon? It would look bad. That's how it would look.

Still, the bus journey was no walk in the park. Every jolt and bump sent a wave of biliousness through my stomach. And now, every gurgle sends the taste of sausage and mash or spotted dick and custard to my mouth. My undercarriage still smarts from where all the hair was ripped out and my poor feet are covered in blisters. It might have been a good night, but this is going to be a long, long day.

Seymour raises his eyebrows when he sees me. I forgot to mention that I'm also striped. Here's a tip. Never let your friend apply fake tan to you when she is half-cut. I look like an orange-and-white striped zebra.

'Oh dear,' Seymour says when he sees me. 'Someone looks as if they had a heavy night.'

'It was my birthday,' I tell him by way of explanation. 'Things got a bit out of hand.'

'I've heard that they know how to party down in Netherslade Bridge.'

'We went to Bistro Live,' I fill in. 'School disco.'

Now he does look surprised. 'Wouldn't have thought it was your style.'

'Me neither. But I had possibly the best night of my life.' I need to sit down in less than a minute or there might be a sausage and mash surprise on the floor of the shop. 'I am now, however, paying the price.'

Laurence was extraordinarily solicitous this morning and, when I awoke, found Tracey asleep on the hideous blue velour sofa. If possible, I think she looked marginally worse for wear than me but, clearly, without trolley damage. My husband escorted her home to her own bed, still dazed.

'I had no idea that it was your birthday,' Seymour says.

I shake my head and wish I hadn't. 'It hardly seemed worth marking. Laurence and I normally go out for a romantic dinner.' I leave out the part where it might be weeks after the event when he gets round to it. 'And he buys me jewellery.' Several pieces from here in the past. 'No dinner, no jewellery this year.' I miss out the no making love bit. 'My neighbour decided we should try a different kind of celebration.'

'Looks like it worked a treat.'

'Maybe a bit too well,' I agree. Then, in a faint voice, 'Seymour. I really, really need to sit down.'

'Of course,' he says. 'I'll put the kettle on.'

Not a moment too soon, I slump into the armchair in the office and cover my eyes with my hand, trying to block out the light.

'Can I just stay in here today? Give me your most heinous task. One that you've been putting off for ages and I'll slowly work my way through it. I'll do anything, just so long as it doesn't involve me moving my head too much.' I do a test movement. 'At all,' I correct.

'I do have some expenses to enter into the computer,' Seymour admits. He tips two heaped spoonfuls of sugar into my cup and stirs. Then he hands over an extra strong black coffee.

I sigh with relief as I sip it.

'Think you can cope with that? A jumbled pile of receipts?'

Sensibly, I resist the urge to nod. 'Yes.'

'That should keep you busy for a few hours,' he says.

'Thank you for being so understanding.'

'I'm just disappointed that I didn't know it was your birthday. We could have had our own celebration.'

'No more celebrations.' I shake my head before I think better of it and regret the vibration it sets up in my brain.

'We'll see,' my boss says enigmatically. Then the shop bell rings and he excuses himself and heads off to deal with the customer, leaving me to groan to myself and vow to be teetotal from now on until my dying day. Which, if I come home drunk again like that, might be sooner than I planned.

Chapter 79

Somehow I manage to struggle through the rest of the day. I even try not to cringe too much as Seymour whistles his way happily through the afternoon. At three o'clock, when it's time for me to go home, I can't tell you how relieved I am not to have disgraced myself by barfing on the computer keyboard or anywhere else.

Everything still shifts unpleasantly when I move. I wonder whether someone spiked my drink and then I remember the handbag bottles of vodka that were empty by mid-evening and think probably not. An involuntary shudder runs through me. I need to go home to dry toast for dinner, a hot bath and a very, very early night. I never have been and am never destined to be, a party animal.

Seymour is in the shop. He smiles when he sees me. 'Thought I'd stay out of your way today.'

'Yes,' I say to him, returning his smile. 'You're too cheerful by half.'

'I'm not letting you get the bus home tonight, Lily. Not on your birthday.'

'It was my birthday yesterday,' I remind him. 'This is just another ordinary day.'

'I hope not,' he says and, from behind the counter, he produces the most exquisite bouquet of red roses wrapped in delicate pink tissue and adorned with pink ribbons.

'Oh, Seymour,' I say. 'I do hope these aren't for me.'

'Who else would they be for, Lily?' He hands them over to

me and then he rests his hands on my shoulders and eases me towards him. I stand there, powerless to resist as his lips brush gently against my cheek and I feel them burn like a brand. 'Happy birthday.'

'They're beautiful.'

'There's something else.' He takes the bouquet from me again and puts the roses on the glass counter. Then he takes up one of the small white Ornato boxes bound with a sliver of silver ribbon and holds it up. 'I hope you like it.'

'I can't accept this, Seymour.'

'You don't know what it is yet,' he points out.

But I know that if it's from here then it will be exquisite and expensive.

'Open it,' Seymour urges.

My heart is pounding as, reluctantly, I do. Inside the box is a link clasp bracelet in eighteen-carat gold. A delicate, diamond-encrusted heart hangs from it. 'This is too much, Seymour. Way too much.'

'I want you to have it,' he says plainly.

This is worth thousands of pounds. Seymour knows that this is utterly beyond my price range at the moment and, probably, for the rest of my life.

'Try it on.' Before I can protest further, he takes it out of the box and fastens it to my wrist. Then he stands back and admires it. 'It suits you,' he says. 'I knew it would.'

Tears spring to my eyes. 'It's so lovely. But I can't . . .'

'Nonsense. I insist,' my boss says. 'In fact, I shall be mortally offended if you don't.'

'Oh, Seymour.' I can't stop the tears and so I let them flow down my cheeks.

'Now, now.' He takes me into his arms and I rest my head on his shoulder. 'You deserve the world, Lily.'

It's left unspoken that he could give it to me. I am well aware of it. I could fight this and refuse Seymour's generous gift. But I can't. I hate to admit it, but my head is being turned by this kind and attentive man. He makes me feel like a woman again. Like I'm loved and cherished. And it's not just this lavishly generous gift – my God, I've learned enough in the last few months to know that doesn't matter – it's his kindness of spirit, the way his eyes shine when he looks at me, the special smile that he reserves for when he glances my way.

I tilt my head and he looks down at me. 'Oh, Lily.'

'What am I to do?' The sentence catches in my throat. 'Tell me.'

'I don't know,' he says softly.

My fingers stroke his cheek and then his lips find mine and I don't pull away. No, I don't pull away. Instead, I twine my arms round his neck and draw him into me as deeply as I can and lose myself in his embrace.

Chapter 80

Laurence was sitting talking to Christopher Cherry. It was three o'clock and this was their afternoon tea break. Alongside the required cup of tea, Laurence was enjoying a freshly-baked scone topped with homemade strawberry jam and a dollop of clotted cream that came from a small farm in Cornwall belonging to relatives of the Cherrys.

'It's important to test the products every day, lad,' Christopher said, when he'd caught Laurence glancing at his watch. 'Twenty minutes out of the afternoon to sit down and take stock never hurt anyone.'

'I'm just finding it hard to adjust to the pace of life,' Laurence admitted. 'Though I am enjoying it.'

This morning they'd had a school party in. Twenty-five seven year olds had been shown around the farm and the animal petting area, then had been served orange juice and flapjacks in the field outside.

The lunch service had been busy too, with a steady stream of people coming and going even in midweek. Christopher had been out and about sourcing a new supplier of home-made cakes and had brought back several samples required for testing. The butcher's counter was always busy, particularly from Thursday onwards as people came in for their weekend joints or barbecue supplies.

'We all need to slow down in life. It goes by quick enough.' Mr Cherry waved his hand expansively round the barn. 'Since I started this place, I've never been away on business for a night, nor missed a family dinner. Never needed to. The business doesn't suffer for it.'

'You're so right,' Laurence agreed, wiping cream from his lip. 'But there are many aspects of Cherry's where I could make a big difference.'

'In good time,' Christopher assured him. 'No need to run at it like a bull in a china shop. If it's a sound business idea, it'll still be a sound business idea in a couple of weeks or a couple of months. You need to decide what your priorities are.'

'I'm thinking about a range of organic meals, high quality, all natural ingredients under Cherry's own brand.'

'It's your family I'm talking about,' his boss said. 'We're ticking over nicely here. I've cash in the bank. I don't owe anyone money. You've only been here five minutes and you're on top of it. I've no regrets in choosing you, lad. You're a credit to the business.'

'That's good to hear.'

'But you and that young family of yours have had it rough the last couple of months. Focus your efforts on them. Get home while it's still light and play out in the garden with them.'

If only Christopher Cherry could see what their garden was like.

'I bet you didn't get much chance to do that when you were in the City, eh?'

'No,' Laurence agreed. 'I was rarely home before they were in bed then.' Plus he'd been at his desk at some ungodly hour in the morning. Lunch was either non-existent or hours long with clients, and then he was usually out entertaining at least two if not three nights a week. Even his golf at the weekends had usually been a way of networking and drumming up business. He couldn't actually think of anything that he did for the sheer love of it. Quite often, and he could hardly bear to admit this to himself, his children irritated him as he was so unused to dealing with them. How differently he felt towards them now. He was overwhelmed with love for them and the way they'd dealt with their change in circumstances.

'That's no way to live your life,' Christopher said. 'I might not be paying you top dollar, but I can help you to have a balanced family life. You won't find me asking you to be here at midnight.'

Laurence was already enjoying his cycle ride to work and back every day. The tummy that he'd started to develop was disappearing already. He felt fitter, freer than he had in years.

'No one ever had put on their headstone, *I wish I'd spent more time at work.*'

'It was Lily's birthday yesterday. It will certainly make a change to be at home to celebrate it.' Normally, it fell when he was on the other side of the world somewhere. He'd missed it more times that he cared to remember, but never intentionally. This year, when he had the time to spoil her, there wasn't the money.

'Take something home to cook,' Christopher offered. 'What about one of those new cakes too? You can all give one a test drive.'

'That's very kind of you.'

'I want you to be happy here, lad. Once someone comes to work here, I don't like to see them go.'

It was fair to say that most of the staff had been with Cherry's for years. It was only the young weekend staff who came and went, usually on their way to university. Oh, to be that young again. Laurence shook his head. He'd do it all differently if given a second time around. There was no way that he'd ever devote every waking moment to a company which could then turn round and dump him the moment the going got tough.

No, second time round, he'd devote himself to his family. As Christopher Cherry so rightly advised, they'd come first now. And, bizarrely, finding themselves in this situation had given him a chance to put that right. From now on he was going to be the best husband and father that he could possibly be.

Chapter 81

Seymour drives me home. We hold hands when he isn't changing gear. I try not to steal glances at him but, instead, try to look straight ahead and think about what I'm doing. But I can't. My head is whirling, my stomach is roiling and I can blame none of it on last night's excesses.

Seymour has kissed me. I have kissed him. And it has changed everything.

He squeezes my hand tenderly and my heart flips. 'Okay?'

I nod.

'You don't regret it, do you?' Seymour asks. His voice sounds uncertain.

I shake my head.

'We'll talk about it tomorrow?'

'Yes.' Then, thankfully, I see the sign for Netherslade Bridge. 'Could you drop me here, please.'

Seymour sighs. 'I'd be much happier if I could take you home.'

I'm not sure if he means to my home or to his home.

'This will be fine. Really.'

So he pulls the car over and then turns to me. His fingers trace the outline of my face and my skin shivers deliciously at his touch. I put my hand over his and hold it there, breathing in his scent. 'I'll see you tomorrow,' I say.

'You will, won't you?'

'Of course.'

'I don't want you to slip away from me, Lily.'

I risk a smile. 'I'll be there. Ten o'clock.'

'Promise?'

Another nod. 'Promise.'

'I know that this has happened very quickly . . .'

I put my finger on his lips. 'Tomorrow,' I say. 'We'll talk tomorrow.' Now, I just need time to think.

Seymour pulls me to him; his lips find mine and my head spins again. I'm the first to break away. 'I have to go.'

'Don't,' he pleads.

But, before I lose my will, I get out of the car and watch as Seymour drives away.

Dazed, I clutch my bouquet of roses to me and then walk into Netherslade Bridge, still wearing the beautiful diamond bracelet which seems so incongruous the minute I step back into my own life. When I get to the tatty local shop, I sit on the bench outside. It's covered in graffiti and surrounded by litter and broken glass. A few bad apples seem perpetually determined to spoil this place, but it often feels as if they are winning, grinding down all the decent people. I kick a dumped beer bottle out of my way. This is my life now, I remind myself. This is how I live.

While I'm gazing down at my bracelet, my brain battling against the turmoil, Len comes and sits down next to me. The dogs follow suit and, absently, I pat the nearest head.

'Wotcher,' he says.

'Hello, Len,' I reply as I undo the bracelet.

'That's nice,' he notes.

'Yes.' I can't deny that. I slip the bracelet back inside its pretty box then bury it deep in my handbag. 'How are the dogs?'

His multi-coloured, multi-breed pack mill around my legs, sniffing happily. I reach out and stroke a couple of them on the muzzle.

'Good,' he says. 'Sally's going to have pups.' He nods at a young spaniel.

'That's nice.' I wonder how he will feed even more mouths but, clearly, Len isn't worried about it.

'Are you likin' it round here?' he asks.

'Yes,' I say. 'I am.'

'Stayin'?'

Unbidden tears burn my eyes. 'I don't know,' I answer honestly. 'I really don't know.'

'Oh.' Then he stands up. 'Wotcher,' he says again and then, en masse, he and his dogs are on their way again.

I *am* liking it round here, despite everything, but now I do wonder what Seymour's home is like, and what he'd think if he saw where I am currently living. Can I stay here? Forever? Can I make Netherslade Bridge my permanent home? I thought that this would be a temporary situation, but it isn't. We're here for the foreseeable future, the long term, until we pay off all our debts and scrabble back onto the property ladder – if we ever can.

I close my eyes. I'm tired and I don't think it's entirely to do with my late night. What I wouldn't give for a life of ease again right now . . .

'Come on,' I say to myself. 'We'd better go home.'

Wearily, I stand and pick up my bouquet of beautiful roses. Then, trying not to look at the cracked pavement, the rundown houses, the weeds, the rusting bicycles lying around, I trudge home.

Chapter 82

In the kitchen, the smell of cooking wafts from the oven and, on the hob, two pots are boiling away, unattended. I turn them down, aware that the smell is making my stomach turn. Laurence and the children are in the garden playing cricket on the one mown strip.

Putting my bouquet in the sink, I run some water to keep the stems damp. I'll have to borrow Tracey's vase for them later. Then, taking a steadying breath, I go outside. My world feels different since Seymour kissed me and I can't for the life of me explain why.

It is the first time I have kissed another man since I married Laurence and the knowledge of it weighs like a lead ball deep inside me.

'Hello.' I try to sound brighter than I feel.

'Hello, darling.' Laurence kisses my cheek and I notice how different my husband's lips feel to Seymour's. 'Feeling better?'

'I'm still not that great,' I admit. Then to deflect attention from myself, 'Where did you get that from?' I nod at the cricket stumps and the bat that the children are currently using to hit each other.

'Borrowed it from work,' Laurence tells me. 'You know that selection of outdoor toys for customers to use? Well, Christopher said I was welcome to borrow them.'

'Of course. That's kind of him.'

'It was a bit of a devil to carry them home on the bike, but I managed somehow.' My husband affords himself a laugh.

'I don't think I've ever had a boss who's been so laid-back before,' he says. 'I'm sure I'm going to like it there.'

'That's good. I'm so pleased.' I try not to think about my own boss.

'I brought some local sausages home too. They're in the oven now.'

Sausages. A flashback to last night's dinner makes my stomach flip.

'Christopher has given us a lemon drizzle cake too, from a new supplier to road test. It might not be the most romantic of dinners for your birthday celebration, but I thought the children would enjoy them.'

'It will be lovely,' I say, even though I feel sick at the mere thought of eating.

'I'd better check the potatoes,' Laurence says.

Not mash too, I think. Please God. 'I can take over.'

'Wouldn't hear of it. I've bought a bottle of cheap and cheerful wine and I'm going to pour you a glass while you put your feet up. Well,' he corrects, 'a mug.'

'Play nicely,' I shout at the children who are doing anything but that, now our attention isn't on them.

I follow Laurence inside and then nearly crash into the back of him when he pulls up short. He points at my roses. 'Who are they from?'

'My boss,' I say, and my voice sounds steadier than I feel.

'My goodness.' His voice is tight. 'You must have made an impact there.'

I try to smile. 'I think Seymour just felt sorry for me today as I was suffering.'

'All self-inflicted,' Laurence points out.

'Absolutely.' I can only hold my hands up to that accusation.

My husband's face has darkened. 'I'm sorry that I've not been able to do more this year.'

'It doesn't matter,' I assure him. Though, as yet, I haven't had so much as a card from Laurence – and how much would that have cost?

If he's so unhappy about another man giving me roses, there's no way that I can show him the expensive diamond bracelet – not, if I'm brutally honest, that I ever intended to. I will have to hide it somewhere and take it out to look at when Laurence isn't here.

Then I think about the road I'm going down. I know that I've only taken one step, but is this really the way I want to carry on?

Wrapping my arms round Laurence's waist, I say, 'Dinner is a lovely thought. I'm really looking forward to it.'

The tension in his jaw relaxes.

What would he think if he knew that I'd just been kissing another man? A man who could offer me the type of life that I used to have. I push the thought aside.

'Go and sit down,' Laurence instructs and turns me round to face the living room. 'I'll bring you some wine.'

So I do as I'm told and I sit on the sofa with a mug of warm white wine that I don't want while my husband makes me sausages and mash that I don't want either. And it gives me far too much time to think about what I do want.

Chapter 83

When I've dutifully finished my supper and I've helped with the washing up, I kiss Laurence on the forehead. 'Thank you.'

He holds me tight. 'Happy birthday, darling. Next year it will be better.'

'This year it was fine,' I tell him.

'You know what I mean.'

And I do, but Laurence doesn't really know what I mean. 'Is it all right if I go next door for five minutes?'

'That'll be an hour.'

'I haven't got a vase for these roses and I'd like to donate them to Tracey as she's been so good.'

'That's a nice thought.'

Plus I don't want them sitting here staring us both in the face. I don't know what Laurence will think and I don't *want* to think what I'll think.

'I'll be back soon.' So, I scoop up my roses and my handbag – I can hardly leave that lying around in case Laurence or the children go fishing for something – and carry them out into the cool night air. I knock at Tracey's and then lean on the brickwork of her wall with my eyes closed trying to still my brain while I wait for her to answer.

When she opens the door, my neighbour stares directly at me. 'You look like someone who's found a pound and lost a fiver.'

'Something like that,' I agree and then, when I'm inside, I produce my bouquet of two dozen ruby red roses.

'Wow,' she says. 'Someone loves you.'

'How observant,' I say wryly.

'Tell all.' She puts the kettle on rather than reaching for the wine box and I assume that means that Tracey's capacity for alcohol has somewhat diminished today.

'They're from my boss,' I say, and she raises an eyebrow. 'Laurence is very cross about them and I'm not sure how I feel, so I would like to regift them to you.'

'Plus you don't have a vase,' she points out.

'There is that small practical consideration,' I concur, and hand over the bouquet.

'Well, I'm not going to look a gift-horse in the mouth,' Tracey says. 'They're beautiful.'

'I know.'

'There's a big sigh lurking just behind that comment.'

Letting the sigh out, I dig in my handbag. 'Seymour bought me this too.' I show my friend my bracelet.

She whistles through her teeth. 'What is it about you that makes men want to shower you with jewellery? And can you give me some tips?'

We both laugh. Then Tracey sets down two cups of tea and we sit at the table. 'What am I going to do with it?' I say. 'I can't wear it. Laurence would go ballistic if he saw this.'

'Is there good cause for him to do so?'

I flush and then mumble, 'Seymour kissed me today. I didn't exactly fight him off.'

'You can't even blame it on being drunk.'

'No.'

'It was a very good night last night,' my friend says.

'Too good. Thank you for organising it all.'

'You're very funny when you're drunk, Lily Jones. You should let your hair down more often.'

'I'm not sure that's a good idea at all! This is the first time I've gone off the rails in my entire life – and look at the result. I've no pubic hair and a variety of trolley-based injuries. What a mess.'

My friend puffs out a breath and fixes me with a stare. 'Is this serious? With Seymour?'

'I don't know.'

'But you adore Laurence,' she reasons. 'You adore the kids. Think of the fallout, Lily.'

'I'm trying to.' I massage my temples. 'This all happened today and I'm still struggling to make sense of it.'

Tracey dangles the bracelet over her wrist and the diamonds catch the spotlights in the kitchen and sparkle like starlight.

'I could wear it for you,' she offers and then holds up a hand. 'Just joking.'

'I can't keep it.'

'You must,' Tracey insists. 'Hide it. Laurence doesn't have to know about it.'

'This is the first secret I've ever kept from him.'

'Be mercenary. You never know when you might need it.'

But I don't want to be mercenary. I want to keep it because I love it and I wonder if I also love the man who gave it to me.

Chapter 84

It is, of course, two hours later when I leave Tracey's house and go home. I should have learned by now that a quick visit to Tracey's is always impossible. Plus I needed to talk to her, to confide the events of the day in someone before my head exploded trying to hold it all in.

Laurence is waiting for me in the living room. 'The children are in bed already, darling,' he tells me, 'but they're not asleep yet.'

'I'll go straight up and kiss them.'

'I thought we'd have an early night too.'

And I don't know if he means *early night* early night or just an early night to go to sleep. What I need, what I want, is the latter. 'That's fine.'

Laurence catches my hand and pulls me down on the sofa next to him.

'You shouldn't have given your flowers to Tracey,' he says. 'You should have kept them.'

'She was very pleased with them.'

'But they were yours. You deserved them. I was just jealous because I didn't buy them and I should have.'

'We don't have the money for rose buying,' I remind him.

'We will do again,' he assures me.

'I'm going to go up,' I say. 'After all the excitment of last night, I'm dog tired.'

Laurence grins. 'I've never seen you like that before.'

'It will be a very long time until you see me like that again,' I promise.

'Oh, I don't know,' he says. 'I rather liked it.'

This is so the wrong time to be flirting with me, Laurence, I think. I'm tired, I'm wracked with guilt and I'm sick to my stomach. Your timing couldn't be more ill-advised.

'Do you still have that sexy little skirt?' His eyes twinkle. 'You haven't had your birthday present yet.'

'Laurence, the skirt is in the laundry basket and, after it has been washed, it's going straight back to the charity shop where it came from.'

'Couldn't you keep it just for fun?'

'No.' Now I'm irritated. Is that what it's going to take from now on to get my husband interested in me – dressing up in tarty outfits? There are some men – and I can name one in particular – who would like to have me just as I am. 'Let's just go to bed, Laurence. I'm very tired.'

With that, I take my handbag and go up to bed. I hear my husband locking the back door and turning off the lights. I kiss the children goodnight and I have to resist squeezing the living daylights out of them as I'm feeling so emotionally over-wrought. It's not just Seymour's kiss that has turned me into a crazy lady; all the stress of the last few months has bubbled up to the surface again just when I thought I was making a good job of keeping it all buttoned down and under control.

I don't bother with the bathroom and am in my nightdress and in bed by the time Laurence follows me a few moments later.

'Goodnight,' I say briskly and then turn over, pulling the duvet up round my chin. There can be no doubting that all I want tonight is sleep.

Laurence strips his clothes off and slides in beside me. I feel him kissing my hair, his hand stroking my shoulder. 'I love you, Lily,' he murmurs.

My stomach is a ball of knots. I can count on one hand the number of times in my married life when I have refused my husband's attentions. I have always, no matter how I'm feeling, tried to make myself *available* to him. Now, I just don't want him to touch me. I can't make love to him tonight – I simply can't. Not while I'm thinking about another man. God help me. So I lie stock still, unmoving. A few minutes later and Laurence gives up. He turns onto his back and lets out an unhappy sigh.

And I think, Serves him right. Let him experience what it feels like to be unloved. Let him experience what it feels like to be unwanted. Let him experience what it feels like to be betrayed.

Chapter 85

Laurence was enjoying a social pint of beer in The Nut. Relations were still strained with Lily and he was glad to get out of the house for an hour. Their argument last night – if one could call it that – had come out of left field. Suddenly, when they were in bed, his wife had gone all cold on him and he couldn't entirely understand why.

Perhaps it was because her birthday had largely gone unmarked, but it wasn't like Lily to make a fuss about such things. She was usually so understanding. But clearly something had rankled with her. He'd tried to talk to her about it in his clumsy, bloke-like way, but nothing he had said could get through. It seemed that he was as well staying out of the way.

'All right, Lozzer?' Skull said when he came in.

'I've been better,' Laurence admitted.

'Work okay?'

'Work's fine,' he said.

'Problems with the missus then?'

Laurence nodded. 'You've hit the nail on the head.'

'You need a game of arrows,' Skull advised. 'That'll take your mind off it.'

'Darts?' Laurence swigged his beer. 'I've never played before. Well, not properly.'

'Nothing to it,' Skull said. 'Get your pint. There's no one on there now.'

They both took their drinks and went over to the dartboard. Skull picked up the darts and handed a pack to Laurence.

'You don't throw them at the board,' his friend instructed. 'You *propel* them *smoothly* towards the *target*.' Skull demonstrated the action. 'Propel,' he reiterated.

'Propel,' Laurence echoed. He threw – propelled – the dart and hit the tiny red section of the bullseye.

His tutor frowned. 'Are you yankin' my chain, Lozzer?'

'No, no,' Laurence assured him. 'Beginner's luck.'

'We'll play 301,' Skull said. 'All you've got to do is get your score down from 301 to zero. We'd normally double in – hit a double to start – but we'll skip that for this game.'

'Right, right.'

'I'll go first,' Skull said. He threw the darts.

Three hours later and too many games to remember, Laurence had progressed to playing Jumpers and Killer. He'd also been invited to join the darts team. He was a natural with the arrows, they all insisted.

Later, the two of them sat down with Digger and Danny, discussed where he could source bikes for the kids and Lily, then watched football on the pub's Sky Television.

At closing time, they all walked together down to Greek John's kebab van that was permanently parked near the local shop.

'There's always a queue a mile long here,' Skull said as they slotted in line. 'Very popular. Best kebabs for miles.'

As they waited, joshing each other mercilessly, Laurence thought that he had never expected to feel a sense of belonging here. He'd expected to be the outsider. It was strange that he felt more comfortable with Skull, Digger and Danny and all the other blokes whose names he'd already forgotten in a beer haze than he ever had with his well-heeled neighbours in their exclusive village. There, he'd always felt as if he had to compete, maintain a certain status – in plain language, keep up with the Joneses. But as the Joneses themselves, they'd often in reality been the ones to keep up with. Here, the others knew him for what he was and treated him no differently because of it.

Ridiculously, he felt settled when once he had been so sure

that he'd be wanting to move on just as soon as he humanly could. Everything was working out well.

Skull slapped him on the back and he came out of his reverie. 'What are you wanting on your kebab, Lozzer? Chilli sauce?'

He nodded and then reached into his pocket.

'It's on me, mate,' Skull said. 'Got to keep our new darts ringer happy.'

'Thanks.' Laurence received his kebab gratefully. The lamb was hot and greasy, the chilli sauce raw and even hotter.

'Good?' Skull wanted to know.

'Yes.' He'd eaten at some of the top Michelin-starred restaurants in the world, tasted the best of foods, had drunk the finest of wines known to man. Yet a pint and a kebab with the boys of Netherslade Bridge had offered him more succour and pleasure than anything he could remember. 'It's good. Very good, indeed.'

And the same could be said about the rest of his life. He just had to work out how he could make things right with Lily.

Chapter 86

It's late afternoon and Seymour Chapman and I have spent the day trawling round diamond merchants in Hatton Garden and little back-street jewellery suppliers. I've seen rough gemstones transformed into beautiful contemporary jewellery – elaborate necklaces, simple bracelets, rings for every finger. I've drooled over diamonds in every hue – even chocolate-coloured ones which I've never in my life seen before. Trays and trays of glittering baubles have taunted and tempted and teased us. We've walked until my feet are sore and my throat is dry from talking.

Seymour takes my hand as he crosses the street, towing me behind him. 'That's it,' he tells me. 'Business is all done. Now for some pleasure.'

And despite the fact that we're on a busy street in full public view, he pulls me close to him.

A week has passed since the first kissing incident and I'd like to be able to tell you that it was all a silly mistake, nothing but a misunderstanding between Seymour and me. But it wasn't. It isn't.

We've had a week of holding hands over the table at lunchtime in the courtyard garden behind the shop, a week of stolen kisses, a week of long, lingering looks. We've talked about our pasts, our relationships, our likes, our dislikes. The only thing that we haven't discussed is the future.

Now we've closed the shop for today and escaped to London – ostensibly on a buying spree for next season, but that has been despatched much more deftly than I imagined.

'What now?'

'I have a little surprise for you,' Seymour says.

'Oh, Seymour.' I've already had to turn down a dozen offers of jewellery that he was keen for me to have. 'I don't want anything.'

'You'll want this,' he assures me and he turns to hail a cab.

We jump in and Seymour says, 'To the Ritz!'

My eyebrows shoot up. 'The Ritz?'

'Afternoon tea,' Seymour says. 'I hope you'll like it.'

'I'll love it,' I assure him. Hand-in-hand in the back of the black cab, we speed off through the streets of London. A short time later, we pull up outside the splendour of the famous London landmark at 150 Piccadilly.

Seymour has reserved a table for us in the spectacular Palm Court and, suddenly, I'm reminded of how my life used to be and sadness wells inside me. This is just the sort of thing that Laurence used to do for me. We're ushered in to the marvellous room and take our seats.

The pianist is playing 'Putting on the Ritz' when the waiter brings our selection of sandwiches and pastries on a tall, tiered, silver server: delicate little morsels of chicken, cucumber, smoked salmon, then whirls of cream and strawberries and the tiniest, lightest piece of chocolate cake that I've ever eaten. I have tea and champagne, then more tea and more champagne and the pianist plays, 'Smoke Gets in Your Eyes' and 'Cry Me a River'.

By the time we've finished our tea it's nearly seven o'clock and my head is spinning. While I don't want to spoil the mood, I say, 'Look at the time. Laurence will be wondering where I am.'

I told my husband that I would be late back and, though he's done this a thousand times to me, guilt is beginning to kick in nevertheless.

Seymour reaches across the table and takes my hand. 'You don't have to go home, Lily.'

'Yes, I do. Of course I do.'

'I've taken the liberty of booking a suite for the night.'

My heart sinks. 'I can't do that,' I tell him. 'I'm not free, Seymour. I have my family to think of.' Though it occurs to me that I haven't done very much thinking about them today. I've been wrapped up in myself today, taken away from the struggle that my life has turned into and shown a glimpse of the past once more – and perhaps, though I don't want to admit it, a glimpse of what a future with Seymour would be like. With Seymour, my life would be one of ease again, of luxury, of freedom from worry. The children could go to a nice school again. I could have a car. Laurence would . . . What would my husband do?

'Stay with me,' he cajoles, breaking into my angst. 'There's nothing I'd like more.'

And, at this very moment, I'd like to stay here too. I'd like to find out quite how elegant a suite at the Ritz is. I'd like to stay here forever in this extravagant, elegant, excessive bubble and never go home to shabby, shoddy, scary Netherslade Bridge. As much as it pains me to say this, I'd also like to find out how it would feel to lie in Seymour's arms. I try to block out the vision, but I can't make it go from my mind. Seymour's naked body next to mine is a very persistent image.

This last year, my husband has done nothing but betray me, pull me down into the gutter and now he can't even bring himself to make love to me. Yet in front of me there's someone desperate to be with me, to care for me, to cherish me, to love me.

Seymour drains his champagne flute and pays the bill. Then his eyes meet mine. 'Moment of truth.'

'I can't stay,' I tell him, although my body is yearning to be wanted. 'I've brought nothing with me. I've made no arrangements for the children.' The fact that I have a husband to consider remains unspoken. Perhaps all the fizz that I've consumed is clouding my judgement.

'All that can be fixed,' he points out. 'We've had a lovely day, Lily. I thought this would be an equally lovely way to end it.'

'I can't stay,' I repeat, trying to drive it into my brain as well as Seymour's. 'I really can't stay.'

'What if we take a bottle of champagne to the room and you stay as long as you can? Just for an hour, no more, if that's what you want. Shall we?'

I should say no, I know that I should. But when I open my mouth, 'Yes' comes out.

Chapter 87

The suite is every bit as sumptuous as I thought it would be. The period room is furnished exquisitely in a muted palette of vanilla, rose pink and the palest powder blue. There's a lounge area, an alcove with a table set for two and, at one end, an enormous bed beneath the most sparkling crystal chandelier that I've ever seen. Lavish bowls of cream roses grace every surface.

Seymour takes my hand and leads me inside and I realise that I'm not here to admire the décor. Far from it. I'm here to consider the possibility of committing adultery for the first time in my life. I have been married to Laurence for nearly fifteen years and have never once in all that time been tempted to stray. Now look at me.

I had convinced myself that we could just have one drink, relax here for a while, perhaps cuddle up together for a precious hour. But I know that's not to be. It's either all or nothing.

Seymour helps me to take off my jacket and then shrugs out of his own. I abandon my handbag on one of the myriad chairs. We ordered a bottle of champagne at the front desk and, in the time it's taken us to reach the room, the bottle is already waiting for us in a cooler filled with ice. My mouth is as dry as a desert as Seymour pops the cork.

I should call Laurence and let him know that I'll be late back, perhaps very late. But how can I? How can I call him when I'm in a room with champagne, deceit in my heart and a man who is making my insides turn to water?

When Seymour has poured the bubbles he hands me a glass and we raise a toast. 'To us,' he says.

But I can't toast us. My mind is in turmoil. I want to be here and I don't. I want to make love with Seymour and stay faithful to Laurence. And, when I thought I was resigned to – was even embracing – my fate, my lowered circumstances, instead I find that I want to lie in this enormous bed, swathed in Egyptian cotton sheets. I want to bathe in the marble bath and drink champagne from crystal glasses. I want pure, unadulterated luxury if only for one night.

Is that wrong of me? Is it so very, very wrong? There are women out there sleeping with men other than their husbands every single day of the week, in every city and every town and every village. Why should I be any different? Why shouldn't it be me breaking my vows? Haven't I had undue provocation? Haven't I stood by Laurence when he has taken us to the brink of despair and beyond? Hasn't he broken his vows to me? I thought that I had forgiven him for all this, but I don't believe that I truly have.

'Okay?' Seymour speaks into my confused reverie.

'Yes.'

'You were a million miles away.'

No, I think. Only at the other end of the motorway. Only in Netherslade Bridge.

'I'm sorry.'

I knock back my champagne and Seymour takes my glass then twines his arms round my waist. 'All I want to do is be with you, Lily. We'll spend it exactly how you want to.'

Then his mouth finds mine and any resolve that I'd had about coming here and having a pleasant chat and drinking some nice champagne go out of the window. With fingers that don't feel like they belong to me, I fumble with the buttons on Seymour's shirt, I tug at his tie, I yank frantically at the belt on his trousers. He returns the frenzy and his hands are in my hair, on my breasts, exploring beneath my skirt. It's as if by moving at such a frantic pace, I can block out any thoughts that this is wrong, wrong, wrong.

313

If it's fast and it's furious then it can't be love. It can't be the same as the slow steady rhythm that Laurence and I have settled into over the years.

Seymour strips off my blouse as we stagger and stumble towards the bed. I should have put on better underwear and then I remember that my better underwear is still trapped inside our repossessed house and, even in my wildest dreams, I hadn't planned on showing my pants to anyone.

As we kiss madly and snatch and tear at each other's clothes, I knock over a side table and a bowl of beautiful roses. The roses tumble to the floor in a torrent of water and I step on a thorn and hop the rest of my way to the bed, still wrapped tightly in Seymour's embrace. I can hardly breathe, hardly think, hardly comprehend what I'm doing when we fall together on the bed. I think I'm giggling but I might be crying. Then all time slows. I can hear my own heart beating. The vanilla, the rose pink, the powder blue all appear in sharp relief. I can feel Seymour's heart against mine. Everything is still, suspended in motion.

Then he kisses me tenderly, so tenderly that my heart almost breaks and his breath is on my face, in my hair, on my body. I feel myself high, high, floating high on the ceiling looking down on myself and what I'm doing. I watch myself lie back, naked, my hair spread around me. Then Seymour sloughs off the rest of his clothes until he too is naked and I see his toned, hard body move above me. My head is thrown back in ecstasy and, if I didn't know better, if I didn't know for sure that it was me down on that bed, I wouldn't recognise myself at all. I wrap my legs round my lover and urge on his delicious, ponderous rhythm.

Then my breathing changes and I writhe beneath Seymour, clutching at his damp skin and, once again, I hear myself, the strange woman that I've become, crying out, 'Yes. Yes. *Yes!*'

Chapter 88

Later, lying in Seymour's arms, I'm quiet and content in my body if not in my mind. My head is resting on his shoulder, my leg is thrown over his and I listen to his breathing as he slips into sleep. His body is so different to Laurence's. The feel of him against me is new and so exciting that I feel as if all my nerve-endings are on fire. I kiss his cheek.

'Seymour,' I say. 'I have to get up. I have to go now.'

'Hmmm?' He tries to rouse himself, but there seems to only be one part of Seymour that's wide awake and raring to go.

Oh, God. How did I get into this situation? Think what Amanda Marquis would have to say down at the Golf Club if she could see me now. Think what my *husband* would say if he could see me now.

I look at my watch. It's nearly ten o'clock and I know that I must go home.

'Seymour.' I shake the man I have just made love to. 'I have to go. Really I do.'

Now he opens his eyes. 'Stay.'

'I can't. I'm so sorry.'

'Sure?' He snuggles into me again.

'I have responsibilities,' I remind him. Even though I have sorely neglected them.

'Then I'll call a car.'

'You stay here,' I urge. 'I'll take the train home.'

'Wouldn't hear of it,' he insists. With a sleepy yawn, he punches

315

a number into his mobile phone and orders a car to come and collect us.

'You have just over half an hour,' he tells me. 'How would you like to fill it?' He pulls me to him again and runs his hands over my body and, despite myself, I want to respond once more.

Instead, I still his hands. 'I should take a bath.'

'I thought you'd say that.' He gives his most endearing smile. 'But I hoped you wouldn't.'

Before I'm tempted to do otherwise, I slip out of the bed and disappear into the bathroom. I turn on the taps of the big, white marble bath and pour in some of the jasmine-fragranced bath foam, inhaling the scent to calm my whirring mind. A few moments later, while I'm running the bath, Seymour appears behind me. He nuzzles into my neck.

'You know that this can't continue,' I tell him.

'We'll work something out.'

What, I wonder as I turn off the taps. Seymour holds my hand as I step into the bath. 'Mind if I join you?'

We settle down into the bath together, my back against his chest, and let the soothing water wash over us. Seymour's hands gently cup my breasts and I want to remember every moment of this night as much as I want to erase it from my memory.

He washes my back and kisses my neck. Then I lie against him until we really can't put off the moment any longer.

Together we get out and Seymour dries my back and the ends of my wet hair and he kisses my face and I think I'm crying again.

Just as we've finished dressing, the car arrives. Seymour has torn my blouse. He has two buttons missing from his shirt and can't find them. He says that he'll have them put the cost of the vase on his bill.

In the car, we hold hands in the back like teenagers and I can still smell him on my skin despite the jasmine-scented bath. The nearer we get to home, the more melancholy I become.

Tonight was a dream, a ridiculous dream and now I'm heading back to reality.

When we get to the first Netherslade Bridge sign, I say, 'Drop me here, please.'

'No,' Seymour says and, instead, we swing into my hideous, horrible, horrendous estate.

The black car purrs along. 'Turn right here,' I instruct the driver. 'Then left.' When we reach my door, I say, 'Here it is.'

We stop outside. There are still lights on inside even though it's now past midnight.

Seymour's face doesn't betray what he thinks about my humble abode. Instead, in a low voice, all he says is, 'Leave him.'

'I can't.'

'We'll talk about this tomorrow.' He takes my hand and holds it to his lips.

I open the car door.

'I love you,' Seymour says, and there's a desperation in his voice that makes my throat close up.

The light goes on in the hall. Any moment now Laurence could fling the front door open. He could see Seymour and me frozen like this and he would know, instantly, that we were lovers.

'I could take you away from all this.' He stares bleakly at my home. As do I.

When I don't speak, he squeezes my hand tightly. 'We'll sort it out. I promise you,' he says. Then, 'I'll see you tomorrow.'

'Yes.' I walk down the path to my rundown home and I wonder how many times I am going to keep saying, 'Yes,' when what I actually mean is, 'No.'

Chapter 89

Laurence's face is rigid with rage when he opens the door. He watches the car as it drives away.

'Who the hell was that?'

'My boss,' I say flatly.

'Where the hell have you been all day?'

'Working,' I remind him. 'Then we had dinner.'

'Did you forget that you had a family?'

'Yes,' I want to shout. 'Yes, I did. When I was in my lover's arms, I didn't think of you at all.' Instead, I say nothing.

'Would it have been too much trouble to call and let me know what was happening?'

Then something inside me snaps. 'How many times have you done this to me, Laurence?' I yell, even though I know it will wake the children. 'How many times?'

My husband looks taken aback.

'For years and years you did exactly as you liked, never thinking once of me or the children. And look where that got us.' I gesture at our crumbling surroundings. I wonder now what Laurence was doing at all those corporate dinners, all those bonding days out that didn't end until the early hours of the morning 'Did I ever know where *you* were?' He could have been doing exactly the things that I have been doing for the last few hours and I would have been none the wiser. 'You have come and gone as you pleased, whenever you've wanted to, and I have never uttered a word of complaint.'

'I've changed,' my husband says quietly. 'I have changed.'

'Perhaps I have too.'

'I have always tried to give you the best,' Laurence says. There's a catch in his voice.

'Now look at us.'

'I thought this was bringing us closer together.'

I snort at that.

'I'm going to handle this job differently,' he swears. 'I'll be here for you and the children more. We might not have the material goods that we did, but we have each other and I want to build a better quality of life for us.'

I don't point out that we don't have *any* of the material goods that we did. Unless you count a knocked-off telly. My mind drifts back to the Ritz, to making love with Seymour, to the sheer decadence of it all.

Then, it's as if a light dawns on Laurence. He takes a step backwards and I wonder if he can smell the traces of Seymour on my skin. Can he see the brand of another man's kiss on my lips?

'You promised, Lily,' he breathes. 'You promised that you would never leave me.'

'I know.' But that was then and this is now, I want to tell him. I never intended for any of this to happen. I was happy with Laurence. Happy with our life. Then it was snatched away from me. And I have done my best, really I have.

But it's all such a struggle. Every time I think we might be getting somewhere, something else comes along to punch us down. A few hours ago, the view of my world and the hopelessness of it was turned upside down.

Now I have met someone who can give me our old life back. Instantly. I could leave here, leave Netherslade Bridge tomorrow and never come back. I could take the children away from here, they could go back to Stonelands School and both have the chance to become a lawyer or a plastic surgeon once more and not be fit only for a job in B&Q.

Seymour wants me and he could give me the world. He loves me. And I'm horrified as I acknowledge that I might feel the same. If I go with him, I never need struggle again. I'm not doomed to a life of drudgery in Netherslade Bridge as I had resigned myself to. I have found a way out.

I just don't know if I can bear to take it. But then, I just don't know if I can bear not to.

Chapter 90

Laurence and I both lie awake all night staring at the ceiling, both pretending that we are sound asleep.

In the morning he gets up early, ready to cycle to work. He brings me a cup of tea, the standard peace-offering for married couples. 'No work today?' he asks hesitantly.

'My boss gave me the day off,' I lie. 'As I was back so late.'

'I'm sorry about last night. I acted like an arse.'

'Me too,' I concede. 'I should have phoned.'

'You should have brought your boss in,' Laurence continues. 'I'd like to have met him.'

I glance around the dilapidated room.

'Perhaps not,' he concurs. Then he kisses me lightly, a troubled expression on his face. 'We will be all right, won't we, Lily?'

'Of course,' I say, but I fail to keep the weary sigh out of my voice.

'I'll bring something home for dinner,' Laurence says. 'So that you don't have to worry about it. Just have a relaxing day to yourself.'

Fat chance, I think. My mind hasn't rested for a second all night, churning over my options.

When I hear the front door close, I get up and go to the window and watch Laurence cycling away with a sick feeling in my stomach. What if there comes a time when I watch him walk, cycle or drive away from us for the very last time? How would I feel if he didn't come home tonight? How would he feel if I wasn't here, if the children weren't here?

Then, in zombie mode, I get the children up, throw on some clothes while they eat their breakfast and then set off to walk them down to the school while trying not to to listen to their constant bickering. As we pass Tracey's front door, Charlize and Keanu come out by themselves. Unusual. 'No Mum today?' I ask.

'She's not feeling well,' Charlize tells me.

'Oh, I'm sorry to hear that. Does she need anything?'

'Dunno,' is her daughter's conclusion.

'I'll drop in on my way back home to check that she's okay.' I can always pop out to the shop for her later if she does need me to get some bits. So, when I've escorted them all to school, I make my way back to Tracey's place, still trying to marshal my scattered thoughts.

Knocking at Tracey's door, I wait for ages and, finally, as I begin to wonder if she's gone back to bed, my friend opens her door. She peers out of the crack.

'Hello,' I say. 'Charlize told me you're not feeling well.'

My neighbour sighs and opens the door to me. Her eyes are red from crying.

'Gosh,' I say. 'What's happened?'

Tracey risks a glance up and down the street before ushering me inside.

'You sit,' I tell her when we're in the kitchen. 'I'll put the kettle on.'

'It'll take more than tea, Lily,' Tracey confides and then I notice that there's a bottle of brandy open on the table.

'It's only just gone nine o'clock,' I remind her, casting a glance at the half-empty glass.

'I need this,' she says. 'Believe me. I might not stop until I've drunk the whole lot.'

I leave the kettle to boil and sit down next to her, putting my arms round her shoulders. 'It can't be that bad.'

'Oh, it is,' she assures me. 'Think of how bad it can get and then double it. Or maybe treble it.'

'It must involve money.'

'It does,' she agrees with a teary laugh. 'Clearly you've lived around here long enough to know that.'

'Anything I can help with?'

The tears start to fall again and splash on the table between us. 'I've messed up badly this time,' she says. 'Really badly.' Surreptitiously, I move the brandy bottle away from Tracey before she's tempted to reach for it again. 'I told you that I went to that loan shark.'

I nod.

She blows out a sigh. 'Big mistake.' She turns her face to me. 'I had five hundred quid off him. That's all. Just to get me out of a hole. Five hundred measly quid.'

'And you can't pay it back.'

'I should have read the small print.' Tracey laughs and she sounds completely unhinged. 'I now owe him five grand.'

'That can't be right.'

'Oh, it's right for sure. This bloke makes up his own interest rates. It's simple extortion, and I fell for it. Jamelia warned me. Her cousin got done by him a year ago. They had a devil of a job to get him off her back. I should have listened to her, but I didn't. I was desperate, Lily. Do you know how that feels?'

Only recently can I even begin to relate to this.

'I'm never going to get out of his clutches. This is what he does and then you're trapped.'

'There must be something you can do,' I say. 'Can't you go to the police?'

'I'd end up at the bottom of Furzton Lake wearing concrete stilettos if I did that.'

'Can't you pay off more?'

'With what, Lily?'

I sigh. Making money appear out of nowhere isn't a trick I've yet mastered.

'There is one way I can pay off my debt,' Tracey admits.

'Then you must take it.'

'I can have sex with him,' she continues bleakly. What's left of her composure cracks. 'Or anyone else he chooses. I can work off my debt that way.'

'No way.' I say. 'You can't even consider it.'

'What else am I to do, Lily? He's demanding that I give him

323

an answer. I have nowhere else to turn. He'll never let me alone and all the time the amount will be racking up.'

'I won't let you do this. We have to think of something.'

'Then we have to do it quickly. He'll be round any day now and he'll want payment – one way or another.'

I bite my lip, willing myself to think clearly. And I reckon *I've* got problems.

Chapter 91

As soon as it's gone ten o'clock and it's apparent that I'm not going to be in the shop today, Seymour starts to call me. I switch the phone to voicemail and, finally, make Tracey that cup of tea.

She's sobbed on my shoulder for the last half-hour and is currently all cried out. We're no nearer to a viable solution.

Fifteen minutes later and Seymour has phoned the equivalent number of times.

'Someone *really* wants to talk to you,' Tracey notes.

'I have my own spot of bother,' I confess. 'Nothing like yours, but difficult enough.'

'Tell Aunty Tracey.'

'It's my boss on the phone,' I tell her. 'He and I . . . well, we're getting a little too close.'

'Oh, yes?' My friend's eyebrows rise. 'How close?'

We both laugh at that. 'Just about as close as you can get,' I admit, shamefaced. My body still shivers when I even think of Seymour. Pictures of his naked body keep flashing, unbidden, into the front of my mind.

'Lily Lamont-Jones,' she says, scandalised. 'You, who looks like butter wouldn't melt in her mouth? They say it's the quiet ones that you have to watch!'

'What can I do? I want to stay away from him, Tracey, but I need the work. We can't manage on Laurence's money now. I might not bring in much, but we'd be lost without it. I wanted to use my wages to start paying off our debts.'

The credit-card company are currently working out a

325

repayment plan for us. Our building society have had an offer on the barn which will just about cover the mortgage. The apartment in London has proved more tricky and, though it has gone now, there is still an outstanding amount that we owe. They're currently offering us a forty-year mortgage to clear it, which means I'll still be in debt to them for a property we no longer possess until I have one foot in the grave. Perhaps it would have been easier to simply declare ourselves bankrupt and just walk away from it all. But then we would never have been able to hold our heads up anywhere ever again.

'And now it's going to be tricky?' Tracey asks.

'He wants me to leave Laurence.' I look up at my friend. Now it's my eyes that are filled with tears. 'What am I to do?'

'Do you want to go?'

'I still love my husband. That hasn't changed.'

'But?'

'But Seymour can offer me a life away from here. He's young, he's handsome, he's very wealthy.'

'Does he have a brother?'

'I don't think so.'

'Then if you don't leave Laurence, can I have him?'

'It's not a joking matter.'

'Oh, Lily,' she says. 'What are *you* going to do?'

'Concentrate on your problem first.' My phone rings again.

'Talk to him,' she implores. 'You can't just run away from this.'

'No.'

'Go in the other room. I'm going to get that brandy out again. I'll try not to eavesdrop if you promise you'll tell me everything.'

So I call Seymour and his relief is palpable when he hears my voice.

'I'm trying to get my head round this,' I tell him. 'I just couldn't face coming in today.'

'I'm missing you, Lily.'

I'm missing Seymour too, but I decide not to tell him that. I don't know if it would make the situation worse, not better.

'Come in,' he urges when I fall silent, 'and we'll talk everything through. We can't leave it like this.'

'Tomorrow,' I promise. 'I'll be back tomorrow.' What I don't tell him is that I'm now, despite the earliness of the hour, going to get blind drunk with my neighbour.

Chapter 92

Life was good, Laurence thought. Despite everything. Hugo and Hettie were, admittedly, talking like they'd been born in the 'hood rather than in a nice middle-class village in Buckinghamshire, but he was sure that it would have ruined their newly-acquired street cred to point that out to them. He was learning a whole new vocabulary from them and one that he wasn't sure he'd ever understand. Still, it was a small price to pay for the fact that they seemed to have settled into their new school and their new surroundings without too much trauma.

He was really enjoying his job at Cherry's Farm. There was no stress, no pressure. It was hard work physically, but there wasn't the mental strain or continual and impossible targets to achieve. Christopher Cherry was the model boss – as far away from Laurence's former paymasters in the City as it was possible to be. Laurence cycled to the farm every morning and back in the evening, taking the path alongside the Grand Union Canal for as long as he could – which was virtually all the way home. That route might prove more taxing as the winter set in, but he could stick to the roads then if needs be. He couldn't even begin to compare it to the daily three-hour commute that he'd endured before.

He was home every night by six o'clock at the latest and had become a dab hand at feeding a family of four for a fiver by following the supermarket crib cards that he picked up every time he went shopping. Their bought food was supplemented by plenty of fresh vegetables courtesy of Skull's allotment, and

Laurence tried to get down there a couple of nights a week and for a few hours at the weekend to help his friend out with the work. He'd discovered a passion for digging and weeding that he'd never previously known that he had.

Tonight there were pork chops, bought from the local supermarket on their sell-by date, with Skull's cabbage and potato wedges for supper, and it was almost ready. The children had set the table and were now watching the television that Skull had found for them for fifty pounds – a small and necessary nod to the indispensable creature comforts of modern life. Hugo and Hettie had been beside themselves with joy when it arrived. Plus it meant that they didn't have to play Cluedo each and every night. It had been money well spent.

The only cloud on the horizon was his relationship with Lily. He couldn't avoid the fact that their marriage was under strain. And he understood perfectly why. He'd expected a lot of Lily. Her comfortable life had been taken away from her without warning and, not six months later, she was bound to be struggling to come to terms with it.

Take her job. She'd never had to work before and he could sense a reluctance from her every morning. But it was difficult. They needed the money. Lily would have to pull her weight. There was no doubt that it had caused a tension between them. They hadn't made love in weeks, months even. Before, it had been he who hadn't been interested – there was always so much else on his mind. Now that things were settling and he could relax more, his . . . *joie de vivre* had come back somewhat. These days, it was Lily who turned her back on him.

Then, before he could dwell on it further, the front door opened and Lily herself came into the kitchen. 'Hi,' she said, and threw down her handbag.

She was supposed to finish at three o'clock, but she was rarely home before him and he wanted to complain about that. The children had to go to Tracey's house after school – not that their neighbour seemed to mind – and he was the one who cooked dinner every night, which was fine. He came home with loads of energy and was still raring to go at night for the first time

329

in years. Now it was Lily who was tired all the time. Weariness cloaked her face and she looked as if she was carrying the weight of the world on her shoulders.

'Tired?' Laurence asked as he kissed her cheek.

'Yes.'

'Cup of tea or something stronger?'

'Tea's fine.'

His wife leaned against the work surface and smoothed her hair back from her face. There were dark shadows beneath her eyes and he wondered why he hadn't noticed them before.

'Anything wrong?'

Lily gave a deep sigh. 'I'm thinking of leaving my job.'

'Lily, darling,' Laurence said, 'we've had this conversation before.'

'I know, but—'

'But nothing,' he continued. 'We need the money. It's a nice little job – you said so yourself. It pays quite well. You could change and do something else, but what would give you the same rate? Your boss is very generous.'

'I know, but—'

'We're just getting back on our feet. Don't spoil it now.' Laurence put his hands on her shoulders. She did look very tired and he felt bad about that. Lily had never had to work, had never needed to contribute to the family income – it must be hard for her. He could appreciate that. 'Hang on in there. For me.'

'Okay,' she said, holding up her hands in resignation. 'Okay.'

He wrapped his arms round his wife and was surprised to feel her stiffen. 'We'll get through this,' he assured her. 'And we'll be stronger for it.'

But from the look on Lily's face, it was clear that she didn't agree.

Chapter 93

Laurence has made a marvellous dinner again. He's very proud of his new culinary skills and his budget management. It was just a shame that I could barely bring myself to eat it. I feel permanently sick to my stomach with nerves and guilt and have done since that fateful night at the Ritz Hotel.

I'd like to tell you that I had the strength to go into work the very next day and tell Seymour that it was over, that it couldn't happen again – all the things that I'd rehearsed in my head – but I couldn't. I saw his handsome face, his warm smile, his eyes that soften when they see me, and I couldn't end it. I couldn't.

'I want to sell everything that we don't need,' Laurence says into my musing.

We're in the bedroom. We have our holiday suitcases out and my husband is on a mission. I'm not sure what has brought this on.

'We could do a car boot sale,' he suggests.

'Yes.' For the first time I can see the joy in saying 'Whatever' as Hettie does so often now.

To be honest, all my waking moments are spent trying to think about what I'm going to do with my future and I can barely concentrate on anything else. If Seymour has his way, I will leave Laurence and the children and I will go to live with him. He has an enormous house in the country and I'm resisting going to look at it as it might be the undoing of me.

'My golf clubs can go,' Laurence says.

They're still by the back door and have been since the day we arrived. 'Are you sure?'

'When am I going to use them again?' He carries on rummaging in the cases. 'Besides, my interests have changed. I'd rather spend a few hours on Skull's allotment than on the golf course.'

That is a major turn-up for the book. When we had acres and acres of beautiful garden at the barn, my husband wasn't the slightest bit interested in it.

I haven't made love with Seymour again since the night of the Ritz. But that isn't because I don't want to. It's just that there hasn't been the opportunity – unless we get down and dirty on the office floor and, to be honest, the thought has crossed my mind more than once. Instead, we have lingering lunches in the courtyard garden where we hold hands and talk of things we will do in a future that we might never have, we touch tenderly as we pass each other in the shop and we kiss as lovers do when no one is there to see us.

'The video camera.' Laurence produces said object. 'This can go. We might get a few pounds for that.'

The last footage that we took was of our Tuscany extravaganza and, frankly, I don't want to be reminded of that. Not now. Perhaps I will put the tape away for posterity as we have so little physical evidence of our memories left. One day I might be able to bring myself to look at it.

In the case there are also five bikinis that I took on holiday. Every one costing over a hundred pounds. Who needs five bikinis? What's wrong with one and rinsing it out each night? What's wrong with buying one for ten pounds from Primarni or TK Maxx?

But then, I remember that my head is being turned by a man who's offering me a life of luxury and ease once more.

'Oh,' Laurence says, bringing my mind back to the present. 'What's this?'

He pulls out the bracelet that Seymour bought me for my birthday. I'm so distracted that I'd completely forgotten that

I'd hidden it there. My husband frowns. 'I thought you'd taken all the jewellery to that chap that you work for.'

'Seymour.' Even speaking his name sets my heart pounding. 'Did you miss this one?'

My mouth is dry. 'I must have.'

He lets the exquisite diamond heart dangle in his hand. 'I don't remember buying you this.'

'It was for a birthday, I think.' The lies come so much easier to me these days. I tell Laurence that I have to work late when it's just because I want to spend as much time with Seymour as possible. Is that bad of me? Yes, of course it is.

With Seymour I feel as if I have stepped outside of my real life. I feel as if none of it is really happening to me but to another person.

'I don't remember ever seeing you wear it.'

'I do.' More lies. 'Just not very often.'

'It's pretty,' Laurence says. 'I have very good taste.'

Clipping the bracelet to my wrist, I try to hide the flush that comes to my face. 'Yes.'

'You should keep that. It'd be nice for you to have at least one piece of good jewellery.' Laurence sits back on his heels and looks at me. 'I've been trying to resist it, but we really do need to sell the rest of the stuff.'

By that I assume he means the 'stuff' that's in Seymour's safe. All of my jewellery and Laurence's watch. 'I know.'

'I want to clear our debts completely, Lily. Now. Not in five years' time of paying them off in dribs and drabs. If we sold the jewellery – all of it – then we could do it. Just about.'

'I'll speak to Seymour.'

'It's for the best.'

'I know.'

'I'm sorry,' my husband says. He takes me in his arms and I go limp against him. 'I'm sorry for everything.'

But whatever Laurence has done, it isn't as bad as what I'm doing and I have no idea how I'm going to tell him that.

Chapter 94

When I'm marshalling all our worldly goods that have been deemed surplus to requirements into a big pile in the corner of the bedroom, my eyes alight on the video camera again and a little light bulb pings in my brain.

'Can I borrow this before we dispose of it?' I ask Laurence.

'Sure. What for?'

'Tracey's in a spot of bother. This might come in handy. I think I'll pop round there now.'

'I'll finish up here,' my husband offers and, gratefully, I take the opportunity to escape.

Next door, Tracey opens a bottle of white wine and we sit at the kitchen table together. I put the video camera down. 'When were you expecting the loan shark to come back?'

'He called earlier,' she says.

'Hence the bottle of wine?'

She nods. 'I don't know anyone else in the world, Lily, who would use the word "hence".'

We laugh together and then Tracey goes on, 'He said that he was going to "call on me" tomorrow.'

'What time?'

'Late afternoon.'

'I'd like to be here when he does,' I tell her. 'I don't want you to have to face him alone.'

'I think the whole idea is that I'm to be here *alone*.'

'You can't,' I remind her. 'I won't let you.'

My neighbour sighs. 'I'm sending the kids straight to my mum's. She's picking them up from school.'

At least he hasn't threatened them. I don't voice that thought as I don't want to give Tracey any more to worry about than she already has. 'I'll leave work as early as I can and try to be back here for four at the latest.'

'I'd appreciate that,' she says. 'I'm terrified of him.'

'That's why I brought this.' I nod towards the video. 'I'm wondering if we can set it up in your living room somewhere so that you can record what he says to you. Just in case you ever need it.'

'He'd kill me if he found it.'

'Then we'll have to think of somewhere to put it where he won't see it.' I down my wine. 'Come on, let's strike while the iron's hot.'

In the corner of the living room, there's a tall display stand which houses a few ornaments and some books. On one of the lower shelves, there's a grey tatty teddy that catches my eye. 'What if we put it in the teddy?'

'Charlize won't be best pleased if I cut a hole in its tummy.'

'Needs must,' I tell her. 'If this gets you off the hook, then I'll buy her another teddy myself.'

'Let's go for it,' Tracey decides.

So we cut a hole in the teddy's tummy and I show my neighbour how the recorder works. Then we place it on a higher shelf, but somewhere that's still easily reachable and that, hopefully, will record everything that goes on.

'As soon as he comes to the door,' I instruct, 'before you even open it, make sure that you press the record button.'

'Will do.'

'There's a new tape in there and it will record for an hour.'

'I hope he's not here that long.'

'He won't be,' I assure her. 'Not if I have anything to do with it.' Tracey is trembling just thinking about it. 'I'll come round as soon as I'm home. Don't worry. I won't let you face this by yourself.'

'You're a good friend, Lily,' she says. 'What would I do without you?'

I'm hoping that we'll never find out as I feel the same.

We hug each other. I've never had a friend as kind or as thoughtful as Tracey. If I do leave with Seymour, will our friendship survive that, I wonder? I'd have to take the children out of the local school, move away from Netherslade Bridge and from Tracey. There's so much to think about, so many decisions to be made and, currently, my head and my heart just can't seem to agree what they want to do.

Chapter 95

My stomach is twisted into knots of anxiety as I bounce my way to work on the bus. It feels like that every morning now. The mixture of anxiety, pleasure and guilt is a painful one, I've discovered.

Seymour comes out of the back to greet me as soon as he hears me enter Ornato. He takes my hands and kisses me softly. We go through to the office and, as is our routine now, I make us both a coffee.

'Laurence and I had a long talk last night,' I tell him.

'About us?'

'No.' I shake my head. 'About our financial situation.'

'There is a very easy way out of that,' Seymour reminds me.

'We're up to our eyeballs in debt, Seymour. We owe friends of ours, Amanda and Anthony Marquis, nearly twenty thousand pounds. All our credit cards are maxed and the companies are baying for blood. Plus I want to help out my neighbour. She's in trouble with a loan shark and I want to give her the money to pay him off.'

'Let me help,' he says.

'I will. What I want you to do is give me a good price – a fair price – on the remaining jewellery of mine that you have in the safe.'

'There's no need for that, Lily.'

'There is. That's the only way I'll take money from you, Seymour. I still have my pride.'

'If we were together,' he presses on, 'if we were a couple then your troubles would automatically be mine. They are now. I don't want you to feel that this is all on your shoulders.'

'If I'm going to leave then I need a clean break, Seymour. Paying our debts off is the first step in that. I can't even think straight until I've done that.'

He holds up his hands, knowing when he's beaten. 'Then I'll buy your jewellery. All of it.'

Seymour opens the safe and pulls out the brown envelope that contains all of the pieces that Laurence has bought me over the years. The sight of it brings tears to my eyes. Seymour spots my distress immediately.

'Lily, there's no need to do this.'

'Your best price,' I say shakily. 'Remember that.'

With a sigh, he starts to examine the pieces and I make myself busy while he does so. I watch him as he picks up some of the things that I have loved most dearly. They're only material possessions, but each one marks a special moment in my life and, much as I'd like to deny it, it does hurt to watch them go. I can only hope that they'll all be given good homes in the future.

Half an hour later, Seymour pushes back from his desk. 'Thirty thousand pounds,' he says.

'How much?'

'Thirty thousand.'

'That's too much!'

He laughs. 'I thought you'd be pleased.'

'I said to give me a *fair* price.'

'That is fair, Lily. You have some very beautiful jewellery. Are you sure you still want to sell it all?'

'Yes.' My palms have gone sweaty and my heart is beating erratically. A bubble of sheer joy – something which I haven't experienced in a long time – floats through me.

Thirty thousand pounds will just about clear the worst of our debts. It will also allow me to help Tracey out. I wonder, would I have got this sort of money if I'd taken my sale elsewhere? It's suspiciously close to the amount of cash that Seymour knew I needed. Still, should I look a gift-horse in the mouth?

I'm sure that Seymour can sell them on and recoup his money. I don't feel that I have any choice but to accept his kind offer.

'I haven't banked this week's takings yet,' he says, 'so I have the money here. But is it sensible, taking all this home?'

He has a point. Our bank account has been frozen, so I can't put it there. I realise that we will have to open one again for Laurence's salary when he gets paid again but, for now. I'm using a jar in the kitchen cupboard.

'Just give me five thousand,' I say, as if it's an everyday occurrence for me to be dealing with this kind of money. 'Can you leave the rest in the safe for me?'

'Of course.' He counts out the money and hands it over to me. My fingers tremble as I slide it into my handbag. This is enough to get Tracey off the hook and that's infinitely more pressing than *our* needs.

'I need to go home right on time tonight, Seymour.' His face is a picture of disappointment and I reach out and stroke it. He turns my hand and kisses the palm.

'I love you, Lily Lamont-Jones,' he says. 'I will wait forever for you.'

Whatever happens in the future, I have loved him for this moment as deeply as I have ever loved anyone. And I want to tell him that. I so want to tell him that. But I don't know how.

Chapter 96

At three o'clock I am, of course, busy. I'm gift-wrapping a diamond pendant for a customer who is buying it for her mother's seventieth birthday and she is insisting on telling me all the details about the surprise party she has arranged.

'I'm having that lovely florist, Susan . . . Oh, you know her name.'

I do. 'Morris.'

'Susan Morris. She's wonderful.'

I keep glancing at the clock and at the office. I can hear that Seymour is on the telephone and is unable to come and rescue me as I know he would.

As she tells me the colour theme of the flowers, where she's ordered the cake from and how much the catering alone is costing, the credit-card machine keeps spewing out her card and I'm on the point of throwing the damn thing on the floor when it finally accepts the payment with a guileless beep.

I usher her out of the door as quickly as I can without looking like I'm throwing her out.

'Seymour, I have to rush,' I shout into the office. But that's not good enough for my lover, new as we are in the throes of lust, and he comes to me and kisses me and I go weak in his arms. 'I have to go. Tracey's waiting for me.'

I don't tell him that she has an appointment with a ruthless thug and that I need to be there for her, as he'd only worry himself sick or insist on coming along to protect me. Probably quite rightly too, I think. 'I'll see you tomorrow,' I promise.

And with that, I dash out of the door, five thousand pounds in my handbag to pay off my neighbour's creditor.

I used to think that doing my bit for charity was enough. By giving money to every collector who knocked on my door I thought it made me a good person. But what were a few pounds here and there to me? In reality, it meant nothing and even the charity work that I did just helped to fill days that otherwise would have stretched on endlessly. This is the first thing that I have ever done because I want to be a good person, a good friend.

Of course, with all of my best intentions, I still miss the bus and have to stand, foot tapping, at the bus stop for the next half-hour. How wonderful it would be to have a car again and not be reliant on the vagaries of the public transport system.

I'm running late by the time I hit Netherslade Bridge and walk as fast as I can down the street from the bus stop without running. When I turn the corner, I see a flash, black 4x4 parked outside Tracey's house. It looks like the loan shark is already there. I put a sprint on and then, I don't know what makes me think of them, but the sight of Laurence's golf clubs by the back door flashes into my mind. Taking a detour, I rush into the house, grab the first club that I can lay my hands on – a six iron – and head back out to Tracey's as fast as my legs will carry me.

As I get to Tracey's open front door, I notice Len and the dogs coming from the other direction. I sprint up to him.

'Wotcher,' he says.

'Len,' I say breathlessly. 'Can you lend me one of your dogs for five minutes?'

If he's surprised, then his deadpan face doesn't show it. 'Which one, Mrs Jones?'

'Which is the most ferocious?'

We look down at the dogs and they're all wagging their tails happily. I eyeball the Great Dane. He might not look ferocious – in fact, he has a very happy face – but he's a big bastard and he's the only one on a lead. 'This one will do.'

'Tiny, go with the lady.' With doe eyes, the hulking Tiny

complies. Len frowns as he hands over the dog. 'Is there trouble, Mrs Jones?'

'There might be.' I sling my bag across my body to enable me to keep a good grip on the dog and the six iron.

'Do you want me to come with you?'

'No,' I say. 'Can you stand here though please, Len? Don't move an inch. Just in case.' Then I hear a blood-curdling scream and my heart drops.

'Come on, boy,' I say to the massive dog and sprint down the path. With gritted teeth and deadly determination in my step and several stones of Great Dane in tow, I push through Tracey's front door and into her living room.

Chapter 97

My friend is on the floor. A burly man is on top of her. He has one hand over her mouth, the other is undoing the belt of his trousers. Tracey's skirt is up round her waist, her blouse dishevelled. Her eyes widen as she sees me over his shoulder.

'Get off her,' I say, voice steely, feet planted firmly on Tracey's carpet, Tiny at my side. 'Get off her, now!'

The man turns to see me with my six iron raised and a Great Dane straining at his leash.

'What the f . . . ?'

'You heard me,' I say again. I'm shaking all over but, thankfully, my voice sounds as steady as a rock. For good measure, I prod him in the buttocks with the golf club. Tiny gives a timely growl which rumbles from his belly. It sounds terrifying.

'Get out of here,' he says. His hand moves to Tracey's throat and then he grins at me, gold tooth glinting. 'Or you could stay and join in.'

At that point, a red mist descends. No one, not even a hardened thug, treats my friend like this. I take a wild swing with the golf club and crack him as hard as I can across the bottom and he shouts out. Tiny thinks this is great fun and takes it as his cue to join in. He bounds towards the loan shark and fixes his great slobbering jaws on the man's trousers and shakes his head fiercely. There's a tearing sound and the seat of his pants is torn asunder. Tiny is delighted and retreats to shake the rent material with gusto. With the dog out of the way, I give him another hefty thwack with the six iron.

The loan shark jumps up. 'Lady,' the man spits, 'you don't know who you're messing with.'

'Neither do you,' I reply. Tiny growls again and lets out a deafening bark. I'll swear that Tracey's light fittings rattle. My fillings certainly do. 'I can't hold this dog much longer,' I warn. 'Next time it might be a more tender part of your anatomy, not just your pants.'

The loan shark, covering his private parts, zips up his trousers, buckles up his belt. Tracey, looking shell-shocked, wriggles away from him and rearranges her clothing.

'I have your money,' I say, delving into the depths of my handbag.

'No, Lily,' Tracey says.

'Shut up, bitch,' the loan shark snarls.

I pull out the bundle of notes. 'Five thousand pounds,' I say. 'Does that clear the debt fully?'

He lunges at the money, but I'm quicker than he is and Tiny has clearly decided whose side he's on as he lets out another threatening growl. The loan shark takes a step back.

'That'll clear it,' he says.

'In full?'

He nods.

'I want it in writing,' I tell him.

'You what?'

'In writing. Tracey – get some paper and a pen.' My friend does as she's told and then sets it down on the coffee table.

'Write out that the money owed by Tracey Smith has been received in full and final settlement.'

He looks at me as if I'm mad.

'Write it,' I insist.

The loan shark sneers at me but does as I ask.

'Sign it.'

He scribbles his signature. I hold out my hand and he gives me the paper. It all seems to be in order, so I hand over the money.

'If I ever see you round here again,' I tell him, 'I will go to the police with this.' Then to Tracey, 'Did you start the camcorder?'

She nods at me.

'Then we have all of this little exchange recorded too. Just for posterity.'

To my surprise, he smiles at me. 'You're a piece of work, lady.'

'I have been told that before.'

'I'm not going to count this now,' he says, 'but if it's not all there, I *will* be back.'

'If you ever come near here again, it won't just be me that you have to contend with.'

The loan shark strides towards the door and Tiny growls as he passes him by, which makes the man walk quicker. I follow him to the door and watch as he skirts round the bemused Len – who hasn't dared move an inch as I instructed – and the rest of the dogs. He jumps into his flash motor and drives away, tyres screeching.

Back in the living room, Tracey runs to hug me. 'Bloody hell, Lily. You were marvellous.'

'I'm shaking like a leaf.' Now my bravado has all gone and I'm trembling from head to foot.

'I'll get the brandy.'

'He didn't hurt you?' Our eyes meet.

'You got here just in time. I dread to think what might have happened.'

'We'll check that camera later and you can put it in a safe place in case you ever need it.' I hand over the scribbled receipt. 'Put this with it too.'

'I don't think he'll be back now.'

'I do hope not.'

Bemused, Len pops his head round the door. 'I don't like to intrude, ladies,' he says nervously, 'but is everything all right?'

'Come in, Len,' Tracey says. 'Want a brandy?'

His eyes light up.

'Find this dog a biscuit too,' I say. 'He was wonderful.'

Tiny's tail goes into overdrive and knocks everything off the coffee table.

Moments later my friend reappears with three generous

glasses of brandy and a packet of digestives for Tiny. After the dog swallows five biscuits whole, we hold the glasses up and make a toast. 'To a job well done,' I propose.

'To a job well done,' Tracey and Len echo, even though dear Len Eleven Dogs has no idea what we're talking about. We knock back the brandy. Len wipes his finger round the glass and lets the dogs take turns in licking it off.

'I'd better go, ladies,' he says, and I give Tiny a last ruffle behind his ears. Then, doffing his non-existent hat, Len leaves us.

When we're on our own, Tracey and I flop onto her sofa. 'I'm emotionally exhausted,' I say.

'Me too,' Tracey agrees. 'I'll never borrow from anyone like that again, no matter how tight for cash I am.'

'That would seem a very sensible idea.'

'Where did you get the money from, Lily?'

I sigh. 'From Seymour.' I turn to her. 'I've sold all of my jewellery. Everything.' I think of the one bracelet that I've hung onto and flush. Nearly everything. 'Laurence and I want to clear all of our debts and we can just about do it now.'

'That must feel good.'

I allow myself time to contemplate it. 'Yes,' I say. 'Very much so.'

'I'll pay you back,' my neighbour promises. 'Every last penny.'

'In time,' I say. 'All in good time.'

'You're a star, Lily. An absolute star. I'm so glad that you came into my life.'

I feel the same.

'I got my mum to take the kids, Hugo and Hettie too. I'll text her to tell her that the coast's clear.' She punches a message into her phone. 'They'll be back soon,' she says when she receives a reply.

We take another swig of our brandy.

'So,' Tracey says. 'While we've got five minutes, tell me how things are with Seymour?'

'Difficult,' I confess. 'I think things are coming to a head. I have to make a decision one way or another. I can't carry on like this. It's not fair to anyone.'

'You can't go, Lily.' The brandy is clearly taking effect. 'We all love you round here. It won't be the same without you.'

I have to acknowledge that I've never felt so at home, so comfortable anywhere else in my life. I feel that somehow I've discovered who I really am while I've been living in Netherslade Bridge. How can I ever contemplate leaving here now?

'Go home,' Tracey instructs. She takes my glass from me. 'Go home and make it up with Laurence.'

'How am I supposed to do that?'

'You've just seen off one of the most dangerous loan sharks in the area, Lily. You're a very resourceful woman. You'll think of something.'

Chapter 98

So, flushed and somewhat unsteady from the result of several medicinal and restorative brandies, I weave my way to my own home. We've been here so long now that I don't shudder whenever I see the wood chip or the psychedelic wallpaper. I've even got used to the terrible carpet.

'You're late,' Laurence says.

'Been next door,' I slur.

'What are you doing with my six iron?'

'Long story,' I tell him.

'Where are Hugo and Hettie?'

'At Tracey's mum's. On their way back now. Tracey's going to give them dinner.'

'I've made a lasagne,' my husband says. 'It's in the oven.'

Now that he mentions it, there's a delicious smell wafting towards me. 'Hmm.'

'You've been drinking.'

'Brandy,' I concur. 'I deserved it. Believe me.'

'The food will be another half an hour yet.'

'Really?' I try to flutter my eyelashes but think I might just be pulling a leery face as Laurence merely smiles at me.

'Are you all right, Lily?'

I go and wrap my arms round Laurence and breathe my brandy breath on him, which only serves to amuse him more. 'I want us to get back to how we were. I want us to be happy again.'

'I want that too,' he says, kissing my hair.

'I got thirty thousand pounds from Seymour today,' I tell him. 'For all of our jewellery.'

My husband gasps

'I've lent five thousand to Tracey,' I confess. 'She's in desperate need.'

'More desperate than us?'

'*As* desperate. She's a good friend, Laurence, I needed to help her.'

'That's just like you, Lily. Always thinking of others.' But that isn't true. Recently, all I've thought about is what *I* want from life. I haven't considered what my behaviour, my decisions would mean to other people, the ripples it would cause for years.

'Tell me we'll stay together,' Laurence says. 'That's all that matters to me.'

'Make love to me,' I say.

'Now?'

'The children won't be back for a while yet.'

He takes my hand and starts to lead me upstairs. 'Not there,' I tease and, instead, I tug him towards the back door.

'Whoa,' he says and turns down the oven. 'Don't want dinner to spoil.'

'I have my mind on other things.'

'So I can see.' Laurence follows hesitantly as I pull him into the garden.

'Out here?'

'Not quite.'

With both hands, I lead him down the one mown strip towards the children's car.

'In there?'

'I think so.'

My husband laughs. 'What's got into you?'

'Oh, I don't know,' I murmur. 'I just thought it would be fun. Remember when we were students?'

'Just about.'

'We didn't think the back of a car was a bad place then.'

'But that was then . . .'

'. . . and this is now,' I finish. Opening the back door of the car, I slide inside. 'Hmm. Quite roomy.' It smells of old leather and motor oil and damp grass. The seats are smooth with years of wear and shine like conkers.

'You can't be serious, Lily.'

'Oh yes, I am,' I say. Grabbing my husband's shirt, I pull him down towards me. 'I've never been more serious in my life . . .'

Chapter 99

Laurence was five miles into his cycle to work when the call came. It was a cold morning – the first when the chill had pierced his flimsy jacket. The mellow autumn mists were slowly giving way to winter chills. It was staying darker later, the sun – rather like his children – reluctant to rise. He wondered how much longer he would still be able to ride along the canal path, and shivered in anticipation of the predicted early snows.

He still had a big grin on his face. Laurence wasn't sure what had got into Lily last night, but he was very sure that he liked it. They'd made mad passionate love in the back of that clapped-out car for hours, until it had gone dark and Hugo and Hettie had come home – luckily, as they had just rearranged their dishevelled clothing – and wanted to know what their parents were doing playing in their car. Proving that their parents weren't yet as clapped out as the vehicle they were in, he was tempted to answer. Dinner had been a dried, blackened mess, but they'd eaten it smiling nevertheless. It wasn't just the sex; he felt as if they'd somehow, without even speaking, connected on an emotional level that had been missing for a long time.

He'd felt closer to and more in love with Lily than he'd done in years, and it made him feel twenty years younger this morning.

Now this. He'd had to stop and take the call. When the caller ID showed who was on the line, he instinctively knew what it was about. The hairs on the back of his neck had stood up, his stomach had flipped with nerves. Now Laurence sat on the lock gate feeling dazed.

351

He'd been offered his old job back. Just like that. A bolt from the blue. The present incumbent, his old boss had told him, had been given the bullet and Laurence was to be offered a second chance. A second chance at the six-figure salary, the company pension, the private healthcare. The whole package. Helston Field – and Gordon Wolff in particular – were *desperate* to have him back. Gordon's very words.

There was a new project to head up and Laurence was the man to do it. Christopher Cherry had predicted it, but Laurence had been certain, so certain, that his new boss was wrong. He was washed up as far as the City was concerned. Now the olive branch was being offered to him and in some style. Looked like Laurence was the one who'd been wrong.

He had been punished enough in the wilderness, it seemed. Without further explanation from Gordon, he was to be the golden boy once more. They wanted him to start back as soon as possible, Gordon Wolff said. How much notice was he on? Could he do a deal to leave before then? All the questions made Laurence's head whirr. Was he interested?

Of course he was interested! Then he needed to let them know his start date as soon as possible. There was an important meeting in New York in ten days' time and his old boss wanted him in on it. Tomorrow? Could he let them know tomorrow?

Laurence said that he would. And then he hung up.

How was he going to get through the day thinking about this? As the weather had turned cooler they hadn't been quite so busy with customers at the farm and he'd been able to turn his mind to planning for the future, considering new product lines, different ways of marketing, capitalising on the Cherry's Farm brand. He'd been so excited about it. Now this unexpected opportunity had thrown him completely.

What would Lily want him to do? He knew what Christopher Cherry would want him to do. He'd want him to send his old boss scuttling away with a flea in his ear. Laurence was so grateful to Christopher for giving him a break when everything had seemed hopeless – and he'd never forget that. And he really enjoyed working at Cherry's. He might not be setting the world alight, but the work was good, honest toil and the remuneration was, for the hours and effort involved, quite fair.

Did he really want to go back to the manic hours? He'd got used to having lunch breaks, meetings over coffee and home-made fruit scones with Christopher every morning. Did he really want to relegate his newly-acquired bicycle to the garage and go back to a three-hour commute, lengthy overseas travel and a burgeoning ulcer?

But then, on the other hand, it was the answer to all of their prayers. They could get away from Netherslade Bridge, buy a house in one of the villages once more. They could both get new cars – perhaps nothing as flash as they'd had before, but it would be a joy to have their own transport again that had more than two wheels. Hugo and Hettie could go back to a decent school, though he wasn't sure he'd want them to go away to Stonelands now he and Lily were both used to having the children at home. Somewhere local would be fine. But then, would that matter, if he was never around again?

He'd been worried about what was happening between him and Lily. That bracelet, for instance. He knew that he hadn't bought it for Lily; he was sure of it. So, where did it come from? Was it a present from someone and she hadn't wanted to admit it, or had she splurged some cash she'd got hidden away and was too embarrassed or afraid to tell him or, God forbid – and this was the most unlikely scenario, he had to admit – Lily had stolen it from the place where she was working?

There was no way that he could confront her about it. What would he say? For a time he had felt that his wife had gone from him but now, thank all that was good, she seemed to be back. Lily was his wife once more. Didn't he owe it to her and the family to take this job whether he really wanted to or not? Would it make her happy again?

Laurence glanced at the time on his phone. If he didn't get a move on, he'd be late for work. He wouldn't mention this to Christopher yet. He'd dwell on it some more first and talk it over with Lily tonight.

But as he cycled on his way, he realised that his smile had disappeared and a frown had taken its place.

Chapter 100

This is hard. The hardest thing I've ever done? I don't know, but it is certainly up on the Top Ten of my list. I have to end my affair with Seymour. Last night Laurence and I not only reconnected on an intimate level, but I somehow discovered that my love for him had never died, it had just grown dim because of outside influences, worries, distractions, stress and a dozen other things that clouded my view of him.

The shop has been busy today. Busier than usual. Christmas is looming large and it seems as if the annual shopping ritual has already started in earnest. Despite the credit crunch, the economic downturn, the doom and gloom in the country, diamond necklaces and pendants are still flying off the shelves. Some lucky women will be – as I always was – unaware of the giddy sums racked up on credit cards on their behalf.

This morning alone, I've taken thousands and thousands of pounds on pretty trinkets to adorn manicured fingers or necks kept firm and young with Crème de la Mer. And I love it. I'm so suited to this work. I know which jewellery complements which outfit, which is the perfect gift for each occasion, and can judge instantly how much someone is planning to spend. Seymour says that I have a natural flair for it, and that his takings have soared in the weeks since I've been here.

Ah, Seymour. My most pressing problem. He is holding off on the festive decorations for now, but has some tasteful sparkly snowflakes to put in the window that I ordered from a specialist catalogue. They'll look beautiful when he does put them up. It's just a shame that I won't be here to see them.

At lunchtime, I avoided our usual cosy tête-à-tête and went and sat on a bench in the nearby public car park in the cold to think about what I'm going to say to end this.

Late afternoon and it's time that I was leaving. Seymour comes into the shop. 'Is that the time already?' he asks.

He's been preoccupied with paperwork for most of the day, so it's been easier to avoid him. Now he winds his arms round my waist and I lean back against him, breathing in the fresh scent of his aftershave and feeling the slight graze of his stubble against my face.

'You're quiet today,' he notes. So, he doesn't miss that much.

'Deep in thought,' I confess.

'I know I said that I'd wait for you, Lily, but it's been so long. When are we going to be able to spend some time together again?' my lover asks.

Letting out a shaky breath, I don't turn as I speak. I don't want to look into his handsome face as I say this or gaze into his kind blue eyes or have him look at me like I'm the best thing that's ever happened in his life.

'We can't, Seymour.' My voice trembles. 'I've been quiet because I've been thinking about us. And how best to end this.'

Now he does turn me towards him, hands on my shoulders. 'No. Tell me you don't mean this, Lily.'

'I can't go on with the lies, the deception. It's not who I am. I've never been unfaithful to Laurence before and I don't want to again.'

'I love you,' Seymour says baldly as if that is the answer to everything.

But I'm older than him and, by default, supposedly wiser. I know that love isn't always enough.

'I want to get back to how I was with Laurence.'

'But everything's changed. You said so yourself,' he argues.

'I have to try.' I let my fingers run along the top of the glass counter. I'm going to miss working here so much. This place, this man, have been a sanctuary for me. He has helped me when

I was desperate and needed him. His kindness has put food on my table and comfort in my heart. It's killing me to turn my back on him now. 'I have to leave this job. Never see you again.' My voice wavers. 'For the sake of my family.'

'What about me?'

Now the tears fall. 'I can't love you, Seymour. I can't allow myself to do it.'

'I can give you everything,' he says. 'Everything that you had before and more.'

'I know.' It would be so easy now for my resolve to crumble. To fall into his arms once more, to enjoy the heady rush of illicit passion and think that I could be with him without causing pain or heartache to Laurence or to the children.

But, in reality, I know that I can't do that. I must protect my family from this. God knows they have suffered enough. We all have. I must sacrifice myself and my lover to do that.

'Your mind is really made up?' Seymour sounds devastated and I wonder how I can have done this to another person when it all started out so lightly, so innocently.

'Yes.' I nod my head, to try to convince myself as much as Seymour.

He takes me in his arms again. 'I won't stop loving you, Lily.'

'You must,' I tell him. 'That's absolutely what you must do.'

Just as I must stop loving Seymour and love only Laurence once more.

Chapter 101

By the time Laurence comes home, I have made dinner. Tonight we have steak and kidney pie with value beef and ready-made puff pastry on the top. I've teamed that with some of Skull's mashed potatoes and some cabbage. Good hearty fare is the order of the day, none of the finickety, faddy food that I used to force on them all.

When he's had a quick shower after his cycle home, we sit down together as a family. There's a twinkle in my husband's eye as he bounds up the stairs and I wonder whether it's still the aftermath of last night's long and lustful love-in.

I'm dishing up as Hettie says, 'The school are having a day out at Alton Towers. Can I go?'

At Stonelands their day trips took in London art galleries, the Shakespeare trail of Stratford-upon-Avon and stately homes. I don't think I ever remember the educational delights of Alton Towers being on the agenda. Hettie will enjoy it far more than any of the other highlights. Anything that makes her scream and feel sick, my daughter adores.

'I'll have to think about it, darling,' I say as I spoon mashed potatoes onto her plate.

'We can get vouchers from the supermarket and then it's half-price.'

I glance at Laurence. This may not be the best way to break my news but, in for a penny, in for a pound. 'Mummy's given up her job,' I say. 'Money is going to be tight until she finds a new one.'

My child, who had been accustomed to getting everything that her heart desired whenever she asked for it, says, 'Perhaps I could write stories and sell them.'

My throat closes as I realise that she fully appreciates the change in our circumstances. She doesn't whine that 'everyone else is going'. Instead, she quietly tries to find her own solution and my heart, which is already feeling bruised and battered, dissolves. It's all I can do to focus on the rhythmic repetition of serving supper.

'We'll think of something, Hettie. Don't worry.' My husband returns my gaze as he steps in to rescue me. 'Then Mummy and I will have a little talk later about why she's given up her job.'

'I can explain,' I say.

'Later.' Laurence holds up a hand. 'Now let's have this lovely dinner. I've brought home a cherry cake from work that's a bit bashed about.'

'Thank you,' I say to Laurence.

'Dad,' Hugo says, 'there's a five-a-side football scheme starting up at school. Dads are supposed to go. You'll be able to make it now you don't work late.'

Now Laurence is the one to glance at me and I don't know why. 'We'll see,' he says.

'But you want to, don't you?' Hugo presses. 'I've told my mates that you're okay at footie.'

An accolade indeed.

'You must,' I say to Laurence.

'We'll see,' he says again, and then he concentrates on his meal.

Laurence and Hugo have really bonded well in the time we've been at Netherslade Bridge. Before, they hardly saw each other and I know now that every boy needs a male role model in his life. I thought that Laurence was a good father because he provided everything for us, but he wasn't. Boys need so much more from their dads than that. They need someone to be there for them constantly, not just a father who buys them the latest computer and turns up every now and again to rugby matches when he's in the country.

When we've eaten, Hettie slides onto my husband's lap. 'Do my reading with me, Daddy,' she demands.

'I'll wash up with Hugo,' I say. I turn to my son. 'Is that all right?'

He nods and, with that, we take the dirty dishes and go into the kitchen. 'I'll wash, you wipe.'

'I want to wash,' Hugo says. So we change roles and it takes twice as long as Hugo is, at best, ponderous with the dish mop. I can see his mind is whirring busily, so I don't try to hurry him. From the living room comes the sound of Hettie's dulcet tones toiling over her reading.

'Everything okay?' I eventually say to Hugo as he's done his thirtieth round of a now very clean plate.

'I'm just thinking,' he says. It must be contagious. He shrugs. 'I like it here. I didn't think that I would, but I do.'

'I like it too.'

'You and Dad are different. You're nicer. You don't get so stressed.'

If only my child knew what was going on in my head. 'That's good.'

'Yeah. You're both around more. Especially Dad.'

'I know. That's nice too.'

'You and Dad are okay, aren't you?'

'Of course we are.'

'Everyone's mums and dads are divorced here. I don't want that to happen to you.'

'Wherever you live you have to work very hard at relationships,' I tell Hugo. 'But Dad and I are fine.'

'Cool,' he says, and moves onto another plate.

I put my hands on Hugo's shoulders and kiss the top of his head. In the window's reflection, I see him grimace. 'What was that for?'

'Being a good boy.'

'*Mum!*' He brushes me away. Business as usual.

Chapter 102

Laurence pops his head round the door. 'We're all finished,' he tells me. 'Harry Potter saved the day. Why don't we pop down to The Nut for a quick drink?'

Folding the tea towel, I say, 'I'll ask Tracey if the children can go in with her for an hour. They need to be in bed before nine, it's a school night.'

'One late night won't hurt,' my husband says easily, and I smile as our children's faces light up.

'Tracey can come with us,' he adds. 'Tell her to get her coat on. She hardly ever goes out. I'll buy her a vodka or two.'

'I bet you say that to all the girls,' I tease. Then, 'What about the children? Are they allowed in there?'

'There's a family room,' Laurence says. 'Away from the bar. There's bound to be something in there to entertain them. See if Tracey wants to bring Charlize and Keanu too.'

So, ten minutes later, both of our families troupe down to The Nut in the cold. It's already dark and the nights are drawing in faster and faster. This house is shaping up to be a pig to heat, like Tracey said, and I'll need to find another job pretty fast. But I've done it once and I'm sure that I can do it again.

In The Nut, Laurence buys Tracey a vodka and Coke and treats her to a double. I have a glass of wine and it's Coca-Cola and crisps all round for the children. My husband has a pint of beer and puts the money on tab for one for Skull when he arrives.

The family room, which is well away from the bar area, holds a table football game, a dartboard for the older children and a small ball-pit tucked in the corner for toddlers. It's brighter in here than the rest of the pub, but it's still scuffed around the edges.

We take a table in the corner and the children automatically gravitate towards the table football. Tracey puts down her drink and then says, 'Back in two ticks, loves,' and disappears.

'Dad! Come and play football,' Hugo begs.

'Five minutes,' Laurence promises, 'and I'll be there.' He turns to me. 'This might be our only chance to talk.'

'I couldn't stay in my job,' I blurt out. 'I just couldn't. It wasn't . . . possible.'

'Should I ask why?' His eyes search mine for clues.

'It just wasn't right for me,' I tell him, looking away. 'There's nothing else to say.'

My husband doesn't look convinced, but clearly he decides not to pursue the matter now.

'I'll look for something else straight away,' I promise. 'Tomorrow.'

'There might not be any need.' Laurence puts his hands behind his head and sighs.

'What do you mean?'

'I got a call today,' he explains. 'Gordon Wolff. I can have my old job back.'

My eyes nearly go out on stalks. 'No!'

My husband nods emphatically. 'Very much yes.'

I swig at my wine, in a state of shock.

'Same salary,' he continues. 'Slightly better, if anything.' His hand covers mine. 'I could go back to Helston Field, to how things were. It could get us out of here – if you want to.'

Shouldn't I be running round the room, shouting from the rooftops? Laurence has got his old job back! I don't need another job, I don't need to stay in Netherslade Bridge. So why does my heart feel cold instead of warm and fuzzy?

'You don't look so sure,' my husband ventures.

'Have you accepted it?'

'No,' he says. 'I wanted to see what you thought first.'

And that tells me that he has his doubts too about re-entering the world of corporate high-flyers.

'We should be pleased,' he says. 'Shouldn't we?'

'We should.'

'But we're not.'

Resting my head on his shoulder, I say, 'Do you really want to go back to all that? All the stress, the back-biting?'

'No. But would I be content at Cherry's Farm, long-term? Would I regret not taking this chance?' He squeezes my hand. 'What about you and the children? You wouldn't have to work. The children could go to a better school again.'

'This one seems to be suiting them more than Stonelands, if I'm honest. They're not so stressed either, much like us.' They play like children are supposed to and neither Laurence or I are so obsessively focused on making them into fully-rounded citizens. Not everything in their lives has to be 'educational'. They don't go to a million different 'fulfilling' activities and, instead, we do more together as a family. 'And I like having a job,' I add. 'Really I do. It gives me something useful to concentrate on.'

Again, my husband doesn't look convinced.

'Just because Ornato didn't work out, it doesn't mean that I can't find something that will suit me. Even if you do go back to the City, I'll still want to find another job.' The thought of getting back on the treadmill that we were on suddenly fills me with absolute dread.

'So what shall I do?'

'I'm pleased that you're even talking to me about it. Before, you would have made the decision yourself without even involving me.' I take his hand. 'What do *you* want to do?'

'I don't know.'

'We'll manage,' I reassure him. 'We're doing okay here. Things can only get better.'

'I should take the job,' Laurence says, suddenly decisive. 'It would be madness not to. How can I look this gift-horse in the mouth? Even if I only do it for a few years, it would get us back on our feet.'

'We're getting there now,' I point out.

'It'll take us years if we do it this way. If I go back to Heston Field, make that sacrifice for a couple of years . . .' His voice tails away.

'Sacrifice?'

The word hangs in the air between us.

'Is that really what it would feel like?'

My husband puts his head in his hands. 'I've got used to being at home,' he confesses. 'I like being around. I like being part of my family, not just someone who flits in and out. But if I have to give that up to get us straight . . . I'm the one who got us into this mess.'

'And we'll *both* work to get out of it.'

'If I'm honest,' Laurence says, 'I don't think I have the stomach for the fight in the City any more. I'm really enjoying working at Cherry's. The job is rewarding. The pay is never going to make us rich, but we'll get by. I'm home every night and my relationship with my children is better than it's ever been.' His eyes search my face. 'And with you, I hope.'

I wrap my arms around him.

'I don't want to give that up.'

'I like this Laurence better than the old one.'

'Me too.' He sighs. 'We have the money from the jewellery you sold. That will tide us over.'

Perhaps I should be ashamed of this, but I wasn't too proud to accept that money from the safe when I left Seymour's shop and his life forever. I have to say, to Seymour's eternal credit, he didn't seem to begrudge me one penny of it. If Laurence doesn't take this job, we're certainly going to need that nest egg.

'I'm terrified to spend any of it,' I admit.

'We'll be fine, Lily,' he assures me. 'Whatever happens, we'll be fine.'

'Dad,' Hugo shouts. 'Come on. I'm losing with only Hettie to help.'

'I'm doing all the best shots,' my maligned daughter protests.

'I'd better go and rescue our son.' Laurence pats my knee. 'I won't make a decision until I've slept on it. We have to think long and hard about this offer, darling.'

If my head wasn't spinning already then it is now – and it's going to take more than some cheap white wine to get me through it.

Chapter 103

Tracey and I were called on for table football and darts the minute she returned to the family room, so we didn't get another chance to talk about the situation that Laurence and I now find ourselves in.

The next morning my friend and I walk the children to school even though they're of an age where they'd really prefer us not to.

'No work today?' she asks as I'm not in my usual rush.

'No. Long story.'

'I have time. I have tea.'

'And I have to call into the supermarket to buy a local newspaper before we go home. I need the jobs section.'

'Oh.' Tracey catches my expression. 'Then I'd better buy biscuits too.'

So, ten minutes later, armed with the *Milton Keynes Citizen*, and a packet of chocolate digestives to go with our mugs of tea, we set up camp at Tracey's kitchen table.

'I told Seymour that it was over,' I confide.

'How do you feel about that?'

'Terrible, but better. If you know what I mean.'

'I do,' she says, pushing in the first digestive of what is clearly going to be many. 'Poor love.'

'I can't work with him now.' Although I know Seymour would have me back at Ornato like a shot – even with conditions attached. But it's me who couldn't cope with it. I don't want to be near him again. If I were near enough to inhale his scent, feel his breath, hear his soft laugh then I couldn't resist the temptation. So it's far safer to stay away. Cut all ties. 'It's for the best.'

'Despite the fact that you're out of work again.'

'That's the other thing that I need to tell you.' The words escape with a sigh. 'Laurence has been offered his old big City job back.'

'No way!'

'He has – just yesterday. But they want him to start at once.' Isn't that typical too. Helston Field have, by all accounts, managed to do quite well for themselves in his absence. But now they've decided to snap their fingers again, he has to come running instantly.

'You should be pleased about this,' my friend and neighbour observes. 'Ecstatic, actually.'

'We are. Sort of.' Frankly, neither of us slept a wink last night. We kept going over and over the ramifications of Laurence accepting the job. Or not accepting the job. Or accepting the job. Or not accepting the job. And on it went. At five o'clock I finally caught an hour's rest.

'Why the hesitation?'

'It means big changes again.'

'For the better! You'd get out of this place. There might be a chance of you getting your home back.'

'I don't think so.' That has gone to someone else now. I join Tracey with a biscuit, but I nibble distractedly rather than wolf it down. 'Besides, there's a lot we've enjoyed about living round here.'

'Humph.'

'You're normally the one defending the estate,' I remind her. 'It's just that we're different people now that we're here. Better people. I don't think you'd have liked me very much before.'

'Obviously, I don't want you to go,' she says. 'But you've got to think about what's best for you, for the children. We'll still be friends wherever you go.'

'But it won't be the same if I'm not next door.'

'I'll still let you come round and get Jamelia to do your Brazilian in my kitchen.'

We laugh at that. 'Wherever I live, whatever Laurence does, I'm going to get another job.' I flick open the local paper. There used to be pages and pages of job advertisements. Now the only people who are employing are public services – hospitals, schools, councils.

Tracey pulls a face. 'There's not much there. You're never going to find another position like the one you've just left. I'd love a little job like that myself.'

I look up from the newspaper and to my friend. 'Go to him.'

'What?'

'Go to Seymour. Tell him that you're my friend and that you need work. He'll love you.'

'As much as he did you?'

That makes me flush. 'Maybe not that much.'

And, as Tracey takes the paper from me and continues to flick through the ads and chatter away, I have to push back the image of Seymour's handsome face, his lovely, relaxed manner, his slender, gentle hands before a wave of longing hits me.

I wonder how long I will have to feel like this? When will the hurting end? When will I be happy that I've done the best for my family, no matter what price it has cost me? Now, because of Laurence's job offer, I know with all of my heart that I didn't just want my husband for the comfort and ease he could give me. I wanted the man himself. I still do.

'I'll go tomorrow,' Tracey says. 'Or maybe later today.'

It takes all of my dwindling resources to resist the urge to say I'll go with her.

Chapter 104

Tea finished, we choose Tracey's outfit for her impromptu visit to Ornato then adorn her with some bling, but not too much. After that, she totters off nervously, pushed in the direction of the bus stop by me.

Back in my own home, I phone two agencies and make appointments to register with them. Then I ring two companies – one which is looking for a receptionist and one which wants an administrative assistant. They both offer to send me application forms. The last call is to a shop selling wedding dresses in a little market town that borders the city; they need a sales assistant and I like the sound of that job very much. I'm hoping that it's on a bus route so that I can actually get there. I'll go into the library to check that out. Having had a small taste of it, I think I'm quite suited to retail life. I'm sure there must be a job out there with my name on it. Things will be tight until I find it, but I've done this once and I'm sure that I can do it again.

After I've done all that, I don't quite know what to do with myself. In the fridge there's two lots of stewing beef that was on offer and a few of Skull's carrots and a couple of onions so I whip up a very basic casserole, throw in a few dried herbs. While it's cooking, I clean the house from top to bottom. Anything to stop myself from thinking, to stop myself from picking up the phone.

The casserole is smelling wonderful, despite the paucity of exotic ingredients or fine red wine. I lift them both out of the oven and put one to the side for me and the family to have for this evening's supper. The other one, I wrap in a double layer of tea towels, then I slip on my coat – another of Tracey's rejects – and head out down the street.

On the other side of the estate, I find Len Eleven Dogs's house. I remember Tracey pointing it out to me on one of our meandering routes back from school. Nervously, I knock on the door and all the hounds set up a cacophony of barking. A few minutes later, Len comes and stands behind the glass.

'Who is it?' he asks anxiously.

'It's only Lily Jones,' I answer. 'I just popped by with something.'

'Quiet, boys,' he instructs, and the barking turns to excited whining instead. He opens the door and then beams his gummy smile when he sees me. 'I am honoured, Mrs Jones.'

As the door swings wider, the dogs pour out and bump round my knees, wagging their tails.

'Can I come in?'

The smile disappears. 'It's a bit messy,' he says. 'I wouldn't want you thinkin' bad of me, Mrs Jones.'

'I wouldn't do that, Len. I'll just hand this over then. It's hot,' I add when he holds out his hands.

'Smells lovely.'

'It's for you,' I tell him. 'Not the dogs.'

'They like it when I share,' he admits.

'I'm sure they do.' I can see how Len would never be able to keep such delicious food all to himself. 'You enjoy it then.'

'This is very kind of you, Mrs Jones.'

'I'll bring you one regularly, Len. If you'll let me. You might not like it yet.'

'I will,' he assures me earnestly. 'I will, Mrs Jones.' Even if I'd put nails in it, I'm sure that he'd choke it down, he's so grateful. 'You can borrow one of my dogs anytime you like. Tiny really likes you.'

That brings a lump to my own throat. This man has nothing but his precious dogs and is still prepared to offer to share them with me. That small kindness moves me to tears.

'Are you all right, Mrs Jones?' His concerned expression nearly undoes me.

'Yes, I'm fine. Perhaps you'll let me walk them with you one day.'

His cloudy eyes brighten. 'I'd like that. The boys will too.' He looks adoringly at his rag-tag of animals.

Perhaps one day he'll let me into his house with my vacuum cleaner and polish too, but I'll take it slowly, slowly, one step at a time.

'I'll leave you in peace, Len. Drop the bowl and the tea towels back when you have a moment. Eat it now though. Don't let it go cold.'

'I'll eat it right away, Mrs Jones. Right away.'

As I turn and head back towards my own street, a lone black-bird sings in the tree with the tyres hanging from it and I feel my heart swell so much that I might be tempted to sing myself.

Chapter 105

He'd arrived at work to find that someone had inadvertently left the gate open to the chicken coop and the chickens were now running round the yard like . . . well . . . like headless chickens.

It took Laurence, Christopher and Linda, the lady from the customer services desk, a good half-hour to round them up again. He was breathless by the time he'd finished.

Then one of the customer toilets had overflowed and Laurence had to roll up his sleeves to mop up the flood so that they'd be functional again before the main rush of customers arrived.

When he'd sorted that out, there was a call to say that the day's bread delivery would be late because the baker's van had broken down, so Laurence was despatched in the truck to collect it from the bakery in Bletchley instead so that they had a supply for the day. His job description was certainly all-encompassing.

It was eleven o'clock and he'd barely had time to catch his breath, let alone think about his new job offer. Laurence had let out a heartfelt sigh when he'd finally sat down for five minutes. He certainly earned his money here.

Now Christopher Cherry pushed the keys to his Land Rover across the table. 'It's about half an hour's drive,' the man said once he'd eaten his mouthful of toasted teacake. 'It should already be programmed in the Sat Nav as I've been out there before.'

It was their daily morning meeting – albeit somewhat delayed – and Laurence was due to go off to a local cheesemaker to try their wares for selling at the farm. 'Right.'

371

'You're quiet this morning, lad,' Christopher noted. 'Even chasing the chickens round hasn't cheered you up. Everything all right at home?'

'Yes, yes,' Laurence assured him. 'Everything's fine.'

'Sure about that? You don't seem yourself. You look a bit distracted.'

Christopher Cherry was certainly perceptive. Laurence didn't think he'd ever had a boss who was worried about his state of mind before. In the City, as long as the numbers were right, the business was coming in, the rest of you as a person could go to hell in a handcart.

'Are you settling in here, lad?'

'God, yes. No problems on that front. I'm loving the job.' Even the runaway chickens and the blocked loos.

'Good to hear it.' Christopher allowed himself a ruddy-cheeked smile. 'That big offer from the City didn't come in, did it – like I said it would?'

Laurence's poker face had never fully developed and now his jaw dropped open.

'Ah,' Christopher Cherry said.

'They called me yesterday morning,' Laurence admitted. 'Totally out of the blue.'

'Big salary, big company benefits?'

All he could do was nod.

'If you want to take it you must,' Christopher said. 'But I want to remind you that all these "perks" come with a price. You've blossomed since you've been here, lad, and I'd like to think that the working environment at Cherry's has something to do with it. You looked like a bloody ghost when you started with us.'

'Christopher, I'm so grateful to you for this opportunity . . .'

Mr Cherry waved his protest away. 'I can't compete on salary. Daresay I could find a few extra grand if you're still here and doing as well in six months. If you bring some of these expansion projects in, then maybe a bit more. We might even drop in a little company run-around. But I can't lift you to the next level no matter what you do here. I could make promises about the future, about bringing you into the business, but it's way too early to be talking like that. I don't know what I'm doing myself yet. I'll retire one day and the kids have got their own lives, their own careers. They're not showing any interest in stepping into my size tens. Cherry's might be up for grabs then. But I don't know for sure.' Christopher spread his hands, encompassing the vast barn. 'So, this is pretty much it. What you see is what you get.'

And that was one of the things that he'd liked most about working here. Everything was very straightforward. There was no bullshit to wade through, no monumental egos to contend with, no political back-biting to keep up with. There were just the chickens, the goats, the fine organic produce and a morning meeting over tea and toasted teacakes or fruit scones. The job couldn't be any better. But was it the best use of his talents? His penchant was for making money, lots of it. Not chicken wrestling.

'You must do as you will, lad.' Christopher Cherry wiped his mouth on his napkin. 'I don't want to lose you. You know that well enough.'

'I have to think this through very carefully,' Laurence said. 'I have to do what's best for my family.'

'Aye,' Christopher agreed, 'But that doesn't always mean chasing the money.' He clapped Laurence on the back. 'Don't be late for that cheesemaker. He makes great cheese, but he's a grumpy old bugger.'

'You'll be the first one to know what I decide, Christopher.' The man nodded and walked away.

Laurence checked the time and then strode out to the van. The winter sun was low over the fields and cast a milky shimmer. He stood and took some deep breaths. It was a beautiful part of the British countryside, there was no doubt. Who could ask for a better place to work? Would he really want to be cooped up on the thirty-seventh floor of a tower block after this? Not him. But it wasn't a matter of what he wanted to do right now, it was about what he *needed* to do.

Chapter 106

Three days have gone past since Laurence's job offer to go back to Helston Field and he still can't make a decision. Gordon Wolff, his old boss, has called him three times now and is pressing Laurence to choose one way or the other.

The children are next door playing on Keanu's Wii. Laurence and I take a coffee through to the living room and slump into the blue velour sofa next to each other. I switch the television on and something mindless plays to itself on the screen.

'I'll have to let him know soon.' Laurence continues the conversation that we started at dinner. The same conversation we've had a dozen times. We will have to reach a conclusion to our deliberations soon otherwise we'll both go insane. I think we're both hoping that suddenly there'll be a revelation and we'll see exactly where our future lies. We both also know that it doesn't happen like that.

'Can't we fob him off for a few more days?'

'No. He wants a decision tomorrow. After that it's taken out of my hands and they get someone else. The chance to change everything passes us by.'

But my brain simply refuses to think about it for another minute.

'There's another thing we must address.' My husband sips his coffee. 'I'm getting worried about having all that money in the house.'

After loaning five thousand pounds to Tracey to pay back the loan shark, we currently have twenty-five thousand pounds left, split into two bundles and stuffed into mine and Laurence's pillowcases beneath our pillows. It's utter madness and my husband is right, we shouldn't have it in the house a moment longer than is necessary.

'Yes,' I agree. 'You're right.' We're both well aware of what happened last time we had any valuables here.

'We need to open a bank account. I'll do it tomorrow.'

Then Laurence turns to me. 'I've been thinking about that,' he says. 'As well as everything else.' His eyes lock with mine. 'What if we use it to pay off all our debts? *All* of them,' he emphasises. 'Start with a completely clean sheet.'

'We're going to need that money, Laurence, if you decide not to go back to the City.'

'It's not our money,' he says. 'Morally, it belongs to other people. The credit-card companies, I can just about keep waiting. We're paying them off gradually.'

I don't state the obvious – that it will take years at the rate we're going.

'But Anthony and Amanda deserve better. If we have the cash, we should pay them what we owe them.'

'They wouldn't do the same thing for us,' I grumble.

'It doesn't matter what they would do, it's what *we* do that's important to me. Perhaps if we give them their money back it will free me up to make a clear decision.'

'How much exactly are our debts?'

'Do you want to sort this out now?'

'We might as well, there's nothing on the television,' I joke. So I take myself upstairs and strip the pillowcases full of money from the pillows and go downstairs with it.

Laurence, in the meantime, has pulled together all the paper-work for the bills.

I tip the notes out of the pillowcases and spread them on the dining-room table. It looks like an awful lot of money when you see it like that, and I think that from now on, I'll start to pay for everything in cash. When you have to count out the notes it really drives it home to you how much you're spending. With a credit card, it's far too easy to ignore that it's real money and, at some point, the bills have to be paid.

'We owe Anthony and Amanda twenty thousand pounds.'

Clearly, I'm not as altruistic as Laurence as I think how horrible they were to us when we needed them, how uncaring. Amanda can still afford to splash out on jewellery, so they're clearly not desperate for it – as we are. But I bite back my protest as my husband starts to count out the notes. They're fifty-pound notes and he puts them into piles of twenty. Very soon he's counted out the amount we owe our former friends.

'It doesn't leave us much,' he observes, as we both stare at the tiny pile remaining.

'No.' Even if all of it was allocated to pay outstanding credit-card bills, there's no way that it would cover them. We'll still be in debt, even after giving all this away.

'What about the outstanding mortgage on the London flat?'

'I can't even think about that. Chances are we'll never pay that off, Lily. It's not an enormous sum, all things considered, and the mortgage company are letting us pay it on interest only over the next forty years. All we can do is chip away at it as best we can.'

My hands start to tremble.

He says gently, 'We have to do this, Lily.'

'Do we?'

'This could be our one opportunity to set things right.'

I'm thinking now that Laurence must take this job in the City. He is giving our only fallback away.

'Okay.'

'Why don't we take it to Anthony and Amanda now?'

'In cash?'

'I want it gone,' he says. 'Let's do it now.'

'I'll see if Tracey has a shoe box or something we can put it in.' I need to speak to my friend anyway, as she did get the job at Ornato with Seymour and today was her first day of stepping into my shoes.

With heavy heart, I leave my husband and the piles of money and head off to cadge yet another favour from my saintly neighbour.

Chapter 107

'I'm here to ask two favours of you,' I tell my neighbour as we tread the familiar track to her kitchen.

Since she was attacked by the loan shark Tracey keeps her front door bolted now and I don't blame her. I should get Laurence to fit one of those spyholes for her and a safety chain to give her some peace of mind.

'Ask away,' Tracey says.

'I want to know if you'll have the kids for a couple of hours more for me and I also need a shoe box.'

'The kids I can do easily,' she laughs. 'They're never any trouble. But a shoe box? I can't begin to imagine what that's for.'

'We're going to pay off our biggest debt.'

'Which involves a shoe box?'

'Laurence has decided we need to take a trip out to see Amanda and Anthony this minute. We need something to carry the money in.'

'Oh. I'll see what I can find.'

She disappears while I make myself useful and dry the dishes that are sitting on the draining board. Minutes later she appears with the requested shoe box. 'This do you?'

'Perfect.' Just the right size for squeezing in twenty grand.

'Anyway,' I say, 'more importantly, I also came to see how your first day at Ornato was.'

My friend stares at me, hands on hips. 'You did not tell me that Seymour was hot enough to grill sausages on.'

'It's an interesting analogy,' I remark. 'But you're right. He's pretty hot.' And charming. And kind. And generous. But I won't allow my mind to go there.

'I really enjoyed it,' Tracey says. 'The jewellery is so gorgeous and I get to wear it all day! I'm not sure that I stepped into your size fives that well, but I'm going to give it my best shot. Seymour seemed pleased.'

'Well done,' I say. 'I knew you'd like it.'

'We should drink a toast.' My friend produces two glasses and fills them from the wine box in the fridge. Another downside of living in Netherslade Bridge is that my liver has probably become pickled since I've been here.

'To your new job,' I propose.

'To being debt free,' Tracey adds.

'I'll drink to that.' And I do. If we're going to visit Anthony and Amanda then I need some Dutch courage.

'He misses you,' Tracey says gently. 'He's quite cut up about the situation.'

'Seymour knew that I was married,' I remind her. 'These things always end in tears. For both parties.'

'Are you okay?'

'Handling it,' I say.

'That's not the same.'

'No,' I agree. 'But it's the best I can manage at the moment. Given some time, I'm sure I'll be fine.' I'll have to be.

Love him, I want to say. *Love him for me. I can't bear for him to be alone.* Instead, I choose the more neutral, 'Look after him for me.'

'I will. It's hard not to like him.'

'That was my downfall.' I give my friend a wry smile.

'Thanks,' she says. 'Thanks for making me do this. I wouldn't have had the confidence to apply for a job like that if you hadn't pushed me.'

And this alcohol is giving me the confidence I need. I throw back the wine. 'I'd better be going if we want to catch a bus there and back.' It's only since I have become a regular user of public transport that I realise how sparse it is at night. Actually, it's sparse during the day, it's just even worse at night. Do the transport companies think that no one ever needs to travel after seven o'clock in the evening?

'I'll see you later,' I tell Tracey.

She stands up and throws her arms around me. 'Best friends forever,' she says.

'Best friends forever,' I agree.

'Go and show them what you're made of,' Tracey urges. 'No one puts Lily Jones in the corner.'

It's clear that I don't understand the reference.

'*Dirty Dancing*,' she tells me. '*The* best film of all time. You've led a very sheltered life, Lily.'

I can't deny it. Most of our favourite films used to involve French subtitles – mainly because they were what *The Times* told us to watch, it has to be said.

'You and Jamelia and me are going to have a girly night in with wine, chocolate and Patrick Swayze – God rest his soul.'

I shrug. 'Sounds good to me.' When a few months ago it would have sounded like my idea of hell. Now I'm confident enough to do what I want, watch what I want. I don't have to justify it to anyone. I don't have to think about Amanda Marquis and her like turning up their noses at me. Everything has a place in life and if I want to chill out, swig two-for-a-fiver bottles of wine and watch cheesy films, then I damn well will.

'Wish me luck.'

'You won't need it,' Tracey assures me. 'It will be fine. You're doing the right thing. You must feel good about that.'

But I don't. I feel nervous, frightened even, now that this safety net is to be taken from under us. When this money has gone then we truly have nothing. Unless Laurence takes this job back in the City, we are at rock bottom once more, with nowhere else to go.

Chapter 108

We wait for ages in the cold to take the bus to Anthony and Amanda Marquis's exquisite home. They live a few minutes away from our old home in one of the villages on the outskirts of the city – one that will no doubt in the future be eaten up by the fast-growing development. For now, Calverly is an idyllic rural retreat. There is one bus an hour and the last one leaves Calverly to get back to the city centre just before nine o'clock as I'd suspected. Time is tight. It gives us only just enough leeway to complete our task.

Laurence and I don't speak much on the bus. We just hold hands and nurse the bulging shoe box that rests on my husband's knee as we watch the darkness move by.

The bus stops in the centre of the village and it's a good ten minutes' walk to the Marquis's home. Their country pile is even bigger than the barn, where we lived in Morsworth. It's an enormous Georgian-style residence in one of the prime locations in the area. Money has been lavished on both the interior and the exterior of the property. It's set in acres of ground and Amanda too, as I once did, has stabling here for her own horses.

Laurence and I tramp down the unlit country lane, collars up against the cold. We should have called to check that they would be in, but we didn't. I think both of us want to minimise the contact we have with them. Now as we make our way in the pitch black to their secluded home, I wonder whether this was a wise move.

Laurence has the shoe box under his arm and we hold hands more tightly as we get nearer to our destination. At least there's little chance of us being mugged for our money out here.

Then, as we round the bend and come up to the imposing gates of the house, we see that Anthony and Amanda's home is lit up like a Christmas tree. There are lights on in every room and a gaggle of cars are parked nose to tail in the circular drive.

We stop dead in our tracks.

'Oh God,' Laurence breathes.

'They're having a party.' Some of the windows are open and the sound of a tinkling piano and equally tinkling laughter drifts out into the night air. Two large caterers' vans are parked at the side of the house. There must be a hundred people here. Possibly more.

I wrack my brains to think of a reason they might be having such an extravagant celebration, but I don't think it's either of their birthdays or their wedding anniversary, if I remember rightly. They must be having a party just because they can. If we were still included in their social circle, I would know the reason they have pushed out the boat. But we're not. Laurence and I are standing here in the dark and the cold, noses pressed up against the window.

'We could just go straight home,' I say. 'Call them tomorrow to arrange to see them.'

'No,' Laurence says firmly. 'I'm not coming all this way to turn back now.'

A journey that would have taken ten minutes in the car has turned into a marathon of nearly two hours if you include waiting for the bus, the bouncy drive and then the walk at the other end. I glance at the time on my phone. We have only twenty minutes to do what we've come to do and get back to the bus stop.

'Let's get it over with,' Laurence says.

So, clutching our shoe box, we advance on the front door.

The knocker is a big brass lion's head and, taking a deep and shuddering breath, with a final glance at me, Laurence raps at the door with it. We stand for one of our precious minutes and nothing happens, so Laurence raps again.

A few moments pass and I'm about to suggest that we turn on our heels and run when the door swings open. Amanda Marquis is standing there, glass of champagne in hand, dressed in a gold sheath that has 'designer' written all over it. I don't think she'll have found *that* at the swishing party. With shoes to match, I doubt she'll have had any change from a thousand pounds.

My former friend stares out at us, eyes flicking up and down and, for a moment, I don't think that she recognises us. Then it dawns on her. 'Laurence, Lily. What are you doing here?'

'Is Anthony available?' Laurence asks politely. 'I'd like to speak to both of you.'

'We *are* busy.' She gestures at the party going on behind her.

'It's rather important,' Laurence presses.

'I'll find him,' she says, and leaves us standing at the door while she disappears into the crowd of revellers in the hall behind her, and while Cole Porter's 'I Get A Kick Out Of You' competes with the conversation.

Laurence and I exchange a glance as we stand there like a pair of abandoned orphans. Inside, I can see more of our old friends, but they're too wrapped up in having a good time to notice who is waiting patiently at the threshold.

Eventually, Amanda returns with Anthony in tow. He has put weight on since we last saw him and his face is flushed with alcohol.

'You two!' he cries. 'Amanda said it was you and I didn't believe her.'

I'm aware of our time ticking away.

Laurence thrusts out the shoe box. 'We've brought this,' he says. 'It's all that I owe you. Twenty thousand pounds.'

Anthony's eyes threaten to bulge out of his sockets. 'In a shoe box?'

'It was the only way,' Laurence says. 'We don't currently have the benefit of a bank account.'

'Christ.' Anthony takes the proffered box from my husband's

hand then runs his fingers through his hair. 'I don't know what to say.'

'I'm sorry that it's taken so long,' Laurence says. 'But we're all square now.'

'Yes. God. Of course.' He looks completely bewildered. Clearly the Marquises had never expected to see the money again.

'We'll be off then,' Laurence says.

Now it's Anthony and Amanda's turn to exchange a wary glance. 'Come in, come in,' Anthony says, bonhomie syrupy in his voice. 'Have a drink with us.'

Obviously, they've now got something else to celebrate. Whereas we have not.

Amanda takes in our scruffy attire – both of us in jeans and winter coats and I can tell that she's assessing how badly we'll blend into her soirée. We'll clash with the canapés looking like this.

'No, thank you,' Laurence says politely and my heart surges with pride at his dignity. 'We have a bus to catch.'

Then he takes my hand and we turn away from the house and walk down the drive, the gravel crunching under our feet, leaving Anthony and Amanda standing at their door, shoe box stuffed full of money in hand.

We have done it. We have cleared our debt to them. It has cost us dearly, but we have finally done it.

'Okay?' Laurence asks as we march briskly back towards the bus stop.

'Yes.' I could weep, and whether it's from elation or despair, I don't know.

This gesture has cost us dearly but, morally, it was the right thing to do and now we can sleep with clear consciences.

Then, as we turn towards the bus stop, I realise that Anthony and Amanda Marquis didn't even say thank you.

Chapter 109

The bus comes on time and we climb aboard for the journey back to Milton Keynes. We will have a long walk back to Netherslade Bridge as there'll be no transfer from the city at this time of night and I wish we'd taken some money out of Anthony and Amanda's stash for a taxi.

We're light of mood as we settle on the bus, sitting at the front and huddling together for warmth. But as we trundle away from Calverly, our euphoria soon dissipates on the way back to our real life.

'What have we done?' Laurence says to me.

'The right thing,' I assure him.

'I'm going to have to take that job in the City. I have no choice. We need the money.'

We do, I think. But do we as a family, having got used to having him around, want to go back to never seeing Laurence from one end of the week to the next?

'I'll call my old boss tomorrow. First thing.'

And, with that, we both succumb to deep gloom.

We get off the bus in the city and begin the long trek back to Netherslade Bridge. It starts to drizzle and neither of us thought to bring an umbrella – and then I remember that we don't actually possess an umbrella. We don't have gloves either and so wedge our hands deep in our pockets.

By the time we reach the estate we are both utterly and thoroughly miserable and are cold down to our bones. As we pass The Nut, the warm glow from the pub looks so inviting.

Laurence looks at me. 'Shall we?'

I nod. I can't face going home just yet, just the two of us looking at each other unhappily across the living room, and the option of drowning our sorrows seems like a damn fine idea.

Inside The Nut the fuggy heat hits us and, even as we go to the bar, we're both stripping off our wet coats. There might not be a roaring log fire in here, but the central heating is certainly working overtime. Though it could do with a serious revamp, tonight the place feels welcoming and cosy. The bar is busy and it's surprising how many people we now know in here. The Nut is more than just a pub, it's the village hall that Netherslade Bridge doesn't have. It's the central meeting place where families and friends get together. Like *Cheers* but without Ted Danson.

'You look frozen through to the marrow, the both of you,' the barman remarks.

'We are,' Laurence confirms, rubbing his red-raw hands together.

'I've got hot chocolate on tonight, Mrs Jones,' he says. 'That'd warm you up nicely with a tot of brandy in it.' He winks at me.

'That sounds like a marvellous idea,' I reply, my teeth chattering.

'And for you, Lozzer?'

'Just the brandy for me,' my husband says. 'But make it a double.'

Despite the cost, I think he deserves it.

Then Skull comes over and claps him on the back. 'Mate,' he says. 'This is an unexpected pleasure.'

To my surprise, I see Laurence choke up. Tears fill his eyes. If Skull notices, he pretends that he doesn't. The difference between the rebuff from his old friend and the warm welcome from his new one has clearly got to my husband. 'Got some parsnips that are just about ready, Lozzer,' Skull says. 'If you want to pop by the allotment in the next few days.'

My husband is unable to answer, but nods soundlessly.

Skull chatters on. 'Want to throw some arrows? Digger and Danny are round there now.'

Laurence looks at me to see if I mind being left alone. 'I'll be fine.' I nod. 'You go and enjoy yourself. I'll text Tracey and see if she wants to come up and bring the children – just for the one.'

The barman hands over Laurence's brandy and my husband buys Skull a pint, then they disappear round the corner to the dartboard just as my hot chocolate appears. It's made with sugary sweet drinking chocolate and has a lavish swirl of synthetic cream on the top. A big pink marshmallow sits on that. When I sip it, the rough brandy cuts through the sweetness and it's the best thing I've tasted in a long time.

'That'll hit the spot,' the barman assures me and I could cry at his kindness.

While I'm sipping my chocolate, nursing the glass with my frozen fingers, Jamelia comes along and kisses me on both cheeks. 'Where you been, girl?' she says and then, before I can reply, 'Hmm. I'm gonna get me one of them.'

'Let me,' I say, and I buy her a hot chocolate with a shot.

'Tracey tells me we're gonna have a girlies' night.'

'I believe so.'

Jamelia high fives me. 'You crack me up, Lily,' she giggles. 'Let's get the other girls over. Sarah, Marcia and Ayesha will be up for it.'

'As long as there are no shopping trolleys involved.'

Jamelia laughs her raucous laugh again, and as it's infectious, I find myself laughing too. And I think that I'd so much rather be here in the less than salubrious setting of The Nut or having a girls' night out with Tracey and her friends – *my* friends – than at any of Amanda's prissy, high-end parties.

Then Tracey arrives with our children. Frighteningly, Hettie and Hugo's favourite place is turning out to be The Nut and with a cursory hello to their mother, my offspring disappear into the family room, no doubt heading for the competitive delights of the table football.

'It's flipping freezing out there,' my neighbour complains. 'What are we drinking?' Jamelia holds up her chocolate and Tracey tastes it. Then, rubbing her hands together, she says, 'Mmm. Yum. Count me in. Let's get us some comfy seats,' eyeing up one of the few vacant tables with a curved banquette around it.

As we stand up, Tracey throws her arm round my shoulder. 'How did it go, love?'

'It went okay,' I tell her.

'You'll feel better now.'

I risk a smile. 'Actually, you're right. I do feel a bit better.'

'Good.' She kisses me on the cheek.

We squeeze into the banquette together, laughing as we always do. I look round and catch sight of Laurence taking his turn at the dartboard and he's chuckling at something, surrounded by friends too. Skull catches my eye and winks at me. Laurence is all right. He's one of the boys and they'll make sure that he's fine.

Then I think that I feel more than a bit better. I actually feel bloody lucky to be alive and well and living here in Netherslade Bridge.

Chapter 110

Far too merry for a week night, Laurence and I weave our way home. One spiked hot chocolate turned into three and now it's nearly eleven o'clock. The children run ahead of us. Normally, I would be hysterical about them still being up at this hour, but now I'd rather them spend time with their new friends and the extended family we seem to be building. They're going to be a nightmare to get up for school in the morning and Hettie will be tetchy all day long. Two late nights in one week is a bad idea. But it was worth it. We've all had a thoroughly enjoyable evening. Next week, I'll get them back on track.

'They're a great bunch of people,' Laurence says wistfully.

I can see his breath in the air and think again that it won't be long before Christmas is here. Normally, my freezer would be filled to bursting with festive food by now, my lavish schedule of entertaining organised like a military campaign. But this year I've made no plans at all. I'm just going to kick back and go with the flow.

'I've been thinking,' my husband continues in a slightly slurry way. 'I'm going to phone up Gordon Wolff first thing tomorrow and turn down that job. Helston Field can stick it. Whatever happens, I don't want to get back on that treadmill again.'

I want to bring in the voice of reason here and remind him that such momentous decisions should be made without the benefit of copious amounts of alcohol. But then I think that perhaps such decisions *are* best made while drunk, as then what truly is in your heart is allowed to give vent rather than be suppressed by what convention expects of you.

The other reason that I say nothing to contradict my husband is because it's what I want too. I want to stay here, I want to find another part-time job that I can do, I want to make my life in Netherslade Bridge – if not forever, then certainly for the foreseeable future. I've found friends here the like of which I've never had before, and I don't think you can price that too highly.

In hindsight, I think I always had a secret fear of losing the money, losing my home. But I've changed. Home is definitely where the heart is. Wherever that may be.

It looks like Christmas will consist of an organic turkey that Christopher Cherry kindly supplies to all of his staff, and some vegetables from the allotment. Perhaps Skull will come and join us if he doesn't have other plans. Maybe Len Eleven Dogs as well. I'm sure that Tracey and her family will feature heavily too. Perhaps we'll have our best Christmas yet.

'You haven't said anything.' Laurence points out. 'Are you happy with my decision?'

I stop in the middle of the pavement by a burnt-out car with a bright yellow clamp. Someone's dumped a shopping trolley and three more tyres have appeared from nowhere. 'I'm very happy. Very happy indeed.'

I wind my arms round his neck and kiss him.

'No regrets?' he asks when we come up for air.

'None at all.'

'I've got lots of plans,' he tells me. 'I'm thinking of starting a scheme for under-privileged children at Cherry's. Do educational days – that kind of thing. I hope that Christopher will be keen on it.'

'I'm sure that he will. Sounds wonderful,' I tell him.

'I want to get a couple of ponies there too, perhaps do some riding lessons for kids who wouldn't normally get the chance to experience it. Do you think Hettie and Hugo might like to help out?'

'I'm sure that they'd jump at the chance.' It's unlikely that they'll ever be able to have their own ponies again, so this would be a wonderful opportunity.

'I've applied for a few jobs myself,' I tell Laurence. 'I'm keen to get something else to do.' And we will very definitely need the money now.

'We're looking for a new supplier of homemade cakes at the farm. Why don't you give that a go?'

'I might do.' It's something that I hadn't considered before but, then again, I quite fancy the job in the wedding shop and I'm hoping that I get an interview for that.

'Are you ever going to tell me why you gave up the job at Ornato?'

I shake my head. 'It was just circumstances,' I offer rather lamely. 'Does it really matter now? It's all water under the bridge. Tracey's filled my shoes — admirably, I'm sure.'

'I'll buy you more jewellery,' my husband promises. 'Sometimes in the future when we're back in the black.'

'It doesn't matter to me any more,' I tell him. 'I'm just glad that we're together and we're happy.'

'You do love me?' Laurence asks. 'Despite all that's happened, you do still love me?'

'Of course I do.'

We kiss again and are locked in our embrace, oblivious to the world when Hugo pipes up, 'You do realise that you're in public? You're *so* embarrassing.'

'I think it's lovely,' Hettie says. 'Mummy and Daddy are in love,' she chants as she skips along the road. 'Mummy and Daddy are in love.'

'Are we?' My husband wants to know.

'Oh, yes,' I say. 'Very much so.'

Then we walk back to the house. There are no lights on and neither is the heating, so it will be cold inside. We're going to have to snuggle up tonight. I smile at the thought. Laurence slips the key into the lock and then shoulders in the warped door.

'Now that we're staying,' he says, 'I must get round to fixing that.'

Chapter III

There was a heavy frost on the ground as Laurence cycled to work, so thick it looked like a sprinkling of snow. Crisp, hard frost that turned the trees to glittering chandeliers and made natural sculptures of the tall grasses and bulrushes. It was, perhaps, a foretaste of the hard winter that the weathermen were predicting.

Each morning it was taking him longer and longer to thaw out when he arrived at work. Soon it would be too cold to cycle and he'd have to start thinking about alternative transport – difficult when there wasn't a suitable bus. Which was a shame because he really enjoyed his daily journey along the canal and, physically, he was in better shape than he'd ever been. Mentally, he was feeling pretty good too.

Having made the decision to decline the job in the City, he felt as if a weight had lifted from him. All he had to do now was make the call. Rather than feeling frightened of what the future might hold, he felt energised – as if this was the first day of the rest of his life. They'd barely a bean to their names, but most of their debts were now cleared, bar the residue of the mortgage on the London flat, some outstanding credit-card bills and a hundred pounds that he owed Peter his old driver. That he would take round to Peter this weekend with a heart-felt thanks for helping them out when they needed it most. From now on they'd budget and live within their means, not feeling that they were entitled to things that they were unable to afford. He was looking forward to a more simple life, getting back to basics, to what mattered most in life – family, friends, love, health.

Laurence cycled into the farmyard and locked his bike in the shed next to the chickens. 'Morning, girls,' he said as he passed them by and swung into the main barn. The hens, he was sure, clucked in response. Wait until they had two pretty-looking alpacas to brighten their day.

'Looks parky out there this morning, lad,' Christopher Cherry said.

'It certainly is.' His nose was throbbing with pain it was so icy.

'Take the Land Rover home tonight,' his boss said. 'Keep it until it's mild enough to cycle in again.'

'Thank you,' Laurence said, touched. 'That's very kind.'

'I don't want them finding you frozen to death like a snowman on that towpath,' Christopher joked. 'That must be against health and safety rules.'

'The Land Rover might end up without its wheels if I leave it parked outside my house,' Laurence warned him.

'It's an old heap,' Christopher says. 'It owes me nothing. I'm prepared to take the risk if you are.'

Laurence took a deep breath. 'I just wanted you to know that I've made my decision.'

'I hope it's in my favour.'

'It is,' Laurence confirmed. 'I'm turning down the City job. I'll be staying at Cherry's for as long as you'll have me.'

Christopher Cherry reached out, gripped his hand and pumped it enthusiastically. 'I knew you wouldn't let me down, lad.'

Laurence shrugged, unable to find his voice.

'It must have cost you dear, this?'

'In monetary terms, yes,' Laurence admitted. 'But I think it's the right decision.'

'I'll see what I can do to soften the blow,' Christopher promised. 'I won't forget this loyalty. I want you to have a long and happy future at Cherry's.'

'Me too,' Laurence said. 'Now all I have to do is make the call.'

'I'll leave you to it.' Christopher went to walk away and spoke over his shoulder. 'Mind, we'll celebrate this at the morning meeting. We'll see what delights Betty can find for us on the cake counter.'

Laurence grinned as the older man waved a hand and continued on his way. It was the right decision. Absolutely the right decision. But his hand still shook when he picked up the phone.

Chapter 112

So. Laurence turned down the marvellous job – or, should I say, the marvellous salary. He's committed instead to the marvellous job and the meagre salary at Cherry's Farm. And he's happier than I've seen him in a long, long time.

Other than that, life goes on, nothing much changes. All is quiet, I believe, on the western front.

It's been a long-winded process, but I've finally got an interview with the wedding-dress shop for next week and I have all of my fingers crossed for that. It's tight managing on Laurence's salary, but we're coping.

Seymour Chapman is being very generous with Tracey. Her salary at Ornato is certainly above the going rate and that means she's able to pay us back a hundred pounds every mouth, which certainly helps. Thankfully, my friend is absolutely loving her job. She's so kind and natural that she's proving a big hit with the customers. I'm so pleased for her. She tells me how Seymour is and what he's up to. And I only get pangs of guilt/longing/grief every now and again. I miss her and our cosy gossips so much during the day, but I hope that I'll soon be out at work again and fully occupied.

In the meantime I've been baking cakes for Cherry's for some pin money. I have three trays of blueberry muffins in the oven now, which are just about ready to come out, and another two batches left to do. Then I'll start on some banana bran ones too. Laurence will take them into work tomorrow to sell – much easier now he has use of Christopher's battered old Land Rover – and he tells me that they're proving very popular.

Hugo and Hettie are working hard on the end-of-term concerts at their new school. No classical piano recitals at Netherslade Bridge school, it seems. Hugo is doing some sort of breakdancing routine and is spending a lot of time in the living room spinning round on his head. Hettie is to sing her favourite Girls Aloud song at the performance, complete with movements. My daughter also currently has nits and is complaining bitterly because I won't allow her to keep one of those as a pet either. I never cease to revel in the fact that our children are home every night with us and wonder how it could ever have seemed right for it to be otherwise.

I have regular girlie nights with Tracey, Jamelia and the others. I still get my Brazilian bikini wax done on my neighbour's kitchen table and still have my fake nails painted alarmingly lurid shades. I still occasionally get 'bladdered' – not my turn of phrase – with them and always vow never to do it again. Though I haven't been near a shopping trolley for some time.

Len Eleven Dogs continues to walk his plethora of mutts round the estate. Sometimes I join him and we walk along the canal banks together and he talks tenderly about the family he lost. I go to see him every week with a plated dinner, for which he is ridiculously grateful.

Our friend, Skull, provides an unending stream of vegetables to supplement our household food, for which *I'm* ridiculously grateful. Laurence's name is creeping higher on the waiting list for allotments and he's hoping to have one by the spring. In the meantime, the herbs I promised myself are flourishing on the windowsill.

In the house, we've invested in some paint and have freshened up the woodchip paper. The rest will have to wait until, as and when we can afford it. We've decided to leave the garden as a semi-wilderness and, strangely, have grown to like it. I even have a certain affection for the rusting car now after our night of passion in it. You never know, perhaps when the weather warms up, we might do it again.

Just as I'm musing on this, the door bell rings. I think the battery must be going as it sounds a bit wonky. Wiping my hands on the tea towel, I head to the door.

When I open it, I'm shocked to see Amanda Marquis standing there. While I am wearing jeans and lots of flour, Amanda looks as immaculate as she always does. She has on black wool trousers and a cream pea jacket in cashmere. Despite it not being sunny she's wearing sunglasses and I think it's probably because she doesn't want to be recognised coming to my door. As if anyone round here is going to know her.

I feel myself bristle, but try to be civil. 'Hello, Amanda. What brings you here?'

We've heard nothing from either Anthony or Amanda since the night we took the money to them at their party. I thought in the cold light of day that they might have remembered their manners and would, at least, call to say a belated thank you. But they didn't.

Amanda glances furtively up and down my street. 'Can I come in, please?' she says. Her voice sounds strained.

I want to point out that we don't have fleas any more, but then I think that it's just petty point-scoring that does no one any good.

Instead, I say, 'Of course.' I stand aside to let her in.

She takes in the drabness of my home and I'm sure that I see colour drain from her face. Amanda leans against the wall, as if she might faint.

'Amanda.' I put my arm under hers. 'Are you feeling all right?'

'No,' she says. When she removes her sunglasses, I can see that her eyes are bloodshot with crying.

'I'll put the kettle on. Then you can tell me all about it.'

At which point she bursts into fresh tears again, so I steer her to the blue velour sofa and settle her in it.

'Now,' I say. 'I'm sure it can't be all that bad.'

Her swollen eyes meet mine. 'It's Anthony,' she says.

And I wonder for a terrible moment if he has died or has left her for a younger model.

'He's lost his job,' she croaks.

'Oh, Amanda.'

'Fifty of them have had to go,' she continues between sobs. 'It's so cruel. Anthony has always been one of the best performers. He's given them everything. Now look what they've done to him. Is that how you treat someone?'

How I remember the all-encompassing bitterness, the sour taste in my mouth that wouldn't go away. I bet Amanda has it now.

If I was mean, I could gloat about this. Who would have thought that the Marquises would be suffering the same in-iquities that Laurence and I have? But I'm not feeling mean and I know exactly what Amanda is going through. My heart goes out to her.

I wrap my arms round her stick-thin body which is rigid with tension. 'When did this happen?'

'Yesterday,' she says. 'He's at home now. On the phone. Trying to find something else.' My former friend turns her face to me. 'How did you manage? How on earth did you cope?'

'I had to. There was nothing else I could do.'

'There are so many cutbacks in the City – what if he can't get another job? What if he's out of work for months like Laurence was?'

'Did he not get a pay-off?' Which would be more than Laurence did.

'It's minimal.' Amanda brushes the thought away. 'The bills are phenomenal on the house.'

The thought that they still have the twenty grand that we returned to them goes through my mind. I don't know that they're on their uppers quite yet. But then I also know how the lifestyle they lead eats up money at a voracious rate.

'I don't know if we'll be able to keep it.' She weeps again. This is like déjà vu for me.

'We could end up somewhere like this.'

'Believe it or not, I like it here,' I tell her.

My friend looks horrified.

'To be honest, Amanda, Laurence was just offered his old job back and turned it down.'

397

Now she thinks I'm lying. 'Perhaps Anthony could apply for it,' she says desperately. Then a shrug. 'If Laurence doesn't want it.'

'Perhaps he could. I'll speak to Laurence.' I wonder what he'll think when I tell him that his old pal has suffered the same fate.

'What if everyone cuts me off?'

'Like they did to me?'

Amanda flushes. Clearly, she is thinking twice about the treatment she's meted out.

'I don't think I could bear it.'

'There are much worse things than being poor, Amanda.'

I am completely unhinged, her expression says.

I sigh. 'Come round for dinner one night. With Anthony. We can talk things through. See if there's anything we can do.'

'I'd appreciate that,' she says, taking a beautifully embroidered handkerchief from her voluminous designer handbag and dabbing her eyes.

'We don't eat anything fancy these days. It'll more than likely be sausages and mash than polenta and monkfish.'

Amanda, who rarely eats fat or carbs, looks slightly faint again.

I pat her knee as I stand up. 'I'll go and make that cup of tea.'

'Lily,' she says. 'Thank you for being so kind. I didn't know who else to turn to. I . . . I . . . I couldn't tell any of our friends. No one else would understand.' She looks down, shamefaced. 'I'm sorry. Really sorry. About everything.'

And I am too. Just because Amanda wasn't a good friend to me, it doesn't mean that I have to be like that too. I could turn her away from our door, smirk at her downfall. Who would blame me? But our own circumstances have taught me the true value of friends and I won't forget that in a hurry.

Chapter 113

Two hours later, when Amanda has eaten two of my blueberry muffins – carbs or not – and has had several cups of restorative tea, she leaves. I stand at the door of my house and wave goodbye to her. She swings round in her top-of-the-range Mercedes and I wonder, sadly, how long that will last.

The day is slipping away from me and I go into the kitchen and think about whipping up my next batch of baking. I'm up to my elbows in flour when the door bell rings again and I give my hands a quick wipe with the tea towel and hurry out to answer it. I wonder if Amanda has forgotten something.

When the door swings open, Seymour's long, gangly form is leaning up against the wall.

'Hello,' he says with a warm smile, unable to tell that my heart has nearly stopped at the sight of him.

'Hello.'

Seymour was the last person I expected to see here. It's even more of a shock than Amanda Marquis turning up at my door.

He's wearing jeans with boots and a brown sweater topped with a leather jacket. His collar is turned up against the cold. His hair needs cutting.

Seymour nods towards my neighbour's house. 'I just brought Tracey home,' he says. 'It's too cold to be catching a bus.'

I think of the times that he did that for me. 'That's nice of you.'

He shrugs. 'It's cold standing here too.'

Moving aside, I say, 'Come in.' Seymour might as well see my threadbare home in all its glory.

We go into the kitchen. It's impossible to keep this house warm, as we are finding out to our cost. The heat just seems to leak out of the walls and windows. I think we can get the landlord to apply for grants for cavity wall insulation and I must look into that. But, at the moment, with the oven on full blast, it does at least feel warmer downstairs. I *will* make this place into a home, given time.

'Something smells good,' he says, and he props himself casually against the cupboards looking as comfortable as if we do this every day.

I, on the other hand, am a mass of anxiety and nerves and can't stand still. 'I'm baking muffins for Cherry's Farm. Where Laurence works.'

'I remember that.'

'Just for the time being,' I add. 'Until I find another job.'

'There was no need for you to leave, Lily. I'd still like to have you at Ornato.'

'What about Tracey?'

'She's fabulous. The customers love her. She makes them all laugh. There's no reason why she couldn't stay too. You're good friends, the best. I'm sure the two of you would work perfectly well together.'

For a moment, my heart leaps and then I dismiss the idea. 'I can't, Seymour. Of course I can't.'

His lips curl into one of his heartbreaking smiles and my insides twist. 'Am I that much of a temptation for you?'

I wring my hands together and lift my eyes to meet his. 'Yes.'

Seymour gives a half-laugh. 'In some ways, that's very good to know.'

I made love once with Seymour, but I'll carry the memory of it with me forever. I'd only have to close my eyes for the briefest of moments and I'd be transported right back there, to the feel of his body, the scent of his skin, the sensation of his mouth on mine. 'I have to stay away from you.'

At that, he sighs. 'I could have loved you very much, Lily Lamont-Jones.'

'Believe me, Seymour, I felt the same.'

'I hoped that you did,' he says.

My voice is shaking when I say, 'Laurence and I are back on track though, and I have to think of my family . . .'

'Of course,' Seymour interjects. 'I didn't come here today to put pressure on you. I just wanted to see you. I wanted to see if we could be friends. And I wanted to give you a gift.' He grins. 'Christmas is coming, after all.'

It's just a few short weeks away, in fact. The shops are full to the rafters with all manner of festive essentials and unnecessary tat. This year it will be different for us. We'll mark it in a distinctly more frugal manner. I won't be spending thousands of pounds on presents or decorations or the mounds of food that invariably ends up in the rubbish bin. The sales have already started in earnest in the stores, prices are slashed, everyone citing the economic downturn. So, perhaps it's not just us who are cutting their cloth accordingly this year.

'I don't need a gift, Seymour.'

He takes in our drab surroundings. 'I thought you might like one though.' From his pocket he pulls out a black velvet pouch. 'Hold out your hands.'

Wiping the remaining residue of flour onto my jeans, I do as Seymour asks, cupping my hands together in front of me.

We exchange a glance and for a moment, I see the pain in Seymour's eyes and I know that Tracey is right. He's missing me. He's missing me desperately. And I hope to God that he can see the pain echoed in mine.

Then he opens the velvet pouch and pours all the jewellery that I sold to him into my hands. My rings, my bracelets and my necklaces tumble out into my waiting palms.

I look at him, bemused.

'This is yours,' he says. 'I don't want it. My gift to you is to return it all.'

'But you've paid me for it, Seymour. An extraordinary amount of money.'

'I can't sell it, Lily. I know how important it is to you.'

'A deal is a deal, Seymour.'

'I have no need of the money,' he insists. 'What on earth would I want with it? Doing this, for many reasons, will make me feel a lot better about myself.'

He takes my engagement ring from the middle of the small pile and slips it back onto my finger where it belongs. Then he gives me a wry smile, closes my hands over the rest of the jewellery and presses them together. 'Keep it,' he whispers. 'But you must promise me that you'll never sell it again, whatever happens. If you need money, come to me.'

'I couldn't do that.'

'I sincerely hope that you would.'

I feel the weight of the gold and diamonds between my palms and don't know what else to say but, 'Thank you. Thank you so much, Seymour.'

'You're more than welcome, Mrs Lamont-Jones.'

Then I put the jewellery down on the work surface and, unspeaking, we move together. I feel Seymour's arms around me and our lips meet. He kisses me deeply and my knees buckle beneath me.

We stay like that for a lifetime, an eternity. I'm not in the ramshackle kitchen of a beaten-up home in Netherslade Bridge; I'm transported somewhere else entirely, somewhere magical, somewhere like paradise, somewhere that I can't remain.

Seymour is the one to break away. He lets out a heavy, unsteady breath. 'I should be going.'

I still have the taste of his lips on mine. 'Thank you,' I say again. 'Thank you. This is too much.'

'Love makes you do very silly things, Lily,' he says and, with that, Seymour walks out of the kitchen, down the hall – and out of my life.

Chapter 114

We wake up to snow. It's still a week before Christmas and I can't remember last when we had a snowfall at this time of the year. Usually our worst months are January and February, but it looks as if the hard winter that has been forecast has arrived with a vengeance.

The ground is blanketed with at least six inches of pristine white powder and even Netherslade Bridge is transformed into a magical wonderland. Tiny icicles hang from the trees and sparkle in the milky sunlight.

Laurence and I gaze out of the window and he slips his arm round me.

'Thank goodness that I'm not working today. The roads will be hell. At least Christopher only has to go across the farm-yard if there are, by some miracle, any visitors. I'll call him to make sure that everything's all right.'

It's Saturday and not my husband's weekend to work. Despite it being mid-morning, we're both still in our pyjamas and I was very tempted to turn over in bed until I saw the snow. Now I say, 'We could go out and make snowmen with the children.'

'We haven't done that for years.'

That's predominantly because since they were both born the winters have been miserably wet and mild affairs.

'Are they awake?'

'No. Still asleep.'

'Wait until they see this.'

Then there's a rap on the door and Laurence goes down to answer it, me trailing in his wake. It's Skull, wrapped up in Artic-style gear.

'It's chilly out here, Lozzer,' he says, stamping his feet on the path.

'Come in.'

'Won't stop,' he says. 'Barbecue breakfast on the green as soon as you're ready. I've got the sausages on already. Bring what you can.'

'Marvellous,' Laurence says.

'See you, bro.' Skull is off up the path and waving goodbye before we have time to ask anything else.

Minutes later my husband is dressed and has cajoled the children out of bed and into as many clothes as possible. I bought them both heavy-duty coats and boots from the charity shops in the city centre and Tracey is proving to be a veritable fund of hand-me-downs.

There's a frenzy in the Lamont-Jones household that I haven't experienced in a long time. Even I'm getting caught up in the excitement and root through my fridge for a suitable contribution to the barbecue.

'Come on, Mummy,' Hettie urges. 'We need to get out there.'

'Just a minute, darling.' I pull out some bacon and tomatoes. 'Here,' I say, 'give these to Skull. I'll see what else I can find.'

I could make some hot chocolate, but we don't have any Thermos flasks. As time goes on, I'm sure we will replace the little things that we lost that we sometimes miss.

'You won't be long, will you?' Laurence is clearly ready to get out and at it.

'I've just got to pull on some clothes.'

He kisses me, distractedly, and heads for the door. 'I love you,' he throws back carelessly.

'I love you too,' I say.

'Yuk,' Hugo says. 'You're being slushy again.'

'I'll catch you up,' I say and push them all out of the front door.

Upstairs in my bedroom, I tidy the bed and then dress. I too am kitted out for winter in previously-owned clothes or 'vintage' as I prefer to call them, even though the vintage of some of them might only be two years old. Oh, and also some bargain finds from Primarni, as Tracey calls it.

I slip off my engagement ring, as the last thing that I would want to do is to lose it in the snow. Then I put it in a sock under my pillow, hoping that it will somehow thwart any burglar. This is the only piece I've kept with me. The rest of the jewellery is in a safety deposit box at a bank other than the one Laurence and I use together. My husband doesn't know anything about it and, to be perfectly honest, I want it to stay that way.

It didn't occur to me at the time – I guess I was swept up in the emotion of seeing Seymour again – but how on earth would I have explained to Laurence that my one-time employer had simply returned all the jewellery he was supposed to have bought. That he'd just brought it back and, out of the kindness of his heart, had given it back to me.

Such a magnanimous gesture would, surely, have prompted too many questions about the true nature of the relationship between Seymour and me. How could I have given Laurence truthful answers to them without jeopardising our marriage? After all that we've been through, I certainly didn't want to risk that again. It was difficult enough explaining away the return of my engagement ring and, though I'm sure he wondered why Seymour was being quite so altruistic, he didn't ask too many awkward questions. Perhaps my husband simply decided that it was better not to know the answers. I don't know. But I realise that it is too easy to keep secrets and can now see why Laurence went down that route. This will be the one and only thing I keep from him, and I assure myself that it's for the best. Perhaps in time I'll be able to come clean but for now, the knowledge has to be mine alone – a scar on my heart.

Plus I promised Seymour that I wouldn't sell my jewellery again and I want to keep that promise, so it's good that it's out of harm's way as I don't want to reach for it the minute that we can't pay our bills. I used to think that having lots of possessions would protect me from the harsh realities of life. It seems that quite the opposite is true.

Pushing away the thoughts, I pull on my boots and gloves and head for the door. Taking a tray of bran muffins that were destined for Cherry's with me, I shut the door of our unlikely Shangri-La and head out into the snow. There's a certain comfort in having a small home, with small overheads, just one door to close behind me. The crunch under my boots automatically puts a smile on my face as I stride along the street, my breath billowing out in front of me.

Tracey's neighbour has had his Christmas lights on for weeks and, even though it's morning and still light, Homer Simpson, Tinkerbell *et al* go through their neon routines. I can already see the rest of the neighbours milling around on the green where the kids playground is and a filigree metal gazebo that's permanently covered in graffiti. Even that looks beautiful today.

Tracey and Jamelia are there, almost unrecognisable in woolly hats and fake Uggs. Hettie and Hugo are heavily involved in a snowball fight with Charlize and Keanu and some other kids that I recognise from school.

Someone with better kitchen supplies than me has brought out a huge Thermos of hot chocolate.

'Hi, hun,' Tracey says. 'Chocolate?'

'Lovely.'

My neighbour fills a plastic cup for me and kisses me on the cheek as she hands it over. 'Everything all right?'

'Fine,' I say and, for the first time in a long time, I can honestly say that it is. My stomach isn't twisted with nerves. Every breath isn't taut with unresolved tension. I break out into a laugh, that brings tears to my eyes. When she frowns at me, I assure her, 'I'm fine. Just happy.'

'God,' she tuts. 'You're a mad woman. Give us one of those muffins to try.'

So, I work my way round my neighbours handing them out. Skull and Laurence are in charge of the barbecue and are already dishing up hot dogs filled with fried onions that have probably come from Skull's allotment.

There's a rash of snowmen dotted around the green, and some enterprising people are busy fashioning a table and chairs out of snow. Two candelabras complete with festive red candles are sitting waiting to go on top.

Len is here with his dogs and I give him a wave and get a gummy smile in return. It might be my imagination, but I think that Len smiles more these days. I must remember to talk to him about Christmas Day. He's joining our celebration and I want to make it a special day for him and the dogs. Then, while Len tucks into a bacon bap, I see Skull slipping a few sly sausages to the dogs who wag their tails in appreciation. Perhaps I could conjure up a special doggy cake for them for the holiday celebration.

I go up to my husband and hug him. 'What's that for?' he asks.

Laurence has dispensed with his barbecue duties and is now eating a hot dog. There's a spot of tomato ketchup on his chin. I reach up and wipe it off. 'Because I love you.'

'Hmm.' He looks pleased with that idea.

Then the children, en masse, run up to us and start pelting us with snowballs.

'Oh yes,' Laurence says, ramming in the last bite of his hot dog. 'Bring it on.' And he spreads his arms and runs towards the children, cackling in a maniacal way. He scoops a shrieking Hettie into his arms and barrels along with her. She loses her hat, but doesn't even notice.

At my side, a breathless and flushed face Hugo urges, 'Let's get Dad.'

'Okay.' But then he's off, back into the thick of the action in the snowball fight, before I can move.

'Go, Lily!' Tracey chants.

'You should be helping me.'

'I certainly should.' She hands her hot chocolate to Jamelia and claps her hands together. 'Let's show them what we're made of.'

And as we bend to scoop up some snow for our weapons to join in the fray, I look round at the happy, laughing faces here – at Tracey, Jamelia, Skull, Len, the dogs, the rest of the neighbours. But most of all at my husband, his hair fringed with snow, smiling, and my children, carefree and chuckling as they wrestle on the ground.

I let out a breath and it doesn't shake in my chest; it's calm, joyous even – and I'm so glad that I'm here and that I belong.